# VILLAINY
# AT
# VESPERS

# VILLAINY
# AT
# VESPERS

JOAN COCKIN

GALILEO PUBLISHERS, CAMBRIDGE

*First printed, September 1949*

*This new edition printed 2022*

Galileo Publishers
16 Woodlands Road
Great Shelford, Cambridge CB22 5LW UK

www.galileopublishing.co.uk

Distributed in the USA by:
SCB Distributors
15608 S. New Century Drive
Gardena, CA 90248-2129, USA

and in Australia by:
Peribo Pty Limited
58 Beaumont Road, Mount Kuring-Gai
NSW 2080, Australia

ISBN 978-1-912916-90-0
epub: 978-1-912916-97-9
Kindle: 978-1-912916-96-2

Printed in the EU

# CONTENTS

# CHAPTER I

HUMAN sacrifice—primitive physical sacrifice—has long been out of favour in England. A considerable stir was, therefore, created when the body of a man—naked and with his throat cut—was discovered upon the altar of St. Poltruan's Church in the village of Trevelley. Murder—and from the beginning it was assumed that not even the most theatrically-minded suicide would make his way without clothes into church, lie upon the altar and cut his throat with a pruning-knife—murder, then, is at least a diversion from the grim perplexities of the daily news. Over its cooling breakfast the British Public studied with pleasurable horror the details— the awesome setting of a deserted church in Sunday twilight, the little child (well, a gawky sixteen but anyway a mental child) who found the horrid sight, the historic wickedness of Trevelley itself, the mystery of the corpse's identity. Anything which happens in Cornwall is news and this promised to be a good family murder—instructive for the children, since the British press on this first day was already plying its readers with learned reports on the historical and social significance of sacrilege and sacrifice, and yet entertaining for less seriously-minded adults. Not that the average Briton was unmoved. The combination of brutal violence with sacrilege made the crime excitingly repellent. Non-church goers were particularly aroused. On suburban trains they said to each other that if this was what the Church of England was coming to it was just as well that they had given up regular attendance. Nevertheless, they read and re-read the Monday morning accounts of the outrage, for there was a macabre quality about the scene and details of the crime and the British Press—Fat Boy fashion— set manfully about making its readers' blood run cold.

Amidst this happy communion of interests one voice could be heard in lament—heard at least by the four other late breakfasters

1

scattered widely around the dining-room of the 'Three Fishers Inn', Trevelley's ancient and solitary hotel. These four thought it best not to jeopardise their splendid isolation by paying any attention to the mourner, so John Briarley groaned alone. Only the waitress responded to the cry and she, remembering his sausage ordered twenty minutes ago, rushed to the kitchen with compunctionate zeal. John Briarley, however, thought only of the headlines before him: CORPSE ON CHURCH ALTAR, and in smaller, but still vociferous type, AMAZING DISCOVERY IN FISHING VILLAGE, and in smaller type again, but with a sibilant quality all its own: Sacrilegious 'Sacrifice' in Seaside Haunt. Re-reading this climactic series John Briarley muttered an oath and a paunchy man in a yellow turtle-necked sweater four tables away looked at him reprovingly. He himself had been waiting for breakfast half an hour and failed to see why a delay of only ten minutes should provoke such a fuss.

A more sympathetic and knowledgeable observer might have credited the young man with sounder reasons for complaint. The smallest, quietest, least advertised seaside village in England—a place known only to fishermen and antiquarians—a village barely detectable on the three-inch Ordnance Survey—a holiday resort where hermits felt at home—in short, the village where John Briarley had come three days ago to spend his last fortnight of demob. leave had suddenly become notorious. A swift glance at the news story had told him the worst. In the summer doldrums of news the Trevelley affair had taken on exaggerated importance. 'Wide interest' the paper said. 'Our special correspondent sent down in order to keep *Daily Clamour* readers fully informed!'; 'Scotland Yard being consulted by local police'; 'Primate expected to make statement this afternoon'. Trevelley had hit the headlines. Privacy and peace were disappearing in a cloud of journalists.

Briarley was starting with furious intent to re-read the whole report when there was interposed between himself and the newspaper a large hot plate bearing a small cool sausage.

"Sorry, Mister Bri'ley," said the little waitress. "I'ope you ain't *too* 'ungry." Her sad Cockney voice recognised that nowadays all customers in the 'Three Fishers' were hungry. There was merely a variation in degree. It was only when customers were youngish males, agreeably free and easy, that she took time to care. They reminded her of the young men who had made life so pleasant when she, an evacuee from Bethnal Green, had first gone into service at the 'Fishers'. Those last four war years had been her *fête-champêtre*. Now, at the age of twenty-five, she knew her best years were past, but Trevelley still had for her a romantic flavour which Bethnal Green could never rival, so she stayed on—the last evacuee. John Briarley and similar young ex-servicemen reminded her of the gay past. He had benefited during the last two days by comparatively rapid service. He smiled at her now with absent-minded thanks.

"No, no; I'm in no hurry. In fact I hardly feel like eating at all. This awful news really puts one off?"

The waitress looked at him curiously. All that she had seen in the paper was the exhilarating report that a murder of national interest was to enliven Trevelley and life. What could the lad be talking about!

"It's such a damned nuisance, you know," he tried to explain. But Lucy was far more interested in her own views on the event.

"It sure is putting Trevelley on the map," she observed, with that old-fashioned American slang which dated her as a wartime débutante. She leaned upon the table, her eyes glowing with excitement. "Manager says 'e's got eight bookin's from London already—newspaper fellers an' p'licemen and I don't know what all. Gawd knows where we'll put 'em. The billiard table slept six in the old days—p'r'aps we'll 'ave to fix that up again. Then there be three sofas in the lounge an' a couple of easy chairs. Wot larks, eh? There won't be many rooms goin' beggin' 'ere for some time, I reckon." Her eyes sparkled with expectation. "Soon's I've finished breakfasts I'm off to Church, I am. First time since confirmation, I guess! This'll make a lot of churchgoers, eh?" She nudged John slyly and giggled with unsuppressed delight until a loud snort from the window table interrupted her pleasure. The turtle-necked visitor was regarding them with remarkable fury. Not only had Briarley been served out of turn before him, but it appeared that the guilty pair were using the entirely unsuitable hour of nine-thirty a.m. for convivial conversation.

"All right, all right!" said Lucy with quite unjustified hauteur. "I can't serve everyone at once, can I?" She hastened into the kitchen however. John felt himself blushing under the indignant glare of the window table. Here was a crime against society, if you want one—to be fed out of order in the queue! There was no reasonable excuse so he turned to his sausage and began to eat with a furtive air. From the tremendous sound of rustling newspaper behind him he was aware that the window table intended him to choke with shame over every mouthful. As a matter of fact he did choke, but that was probably because one of the lesser known portions of the pig had found its way into his sausage.

A large hand descended powerfully upon his back and with six blows cleared his windpipe.

"You almost killed me," said John resentfully, picking up his fork. "What with one thing and another I've a good mind to go back to bed. This is going to be a rotten day."

The man who sat down opposite him chuckled without perturbation.

"Nothing like the peace of the English countryside, eh, Jack? O for a rural bower where the hand of man has not set its evil stain! O for the uncorrupted peasant going his tranquil way through the bosky woodland...."

Inspector Cam of Little Biggling had the round, bland cheerfulness of a well-nourished two-year-old, but there was a watchful sparkle in his deep-set blue eyes which marked him as experienced in the ways of sin. He combined a very searching and lively imagination with a curious admiration for the inferior poets. His attempts to speak in a poetic vein, therefore, were always painful to sensitive friends. John Briarley, after four days in the same hotel, was sufficiently acquainted with him to express his feelings freely. He regarded him without pleasure.

"Is that supposed to be poetry? This kind of affair doubtless brings out your softer side. I suppose all your foul friends from Scotland Yard will be coming down to spend the holiday with you! Not a beach will be free from flat feet paddling in the brine." His eyes narrowed suddenly. "I wouldn't be at all surprised if this wasn't a put-up job by the Yard just in order to give the boys a seaside holiday. I've often wondered why summer murders always take place in pleasant rural surroundings and winter ones never outside London. Well, I don't mind your corrupt little practices, but in God's name why choose Trevelley? There isn't even a dance-hall here for the boys—and all the pretty girls have gone off to America!"

Cam smiled with galling understanding. "Don't get too edgy yet, Jack. For all you know the Yard may never come into it. Wouldn't be surprised if the local fellows hadn't got the man under lock and key already and it was just a twenty-four hours' wonder. Anyone who's show-off enough to put the corpse on an altar with all that hocus-pocus will give himself away soon enough. Funny thing that! What you said about put-up job. That's how it struck me, too. The thing reads in the paper like a ruddy detective story. There's something phoney about it. Mark my words!"

The older man had drifted into a ruminative drawl as he spoke and his piece of toast and marmalade, borrowed from Briarley's plate, hung suspended between plate and mouth. The young man struck the table with such urgency that the toast almost hit Cam's nose as it flew up. He looked at the other reproachfully. But Briarley was past reproach. A terrible thought had apparently struck him.

"By God!" he exclaimed in horror. "The Pollpen brass! They won't let me get at it! They'll be locking up the church for their beastly finger-prints and foot-prints." He threw his newspaper furiously to the ground. "All wasted! All the time wasted! That lovely brass shut away...." He stopped, choked with frustrated anger.

Cam, chewing vigorously, looked at him with more calm than such agitation seemed to warrant.

"Still rubbin', rubbin', rubbin'?" he asked cheerfully. "Well, well! That'll be a good one, I suppose." He poured himself a cup of John's tea.

"Unique," said the mourner in muted tones. "1365—civilian—man and wife—reticulated head-dress—enamelled shields—complete marginal inscription—fine double canopy. Lovely bit of work. I saw it first during the war when I was stationed near here. You remember I told you. That time they boarded it up for A.R.P. reasons. This time they have a murder. I believe the thing must be cursed! Or I must be."

"Can't see what you get out of it myself," said Cam. "But then perhaps it's because I can't get a clear view of 'em nowadays, eh?" He patted his projecting waist band affectionately. "Rubbin' brasses doesn't seem quite the thing for a holiday; too much like scrubbing floors. But it takes all sorts. That Pollpen brass is the one you were going to use to educate me in the finer points, wasn t it?"

John nodded gloomily.

Cam shook his head. "Can't go neglecting my education. I know the Inspector here. I'll see if I can get you in. But don't tell a soul or I'll have the whole hotel round my neck."

He brushed aside John's thanks, borrowed his morning paper and with resolute determination set himself to meet and master the economic enigmas which every morning face the conscientious Briton.

Soon the young man gave up a half-hearted attempt to save his breakfast from Cam's unconsciously wandering hand and getting up he strode moodily out of the room.

His exit was followed even to the door by the unsympathetic eyes of the window seat, who seemed incapable of forgetting his grievance. Cam caught the glance as his eyes flickered from the newspaper. Their glances met and the man seemed to feel that the occasion called for comment.

"Queer bloke, that," he whispered in an almost inaudible voice that seemed to come from deep in the fat recesses of his body. The fact that he always whispered gave him a conspiratorial air out of accord with his otherwise hearty appearance. "Always in a hurry. Never still. No perspective, that kind. Give me the jitters." His little rosebud mouth, rather too pretty for a heavily-jowled face, pouted disapprovingly.

Cam shrugged. "He's had a pretty rough trip, I should think. Has to start work in civvy street soon and was counting on this holiday to get readjusted—as they say. Bad luck having a hubbub like this when all you want is peace and quiet."

The fat man—who Cam had heard was a Covent Garden potentate, presumably the vegetable market, not the Opera—nodded doubtfully and looked less petulant. He had in fact one of those unusual faces which when relaxed fall naturally into a smile. This gave him a jolly, eager appearance which was strangely touching in such a large man. At first glance he seemed rather vulgarly conspicuous. And then you realised that you had met him a thousand times before—looking conspicuous in every pub or men's club or sports meeting you had ever entered. He was a standard sports model.

"Hard on all of us," he remarked. "I don't suppose any of us came'ere, here, with this sort of entertainment in mind. Even you," he added after a pause. "Police officers don't like busmen's holidays any more than the rest of us, do they, old man?" He smiled with man-to-man familiarity.

"I probably won't get mixed up in this," Cam explained kindly. "The police here, can handle their own case quite competently. If they need help they'll get in the Yard. I'm not biting *my* nails over it. Thank you, Lucy, my dear. That's a very handsome sausage, if I do say so. Reminds me of myself at the age of two days; same colour; same shape; same size. I hate to eat it." Cam attacked the creature with relish and Lucy smiled tolerantly.

"You're late," she said. "Five minutes later and I wouldn't have waited on you, no I wouldn't. Mrs. Cam and the children were out in the sunshine hours ago. Ain't you ashamed of yerself, givin' the kids such a bad example? "

"The only privilege of power which is worth having," pontificated Cam, "is that of lying in bed after the powerless have got up. I am teaching my children that being grown-up does have some compensations. I am setting them a goal towards which to work and strive. As the poor little beggars were dragged out of bed this morning probably all three lisped an oath that one day they would grow up to be like their papa and lie in bed till tea. It gives them something to live for."

"Well, you almost missed breakfast anyways," Lucy persevered, "and you did miss Mr. Honeywether. 'E was 'ere about nine wantin' to see you. I wouldn't be surprised if 'e wasn't arter you ter go up to Church an' see The Body." She lowered her voice with awful reverence. "But when I says you was still asleep 'e said it could wait, that 'e 'd call back later. So now you see what you misses by being late abed," she ended triumphantly.

Cam looked at her gravely.

"You convince me," he said. "If dangers Like Honeywether hang about this place in the early hours I shall henceforth take my breakfast in bed. Lord," he said, pouring another cup of tea, "for that from which Thou hast preserved me, I thank Thee." He patted Lucy with fatherly affection and bade her be off about her work while he solved the problems of the Middle

East. It was twenty minutes before, having accomplished this, he rose to go.

★ ★ ★

Inspector Cam on holiday allowed his natural friendliness to have full play. There was about this friendliness something of the serpentine persuasiveness which he used upon difficult witnesses, but Cam himself was unconscious of a habit of questioning strangers more closely than is conventional. To do his technique justice, they were usually equally unconscious of the cross-examination process and only flattered by the interest this simple-hearted fellow took in their opinions and their problems. As a result Cam on holiday was seldom alone. Wherever he went he knew everybody and everybody's affairs—from the chambermaid to the most aloof visitor— within two days of arrival. He was not particularly gregarious. People in crowds rather bored him. Parties were only tolerable amongst old friends or amongst individuals so much at odds that their individualities sharpened from the friction. But people on their own were the incurable fascination. He was not discriminating. Anyone human would do. With first one person, then another, he would retire into a comer or go for long walks *a deux* and could be seen for hours on end nodding patiently, speaking little, while the life stories of his various companions bubbled forth. To Mrs. Cam his tastes in this were a constant mystery. Her idea of a holiday was to get out into the fresh air, preferably upon some unfrequented beach, and spend her days speaking to as few people as possible. She was, in fact, a normal English holiday-maker. She did not criticise her husband for his peculiarity. She was a woman who got the best out of what she had. It was nice, she told her friends, to get into bed at night and have Bill tell her the life stories of the other guests. It gave her something to think about at meals, when she could watch them and try to reconcile Bill's stories

9

to their expressionless outward appearance. The two hardly saw each other from beginning to end of holidays except in bed—and this again was well-advised, Mrs. Cam confided in the doctor's wife, because one had a holiday to get away from familiar troubles of which Bill was the outstanding example.

On this Monday morning Inspector Cam had already spent a week at the 'Three Fishers' so he was well acquainted with all the other late breakfasters except the fat man who had arrived on Friday and had not been around the inn very much. He talked his way out of the dining-room at a leisurely pace. The residents were a dull lot on the whole so a nod and smile did for them. But there were others. Miss Cornthwaite, headmistress of a school for delinquent girls and source of some of his most effective bedtime stories for Mrs. Cam, wanted him to play bridge that evening. Her dour but undemanding independence pleased Cam. It was good to meet someone of such self-sufficiency. Physically she was rather stockily robust. She went for ten- or twelve-mile walks along the cliffs every day, always alone, and returned every night prepared to sit up until the stroke of midnight, but no later, with whoever she could find for bridge. As her bridge was depressingly competent Cam excused himself on the grounds of another nebulous engagement.

Roland Magnuson he passed by quickly with a nod and good morning. He was not an agreeable young man. His rather obvious attempts to 'get himself a girl' as part of the holiday routine had been as futile as they were persistent. Cam tried to pretend to himself that it was the attempts which disgusted him—and the random way in which Magnuson pursued first some holiday-making London typists, then a village girl, then the hotel servants, with apparently indiscriminate lust. It was probably his dismal failure, however, and the obvious incompetence with which the young man tackled his project which really offended Cam's masculinity. For his first few days he had been the object of considerable distaste and alarm by those resident ladies who customarily appoint themselves guardians of the hotel conscience. The measure of his failure was that after a few days these stalwarts came to refer to him as Poor Mr. Magnuson.

At the table by the door was a more attractive personality, and Cam lingered here though she was so obviously concentrated upon completing breakfast with the minimum waste of time. Betsey Rowan smiled briefly between mouthfuls.

"Howdy," she said with that conscious Americanism which Americans in England come to adopt in order to preserve the illusions of the natives.

"Hiya, sister," said Cam with equal civility. "How are the kids? Are you going soft on them—eating your sausage under cover?"

Betsey took the accusation seriously. "No, really. I like camping out, Mr. Cam. I had to come into the village early to get some fish-hooks, though, so I thought I'd breakfast here. The kids are fine. You can't tell them anything is wrong with the English climate now. They think this last week is typical."

"It can't last," Cam stated. "Ten days of summer is more than enough in my opinion. Your children are getting spoilt. Tell them that they can't really know England until they've camped out for a fortnight in pouring rain and done all their swimming in the puddles between tents. Still, I'm glad the camp is a success."

"Next year I'll bring over twenty kids," Betsey said firmly. "It's a wonderful educational experience and I should easily get that number when these nine tell their friends about it. I know myself," she went on, "what fun travel can be when you're just that age and have someone the same age to talk things over with. Most of these kids are only children and if it wasn't for the camp they would never have the experience."

"Did you go to a camp like this?" asked Cam. "Or did you travel with brothers and sisters?"

"I had a brother," she said briefly. "He's dead now—killed in the War."

Cam muttered some time-worn but sincere expression of sympathy.

She changed the subject abruptly. "Has Jack gone for good? He rushed past me as I came in."

"I'm afraid so," Cam said regretfully. A nice little romance had apparently turned sour. "He's a bit upset today. The Body, you know. It means an end to all peace in Trevelley. And to rubbing brasses. What a terrible thing murder is to be sure!"

Betsey laughed rather harshly. "Just like Chicago, isn't it? The kids are thrilled. They want Jack to show them round the church again, but I'm afraid it's not just antiquarian interest. I suppose the church will be shut anyway."

Cam shrugged. "I don't know. Probably. That's the trouble. Jack can't get at his brasses and he's like a bridegroom kept from his bride. But I don't know the drill. Closing a church is something of a procedure. It's not my pidgeon, thank God. You have to get the Archbishop's permission, I believe."

Betsey had forgotten her breakfast.

"Have you got any inside dope about the affair?" she asked, tipping her head back to look more directly at Cam, so that her long, bobbed brown hair, shining with a gold underglow, hung loose from her shoulders. "Do you think it was one of the villagers? And why that horrible stage-setting on the altar? I was reading a book about Black Magic not long ago. Do you think something like that might be mixed up in it?" She did not pause for answers. "At the shop—Finnegan's—there was quite a crowd of fishermen talking about the murder like a lot of gossiping housewives. They shut up when I went in— foreigner, you know, and a woman to boot—but one little guy was saying that it was probably God's judgment on the village. He sounded kind of serious, even if he was a bit squeaky. And all the other men just nodded solemnly. *Is* there something wrong with the village, Mr. Cam? I don't mean that I would fall for this 'judgment' stuff, but is there any reason why anyone else should?"

Two deep lines furrowed between the girl's eyes and made her appear much older than she was. Cam laughed kindly.

"Thinking about your duties as chaperone, Miss Rowan? Well, I shouldn't worry about it too much. There's nothing in this village could hurt your wards, I'm sure. But you know and I know what those old fishermen were talking about." He shrugged shyly. He was too old-fashioned to like discussing these things with a girl, through Betsey Rowan was probably well enough acquainted with them. "The village had quite a time during the war: you know, as a submarine and invasion base. Lots of strange types of all nationalities stationed here. Glamourous chaps, some of them; espionage agents, saboteurs, commandoes as well as plain army and navy tykes. Naturally it gave the local girls quite a lot to think about and from what I hear some of them didn't think quite far enough. Anyway, if you keep your eyes open you see quite a lot of interesting-looking children running round Trevelley these days. I don't hold with such goings-on myself, of course. Still, a mixture of blood never hurt England in the past or your country either, eh?" He grinned slyly but Betsey seemed very serious about it. She nodded slowly.

"Yes, I see. I had a nice chat with the greengrocer's wife last week. She told me that about twenty local girls married G.I.s and as many more should have. Quite apart from the other nationalities here! But the village fathers wouldn't see it your way, I suppose. They must have thought Trevelley was doomed like another Sodom or Gomorrah. Poor old things!"

"I shouldn't waste pity on them, my dear," laughed Cam. "Fishermen in this part of the country usually know how to keep command of the situation in their own families. They've got the upper hand again now and those girls who didn't marry their friends and leave the village are the ones to feel sorry for."

"They had their fun," Betsey said sharply. "I guess most of them were just little—hussies."

There was just the slightest pause before the last word. Cam wondered which of the many obscene words on the subject she had been going to use—and whether American women from her background were accustomed to use such words. Not that he knew anything about her background and his assumption that it was comfortable middle class may have been merely the result of ignorance of American standards. He would have expected a broader tolerance of the shortcomings of others, but this, he recognised, might be just another of his misconceptions of America. In Kansas, he had heard, the citizens still endure prohibition.

"Are you from Kansas?" he asked abruptly and without thinking.

"No," she said. "Rhode Island. Why? Do you know Kansas?"

"Never been there in my life—nor in the States either," said Cam blandly. He had long ago discovered that it is easier for everyone not to explain the inexplicable. "Come. Will you let me walk back with you to the camp? I'd like some exercise before lunch."

Betsey, who had been looking more and more like a chaperone during the previous conversation, brightened up and looked sixteen again. Cam had estimated twenty-six and the rapid changes in her manner amused him. She leaped to her feet.

"Of course! Why not lunch with us? We have coca-cola, you know, and canned hamburgers for the main course. And you can tell the kids about the organisation of the British police. That will be educational and they'd love to hear about it—especially now."

Cam winced at the educational motif but he liked Americans and American-style hamburgers. They left the dining-room together, leaving Mr. Magnuson looking after them with glum discontent. He had thought of asking Betsey to go to the flicks with him. But she was always so snooty and whisked out of sight now before he had time to get going with her. It was being a lousy holiday. Not a girl in the place worth going out with. Except one, and he'd mucked that up all right. These country types were no damned good to anyone anyway. He felt he would be quite sick if he had any more fresh air rammed down his throat.

"Now, Mr. Magnuson!" Lucy rattled her tray at him. "You mustn't sit here all day, you know. I've got to get lunch tables ready. You get out into the lovely sunshine, eh?"

He gave her a look of unspeakable distaste and slouched out. As there was nothing else to do he went up to take a look at the church.

Other people had the same idea and there was a crowd of some thirty villagers and farmers clustered in muttering groups round the lychgate. A constable kept them from entering the churchyard, which was already so crowded with brief gravestones that there was hardly room for a man to stand except on the one narrow path. Churchyards in fishing villages seem more populated than elsewhere. Magnuson had no eye for the lichen-covered charm of the graves, however, nor for the perfection of the thirteenth-century architecture which made this small church famous amongst antiquarians. He wanted action. To his delight he got it in a form which sent the whole crowd scattering in bewildered consternation. Down the church path, his black gown billowing magnificently around him, swept a great gaunt figure with hair as black as his robe and face as grey as the tombstones. He did not run but he came so swiftly that he seemed to appear amongst them in a cloud of dust. Without touching the constable he swept him aside with a gesture and turned upon the gaping crowd fiercely contemptuous eyes.

"Fools!" he exclaimed in a harsh grating voice which set the ears on edge. "What do'ee want here at God's House, eh? Not religion, I'll be bound. Why, there be hardly a one o'ye bin here to church in living memory, there bain't! Impious fools!

D'ye think God doesna see ye now—gathering like vultures because sacrilege has been done in His House? D'ye think this be another o' your scand'lous picture shows, eh? Away wi' you, Gadarene swine! God's curse on 'ee for not being at home on yore knees, praying that He will forgive the village its sins! An' on your daughters too, for bringing this sorrow on us. How darst ye look upon the church, you fools? Rundle, you lazy lug, drive them off! Must I do yore duty meself?"

And forestalling the bewildered constable the old man, whose voice cracked with rage, started to lay about with a branch he picked from the ground, scattering the crowd in every direction. Magnuson, scampering safely to the other side of the road, saw with surprise that he was the only person laughing at the old fool. The villagers seemed to take even the blows without resentment and he could see by their muttering and nodding amongst themselves that they thought the spectre was pretty much in the right. The crowd quickly broke up and started drifting downhill towards the 'Three Fishers'. Further discussion would obviously take place there.

The old man in his torn black gown stood triumphant in the middle of the street, holding his branch crooked over one arm like a sceptre. His eyes turned towards Magnuson and for an instant seemed to blaze antagonism in the young man's face. With a momentary twinge of panic he stepped into a garden gate, falling over the feet of John Briarley who stood in the shadow of the high wall sombrely watching the scene.

"Isn't it the ruddy limit?" Magnuson allowed his disgruntlement with life to overflow. "Can't even look at the scene of the ruddy crime without some ruddy old fool interfering with the fun. Who does he think he is, anyway? The Vicar, or whatever he calls himself?"

Briarley looked at him with scarcely hidden contempt.

"That's the Verger. He's devoted to the church. He doesn't like it being regarded simply as the scene of a 'ruddy crime' I suppose."

"This is a free country, isn't it?" Magnuson snarled. Another thought struck him. "Are you sight-seeing too? Not too nasty to be interesting, eh? But I'm not blaming you. I guess we're all human, old man!"

His tone of would-be comradeship infuriated John Briarley, who stepped quickly out into the sunshine. He condescended to explain his presence, however.

"I came to see if brass-rubbing might be permitted," he said briefly. "It isn't. And if you want a further report on my movements I am now walking over to Powey to rub their palimpsest." He waved his roll of white paper in ironic farewell and strode rapidly towards the ferry down the lane which branched from Fore Street at this point.

"Brass-rubbing?" Magnuson was muttering. "P-pal—? What the hell is he talking about? Touchy fellow, too. Crazy! This place is full of lunatics. I'll be crazy myself unless I get out of here while the going's good. Better have a drink and think it over. Yes, that's the ticket." And so the little man wandered off towards his personal disaster.

# CHAPTER II

IT WAS a day in June when workers in city offices look out through grimy windows at the sun and curse their luck in having decided to take their summer holiday in August. It was a Monday when housewives eye the cloudless sky suspiciously and wonder whether it isn't really too good to last until their laundry is blowing on the line. It was a morning when children dance in agony upon their toes, certain that if they wait until afternoon for the picnic the clouds will open and the heavens pour down upon them.

But for Inspector Cam the month, the day, the hour and the place were all correct and he was filled with comfortable sensations of well-being as he followed Betsey Rowan along the cliff path which lay between Trevelley and Poltherow. To his left a hundred feet below was the blue Atlantic, scintillating with theatrical intensity. To his right was the electric green of cultivated fields which in this hoarded earth were brought as close to the unprotected cliff-side as the safety of plough-horses permitted. Before him, winding closely to the edge of the cliff like a devil-may-care school-boy, ran the yellow strip of a narrow footpath. The Gulf Stream brought with it today the warm tang of tropic seas and Cam executed a tentative little tango step on the very edge of the solid English cliff as he pounded along behind his guide. The frosty common sense of maturity melted as the sun soaked into his big frame. Strange thoughts of romantic adventure, of sea-faring heroes and piratical deeds welled up from boyhood memories. This was the land where he had spent holidays as a boy. Down the sides of these cliffs were the tiny coves and imperceptible caves which as a lad he had explored and in which he had dreamed of magnificent and unperpetrated crimes—caves known only to smugglers, pirates, himself and a thousand daring Cornish boys. In Cornwall, that alien appendix to the solid body of the British island, he felt that improbability ceased to exist. Almost a thousand years of union had not erased the invisible boundary between Saxon England and the Celtic hinterland. The Cornish language was dead now. There was much more migration to England nowadays than in his youth. But the Cornish people remained obstinately different.

Strangers—and Cam candidly counted himself a stranger after an absence of twenty years—were always conscious of a stratum of independent life in the village in which they had no share. Some did not like this. They liked everything familiar and above-board—on the gifte-and tea-shoppe level. Cam was never happier, however, than living on the edge of mystery. His boyhood sense of the romance of crime had suffered considerably during a lifetime devoted to its examination. He never regretted nowadays that circumstances had placed him on the opposite side of the legal fence from that which he had originally planned. But in this part of the country, and on vacation, he was happy to believe again that all law-breaking was not sordid and rather commonplace. He even hoped in his unofficial heart, off duty, that blood feuds and smuggling and even piracy still flourished in their secret places with an old-fashioned vigour uncorrupted by modern commercialism.

His friend Honeywether, the local Inspector of Police, derided these illusions when Cam hinted wistfully at them and swore that crime in his district was as crude an affair as anywhere else. Traffic offences and wife-beating, he would say complacently, provided the little Honeywethers with their bread-and-butter. Cam accepted derision blandly in the inner conviction that Honeywether himself—a foreigner from Sussex—probably didn't know what was going on under his very nose. In a complacent mood the Gloucestershire man had once boasted that he could smell crime—that every crime had a different odour, all for the most part equally nauseous. The criminal atmosphere near Trevelley had a uniquely exotic and aromatic flavour. He had always as a boy enjoyed here the exhilarating conviction that he was on the very doorstep of a thousand mysteries. Now the old tickling expectancy was coming back and the cream of the pleasure was that it was not his official duty to solve one of them.

> "Tis my delight on a moonlight night
>   In the season of the year. . . ."

sang Cam. He was aware that his dancing was not very graceful, however, and blushed shyly when Betsey, turning suddenly, found him in the middle of a complicated caper.

She looked at him wryly, as nostalgic age looks upon a small and awkward boy.

"Watch where you're going," she warned. "These cliffs aren't very safe. I wonder they don't put fences up."

"God forbid!" said Cam reverently. "They've got too many as it is. Can you conceive an England completely encompassed with wire fences six feet high and Office of Works brown? Is this or is it not a free country? If people want to be careless and fall off the cliffs I say let 'em—and I say it in all consciousness that it is the duty of me and my kind to pick up and identify the pieces! But I'd rather spend all my time matching arms to torsoes than lose my inalienable right to risk my own life on the edge of eternity."

He exercised his right by waving a large leg in space.

"You are a child," Betsey said kindly. "I'm sorry I suggested such vandalism." They climbed a little bank at the edge of the cliff. "Look," said Betsey, pointing ahead. "There's Miss Comthwaite."

Cam looked past her and saw in the blue distance a grey figure in a too-short skirt which looked workmanlike rather than indecorous, striding briskly along looking neither to right nor to left. The two glanced at each other and laughed mischievously. Somehow Miss Comthwaite looked out of place amidst Cornish scenery. But even as she laughed Betsey's mood seemed to change.

Unexpectedly she turned off the path, sat down on a tussock of grass and, cradling her chin in her hand, gazed moodily over the sea. Cam, amenable to anything today, lay down beside her and thought sentimentally about the days when Mrs. Cam and he had lain side by side on these same cliffs. In the hush that followed the cessation of their tramping footsteps a lark sprang up from a nest amongst cowslips and in sudden exaltation of spirit poured out its song in such abundance that even the seagulls seemed to still their screams to listen to this small brown creature. Foot by foot the lark rose into the sky, propelled by the force of its own ecstasy. And then while it seemed still in full flush the song ceased and the lark swooped silently back to earth. The sun seemed then a little cooler.

Cam was unconscious of his companion except as a vague presence.

"This is a terribly *wicked* place, isn't it?" She spoke suddenly in a voice which was harsh and old. There was such blunt dogmatism in the words despite their questioning form that Cam was jerked abruptly to a sitting position and looked at her in amazement.

"Well, now," he answered slowly after a blank pause, for her remark fitted strangely with his own previous thoughts. "I don't think I'd say that. It's no worse really than other places, though I don't suppose it's any better either. I mean the same old crimes go on here probably, perhaps a few others. But 'wicked' is a strong word. Why, it's a nice little place...." He felt he was protesting to someone who hardly heard him.

"I feel it all around me," said she grimly. "Of course I've read lots of stories of piracy and smuggling in these parts, but that was long ago and I don't think what I feel is just imagination. There's something crooked here now—right now. Why, even the natives have the same idea. Remember that old man in

Finnegan's I heard talking about God's judgment? And in church last Sunday morning there was hardly anyone except a few old biddies and some tourists. Even the clergyman seemed discouraged. It *is* a wicked place."

Cam shrugged helplessly, feeling that he was arguing against his own inner conviction. Only he rather enjoyed the latent wickedness of Trevelley himself, while Betsey clearly disapproved.

"You have been reading too much ancient history," he declared firmly. "Anyway, I've always thought those smuggling days were pretty good stuff—wrong-headed, perhaps, but lusty and lively." He realised that his tone was becoming rather defensive because his own peculiar sensitivities had been touched. "Don't you like the people here? I mean the people you've met, not those you read about."

"But, of course!" she exclaimed. "Especially the women with their good round faces which I'm sure have never looked in a mirror except to see if they're dirty. Oh, I like them. I like them very much. But it's the atmosphere in which they live I'm talking about. They're as much at sea in it as I am."

"Bosh!" said Cam bluffly, knowing he was right to say so. Yet wondering. The atmosphere of a place derives from its inhabitants and cannot have independent characteristics. Yet, can it? He tried another tack.

"I can't see anything exactly 'wicked' in people not going to church. It's a great pity, of course, but frankly I wouldn't go either if I had to hear a sermon every Sunday like the last one. A full hour! And I never was much interested in Micah's genealogy anyway. Profound enough, I dare say, but personally I like the brief, straight-from-the-shoulder, onward-Christian-soldiers sort of sermon. All this fathers of the chinch history is over my head."

The girl nodded sadly. "Yes, he was very out of touch, wasn't he? I must have a talk with him one day, but he won't be any help," she added dispassionately and to Cam's confusion.

"Help?" he asked. "Why do you want help? You mustn't worry about the children," he added. "It seems to me they are having the time of their lives here."

"I'm not worrying about *them*," she said roughly. "They're all right."

Cam felt at a loss. "Aren't you enjoying Trevelley yourself?" he asked rather feebly.

Betsey shrugged coldly. "It's what I expected," she said inexplicably. "You know it well, don't you? I mean, you seem to know a lot of people here."

Cam sighed regretfully. "I used to, twenty years ago—twenty-one. Spent every summer here with an aunt who's dead now, bless her. But now I don't know the real villagers. Honeywether, the local Inspector, is an old friend because we used to work together, but otherwise I only know hotel people."

Betsey looked disappointed—more disappointed than Cam's reply seemed to warrant. "I thought you knew everyone," she said accusingly and almost rudely. "Oh well, come along. This is no help." She rose abruptly and turned without waiting for Cam up the path towards her camp. He felt that she had suddenly decided that he was not worth talking to, after all, and the thought annoyed him. He got up more slowly and followed up the steep incline, regarding her stiff back with some perplexity.

"What do you mean—no help?" he finally called after her. "What sort of help do you want?"

But she was apparently too far ahead by now to hear and the question went unanswered.

At the next turn in the path, rising to a stile where two fields met the cliff, they saw the camp—a group of one large and three small tents, together with a large lorry, placed about two hundred yards from the edge of the cliffs. The encampment was sheltered from the wind behind a high Cornish 'hedge' of flints overlaid with earth which was sewn together by the

23

roots of sedge and clover, pimpernel and ragged robin. They were fine, handsome tents—so spick and span store-bought as to be unmistakably American. They reminded Cam of the well-appointed kitchen of refrigerator advertisements—neat, hygienic and perfectly adapted to a single scientific purpose.

When Betsey Rowan, the American ex-W.A.C., and her band of fourteen-and fifteen-year-olds from happy American families able to afford two hundred pounds for their children's summer holidays first appeared near Trevelley the villagers, behind a polite facade, sniggered privately at the immaculate tents and laid bets as to the number of days before the amateur campers took shelter in the 'Three Fishers'. But the camp had been blessed by almost two weeks of perfect weather and so far the daisy white of the canvas was unspotted by a single desecration of mud. The bets still held good, a bargain being a bargain, but the attitude of the village had perceptibly changed. At first there had been mischievous anticipation of the day when these luxurious strangers would become refugees from the weather. Within a week, however, the unselfconscious friendliness of the American children, their joyous pleasure in all aspects of Trevelley life and their insatiable appetite for the stories of the fishermen had made them the most popular tourists in the history of the village. Betsey herself was liked and respected as a competent manager, who could combine on her shopping expeditions pleasant conversation with a canny eye for bargains. But Betsey was never received into the homes of the villagers as her protegees were. During the first days of the camp she was worried when children disappeared for hours on end. Now she was reconciled. Either they were playing in the cliff caves with Cornish children or they were out with the fishing-smacks. In either case they were in excellent hands from which it was a pity to remove them. But her prospectus had said in best academic American: "The project envisages a series of camping sites for the study group. These have been effectuated in advance in diverse areas of England and Scotland selected for the purpose of giving the children as wide an educational experience as possible of the life of the natives and the geographical character of all parts of the country during their two months tour." One more week and they must move on to further educational experience.

As Cam and Betsey approached the camp a crimson-coloured figure came out of the black mouth of a tent and looked in their direction. A thin shout came to them across the intervening fields and at the signal a group of vari-coloured young creatures swarmed out and came rushing across the pasture. They seemed in a great state of excitement, Cam observed calmly, but then he had never seen any of them other than in the heat of passionate enthusiasm.

One of the boys reached them first—a debonair figure in blue 'jeans' and a jacket which would have aroused the worst in Jacob's brothers.

"Whaddaya know, Betsey," he was shouting as he came. "Boy, are we seeing England! The bobbies are on to us now, old girl. Bring on Sherlock Holmes! What, what, eh, by Jove!" His excited parody of an English accent wavered from soprano to alto in a sudden adolescent descent and Cam did not refrain from laughing.

"What's the catastrophe today, Bert?" he asked, but the rest of the group, equally incoherent, were upon them now. With admirable calm Betsey induced one of the girls to tell them what was the matter, but not before The Matter itself was approaching down the path.

"Mornin', Cam," Inspector Honeywether said. "Mornin', Miss Rowan. How are you this fine day? Getting a bit close though. I'm afraid your children rather hope I'm going to arrest them just because I was asking them a few questions."

Bert Brinkerman, the liveliest of the group, showed instant despair. "You mean to say you aren't? You can't do tills to us, Mr. Honeywether! Our folks sent us here to see all we could of England and we haven't *yet* seen inside a jail. Betsey, honey, tell him he ought to arrest one of us. I'll confess to it all—I swear I will. Gee, Mr. Honeywether, you wouldn't be so mean, would you?..."

"Bert, shut up a second," Betsey said briefly and turned rather coldly to Inspector Honeywether. "I'm afraid the children can't have been much help. Can I do something?" There was a marked implication in her voice that the Inspector had shown bad taste by approaching the children in her absence. He flushed, casting an embarrassed glance at Cam who with suppressed delight returned only a stare of cold censure.

"I hoped to find you here, Miss Rowan. All I really wanted to know was whether you or the children have seen any stranger round here since yesterday afternoon. Anyone who looked at all suspicious."

Betsey Rowan regarded him with faint derision, but answered him courteously enough. "I haven't, for one. But I shouldn't think we are very good witnesses, Mr. Honeywether. We should hardly know who is villager and who is stranger. After all, we're strangers here ourselves."

There was a murmur amongst the children. One of the girls—pretty as a postcard and indistinguishable from the others in slacks, loose jumper, lipstick and ingenuous simplicity, objected.

"I guess we know most of the villagers now, Betsey. By sight, anyhow. But we really haven't seen any strangers. People don't use this path much, do they? They mostly go by the inland road.'Smatter of fact"—she looked for approval to the others who nodded solemnly—"'smatter of fact, we've been talking about the murder—kinda chewing the rag about what fun it'd be if we solved it—and Bert took notes on whether any of us has seen anyone suspicious." She sighed. "We hadn't. No one."

The group nodded with reluctant agreement.

"We saw Old Red," one of the younger girls said, and added in self-defence against the reproachful glances of the other children. "I don't mean he's *suspicious*. But we have seen *someone.*"

"Red Cowdray is one of our *best* friends," said Bert emphatically. "He was sailing to Poltherow to see his married sister and dropped in to see us."

"Who on earth is Red Cowdray?" Betsey asked in mingled amusement and irritation. "If he's one of your *best* friends I must have seen him."

"*You* know," Jane, the oldest girl, answered. "The old man who is red all over—face, hair, arms. And he wears a red sweater and looks just like the Devil—or at least I thought so when I first saw him, but actually he's a pure darlin'—just the cutest old guy you ever saw. He sends me terrifically. And he takes us fishing. That's why he came to see us—to show us a whopper he'd caught."

Honeywether was looking faintly astonished. "That's the first time I ever heard Old Red called a 'pure darlin'" he commented aside to Cam. "The worst old rough-neck in the county in his day."

"If we are suspecting *everyone*," Bert was saying with bitter solicitude for his fisherman friend, "we might as well mention Miss Cornthwaite! She was out here yesterday evening too, taking her usual walk."

"And I saw Mr. Magnuson," a girl giggled. "He came along last night with a girl-friend. *Not* Miss Comthwaite of course." The other children laughed knowledgeably.

"What time?" asked Honeywether.

"Miss Comthwaite was about five—*tea*-time, you know. She always passes at tea-time. And Mr. Magnuson in the evening. Much more romantic. About six-thirty."

"Who was with him?"

"I didn't see," the girl who had spoken before confessed. "I saw him over the hill when I was looking for four-leaf clovers. It was dusk and he had his arm round her and they were walking back to the village. They'd been necking, I guess," she concluded tolerantly.

"Well, that's that," the Inspector nodded. "It was just a routine check-up. If you *do* remember anything or see anything suspicious letmeknow." He paused for effect. "We suspect that the criminal may have passed this way and with such a lot of keen observers near the path I rather hoped to get a clue here. Never mind! We can't be lucky all the time." He shrugged sadly and the children showed simultaneous delight at such recognition of their ability and disappointment that they could not help this great man. Betsey was eyeing him with some suspicion and Honeywether turned hastily to his fellow-inspector.

"I must go now," he said. "Cam, will you come too? Mrs. Honeywether told me yesterday to ask you to lunch and she'll blame me if you don't turn up."

Cam was perplexed. "I've just arrived," he complained. "I was going to have some coca-cola and hamburgers. And I *don't* want to talk about the murder. Can't I come later?"

The children gave him his answer in loud chorus and to the effect that they would prefer to see him tomorrow after he had been initiated into the secrets of the local crime and could tell them all about it. Betsey laughed wryly, but there was a hint of curiosity in her own eyes.

"You wouldn't be allowed to enjoy your lunch," she said resignedly. "Take a rain check, Mr. Cam."

Cam looked puzzled and she explained. "Come another day, that means. We'll expect you tomorrow—and your story."

"All the gory details," one of the boys enlarged. "No holding out on us." And there was not a hint in the summer air that this pleasing excitement was anything more than an escapade planned for the entertainment of summer visitors to Trevelley.

Honeywether and Cam made their way back along the cliff side by side, first one and then the other stumbling through the long hassock grass. They had know each other for many years. There was no need for formalities.

"Why the devil," Cam exclaimed as soon as they were out of earshot, "are you barging into my holiday? *I* don't want to hear about your revoltin' murders. Can't understand you, Honeywether. How would you feel if I dragged you from your pleasures to some potty Little Biggling larceny?"

"This isn't a pottle little larceny and you needn't help me, as you call it, if you don't want to. It's not," Honeywether explained carefully, "that I need your help. It's just that I want to *talk* about the thing with someone in the trade. I'm puzzled," he exclaimed abruptly. "Puzzled and worried and a bit uneasy, Cam. This is a queer affair."

"It makes a nice story for the newspapers," said Cam more amiably. "Just a bit gaudy, though. Not quite convincing."

Honeywether growled viciously.

"Don't I know! Anything to do with the Church and a straightforward crime begins to look like Anti-Christ. Look at all the trouble they've been having about the Cathedral Robberies case. Archbishops issuing statements ... Questions in the House ... Newspapers playing it up until you would think every church in the country had been sacked and Thomas Cromwell on the tramp again. And now *I've* got to have a church *murder*!"

Cam nodded sympathetically. One cathedral—Manchester—and four ancient churches had recently suffered the loss of some of their treasures through theft. With a fine sense of precedence if not of proportion the Press had christened the series—The Cathedral Robberies. Readers had been regaled for weeks with learned articles on canon law, ecclesiastical art and sacrilege, but now interest was beginning to wane. Eager to put that hard-won knowledge and commissioned articles to further use, the Trevelley murder would be a godsend to economy-minded editors. Professionally speaking, it was for Honeywether a most unfortunate murder.

"Well," Cam said kindly, "I'll be glad to help you if I can, old man. If it doesn't involve any activity. As long as you just want to talk—talk. But tell me first—what's the point about questioning the children? Have you evidence that the murderer really came this way? Seems a long way to come on a wild-goose chase. Why not send a constable?"

"Send a constable!" the other explained bitterly. "Do you realise I've only got two! There's a manpower shortage, you know, and Trevelley doesn't rank high in priority for constables. Perhaps this will show the Superintendent what happens when I'm not given any help."

Cam grunted sympathetically. He had the same problem in Little Biggling. "But you haven't answered my question. Why toil out here?"

"Let's start at the beginning," exclaimed Honeywether impatiently. "I'm mixed up enough." He paused a moment to kick a rock over the deep descent into the ocean and then took up his pace and his story—both slow and deliberate. "I really came into this at twenty-five past eight yesterday evening, but I'd better start before that. At six forty-five Evensong ended at the church. Vespers, as the Rector calls it. It's short enough—just half an hour—and considering that only half a dozen people were there, perhaps that's too long. There's no sermon. The Verger was not there because he was ill—he is subject to bilious attacks, if you want to know. At six forty-five on the dot the benediction was said and everyone—almost—heads for the exit, led by Mr. Copperman himself, who has to water the roses before it gets dark."

"That's the Rector?" Cam interjected, and Honeywether nodded sourly. Obviously the clergyman was not a favourite.

"By six-fifty the church was almost deserted. 'Almost' because one of the congregation stayed late for purposes of his own, so far unexplained. That's a Mr. John Briarley staying at the 'Fishers'. Know him?"

"Pretty well," said Cam. "He has been there since before I arrived. Ex-service; on demob, leave; Going into school—mastering; brass-rubber."

"Brass what?"

"Rubber. It's a thing you do—a hobby. As far as he's concerned, a passion. Brasses are those old engraved metal plates you see in churches. Middle Ages usually—saying, 'Here lies poor old so-and-so; pray for his soul' in Latin—and with a picture of same. Briarley makes rubbings of them and is quite learned on the subject. Lord knows why, but it's not criminal, anyway. Go on."

"Sounds lunatic to me and I'm not sure yet whether it's a lunatic or a criminal I'm after. Anyway, here we are at the critical period of the story—from six-fifty to eight o'clock. For twenty minutes of that time Briarley was alone in the church— six-fifty to seven-ten. Alone, doing I don't know what. No one bothered to lock up. Mr. Copperman—who disapproves of locking churches, anyway, he tells me, but this should teach him—had rushed home to his roses. Mrs. Copperman went to see the Verger as soon as service was over and discovered he was feeling a bit better. She offered to lock up, but Yardley said he wanted to do it so she went on home too and proceeded to get supper. At about five past seven Yardley managed to get on to his feet and went over to the church still feeling rather groggy with his boy, Colly. As he went up the path he passed Briarley, who was coming out of church looking, he says, rather flushed and excited. But to do the young man justice I ought to say," Honeywether added conscientiously, "that Yardley suspects everyone who sets foot in his church of being there for no good purpose. Anyway, Briarley turned down the path towards the ferry and Yardley went in. He went along to the altar first to see whether Briarley had stolen the altar cloth! Everything was all right. And no body there either! But at that point he had another violent attack of pain and after resting a bit on a pew he had to get home as best he could with Colly's help and without locking up the church. That would be about seven-twenty. From seven-twenty to eight the church stood open and so far as we know empty. But during that time the body was placed on the altar and during that time the murder probably took place. The facts show it took place in church and the doctor tells me it could have been any time between six and eight. He's not experienced enough to say to the split second. But that doesn't matter so much in this case."

"A nice warm Sunday evening in June," Cam commented. "There must have been strollers round the place. Surely one of your old village biddies could give a list as long as your arm of suspicious strangers."

Honeywether shook his head. "You know how the church is placed—a little way inland behind the village and on top of the river cliff. It's above most of the houses and the shops and cinema. For summer evenings visitors prefer the sea-cliff walks and the locals like the flicks. There was no reason for anyone to pass except to get to the ferry or to the few cottages inland. We've checked on the cottagers—all respectable labourers— and they saw no one. The ferry wasn't busy either. Not many people would be wanting to walk the two miles to Powey at that time on a Sunday. The ferryman had two passengers— Miss Rowan at seven and Mr. Briarley at seven-thirty."

Cam made a rapid calculation. "Briarley left the church at seven-ten," he said. "It wouldn't take twenty minutes to the ferry. More like two."

"The ferry runs to a schedule nowadays. Seven-thirty was the next trip."

"What about the other routes away from the church? The very fact they weren't much frequented would make it more difficult for someone to escape unnoticed."

Honeywether shook his head moodily. "There are only two ways—down the village itself and eventually out on to the cliff path to Poltherow or past the railway station and Penton farm along the inland road which also leads to Poltherow. Rundle, my constable, was on his beat up and down Fore Street all that evening and he swears that not a stranger passed. I believe him. In Trevelley a stranger sticks out like a sore thumb, even in the tourist season. As for the inland road, old Mrs. Penton sits in her window knitting all day and watching like a hawk for tramps coming to steal her chickens. She says no one passed that evening. Of course anyone could have crept along behind hedges but I've no proof at all. Though God knows I'd like this murderer to be someone from another district!"

Honeywether pondered a moment on the unfairness of it all, then shrugged and exclaimed roughly: "Well, let's get on with it. At five to eight Yardley's boy came along to the Rectory and said that his Dad was feeling too poorly to finish the job of locking up and please would someone else do it. This boy, I might say, is somewhat feeble-minded—harmless but a sight too religious for a fourteen-year-old. You'll see him. It's his father's fault in my view, though you can hardly blame a man nowadays for raising his boy according to the Scriptures. He uses the toughest chapters in the Old Testament, however. Anyway, Mr. Copperman was out among his roses so Mrs. Copperman put on her hat and went back with the boy to the church. They both entered by the South porch which is the only entrance used, and she turned left into the vestry which is at the west end under the tower, just curtained off from the nave aisle, to see if the safe was locked. It wasn't, of course, because Rector had forgotten and she was checking the plate when she heard the boy sobbing in the chancel. Out she goes into the nave and finds him on his knees moaning and groaning something about the 'wrath of God'. (Now, I ask you—is it right that a lad should think about things like that?) Anyway, Mrs. Copperman sees in a moment what it's all about because no one could miss it once they were faced that way. There was this body laid out on the altar with the green Trinity frontal stained black with his blood. You never saw such a sight in all your born days. And the candles in one candlestick at his head burning right down to their base." Honeywether wiped his nose impatiently. "Mrs. Copperman, she went down herself on her knees beside the boy, she says,

33

and knelt there trembling and sick-like for Lord knows how long—three minutes, say. She couldn't move, she says. She felt it was the devil himself lying there and evil all around her and she hadn't even the courage, she says, to take her hands from her eyes. But then the boy started to go off into hysterics. She pulled herself together and, getting up, dragged him to the door. He couldn't walk. Once he was outside he seemed better, though dazed, and she told him to go off for the police double quick. He did it, too, because at eight-fifteen he got to the station and told Rundle, who was just packing up after his beat, that the Lord had punished the unrighteous and he'd better go up to the church and see about it—or words to that effect. Meanwhile Mrs. Copperman waited in the porch, not daring to go in again, but keeping an eye open for suspicious strangers. There wasn't a soul about. We got there at eight twenty-five."

As Honeywether came to an end of his story they had reached the beginning of the village street. From here on to the church Fore Street was sharply uphill, hemmed in by houses. Carts, cars, lorries and cycles played a dangerous game of musical chairs, dodging from one to another of the places where it was wide enough for two cars to pass. The two men trudged with absent-minded skill through the maze.

"You've left a lot out," Cam complained. "Who except Briarley was at Vespers?"

"Three village women—old and safe as pre-war houses— the Rector's wife, some man nobody knew from the hotel who sang at the top of his voice, tenor, and Miss Betsey Rowan."

"Ah!" said Cam with satisfaction. "So now we come back to my Question No. I. Why did you go all that way yourself to question innocent children?"

"I'm questioning all the congregation myself, personally," Honeywether replied pugnaciously. "It's the only lead I've got—and I suppose I ought to be thankful there weren't more of them. Though perhaps if we had a more God-fearing village here upsets like this wouldn't happen at all. Things aren't what they used to be round here, Cam." The Inspector paused to think this over a moment and then added parenthetically: "Or perhaps they're too much like what they used to be—a century or so ago. Well, I've seen the Rectory people and the villagers who were at Vespers. Briarley I am leaving for the last. Now I've got Miss Rowan and the Tenor to cover. There's one thing about Miss Rowan that interests me. She stopped to talk to Briarley as she was going out. And Mrs. Tregowan—she was one of the old women—says that he sent her off with a fly in her ear. She was looking pretty pink and peeved, says Mrs. Tregowan, when she left him after a few words. I'd like to know what they had to say to each other."

Cam opened his eyes ingenuously. "Why not ask her? You had the chance."

"In front of that horde? Don't be simple! Anyway, I'd just learned something else about her which interested me. The children say she didn't get back till ten. She apparently told them today—when they started asking her about the crime and whether she had any clues, you know—that she had gone to the hotel to have a drink with Briarley! Why did she lie, eh? We know she crossed over to Powey-side and she didn't go with Briarley. What has she got to hide? It's my guess that she will know pretty soon that the children told me her story and it may be a good idea to let her stew in her own juice for a few hours. She looks an obstinate type to me and I've a hunch that direct questions wouldn't get me far with her."

Cam shook his head regretfully. "An odd girl," he murmured. "She's got something on her mind, I know, but I'd be surprised if it were murder. She's very devout," he added inconsequently. "She went to morning service also." He frowned suddenly and turned to the Inspector. "What about the 'why' of this case, Honeywether? And therefore the 'who'? Have you any idea who the fellow on the altar was? And why one might wish to murder him?"

The other policeman shook his head.

"None. Not a clue. Not even where he came from and how he got here. He was an ugly type—not the sort of face you forget—but the railway porter never saw him come in. The garage people neither, and I haven't found any abandoned car or even a cycle. Nor did he come by ferry. Of course he may have walked in, but none of the neighbouring villages can identify him. He doesn't look the hiker-type either. A good sight too flabby. His clothes are all gone and no identification marks except one. Yet that's a pretty good one, I must say. He has the Stars and Stripes tattooed on his chest! Three inches wide and two high. A clear sign he's American, you see."

"There are one hundred and fifty million, I believe," Cam murmured.

"Not all in England," the other growled. "They've gone back now. Anyway, it's a hint. The Home Office is checking on passports and we've cabled his photo to the F.B.I. in Washington."

"Already?" Cam exclaimed. "Well, you've certainly been on your toes."

"It's almost noon," remarked the other pointedly. "We can't all lie abed till ten." But he looked gratified and added less defensively, "It's a queer case, Cam, and I don't mind saying that the sight of that body—the altar—it gave me a turn. Yet I suppose that when you get down to cases it's just like any other crime, eh?" He was asking for encouragement, but Cam gave gave him none as he looked up the rocky steps on which they climbed to the grey church looming over them.

"If you call it a crime," he said thoughtfully. "It might be worse. It might be called a mortal sin."

# CHAPTER III

WHO St. Poltruan, the patron of Trevelley Church, may have been is lost in the mist of Celtic Christianity. Some antiquarians have associated him with St. Piran, the intrepid Irish saint who built an oratory in the tenth century on the treacherous sands near Peranzabuloe—*Piran-in-sabulo*. Whichever minor saint, however, was honoured through the labour of successive centuries by the church which now stood upon the cliffs of Trevelley might well be proud of his disciples' handiwork. Primarily thirteenth century, the church boasted also a sturdy tower, a north pier arcade and a font of the Norman period, two exquisite curvilinear north windows of the early fourteenth century, a small but finely-proportioned Perpendicular east window and, typical of Cornish churches, some delightfully-carved choirstalls and bench-ends. The harmonious blending of the architectural genius of many generations of craftsmen had created a church with something of the massive vigour of the Normans, the good humour and grace of the thirteenth century, the delicacy of the fourteenth. From the sixteenth century the church had remained untouched, except by weather, wind and salt air.

Its Norman tower, square and determined, looked loftier than it was because of its position at the top of the cliffs. Within living memory a light at its top served as a warning to sailors of vicious rocks below. Now a more elaborate lighthouse stood out to sea, but Cam could remember stirring stories of battles between local parsons and their 'wrecking' parishioners in bygone days, when the latter, according to the hideous legends of these coasts, tried to dowse the fight and lure rich-cargoed ships to their ruin upon the rocks. Perhaps this historical difference of opinion accounted in part for a latent antagonism which still existed in Trevelley between church and parish. At one time during the morning the shadow of the tower overhung the whole village and villagers, judging time by this hour, talked of 'when the church is against us'. Unlike the typical parish church of England St. Poltruan's seemed to stand apart from the village in proud isolation. There was no sense here of the cottages grouped round the church for protection and spiritual shelter. Instead, they seemed to cling fearfully to the cliff beneath a grey threat of the Judgment to come. The church stood between the road and the River Trevelley, its west side facing inland, its east wall so close to the steep cliff-banks of the river that it appeared merely to be their continuation, its south porch overlooking the village and the Atlantic. The road just above the church twisted east and while the main branch drove inland, following the curves of the River Trevelley, a small path turned down to the river itself and to the ferry slip which lay almost directly beneath the church. The eroded banks of the river turned so sharply that the church was precariously perched upon a small peninsula. No doubt those banks could be climbed by Cornish boys or expert mountaineers, but to all intents and purposes the church was islanded between the river and the road and only accessible by the latter.

Despite its charm, it suddenly appeared to Cam as he climbed the steps towards it that this was not a comforting or comfortable church. He remembered nostalgically for a moment the vulgar humanity of his own thoroughly 'restored' church at home in Little Biggling. The Little Biggling church, however, had experienced a quieter history in its sheltered Cotswold valley than St. Poltruan's church upon the wild Atlantic and the untameable Celtic fringe. Cam brushed such mental imageries away impatiently. In all his visits to Trevelley as a boy these thoughts had never disturbed him. Old Mr. Banting, the last Rector, had been the nexus of village life. By kindness and gentle ways he had broken down all barriers between village and church. If he could do so anyone with the right spirit could do the same. It was absurd to imagine that there was any real cleavage between village and church. Absurd! Idiotic!

Cam, it should be mentioned, was accustomed to abusing his imagination with such strictures whenever it ran away with his slower-paced mind.

They passed through the lychgate. This was where coffins had once lain before their brief last journey up the path and into the holy church. Even at high noon it was dark in the gate's shadow. Cam hunched his shoulders grimly as he followed Honeywether up the path. Why the devil, he was thinking resentfully, did I get into this? Let Honeywether manage his own murders. Fine way to spend a holiday! They'll count it against my leave, too.... He stopped abruptly though Honeywether had entered the porch and was speaking to the constable stationed there. When the Inspector came back to ask impatiently that he should get a move on Cam was gazing thoughtfully at a crude picture scrawled in red crayon upon the grey slate of the porch floor. In common with all beautiful or renowned buildings, the whole of this porch was engraved with dates, initials and amorous phrases—the desperate attempt of small people to leave some record for history. But the drawing which Cam was inspecting was newer and more startlingly irreverent than most of the other hieroglyphics— and in even worse taste. It was a face—half a face—looking over a crude wall with fingers clutching at the top of the wall as if in a moment the whole figure would be leaping over. Beneath it was scrawled roughly: '? WAS HERE.' The drawing itself was familiar enough. Introduced by American G.I.s, it had been picked up everywhere, became fantastically popular like a catch phrase or jazz tune, and in public places, docks, lavatories, restaurants, cinemas, you would find the round curious eyes peering over a wall with the words beneath: 'Kilroy was here.' Cam was familiar with it. Sometimes it was placed with a nice sense of incongruity and had the humour of familiarity, but he had a sudden feeling of distaste at finding it in a church. Sacrilege on the grand scale was bad enough, but sacrilege reduced to vulgarity was worse. Honeywether had followed his gaze and snorted with disgust.

"Those foul kids!" he exclaimed. "Rundle!" An anxious constable came out of the church and looked obediently where his Inspector pointed.

"I thought I told you not to let anyone in the churchyard. Look at this! If you didn't do it yourself, and perhaps it appeals to your half-wit sense of humour, how did it get there? Who was it?"

The constable looked aggrieved.

"Nobbudy come in thes mamin', sir. I've had me eye glued on t'gate all day. Sent off a pile o' kids, I did, an' quite a few who should've known better too. If anyone did it since It happened he must'a' bin here afore I came on duty."

Honeywether shrugged impatiently.

"Well, it may not have anything to do with this. Some boys in the choir, perhaps, showing off. Disgusting, I call it. Isn't there any decency left? Never mind now. Come on, Cam."

He marched into the church and Cam followed thoughtfully.

The church was saturated with golden light as sunshine, drifting through the dusty lemon-coloured windows, seemed to reflect and expand off the mellow stone. Inside the church one forgot its external isolation. It was a humane, a civilised if rather lonely harbour. Brutality and violence seemed of an alien world. Cam strolled to the central aisle and looked along the bright nave through the tiny, dark choir to where a pool of sunshine lay in the sanctuary. Even from that distance he could see the splash of red darkening into black upon the altar cloth—a sharp-edged, evil stain. Honeywether hustled him along the stone paving of the aisle and past the rich carving of the choir-stalls to the altar steps.

"See this pool of blood," he said unnecessarily, pointing to the first of the three broad steps. "It must have happened here."

Cam nodded grimly at the great stain.

"That broomstick marks where the other candlestick was lying," Honeywether rattled on, "and the scissors—I borrowed them from Mrs. Copperman—are where the pruning-knife lay. I've taken it for fingerprint tests. The murderer must have knocked him on the head with the candlestick as he stood or knelt here and then cut his throat while he was unconscious. Gouged it, I should say! You can't make a clean cut with a blunt knife. Filthy business!"

"And then carried him up to the altar," concluded Cam. "Why, as you suggest, a blunt pruning-knife?" he asked after a few moments contemplation. "It must have been quite a job. I can't even cut plant-stems with'em unless they're unusually sharp. Prefer to use Mrs. Cam's best kitchen knife. You haven't got much of a blade to work with for a job like this."

"It was handy," suggested Honeywether. "Lying in the vestry from the time when Mrs. Copperman fixed the altar flowers that morning, she tells me. She had been using it to trim stems. Suppose the murderer knocked the man out with the candlestick? Then he would want to finish it off thoroughly so he'd look about for an instrument. Well, there's not much that's suitable here, naturally, but down in the vestry he'd find the pruning-knife lying on the table. After all, the man was unconscious so he could take his time. He certainly hacked that throat about. A butcher's job!"

Cam shook his head. "Why not just bash his head in a bit more with the blunt instrument? Just as effective. Not so much trouble. No more messy. It all seems very unnecessary. Well, well..."

He dismissed that enquiry for the moment and, skirting the congealed pool, tiptoed cautiously up the steps to the altar. He felt curiously ill at ease standing there in the sanctuary. It was a queer place for a murder investigation. By rights, he felt, this was the place for a priest, not a policeman. He remembered Mrs. Copperman and the feeble-minded boy kneeling in the church after the discovery of the body and he could understand how such a scene in such a place might send

41

even unbelievers to their knees. Those two, of course, they would be sincere enough.

His grey eyes narrowed suddenly and shot from the pool of blood on the steps to the stain on the cloth and back again. Honeywether grunted.

"I saw that myself!" he said smugly. "Problem No. I. It's the blood which *isn't* there that we have to worry about."

Cam nodded thoughtfully. Between the blood on the steps and the blood on the altar there lay five feet of a strip of plain green carpet, and upon it was not a mark or stain. If the body had been carried from the steps to the altar somehow it had been done without leaving a trace upon the floor.

"Under the carpet?..." Cam questioned.

"Nothing to help us," replied Honeywether, and taking a corner of the carpet tossed it aside. Cam gasped in momentary surprise. Beneath it there was certainly no trace of blood, but welded to the stone floor was a magnificent sheet of brass, five feet by four, engraved in most elaborate and exquisite detail with the figures of a man and his wife. They lay with then feet towards the altar and although their heads rested upon tassel-cornered pillows they were incongruously standing upon grassy tufts sprinkled with flowers in which two small dogs played. The pair were hand-in-hand, and despite the fact that their faces bore an expression of rather smug placidity Cam saw in them for a moment the reflection of all those moments of matrimonial comfort which he himself had enjoyed. Then robes were simple and civilian but over each figure was an elaborate canopy and around the whole an inscription which Cam knew at a glance was past his own deciphering. The sun shone on the brass at just that angle to bring out every finely etched line upon it. Cam was lost in admiration until Honeywether covered it again with a flick of the carpet.

"That's the Pollpen monumental brass," he said briefly. "Quite pretty. Best in England, they say. People come from everywhere to see it. But we've no time for that."

Cam remembered now that this was the brass of which John Briarley had been longing to have a rubbing. He understood him better now. He would have liked to examine it longer himself and he remembered resentfully again that, after all, this was his holiday.

They went back, however, to an examination of the church. Honeywether gave a succinct description of his work to date but there was little actual evidence to see. Clues were only conspicuous by their absence. Fingerprints of the Rector, the verger and the Rector's wife had been found in places where they might be expected—otherwise there were none. Honeywether had already taken samples of dust on the floor in case they might provide a clue to the owners of the feet which had walked near the altar. Fortunately the church paving was kept scrupulously clean and with any luck such distinctive soil might be traced. It was a faint hope, however. As for the entrance, the church had been wide open. Anyone might have walked in through the south door. There appeared to be no other entrance except a bolted west door in the vestry which was blocked by a small disused hand-organ. It was obviously inaccessible.

"You've examined that, I suppose," said Cam distrustfully, regarding the height of the organ pipes through which he would otherwise have to climb.

Honeywether nodded. "Nobody has opened it in the last fifty years. I doubt if it would be possible to budge it."

"There's no window one could get through—out of sight of the road?"

"No. The north transept windows look straight over the cliff and are unreachable. Why bother to find a secret entrance, anyway, when you can just walk through the door and there's no one on the road to see you? There *is*," he added, "the old smuggler's cache. It's up in the tower above the bells. There's an exit through the roof and down through the stair turret if a man had to get out quickly. At the bottom of the turret is a door that opens stark into mid-air over the river now. It's never open, of course. They used to sling the loot up into the tower from the boats in the river in the old smuggling days and you can still see the worn marks where the ropes were hauled. The men followed by the stair turret. We've looked up there. The cache is as clean as a pin. The Verger gave it a turn out last Friday, he tells me. Why clean that hole in the corner which no one sees? Because he cleans the church for the Lord's benefit, not for man's, he says, and the Lord can see that hole as well as the Communion Table itself. It sounds a pretty unlikely story, I'll admit, but you look round. The whole church bears him out. There's not a corner here which isn't dusted and polished. You'll find even the lock and hinges of that turret door no one can use all freshly oiled. It always is. I've a good mind to bring our char up here some day to see what real cleanliness looks like."

"He must be pretty nimble for an old man," commented Cam, noticing now that even the more remote parts of the organ were free of dust and cobwebs.

"Oh, he sends his boy Colly climbing round the church with a duster. That boy must know what the back of every beam in the place looks like."

"There was nothing at all in the smuggler's hole, then? Not merely an absence of dust?"

"Nothing. If anyone was there since it was cleaned on Friday he left no trace behind."

Cam sighed. "Too careful. So even the church used to play its little part in smuggling," he added. "I never realised that it had the blessing of the church. Is that a local tradition?"

Honeywether scowled. "Everybody smuggled in the old days. In England as well as Cornwall. You can't properly call it law-breaking."

Cam raised his eyebrows in wide-eyed amazement.

"Is this a police inspector I hear? An established servant of the Crown? According to that thesis, when enough people break the law the law ceases to be valid. Shame upon you, Honeywether!"

The Inspector flushed. "I only mean to say that you can't judge those old smugglers too severely. The laws then were pretty iniquitous. As for the smuggler's hole, it was only used a few years with the connivance of one curate—Jeremy Treselly—who was hanged for his trouble. Anyway," he concluded firmly, "it was all two hundred years ago and we aren't here to examine that case."

"Why not?" asked Cam. "It might be very instructive."

Honeywether scratched his head bad-temperedly.

"Don't talk rot," he said crossly, "and let's look at the place as it was last night—not hundreds of years ago in your imagination." He marched back to the altar steps and thought aloud. "Two men—or one man and one woman, I suppose—were standing at the altar steps between seven-twenty and eight o'clock. Where they came from or why they came we don't know. One of them seizes a candlestick from the altar and smashes the head of our corpse with it. Probably he—or she—stood at the top of the steps, while the victim stood at the foot. That would put a lot more power into the weight of the stick—it's not heavy, yet the skull is crushed through. I'll show you at the station. Then the murderer tossed the candlestick aside and went off in search of something else to finish the job. Why? *I* don't know. Anyway he found the knife in the vestry and came back to finish his butchery on the altar steps. Perhaps it was then that he lit the candles on the second holder so that he could see better. Not that it would have been very dark. He removed the clothes, lugged the body up on to the altar and laid him out with the candles at his head. But by some witchery he managed not to get a drop of blood on the floor during the operation—though the corpse is no feather-weight. All this is done in half an hour at most, probably much less."

"Perhaps," said Cam, "he had a rug or something over the carpet so as to catch the blood and took it away with him, along with the clothes."

"Why?" asked Honeywether. "Why all the trouble when he doesn't mind leaving buckets of the stuff everywhere else?"

Cam had no answer to this. He wandered down the nave aisle and stood nearer the west end of the church again looking east. His hand played idly with a bench-end in the form of a particularly vicious little monkey. In a style typical of Cornish church furniture there was a fine variety of carved bench-ends to the ancient pews, many of them secular and some grotesque. He noticed that the woodwork of the church shone with polished care. The thoroughness of the Verger's devotion was everywhere apparent. Even the prayer-books were in perfect order, large blue hymn-books and small red prayer-books alternating in every pew-rack. Beneath them the worn grey hassocks were precisely arranged to accommodate members of the congregation with a good three feet of space for each. Probably, he thought wryly, this orderliness was rarely disturbed nowadays, judging by the numbers of the congregation on Sunday. Not like old Mr. Bunting's day when villagers would come from miles around to hear his homely little sermons.

Cam had the sort of mind which instinctively reaches to set mantelpiece ornaments straight. His eye ran comfortably, therefore, over the ordered pews until it was jarred by a breach of discipline. In the second pew from the front several hymn-books were jammed together in a rack and beneath them four hassocks lay awry. It was a small disorder. No doubt this was where one of the members of that select vespers congregation had sat and the displacement had not yet been corrected. He wandered up and down the other two aisles searching for the places where others had sat. There appeared to have been two on the north aisle near the back, two more on the south side of the central aisle, squarely placed to keep the preacher's eye and probably belonging to a couple of elderly residents, one more on the south side near the door and well chosen for a quick exit as the words of the benediction died, and one more near the front, just under the pulpit, which was unmistakably where the Rector's wife sat, an example to the congregation and a support to her husband. That accounted for the seven, he thought, but the person in the second pew had certainly created more untidiness than all the others. The displacement of hymn-books and hassocks was such that he must have used three or four of each.

He wandered back to Honeywether who was peering into the interstices of the altar rails.

"Ever done any brass-rubbing?" Cam asked.

Honeywether straightened his back and looked at his friend with some disgust.

"What do you think I am?" he asked. "A tourist? Of course not."

"It's not tourists; it's antiquarians," Cam corrected mildly. "Briarley was telling me about it." At the mention of Briarley's name Honeywether looked more interested. "You see," explained his friend, "you take a sheet of white paper—the sort you use for lining drawers is best and it comes in long rolls. Then you lay it along the brass—like this one here. Oh, I forget. First you dust the brass so nothing on it can tear the paper. Well, when the paper is laid all you have to do is rub in long even heavy strokes up and down the whole plate with plain cobbler's heelball—that black, waxy, crayon stuff cobblers use for marking shoes. If you rub hard enough and long enough you get a handsome picture on your paper because the flat parts of the brass come up jet black and the engraving comes up white and sharp. You've probably rubbed a penny that way."

"What," asked Honeywether, "the h..." He remembered his surroundings just in time and corrected himself ponderously. "What possible bearing does that have upon this case, may I ask?"

"Ah!" said Cam sententiously. "Now doubtless a thought has struck you. How does one hold the paper in place whilst one rubs it violently with a piece of cobbler's heelball? Eh?" Honeywether's expression indicated that no such thought was troubling him. "Well, it struck me, anyway, and I asked Briarley. Obviously if the paper moved during the operation you would get the whole impression out of kilter. He tells me that you have to anchor the paper with anything that's handy. Sometimes brasses are on the wall and you stick the paper up with sticking plaster—or chewing-gum. When it's on the floor—and if no vergers are there to protest—you use hassocks and hymn-books, a few at each corner."

Honeywether still looked uninterested and Cam sighed.

"Let me lead you further, man. It just occurred to me that if John Briarley stayed on after evening service he probably, from what I know of his interests, had one idea in mind. He wanted to see the brass. And no doubt, once he had looked at it again he also wanted to rub it. So what more natural than that he should seize his chance and a few hassocks and set to. On Sunday afternoon, he told me, he went to rub brasses at Powey. He must have gone to vespers on his way back to the hotel so he would have his paper and heelball with him. It strikes me that with that young man to think is to act. Nothing more natural than that he should take the opportunity of the empty church and the evening light to rub his brass."

"Proof?" said Honeywether with interest.

"There are seven displaced prayer-books and hassocks, one for each member of the congregation. But at one place there is a regular convulsion of hassocks and hymn-books. That's perhaps where Briarley borrowed a few to hold down his paper."

Honeywether went to confirm this and nodded at last reluctantly.

"Well, that's an explanation of his delay here," he agreed. "That rubbing would take some time, I suppose. The full twenty minutes, say, we know he was here. But it only provides him with an excuse for staying on," he added, brightening. "We've no proof he actually did rub the thing."

"That's very true," said Cam. "And as a matter of fact when I talked with him about the murder at breakfast today he complained bitterly that he wouldn't be able to rub the brass here. So, unless he was bluffing, he certainly never finished the brass, even if he started it. I wonder why."

Honeywether pursed his lips. "I don't like it at all," he said. "It doesn't seem rational. Not that I, for one, ever expect these intellectual types to be rational. Brass rubbing! And there's another thing, Cam! He went to Powey to rub brasses yesterday afternoon, did he? Well, why the devil did he want to go back again in the evening? Because, according to the ferryman, he did. Now I don't suppose it could be because he wanted to get rid of something, eh? The clothes of the corpse for instance? He was carrying a bag, I do know."

"He always carries a cricket bag with his brass-rubbing materials," Cam explained. "Perhaps he had forgotten something in Powey—dropped his hanky. Perhaps he wanted to apologise to Miss Rowan and was chasing her."

"Perhaps he's as innocent as a babe," said Honeywether impatiently. "But he is still my next port of call. Come on, Cam. We've finished here for a moment."

The two men left the church together. Cam lingered at the door a moment, looking over the village roofs to the blue sea beyond.

"What's the matter with this place?" he asked suddenly. "Prettiest village I ever saw. Every prospect indubitably pleases but man seems remarkably naughty. I don't remember it being like this in the old days, Honeywether. Of course I was only a kid then. But it makes me feel quite old to find the haunts of my childhood turned so sour."

"It's the War," said Honeywether glibly.

Cam sniffed rudely. "It's always 'the War'."

"You weren't here during it or you would understand. Every sort of trouble I had. Everything from shop-lifting to witchcraft. Now we're settling down again, thank God. But you can't expect a village this size to play host to three thousand professional dare-devils and foreigners without losing some of its equilibrium."

"Witchcraft?" Cam repeated with interest. "Now that's one thing I've never had in my district. Did you have a case?"

Honeywether shrugged. "I cleared it up without going that far. Those cases are rather tricky nowadays, though the Witchcraft Act is still on the books, of course. It wasn't straight old English witchcraft, though, so heaven knows what trouble I might have had. Black Magic was mixed up in it too. We had some West Indian troops here who knew a thing or two about that. Together with local superstitions it made an explosive mixture. Regular orgies they had on the cliffs out towards Poltherow, just about where the American camp is! Some went because they wanted a thrill, some because they had nothing else to do when the cinema was closed, some because, if there *was* something in it they wanted to be on the safe side, some because one kind of mischief is as good as another. It was quite a time before I heard about the game. Local people can be pretty close when they want to. You can bet I took quick action when I heard. I had some of the servicemen transferred and put the fear of God into three or four local ruffians so that they closed shop in a hurry. Old Rector," he added wistfully, "wouldn't have allowed such goings-on."

"A fine old fellow," agreed Cam. "He really knew these parts too. Mr. Copperman came quite recently, didn't he?"

"Uh-huh. Early in the war when Mr. Banting died, and he has never really taken hold of things. People never took to him, though he tried to be amiable in the beginning. But now— well, as long as the roses aren't blighted he doesn't worry much. I suppose he thinks the village is a bit beneath him."

"Has he seen better days then?" asked Cam.

50

"He was a Canon of Manchester. Quite a scholar, they say. But he got ill and resigned. So he came to Trevelley. I doubt if he could afford to retire completely. Anyway he certainly doesn't pull his weight here."

"What about his lady?"

"Oh, she's a real saint," Honeywether exclaimed enthusiastically. "Worth ten of him. No doubt who wears the breeches there. Everybody respects her. A fine lady!"

"Do they live alone there?" Cam asked, pointing across to the Rectory.

"No, Giles Allen, the curate, lives with them. A nice young feller who does his best to make up for Mr. Copperman's deficiencies. They have no maids living in. Couldn't afford it, I guess. One of the village women goes up daily."

"Where was Allen at the time of the murder? You haven't said much about him."

"I haven't forgotten him. But he was at Powey taking evening service. He does it every three weeks. It starts there at six-thirty and ends at seven forty-five. He always takes the five-thirty ferry and cycles to the village, arriving about six, with plenty of time to change into his vestments. Then he spends the night with an old friend there. He hasn't returned yet so I haven't questioned him personally. But it looks as though he were out of the running."

Cam laughed. "You know I suspect cast-iron alibis. What about the Verger? Was he really ill?"

"I've no reason to think otherwise. He certainly suffers something awful from his insides and when sickness gets hold of him he's completely out. The son says he was ill and he is too simple to be a convincing liar. Anyway, look at the crime. The old man wouldn't have the heart to desecrate his own church in that way. He lives for it. He is far more broken up by the murder than the Rector is."

Cam nodded absently. "A desecration," he muttered. "Of course it must be that. Honeywether," he asked abruptly, "are you sure that you wiped out that witchcraft—sure that you didn't just drive it underground?"

Honeywether raised a defensive hand.

"Don't even suggest it! There hasn't been a murmur for two years, Cam, and I've kept my eye on the source of the trouble, you can be sure. They wouldn't catch me napping again. There's one family—the Cowdrays—who were at the root of the whole affair and they have too much sense to start the same game again."

There was a long contemplative silence and then Honeywether added slowly:

"I wonder if all this religious hocus-pocus is rather leading us off the track. Perhaps it's meant to. After all, a corpse in a church is no more dead than anywhere else. Once we know who he is—was—the whole purpose of the crime will probably appear quite straightforward."

"I doubt it," said Cam. "It all smells very crooked to me."

"You and your smells!" sneered Honeywether.

"They're not to be sneezed at," Cam defended himself. "I think I'll leave you for a little to sniff it all out. By lunch you'll have the thing solved, I'm sure. And as for me," he turned towards the gate, "I'd rather like to pay a visit to the Rector. I'll introduce myself. He ought to be glad to meet a member of his congregation. An exclusive group, I gather. I'll see you at lunch in half an hour, if that's all right."

Honeywether looked at him suspiciously.

"I've questioned him myself," he said doubtfully. "I don't see what you expect to get out of him." For the Inspector wanted a disciple, not a free-lance, working on the case with him. Cam on the loose was likely to go off at disconcerting tangents. The latter read his expression and laughed.

"Listen, old sleuth, you can't interfere with my holiday and then not let me do things my own way. Where's your sense of justice?"

The other grinned shamefacedly.

"Do as you like, Cam—up to a point—and good luck to you. But for God's sake don't get me into trouble. I've got enough on my hands. Tell you what—I'll give you a free drink for every clue or witness you produce as long as you bring them straight to me and don't try to solve the case on your own. Isn't that fair?"

There was bluff assurance in his voice that as Cam could anyway not hope to beat him—Honeywether—to a solution the drinks were by way of largesse. But incidentally he was taking no chances.

"It's a deal," said Cam, rubbing his hands. In another man's district he had no professional jealousy. "Free drinks let it be. And in pints, Honeywether, don't forget. So then we shall all be happy. You'll have the outward glory and I shall have the inward glow. A fair exchange!"

# CHAPTER IV

THE rectory stood across the lane from the church, its mid-Victorian pinnacles poking above the elms. A rookery high in the branches was filling the air with hoarse complaint. The cadaverous brick building looked a far more suitable setting for murder than the church itself. The upper windows were dirty and uncurtained. Apparently, Cam conjectured, the Rector's wife had solved the profound antithesis between family-minded Victorian living space and inadequate modern domestic help by closing part of the house. As he pulled the knob of the door-bell he could hear it tinkling faintly through remote passages. Even in an abbreviated form the domestic quarters must be extensive. Mrs. Copperman came to the door herself after a few minutes. Her features were thinly drawn and rather pinched about the nose, but there was nothing fretful or tense about her, and her eyes, though a trifle cool, were not hostile. She had the unusual quality of quiet hands, of letting her long fingers he motionless when not in use. Her dress was grey, rather long and almost ostentatiously simple. Even the grey bodice buttons were plain bone. Her only ornament was the unusual one of a long knotted silver chatelaine chain which hung knotted about her waist and supported a cross, a pencil, a small penknife, a thimble-case and a seal of St. Christopher—all in silver. Very high church, thought Cam. Her lavender perfume might have been incense. He found it impossible to imagine her kneeling in terror before the altar. What could terrify a woman of this calm self-sufficiency?

"Yes?" she asked with a tone of cool enquiry which might have received equally a parishioner or a pedlar.

"How d'you do, ma'am," Cam said politely, rather wishing he had a tie on. "My name's Cam. I'm from Little Biggling, up Gloucester way. I hope you're not going to think me impertinent but I used to spend holidays here in Trevelley when I was a boy. The Rector then used to be Mr. Banting—as fine a man as I ever knew. So coming back after all these years I thought it only decent to come on a sort of pilgrimage here...."

He paused, feeling that the fact that his story was half true did not prevent it sounding rather hollow. Mrs. Copperman regarded him with a decided absence of simple trust. It struck Cam now that his introduction was exactly that which any curious sightseer, eager to pry into a sensational murder, would choose. He rebuked himself mentally for not having elaborated a more convincing excuse for the visit. But apparently Mrs. Copperman, suspicious or not, felt that she could not run the risk of turning away a conceivably honest Christian.

"Do come in," she murmured, standing aside. "My husband, Mr. Copperman, is Mr. Banting's successor. I am sure he would like to meet you. He is in the garden. Perhaps we might join him."

She led the way silently through a long hall which was unexpectedly pleasant. Sun poured in through pseudo-Gothic lancet windows and reflected the colours from the stained glass of the transoms upon the uncarpeted stone floors and whitewashed walls. The variety of colour was picked up again by extravagant bowls of flowers, set in dark corners which they made lively with their own exuberance. As they passed through the french windows of the barely furnished dining-room into the garden Cam saw the rich source of this display—a magnificent herbaceous border in full bloom at the far end of a fine lawn which stretched in unbroken perfection from the house for some twenty yards. Against the six-foot wall which encompassed the garden and hid it from the road were espalier trees laden with promising fruit, and beyond the herbaceous border was a glimpse of a well-stocked kitchen garden. The man apparently responsible for all this was bent over one small rose-bush, pruning away suckers. Mrs. Copperman stopped silent for a moment until he had finished the operation. Then she stepped quietly across the lawn.

"Robert dear," she said. "Here is a gentleman to see you. He knew Mr. Banting."

At her first words the figure had straightened and the Rector turned round with an expression of quite youthful animation. Cam had remembered him as an old man in the pulpit and the transformation astonished him. On seeing Cam, however, the corners of his mouth drooped into tired resignation. His shoulders slumped, his age seemed to double and he looked at the Inspector without pleasure.

"Mr. Banting?" he said doubtfully. "Oh, yes, of course!"

Cam plunged into a rather effusive story of his happy childhood days, feeling Mrs. Copperman's eyes upon him and knowing that he was offending the memory of Mr. Banting with every banal word. The Rector listened with weary indifference.

"I never really knew Banting," he managed to say in a pause between Cam's memories of holiday escapades. "Everyone tells me he was very remarkable." There was unmistakable bitterness in his tone. "This is my first parish. I've always been an academic cleric. I made the mistake of thinking I was being lazy and must do some real parish work before I grew too old. Well," he said sourly, "no doubt Banting knew how to handle things. I'd like to know how he did it."

"You don't like it here?" Cam said with honest surprise. "I should have thought it was a delightful parish."

"Impossible people to understand unless you're born and bred here. That's the trouble. Some of them are interesting enough. There's one old red-haired rogue I go fishing with. But how they think and what they think I'll never know."

"Robert dear," said Mrs. Copperman. "Isn't that the Mrs. Henry Bowles rose you are pruning? You should tell Mr. Cam about its history."

It was remarkable how the very sound of his wife's voice changed the Rector's train of thought. His face brightened became younger, his shoulders straightened and he plunged into a discussion on gardening and rose-pruning. This was a subject close to Cam's own heart and within a few minutes they were exchanging weed-killing recipes with great enthusiasm.

In half an hour Cam had almost forgotten the purpose of his visit in the pleasure of talking with a man who was so obviously expert in his hobby. Mrs. Copperman, who had been standing silently by, interrupted.

"Robert dear," she said, and Cam noticed that she usually preceded her few remarks with this form of address and that they always aroused the same quick attention in her husband. "Robert dear, it's one o'clock. I wonder if Mr. Cam would care to stay to lunch so as not to interrupt your conversation."

Equally regardless of Mrs. Copperman's and Mrs. Honeywether's convenience, Cam accepted immediately. He was aware that the latter would be waiting for him, that the former had no choice but to invite him, but he was enjoying his visit. In any case he excused himself, until he had turned the conversation on to the subject of murder he could not, in fairness to Honeywether, take his leave.

There was an interruption to the garden peace of the Rectory as they were going in lunch. The gate on to the road opened with a loud squeal. Through it strode a gaunt figure which Cam recognised as the Verger armed, as if for attack, with a rake. Mrs. Copperman had already disappeared towards the kitchen in search of an extra plate for Cam. The Rector, after one glance towards the intruder turned with a growl to the french windows and stepped hastily in. So Cam with some embarrassment found himself alone with—what was his name?—Yardley. The old man looked at him without friendship.

"Whar be Rector?" he asked abruptly. "Whar did he run off to, eh?"

"He just stepped inside for a moment, I think," Cam said hopefully. "Do you want to see him?"

"O' course I do. Whoy else should I be here? Be you a

newspaper feller?"

"No," said Cam. "I'm just paying a friendly call." There was no reason why he should explain, but he did not want to antagonise the old man. A jaundiced pallor witnessed that the Verger was indeed in serious ill-health. Even now there was a shadow of fever in the savage, deep-set eyes. He did not look like a man with whom it was easy to deal. Cam felt a twinge of sympathy for the Rector.

The old man did not restrain his antagonism now.

"We'm havin' lots o' callers, nowadays," he snarled. "Everyone peepin' an' pryin'. All the riff-raff from the village an' the strangers from the 'Fishers' comin' to see *my* church as though et be a picture-house!"

"I thought it was God's church, not yours," Cam could not resist saying rather self-righteously. To his surprise the Verger was taken aback. A bluish flush spread over his cheeks and he jabbed at the path with downcast eyes.

"Aye," he said after a pause. "You be in the right. Thet war vain-glorious, et war. Mr. Banting wouldna have liked et."

"I knew him," Cam said. "A fine gentleman he was."

The Verger looked at him with something approaching respect.

"Any fool could see ut," he agreed in almost amiable tones. "He knew the Word of God like nobbut else in the world."

"A sad day for the village when he passed on." Cam pressed his advantage.

"Ah!" said Yardley meaningly, with a sidelong glance at the open french windows. "Satan has been goin' to an' fro in the earth an' walkin' up an' down in et. Nothin' but trouble for the flock, mister, since the shepherd war lost. The Lord has given us over an' they that plan iniquity an' sow wickedness reap the same. 'Tes His will, though, an' we must bear et dutiful-like. 'Hast Thou not poured me out like milk and curdled me like cheese,' eh?"

The old man looked at Cam fiercely as one expecting an

answer. The Inspector knew his Bible, but that was new to him and he could not cap it.

"So you think this lovely little place is wicked," he commented weakly. It was the second time that day he had heard such views.

"It looks innocent enough."

"Like the harlot's face," the Verger said bitterly. "Yet there'll be changes soon enough, mister. The Lord es movin' myster'usly Hes wonders to perform. I see the light comin'."

"What about the murder?" Cam asked mildly. That doesn't look very like 'light' to me! 'Affliction,'" he added with some self-satisfaction, "'cometh not forth of the dust, neither doth trouble spring out of the ground.'"

The Verger, to Cam's amazement, brightened and even attempted a rusty smile. "Aye, thet was owld Satan," he said incomprehensibly. "Now he's gone things wull be better."

"Do you mean the corpse was Satan—or the murderer?"

"Et be the end," said the Verger solemnly. "I promise, you et be the finish."

"How..." began Cam, but the Rector at this point appeared suddenly at the door as if in tardy remembrance of his guest.

"Come along!" he said impatiently. Lunch is ready. What do you want, Yardley?"

"I want to clean my... the church," the Verger said a suggestion of truculence underlying his tone. "I want to wash thet blood off et, I do."

"Well, it's no good coming to me." The Rector scowled, more nervously than in ill-temper. "Inspector Honeywether is now in charge and we must wait upon his orders. Perhaps he will allow us in before next Sunday."

"Et's scand'lous!" Yardley exclaimed. "And hev you seen them dev'lish drawings what summun bin makin' in t'porch. Eh, but I oughtta sleep at church, I should, to keep th' ruffians out."

"Drawings?" asked the Rector. "What sort?"

The Verger described in Old Testament terms the crayon

picture which Cam had noticed an hour ago. The Rector was enraged.

He went pale and red in turn.

"Who dared do it?" he stammered. "What beastly vulgarity! It's unforgivable! Who did it, Yardley? My God, man, aren't you ever about when needed?"

"Et's a sad day," exclaimed Yardley, "when the Rector himself taketh the name of the Lord our God in vain! Nay, Mr. Copperman, et's not known to me who's bin defilin' the church an' makin' a mock of our Maker. But one thing I'll say, Mr. Copperman, an' no one shall stop me. Whither the shepherd goes so goes the flock, Mr. Copperman. There be nasty things afoot here from stem to stern o' Trevelley. The devil's at work an' he spareth not the house of God, Mr. Copperman. An' I'm thinking there be too many who take their duties lightly. Not your lady, God bless her soul. I don't mean her. But there be others, there be others. I've bin here sixty years an' more and though I've bin a great sinner I dunna recall such wickedness en all me born days. Et's a purge we be needin', Mr. Copperman, a weedin' out, root an' branch. And I'm thinkin' thet when the Lord moves He'll spare neither t' high nor th' lowly amongst the unrighteous. An' move He will, Mr. Copperman! Move He will!"

The Verger stumped off, swinging his rake angrily, leaving the Rector and Cam in equal embarrassment. But Cam's confusion was mixed with considerable sly interest and the Rector seemed less surprised than exasperated.

"Pay no attention," he said shortly. "The old man's getting on, I fear. Come on. Lunch will be getting cold."

As they passed from the radiant garden into the dining-room Mr. Copperman scrupulously scraped his boots and dropped the gardening gloves and tools which he still carried into a box by the door. Cam picked up one of these tools, a short-bladed pair of secateurs, and examined it curiously.

"Pretty old model this, isn't it?" he asked. "You can get good ones with springs now, you know."

"Of course I know," the Rector said irritably. "But I like a plain knife myself, anyway. My best one is now in the hands of the police so I have to use this thing."

Cam manifested astonishment and the Rector added hastily:

"They found it in the church. Used for the murder, y'know. I'll have to get a new one."

"D'you mean to say the murderer stole his knife from here!" Cam exclaimed. "The one he did it with! What almighty cheek!"

The Rector glared rather helplessly about him and a cool voice spoke from the other end of the dining-room.

"I took it myself to the church for cutting the stems of the altar flowers, Mr. Cam, and left it in the vestry. Robert dear, I feel very guilty about depriving you of it—even unintentionally." Mr. Copperman mumbled something unintelligible about police incompetence. In the embarrassed pause which suddenly paralysed the atmosphere Cam hastily remarked that they must have a fine supply of altar flowers at this time of year. Were they using the roses? Mrs. Copperman said no, she liked the lupins at present and they made a much finer display of colour against the green of the Trinity altar cloth. Fortunately they were seating themselves at this moment and Cam's expression of sudden conjecture passed notice.

There were just the three of them at the great refectory table before the french windows. Mrs. Copperman brought in the omelette.

"Where's Annie?" asked her husband irritably. You shouldn't have to do this."

"Annie can't come," she replied. "I m afraid we shall have to get on without her for a few days."

"Because of the—the murder?..." he questioned after a pause, and she nodded.

Cam assumed a lugubrious expression.

"I'm afraid it wasn't very considerate of me to call upon

61

you at this time, sir. You must be having your difficulties. I noticed," he added with casual duplicity, "a story about it in the paper."

"Insufferable!" exclaimed the Rector, with a glance of concern at his wife. Cam noticed now how alike the two were, both pinched in face and grey in complexion and yet how the strain of his expression and the tranquillity of hers disguised die resemblance.

"Disgusting!" the Rector was exclaiming. "The papers write as though it were a sensation arranged for their special benefit. And their wretched reporters nosing round the place looking for trouble. Possibly not one has been in a church before, but they act now as if their salvation depended on getting into this one. Turning this harbour of grace into a Roman holiday. "Not", he added gloomily, "that my parishioners are much better. I blame myself, God knows, but this morning I had the churchwardens up here demanding that I ask for a re-opening of the church—not from any desire to worship there but so as to get a little extra tourist trade for their miserable shops!... They actually said so! I was astounded. Somehow I never expected commercialism so deep-rooted, though Heaven knows I've never had cause to expect otherwise."

"Robert dear," said Mrs. Copperman warningly. "I'm sure we all know the churchwardens have the interests of the church at heart."

This time he refused to heed her obvious warning that it was better not to wash dirty linen before strangers. Without looking at her he spoke bitterly.

"I don't pretend to understand them. I never have and I never shall. They pretend to be devout, but when God gives them this lovely church they resent paying a penny towards its upkeep. I gave a series of sermons on its history and they stayed away in droves. And why don't they agree to some repairs to this brick heap here? And why don't they do something to make this a reasonable living and not a starvation pittance....

Perhaps I should never have been a parish priest. At Minchester we lived like gentlefolk in the service of God. I confess it's difficult to change to this kind of penury at my time of life."

"The labourer is worthy of his hire—if I may say so," Cam murmured sycophantically. Mrs. Copperman looked at her guest strangely.

"You think so, do you?" the Rector said. "Well, I've not found many here with the same opinion."

Cam believed him. But he preferred the Rector on roses to the Rector on churchwardens. The blindness of countrypeople to their surroundings—both from the artistic and spiritual point of view—was an old story to him. A countryman himself he was only saved from the same indifference by having spent some years in London. He could appreciate natural beauties now as well as any townsman, but he did not expect fellow-villagers to do the same. The Rector's shocked amazement was only a sign of his city origins and city tastes.

The conversation proceeded now into a bitter dissertation by the Rector on the indifference of the villagers to the God-given loveliness of their environment. A little less interest in nature and a little more in people would make for a better parish, Cam thought. But he was silent and the Rector was interrupted only occasionally by Mrs. Copperman making gentle amendments to his exclamations.

Gradually the Rector's anger was expended and he drifted into a more positive description of the beauties of his church. He relaxed. His voice became gentle and urbane and Cam realised now that he was listening to a man of wit and erudition—slightly curdled, perhaps, but stimulating still. The best evidence of the Rector's talent was the rapt attention of his wife. She followed every word with silent enjoyment of its style as much as its content. Cam, who was aware that his own conversation had long since ceased to interest his wife except as a means of conveying information, thought enviously that some genius must be required to be able to amuse one's wife—

and even at lunch.

Eventually there came a pause and Cam reluctantly took the opportunity to return to the subject of the murder.

"In such a place," he said after a pause murder seems inappropriate as well as evil. It must," he said, turning to the Rector's wife, "have been a terrible experience for you Finding the body, I mean. Especially having no idea who the body was, as it were."

"I can't say that made much difference," she said reasonably. "It might have been much worse if I had known him. But it wasn't pleasant." She got up quietly and went into the kitchen for the sweet. The Rector's eyes followed her and there was bitter anger in them again.

"It's intolerable!" he burst out, turning again to Cam. "Exposing *her* to something like that simply because he cannot or will not do his job. I'd have retired him months ago if it weren't for the churchwardens. This time he'll go though—either he or I."

After a second of thought Cam guessed that the Verger was the subject of this attack.

"He was ill, wasn't he?" he asked mildly.

"So he says," muttered Mr. Copperman darkly. "But he was well enough to get to the church. Why couldn't he close it? Bad blood will out, I say. He may have pulled the wool over my predecessor's eyes but he can't do the same with me. He has always been most un-co-operative from the moment I arrived here. As if I were an intruder on his territory. But in that he has not been singular. From the day I arrived here there has not been a word of welcome not a sign of friendliness. Not," he added hastily, "that I seek for friends here. That's too much to expect."

"Robert dear!" his wife said reproachfully as she came back again "You mustn't give Mr. Cam the impression that all the people here are so wicked. Yardley is a very good man. You know you really admire him and you can't blame him for last night. When I went to see him just after Vespers he was in great pain. I wanted to close the church myself then and there but he insisted on getting up. He has a great sense of devotion to the church, Mr. Cam, and was terribly upset at missing the service. It would break his heart, I think, to be retired. The church is all his life. He has suffered enough, I think."

"He looks it," said Cam.

Mrs. Copperman shook her head gravely. "It is not just the big things—though the early death of his wife and a simple-minded son and perpetual ill-health are trials enough. But in every little thing he is so unlucky. There never was a man so plagued by ill-luck—always losing things or burning things or falling down and hurting himself. They even use it as a proverb in the village—speaking of unlucky people as having 'Yardley's luck. He is much to be pitied."

"Like Job," said Cam, remembering the source of those biblical quotations flung at him. Apparently Yardley himself was aware of the likeness.

"Mostly carelessness," said the Rector. "One has to be practical about these things. If he can't do his job he'll have to go." He concentrated on his prunes and custard. Cam wondered which of the Coppermans was really the more practical.

"Yardley looks a very remarkable personality," he murmured.

"He is." Mrs. Copperman hastily anticipated her husband. "A most unusual person. A great sinner once, I'm told—he would tell you so himself for that matter. But our predecessor, Mr. Banting, won a great victory there and converted him to Christ about fifteen years ago. Since then he has never wavered, although he has certainly not gained in worldly comfort. A little strict, perhaps, but where the battle has been hardest the defences must be strongest."

Cam detected an edge of evangelical enthusiasm to her level voice and wondered momentarily what satisfaction her husband could give to that side of her nature. Mr. Copperman could have converted few people in his time.

"A pity the fellow wasn't about, anyway," he suggested. "I suppose his presence would have frightened off the murderer and the whole thing would never have happened."

"Very unfortunate," said the Rector. There was a wealth of unpleasant implication in his voice.

"Giles's absence was equally unfortunate," his wife said unexpectedly and in a tone which Cam did not quite understand.

"If he had been here the church would in any case have been locked up on time."

"Well, it's too late to talk about what might have been," the Rector said impatiently. "Allen *had* to take the Powey service; Yardley *had* to be ill; I *had* to water the roses before it was dark. The day was cursed, that's all."

"Well," said Cam pacifically, "at least you are not the only church to be troubled by criminals. Of course murder is in a different class, but the Cathedral Robberies are bad enough. Sacrilege seems to be taking on wholesale proportions nowadays, Mr. Copperman."

"Of course it is," the Rector growled. "What do you expect in these unholy days? A criminal would as soon rob or murder in a church as anywhere else—and we certainly make things easy for them. Why, at Minchester—I used to be a Canon there—at Minchester they left the library wide open for visitors with only one attendant on duty. When he was out of the room—as he usually was—there was not a soul there to stop the Robarts Tapestry being taken by whoever took a fancy to it. And so it was stolen. I suppose it was the same in all the other churches. The whole trouble undoubtedly is that we've trusted too much in the Church in the goodwill of mankind. It can't go on. We shall have to lock up everything like sensible property owners. Do I leave the house and the garden gate unlocked when we go out? Of course not! It's wicked to put such temptation before people."

Mrs. Copperman sighed. "Of course you're right, dear," she said. "But it does seem that the Church ought to set an example in mutual trust. After all, it's obviously one criminal gang which has been robbing the cathedrals. Once they are caught the whole incident will be closed. I don't think the Church should be frightened into hasty action."

"How do you know it's a 'gang'?" the Rector returned. "It's *my* view that since one criminal showed how easy it was to rob the Church, all the others who are sufficiently literate to read the newspapers have been picking out their own ecclesiastical establishments to despoil. Even our police would surely have traced a 'gang' operating on such a vast scale. In any case," he concluded triumphantly, "'gangs' are American—not English."

"In the criminal world, even here," Cam said ingenuously, "I am told they are not uncommon. Well, I'm sure you lock up *your* church plate carefully, anyway, Mr. Copperman." To his surprise Mr. Copperman looked at him with sudden venom. As their eyes met Cam was taken unawares. For a moment he was faced with naked antagonism. The second passed and Cam took a hasty mouthful to cover his confusion. Mrs. Copperman was talking however.

"You ought to ask Giles Allen about the Cathedral Robberies," she said. "He has strong views on it. Mr. Allen is our curate."

"Is he a young fellow from Bristol?" Cam asked innocently. "I used to know a curate at St. Peter and St. Paul's there. ..."

"No, he's just out of the army," the Rector interrupted rapidly. He was flushing slightly, perhaps embarrassed at having been taken off guard—but off guard against what? "I can't afford a curate, heaven knows, but this living serves two hamlets as well as Trevelley—Powey and Poltherow—so I had to get someone. We spread our ministrations rather thin as it is. I give two morning services out of three here, and one every six weeks at Poltherow and at Powey. Allen takes one morning service at each church every three weeks. Yesterday was his morning at Poltherow, his evening at Powey. We have the same rotation for evening services. It means that one Sunday out of three they have either no morning or no evening service at Powey and Poltherow."

"Do the villagers complain?" asked Cam. "Though I don't see how you could arrange it differently."

"Of course they complain," said the Rector. "It doesn't matter to them that in all sorts of weather either Allen or I have to cycle interminable distances to hold service for a handful of congregation. That's what we're here for, they claim."

"Don't you have a car?" Cam asked with some sympathy, for the Rector was certainly old to have to face such excursions.

"A car!" exclaimed Copperman in mock surprise. "Only the fishermen here can afford cars. No, we have to walk or cycle."

"There is hope," Mrs. Copperman said, "that Powey will have its own rector soon. The village has grown a good deal recently. Then we shall only have Poltherow, which is comparatively near."

"Mr. Allen had a busy Sunday yesterday," Cam commented. "Poltherow in the morning; Powey in the afternoon. The day of rest indeed! He must have been tired when he got back."

"He's not back," said the Rector. "He spends the night in Powey when he takes evening service there. Giles has one advantage. He was born here. Knows the country well and has friends in all the villages. His family, as a matter of fact, used to be the big family here. They lost their money and their house three generations ago and since then the village has had no real squire. But Giles's father was ordained and was rector here before Banting."

"It must be pleasant for a young man to come back from the army to start work again in his own part of the world," Cam said sentimentally.

"It depends on what part of the world is his own," Mr. Copperman said bitterly. "Trevelley holds no attractions for me, anyway. It used to. I even looked forward to coming here, if you'll believe me. But it's worn me out."

"A little more time, dear," murmured Mrs. Copperman. "Just a little more time and it may be better."

There was a thoughtful silence at this gentle comfort. The Rector looked at his plate. Cam looked absently at the centre-piece of lupins and ornamental grasses.

"A charming arrangement, if I may say so," he commented eventually. Mrs. Copperman followed his glance with a certain complacency.

"I just threw them together," she deprecated. "They are very untidy, I am afraid, though the blooms themselves are lovely." She drew one of the flowers out, shortened its stem with a swift cut of the penknife on her chatelaine and put it gently back. "There," she said, "that's better."

"Do you enjoy the garden, then, as much as your husband does?" asked Cam.

She laughed. "There's not room for two enthusiasts in a garden, Mr. Cam. No, while he works in the garden I look after the house—and steal all his flowers for the glorification of my part of the establishment."

"Lucky Mr. Allen," said Cam jovially, "to benefit by the labours of both of you!"

As if on this cue, there came a sudden staccato racket of opening doors in the hall and swift steps approaching the dining-room. An air of strained suspense seemed to seize Cam's hosts. Mrs. Copperman looked round quietly but with a forced and erect attention to the door. Her husband, motionless, sat with fork half raised to his open mouth. The door was flung open and a singularly unalarming young man burst in. Only a clerical collar distinguished him from the mass of even-featured, even-tempered young men who busy themselves strenuously in English holiday resorts—only the 'dog' collar and the anxious, harrowed expression with which he confronted them.

"Robert! Cecily! Is it true? I can't believe it! I cycled over at once when I saw the papers. In the church itself! This is *too* much!"

Mrs. Copperman answered. The Rector had lain down his fork and was wiping his mouth nervously. Even his wife's voice seemed a shade strained.

"It's true, Giles, I'm afraid. We shall just have to stand all together and keep calm now." There was a shade of warning in her tone and Cam, trying to look inconspicuous by burying his face in a serviette, sought for some connection between this and the curious impatience of Giles's 'This is *too* much'. But her next words startled him out of such consideration.

"This is Mr. Cam, Giles. He knew Mr. Banting. He is a friend of Mr. Honeywether's too, I believe. Didn't I see you visiting the church with him this morning, Mr. Cam? I suppose you *are* a policeman?"

# CHAPTER V

CAM was a staunch supporter of the employment of women in the police force. He frequently said that if he had his way he would always use a woman to interrogate suspects—preferably his wife. In later years he was always to couple Mrs. Copperman's name with that of his wife. At this moment, however, he could not objectively admire the timing of her question. He felt himself turning a slow red. She had succeeded in making him look a fool without even the comfort to his self-esteem of appearing a knave. It was a ridiculous situation and he thought he could sense the quiet enjoyment the Rector's wife took in it. Giles Allen, of course, was unconscious of the joke and merely regarded the Inspector with the mildly respectful curiosity which all civilians take in those who dabble with crime. The Rector, however, exploding furiously, lent to the scene a little melodrama which Cam indeed thought preferable to farce.

"A policeman! Do you mean to say a... I never heard of such a thing!... A policeman! In my own house!" He sprang to his feet and glared indignantly at the intruder.

"Robert dear," said Mrs. Copperman. "I didn't mean that Mr. Cam came here to investigate us. That would be absurd. He need only have come and said so if that were the case. I'm sure Mr. Cam came here in good faith."

"As a matter of fact, I didn't," Cam said, brazen now that he was exposed. "I came because I wanted to meet you as ordinary people, not as a police inspector interviewing suspects. I know it's not in the book of rules, however. If you want to complain it's quite within your rights and you should do so." He felt fairly safe in this as complaints would go to Honeywether who in self-defence, as well as comradeship, would know how to deal with and dispose of them.

"Suspects!" burst out the Rector and the curate simultaneously, one in indignation and the other in horror. "You can certainly believe I shall complain, sir!" added the senior. "I doubt if there's been such an infringement of the rights of private citizens since—since 1689."

"Robert dear!" Mrs. Copperman interrupted this historical hyperbole. "Of course we are suspects. Everyone in the village is, I suppose. What I can't understand is why, when we have already given our stories to Mr. Honeywether, he should check up on us in such an underhand way."

"You mustn't look at it like that," Cam defended his colleague and himself. "It wasn't to check up on your stories that I came, but to get an impression of your views of the case—and to meet you as a normal family group. The work of a police officer in a case like this," he continued in a pontifical vein, "is to discover and to explain the abnormal. It is in its deviation from the normal that a crime reveals itself. But naturally one cannot discover the abnormal without knowing what is normal. Honeywether knows it all, you see, through years of experience here. I have to try to put together the pre-murder picture from seeing people under conditions of post-murder strain and suspicion. My only reason for visiting you like this, I assure you, was to meet you as real people, not as witnesses. I'm sorry if you should take it any other way." Cam managed to introduce a note of hurt goodwill into his voice here and he ended on a pathetic note. "I am sincerely interested in gardening, Mr. Copperman!" He got up to go and the Rector's wife rose with him.

"Well, we certainly want to do all we can to help the police, Mr. Cam. We just don't understand the procedure, never having had anything to do with it before. Perhaps you can come back and talk with us some other time."

Cam read into this a promise that she would calm the troubled waters before his next visit. Judging by the Rector's expression this would be quite a task. As Cam turned to the door he bumped into the curate, who was still regarding him with puzzled indignation and curiosity.

"And what do you think of our 'family life'?" he asked, truculently. "Do you find it normal enough? I'm not sure I like this introduction of amateur psychology into police work. Why don't you stick to finger-prints and blood-stains? I should think it would be more profitable."

"It depends what you mean by 'profit'," Cam said pleasantly. "I've enjoyed my lunch a lot."

The young man turned away with an angry shrug. "A humorist!" he exclaimed scornfully to Mrs. Copperman. "Do all our village policemen try to model themselves on Gervase Fen, do you suppose?"

Cam left the room in bleak silence in the wake of Mrs. Copperman. At the door she said good-bye without resentment.

"You must excuse the men," she explained. "This is a terrible occurrence. The desecration of our church—you cannot appreciate what it means."

As he strode down hill Cam mused that it was always on the desecration of the church that people harped. The murder itself, and the terrible nature of the victim's death, were incidentals. Perhaps that was natural enough. The personality of the church was something familiar, powerful and persuasive here. The corpse was only an untenanted body without past or future, name or address. She was wrong, he thought. He could and did appreciate what the church meant to its consecrated clergy, when even he, a layman and stranger, found it difficult to remember that a man as well as the church had been outraged. He was glad to know her not infallible. By God, he thought, a woman like that would be hard to have a reckoning with. A sudden thought crossed his mind, but he dismissed it after brief consideration. She had the opportunity—a free run of the church both before and after Colly's discovery of the body—but what possible motive? He could not believe her, on the available evidence, capable of such violent action for personal motives. A religious maniac? Certainly unlike any maniac he had ever set eyes on. The desecration of the church would go against her grain even if she did not baulk at murder.

A podgy hand grasped him familiarly above the elbow.

"Just in time to have one before it closes, old man." It was the voice of Mr. Potts, the Covent Garden merchant. He can never have worked his way up from the bottom, Cam decided as he smiled a greeting. A voice like that would have made little impression in the morning racket of the Vegetable Market. It would, however, he suddenly thought, be a nice sweet tenor at church.

"Be glad to," he agreed to the implied invitation and they continued towards the 'Three Fishers' together. "Been for a walk?" Cam asked.

"Down to the station," the other said gloomily. "I'm expecting a friend to join me and went down to see when the next train gets in. Not till six. Ruddy inconvenient hanging around waiting. Expected him yesterday. Didn't I see you going up to the church with the Police Inspector?"

"That's right," Cam sighed. No one seemed to be ignorant of his movements. "Lots of blood and nothing else," he added, assuming his most effective Disgruntled Policeman air.

The other man wrinkled his nose in disgust.

"Don't know how you stand it. Never could abide blood myself—even my own. I was at that evensong service, y'know, just before the murder. Thank God I didn't hang around afterwards," he added sincerely. "It might have been me instead of whoever it was."

"What did you do after the service, then?" Cam asked curiously.

"Went down to the river and sat by the ferry. It's pretty there. Most visitors miss it because they're only looking for the sea. Me, I keep away from that! Too much ruddy water! So there I sat chatting with the ferryman while murder was done above me. It's a nasty thought, isn't it?"

"Well at least you have an alibi," Cam said jovially. "If you were talking to the ferryman all the time you can't have been cutting the fellow up in church."

The other looked at him in startled surprise. "I never thought of that! I mean—that they might suspect me. After all, I'm a visitor, ain't I? Good God!" He thought hard for a minute with obviously unsatisfactory results. "But I didn't talk with him all the time," he said uneasily. "He took that American girl over to the other side and I just sat there alone on the bank."

"But not for long, I suppose. Briarley came down then, didn't he?"

"I say," Potts said respectfully, "you do know it all, don't you? Yes, Briarley came down just after the ferry left, trying to catch up with his girl friend." He puzzled it out a little further and then his face brightened. "So that's all right, isn't it? I mean, that's an alibi. If Briarley was with me and I was with him until the ferry came back for him neither of us could 'ave—have done it?"

"That's right, I guess," Cam said comfortingly and forbearing to mention that eight was the dead-line, not seven-thirty. But he asked one more question. "Did anyone else cross while you were there?"

"Not a soul. I sat there until it was getting on for eight and quite chilly. The ferryman came back and we had a few more words. He's a dull chap, though. Then I went back to the hotel—passing the police on my way. Though, of course, I didn't know what they were after then. Gawd," he said bitterly, "this place is going to lose its trade quicker than you can say weasel if visitors get accused of murder just because they take an evening stroll."

He put his arm through Cam's with a curious comfort-seeking gesture. His interest in the case appeared to be quite perfunctory and now that his own innocence seemed established he changed the subject. He pointed across the road.

"There's young Briarley. Suppose we ask him along too. I was a bit hasty at breakfast, wasn't I? Anyway, the more the merrier. I like company. Fat men do, y'know." He laughed shyly and Cam thought what a disarming fellow he was. Without waiting for an answer the other ran across the road and seized Briarley who, cricket bag in hand, was gazing at the display of cosmetics, hot-water bottles, jar covers, aspirins and soap substitutes in the window of the chemist's shop. After a brief argument which Cam could not hear the pair came back together, the younger man rather ungraciously but Mr. Potts beaming with gregarious pleasure.

"This is something like a holiday," he said. "It's not that I mind peace but it's pretty dull here, don'tcha think? People seem kind of snooty too. None of the good old get-togethers I used to have in the bar of the Wattlebury Holiday Camp. If either of you ever want a good cheerful holiday that's the place for you and I'm the boy who can get you in. Never less than eight hundred lads and lasses and all out for a good time. You'd have the time of your life. And I know the Manager. Swimming in the indoor pool, dances, sports, obstacle races, sing-songs..." He sighed nostalgically. The other two said nothing though Briarley looked at him with startled horror.

They strolled on together, Mr. Potts bearing the brunt of the conversation and turning now to the iniquity of having to spend his whole holiday at a railway station. The sex of his tardy friend was not quite clear, but Cam hoped for the best. Perhaps it would be a Piccadilly flower-girl—they might have met each other in Covent Garden and the size of the 'girls' he knew would make a suitable partner for Mr. Potts.

The saloon bar of the 'Fishers' was crowded with tourists and journalists, happily exchanging drinks and gossip about the murder. By common agreement, therefore, they went into the Public which was almost empty at this hour. It was a pleasant timbered room, rich with the scent of sawdust, salt water, strong tobacco and beer. Two old fishermen, permanent fixtures, were wedged on a bench against the wall by a rough wooden table. Cam and Briarley took a table while Potts went to the bar to get drinks from Lucy who served in the bar during off-hours in the dining-room.

As the two joined in heavy repartee Cam turned to Briarley.

"Been rubbing?" he asked genially pointing to the ever-present cricket bag.

"Over at Powey," the other explained, and added in a low voice, "Have you been with Honeywether today?"

Cam manifested mild surprise. "Why yes, I have. Why? Oh, the Pollpen brass! I'm very sorry, Briarley. I forgot to ask about it."

Briarley grunted unhappily. "There's that. But I had another mouldy idea this morning and I wondered... Oh well, there's probably nothing in it."

"Have you seen Honeywether yourself?" Cam asked cautiously. "He's been wandering round town."

"Oh?" said the young man listlessly. "No, I haven't seen him. I got back about an hour ago from Powey." He paused and Cam wondered with surprise what had happened to the Inspector since they parted. He was not usually one to let grass grow beneath his feet. "I say," said Briarley suddenly, "did you know I went to evensong yesterday?" He did not wait for an answer. "I was last out too, and I wondered if that made me a witness or something. Not that I did witness anything, of course, but I just wondered what my legal position was."

"Tricky," Cam said judicially. "How long were you alone there after the others left?"

"About a quarter of an hour—twenty minutes. I was looking at the brass. You know—or probably you don't—I dropped in on Saturday and that old watch-dog of a verger wouldn't let me rub it. Quite right from his point of view, of course. Some pundits say it's not good for them to be rubbed too much, but one always regards oneself as a special case, I suppose. Anyway the Verger wasn't at evensong for some reason so I thought I'd seize the opportunity to do my rubbing after the service. I had paper and heelball with me."

"Did it take only fifteen minutes?" asked Cam. "I thought a rubbing took longer than that."

"This one would," Briarley said. "But I didn't finish. The Verger came along to close up, so I had to get out quickly, looking as though I had urgent business elsewhere. He gave me a very dirty look."

"Where did you go then?"

"Over to the other side and then for a walk along the cliffs to Powey. It's less crowded there than on our side."

"I must go over there again one day," Cam commented. "You seem to like it; yesterday morning, yesterday evening and again today. Are the brasses as good as all that?"

"They're not bad—one late fifteenth century. There's no one to stop you rubbing them, anyway. It's a quaint little church with a fine smuggler's hole in one of the churchyard tombs."

"Do all the local churches have them?" Cam asked. "Have you seen the one here?"

Briarley shook his head. "I've heard vaguely that there is one. In the tower, isn't it? No, I haven't seen it. That sort of thing doesn't interest me very much really. Brasses and architecture—those are what I'm after."

"What about Miss Rowan? Did you meet her on your walk?" Cam asked innocently. The young man reddened. "No. I'm afraid she is—was—rather cross with me. My fault, I was rather rude. We had a vague idea of having drinks together yesterday. She reminded me after Vespers. I tried to explain that this was my one chance to rub a brass I'd been after for years, but she didn't quite appreciate the importance of the opportunity."

"Women have no sense of proportion," Cam commiserated and the other nodded glumly.

"I think," said Cam, "you should tell Honeywether all this."

He brought the conversation to an abrupt close as Mr. Potts came back with three tankards. In better days they would have foamed exuberantly. Now they contained only an agreeable amber liquid, but the pewter was handsome and cool between the hands. Leaning back against the wall Cam and Potts chatted easily—holiday talk about weather and swimming and football pools. They drifted back to the question of smugglers holes, too, about which Potts was enthusiastic.

"It may sound queer from a Cockney," he confided, "but I've always had a hankering for those times. Even when I was a kid books about smugglers were my favourites. And now to think I'm actually here—my first visit!" He looked with enormous satisfaction at the two old fishermen across the room, investing them, no doubt, with every kind of piratical vice.

"The more you know about them the less you like them," Briarley said sternly. "A treacherous lot and vindictive too. The feuds of the Scottish clans take no odds over the vendetta which went on here. The same Celtic streak, I suppose. Revenue officers suffered most, but even amongst themselves—as between villages or between families—revenge for fancied injuries was taken in pretty horrible ways."

"It's all dead and gone now, anyway," Potts said, not without regret. "Unless," he suddenly thought, "that fellow up in the church was mixed up in a feud. Say!" He banged on the table enthusiastically. "I wonder if anyone's thought of that! A family feud! Maybe he had run away with somebody's daughter—or ratted on an old partner—or was cutting in on another gang's territory...." The fertile imagination of Hollywood glowed in his eyes.

"Unfortunately," Briarley said dryly, "the man had never been seen in the neighbourhood before, according to all accounts. So it's not likely that anyone here bears him a deadly grudge."

"Who says," asked Cam, "that he hasn't been seen here before? The body is locked up in the police station, isn't it? So who would know?"

Briarley shrugged. "The police have been talking, I guess. Some villager told me."

The conversation ambled on and even Briarley seemed to relax. The hum of busy voices in the saloon bar drifted restfully through to their part of the inn. Although the two old fishermen made no attempt to invite the three visitors to conversation their nodding heads indicated no disapproval of their presence.

After Potts's round was finished Cam bought another. They spoke of boating and gardening. Potts had an almost childish wonder at the marvels of gardening and confessed that he had never planted a growing thing in his life. Cam mentioned the Rector's fine display of roses.

"Yes, I saw it," said Potts warmly. "What a gardener he must be."

Conversation slowed to a stop as three o'clock and closing time approached. In a minute or two they would have to brace themselves to find other occupations. At the Wattlebury Holiday Camp, Potts said, you could always get a drink if you knew the Manager. At this late hour, however, a group of three fishermen entered the bar and thumped empty glasses for attention.

"Now, now!" said Lucy, for it was the day the cinema was open and she wanted to fit that in before her evening duties. "It's gettin' late for a drink now, lads. You'll 'ave to gulp it down. We don't want no p'licemen in 'ere, with all respects for yerself, Mister Cam." Cam nodded graciously and the fishermen glanced over their shoulders at him with curiosity.

"The p'lice won't bother 'bout us," said one curtly. "We bin helpin' them an' like as not they'll be in themselves by t'back door ask'in fer a bracer free."

Lucy looked at him sharply. She had been here long enough to know what co-operation between fishermen and police usually meant.

"An accident?"

The man nodded. "Hurry up thet pint like a good lass. 'Twarn't a pretty 'un." A hush fell on the bar and Lucy quickly drew four more tankards. The men took deep draughts.

"One o' your visitors," one of them volunteered as he wiped his mouth on a sleeve. "Young feller. Tippled over cliff an' got a might bashed on way down."

"'Struth?" said Lucy, her eyes wide with morbid interest. "Young, was he? Know his name?"

The men shook their heads.

"Th' American lass knewed him," the youngest one remarked. "She found him—heard him shout on t'way down, poor lad. He mun 'a tripped over a tuft o' grass like."

"Magnuson!" said Cam abruptly and with sudden conviction. "Was he rather reddish-haired and undersized, with spectacles?" The young man nodded. "That's him, I'spect. Sounds like the name the young leddy used."

"Well, would you believe it!" gasped Lucy.

Potts had turned a pale green. "That's terrible!" he exclaimed with real feeling. "Poor, poor fellow! So young too! Those cliffs are a menace. Look, Lucy. Let's have another round like a good girl."

Lucy decided that the occasion called for leniency and she had one herself too. Briarley showed conventional distress at the news.

"Wonder what he was doing on the cliffs," he murmured. "Never knew him to walk that far."

"He went the same walk last night," Cam contributed, suddenly recalling the American children's remarks. Briarley looked at him sharply and Cam could have sworn that as he abruptly hid his face in the tankard there was a flash of dark anger in his eyes.

"When did you last see him alive?" Cam asked at large to the group.

There was a pause and then Briarley answered casually as he placed his tankard quietly on the table.

"About ten this morning. Outside the church. I left him there." "That's since I did," Potts contributed with a shade of relief. "I saw him last night before evensong walking up to the church with that pretty American girl. But he didn't go to the service, I noticed. They were quarrelling, I thought.—Oh!" He clapped one podgy hand over his mouth and looked with shamed horror at the others. Cam, however, appeared to take no notice and Briarley merely took another drink.

"Lord," said Lucy reverently. "And to think I'd 'ardly let the poor chap finish his breakfast, that keen I was t'clear the dinin'-room. Told 'im t'git out an' get some fresh air, I did. Ain't it awful? Well, we never knows, does we?" She took a philosophic draught. "I saw 'im up at the church this morning, too, Mr. Cam," she added. "I got there a bit late arter everyone else 'ad gone an' 'e was runnin' down the 'ill. Rushed past me, 'e did, without a word. Looked as though the devil were arter 'im. Indeed for sure 'e must 'a bin."

There was a gloomy pause though no one, except perhaps Potts, seemed deeply shocked by the occurrence. To the fishermen such accidents were not unusual, while none of the hotel visitors had personal reason to mourn Magnuson. Only the common feeling that 'there, but for the grace of God, fell I', induced a sense of awe.

"Was Mr. Honeywether there?" Cam asked the fishermen, wondering if this explained the Inspector's delay in questioning Briarley.

"That he were," agreed one. "The young leddy fetched him and Old Honeywether got us together to hoist him up to cliff. Red Cowdray were there with his boat and helped."

Cam got up abruptly.

"Well," he said bluffly, but with a certain earnest meaning, "this holiday is beginning to take on the appearance of a wake. Next year I'm going to one of those spas where all the visitors are too old even to die."

"That's right," Potts agreed whole-heartedly. "This is getting me down, I don't mind telling you. At Wattlebury we never had such trouble. If it wasn't for my friend I swear I'd get out of here while the going's good." He looked sincerely shaken by the news and took comfort again by draining his tankard.

Briarley gave him an odd look. "At least this is an accident," he murmured. "They're not uncommon on these coasts after all, though it seems rather awful, coming so soon after the murder."

"'E was in 'ere about eleven," Lucy, who had been lost in thought, suddenly announced. "'Alf an hour arter I saw 'im by the church. I wasn't servin' but I dropped in for a quickie meself an' noticed 'im out o' the corner of me eye like. Thought to meself 'e oughta be outside on a day like this, I did. Didn't you see 'im?" She looked accusingly at the two old men propped against the wall, who had so far appeared to take no notice of the conversation. With mournful, misty eyes they peered into their empty mugs, searching hopefully for a few more drops of beer. One of them now looked up from his research with scorn which indicated that he had not missed a word and that if only folks would pay more attention to an old man they wouldn't waste so much time.

"I remembers 'im, o' course I do. Nasty young feller, always buttin' into folks' talk, he wor. Only come in 'ere becorse saloon wor empty, eh, Samuel?"

His companion nodded wisely. "Thet's the feller. Reddyhaired, like you says, mister. Talk, talk, talk! All abaht th' murder. You'd 'a thought he'd done et hisself, he talked so much abaht et." He indicated scornful disapproval of all young men who went in for vain self-glorification.

Cam looked at him sharply. "How d'ye mean? Did he say he knew something about it—anything more than all of us know? Or that he had anything to do with it?"

The old men looked at each other.

"Nay," one said cautiously. "Didn't *say* nothin', he didn't. Not that tiddly, he warn't. Only said as how he'd frightened a year's growth off summun who did know summut an' would do et agin afore nightfall. Looked a bit frighted hisself, *I* thought. He war tipsy, eh, Samuel?"

The other nodded shaking his empty tankard wistfully. "Shockin' tipsy, Matthew."

Further questioning by Cam elicited little more definite. He pieced together that Magnuson had come in very quiet and furtive, but after two double whiskies was talkative again and full of bravado about his own unappreciated powers of detection. It was perhaps the normal reaction to expect of such a youth when there was a crime in his vicinity. He had gone off muttering in general terms that 'he would show them'. It was an old, old story to Cam.

Briarley had been listening, too and with a worried frown. "He didn't say anything to me," he volunteered. "Though I don't suppose there was any reason why he should. We only exchanged a few words at the church." He paused. 'I say...You don't think ... I mean, it *was* an accident, I suppose?"

Cam looked at him grimly. "That's for the police to say." He turned to the three fishermen who had taken part in the recovery of the body and who now looked at each other with lively surmise.

"Any idea how long he had been dead when Miss Rowan found him?"

"She heard him hollerin'," the youngest said bluntly. "Heard him at the camp and skedaddled up to see ef'twar one o' her kids. Couldn't 'a bin more'n two minutes afore her got there. An' there weren't nobbody there then 'cept t'body," he added.

Cam tapped his tankard impatiently on the table. This was

not his work. It was Honeywether's. A sudden wicked thought made him chuckle inwardly. What was that about a pint per witness and a pint per clue?

"It is my opinion," he said impressively, "that Mr. Honeywether ought to know about this. Probably doesn't mean a thing, of course, but if there's anything new... And no doubt rewards may be offered..."

The old men seemed to catch on with surprising speed.

"Us oughta go along away an' see him, I say," remarked one and the other was half-way to the door as he said it. In a matter of seconds they were both struggling down the passage in decrepit haste to be the first to give evidence. Perhaps there was more than one practical incentive. Murder case witnesses are rarely at a loss for kindly strangers to stand them drinks.

"Had I better go too?" Lucy asked wistfully. "Arter all, I seed 'im."

"Of course you should go," Cam said heartily. "Let's all go and see him. Briarley, you want to talk to him, I know. Come along; we'll go together. Potts, haven't *you* got a story?"

The stout man denied it emphatically, so, with one arm round the flustered Lucy, who called over her shoulder to some invisible Jane to lock up, and with the other hand grasping the young man's arm, Cam marched them out of the bar. Briarley tried to withdraw.

"No, no, Cam. I'll see him later. There's no hurry, you know."

"Of course there's a hurry," the other rejoined. "This is murder, young fellow—one murder, at least. Keep still you!" he reprimanded Lucy, who was also pulling away without much conviction. "No, there's no need for you to lock up the bar. Give the boys the opportunity they want for once. Anyway, the landlord will be down soon enough. I'll explain to him when we get back. Don't you want to be a witness?"

They went on together, John with downcast eyes, Lucy trying to think up a fine dramatic statement for the Press and Cam chuckling maliciously to himself. This would be a nice job for old Honeywether. He'd teach the Inspector not to interfere with a man's holiday. Four pints of beer already for himself at Honeywether's expense! If it was work the Inspector was after he would get it. He regretted now that he had not brought along all the saloon bar too. They would surely have something to say. This was going to be a really complicated case before he had finished with it.

Turning the corner into the market he swung Lucy around so sharply that she bumped into another woman who was striding swiftly along in the opposite direction. They recognised each other with mutual displeasure.

"Good old Lucy," the other said. "Always falling over her own or someone else's feet." There was a malicious humour in her voice. It went well with a mass of careless black hair and a pert, dark-complexioned face. Her dialect was local with American variations. Even a white satin blouse, red slacks and high-heeled patent-leather shoes could not disguise a certain gypsy distinction in the way in which she carried her head, any more than they attempted to disguise a very fine figure. Cam found himself staring at her with more than polite interest and took comfort in the fact that Briarley was even more absorbed. A hussy probably, but a handsome hussy.

Lucy took instant if excusable umbrage at the words which were so obviously intended to wound.

"Pardon me, I'm sure, *Mrs.* Luigi," she exclaimed with unpleasant emphasis on the matrimonial form of address. "Per'aps if you didn't keep yer nose so 'igh in the air you might see a lidy comin' round a corner."

"Lidy?" the other giggled. "Well, well! Look who's talkin'. Little Lily the Barmaid!"

Lucy tore her arm free from Cam's control and made a threatening gesture. "Yus, 'Lidy', that's what I said. Just because you're married doesn't make you one, you—you woman!" she exploded. "Married! Ha!" Her whole face was contorted with heavy sarcasm. "And how are the little Luigis, may I ask? Or should I say Jones? Or Wilson? Or 'Orton? It's so'ard to keep up."

"Dirty cat," said the other, but without emotion. "Jealous, aren't you?" She smiled blithely at Cam. "She ain't bin so lucky. And can you wonder? Ta, ta, Lucy darlin'!" and she laughed with tantalising indifference as she passed on—her tightly sheathed hips swaying with rhythmic complacency.

Lucy was left breathless, pink with rage.

"Now, now, Lucy," Cam said tactlessly. "That wasn't very nice, was it? Even if it's true."

"Garn!" Lucy turned the vials of her fury upon him. "Trust a man to get took in by a pretty face. If you call it pretty. Vulgar, *I* call it. Nasty bitch! Only took up wi' that Italian feller because 'e was 'andy when 'er time come. Gawd, I 'ates 'er!" She thrust her hands into her apron pockets and marched grimly on in front of the other two, indifferent to Cam's attempt to take her arm again.

"Who is she?" he asked cautiously.

Lucy gave him a sardonic look over her shoulder.

"Look who's askin' then! Like to see more of 'er, eh? Oh, she 'as a way with 'er all right. Like pisin! She's married now and her 'usband's kinda jealous too. Italian-Yank, he is, an' knows 'ow to use a knife, they say."

"How did they come to live here?" Cam asked curiously. "She sounded like a local girl."

"Local scandal!" sneered the waitress. "She's no girl! Red Cowdray's daughter is what she is. Like father like daughter! Both bad as they come. Luigi was a G.I. 'ere and as soon as th' War was over orf they went to the States with t'babies—twins, she 'ad. Two kids an' ten dads, some said. An' Luigi not one of 'em if truth were told, *which* it never will be. Nine months later back they are like bad pennies—without th' babies. *She* says they's with 'is folks, but it's a queer sort o' mother would leave 'er kids on t'other side o' ocean, I say. Not that she's any sort o' mother, Gawd knows! No one tells why they came back, but it's not 'ard to guess. America wouldn't 'ave 'em, I dare say. 'E's much of a muchness with 'er. An' old Red makes it three of a kind. Bad all through. A disgrace to decent folks, that's what they are! Bargin' all over the pavements in tight pants like she owns the place. Ought to walk in the gutter, by rights, she should. Knockin' decent girls about..."

The monologue went on—cast back in sour lumps over Lucy's shoulder—until they reached the police station.

Cam was translating it all into the romantic terms of his holiday imagination. The sinister red-bearded local pirate; his beautiful raven-haired daughter, temptress and perverter of feeble men; the foreign buccaneer, a match for depravity, who wins her, with a yo, ho, ho and a bottle of rum.

"I'd like to meet the family," he said aloud. "Interesting types; local colour. Where do they live?"

Lucy looked at him in disgust. "Find out for yerself," she snapped unjustly. "I'm thinkin' of yer poor wife."

"Down near the harbour," Briarley said absently. "Anyone will show you there."

Cam looked at him in surprise. "Do you know them then?" he asked.

"I've been fishing with a red-haired fisherman," Briarley said. "There can only be one like him."

"Cowdray," Cam repeated after a thoughtful pause. "Where have I heard that before?" He jerked the arms of both his wards as he remembered. "Witchcraft! The ring-leaders. That's it! And she the chief witch, no doubt. She'll fill the bill."

He was surprised by the startled reaction of both Briarley and Lucy. The waitress shot him a glance of angry dismay as though he had said something painfully rude. Briarley stopped dead in his tracks with eager interest.

"Witchcraft!" he exclaimed. "What the devil are you talking about? Do you mean that still goes on down here?"

"Of course it don't," Lucy said bitterly. "We had a wee spot of trouble in the War, like everybody else, and that's what he's talkin' about, I'll bet. But it's all over now. Don't you mind his chatter." She was so anxious to change the subject that she even forgot her grievance against the Cowdray woman. "Let bygones be bygones," she said firmly. "We don't talk about that 'ere no more that what you'd talk about a granny what drinks. An' 'ere we are at the p'lice station, so come in, do, and let's not waste no more time."

# CHAPTER VI

IN the waiting-room they found the two old fishermen eagerly expressing their views of the case to a couple of London reporters. Cam left his convoy here and entered unannounced into the inner office. Honeywether, scratching laboriously with an ancient H.M.S.O. pen, looked up with dour resentment.

"Having a good time?" he asked bitterly. "What happened about lunch? We waited twenty minutes. I didn't half get a ticking off from Gertrude. And who are those old buzzards you let loose in the office? I haven't time to waste, y'know."

"There are two more now," Cam assured him. "And don't forget I get a pint apiece. They're all Important Witnesses. I'm sorry about lunch and will apologise personally to Mrs. Honeywether. I lunched at the Rectory. Any developments?"

"Have *you* any?" asked Honeywether, determined not to commit himself without compensation.

"Of course I have," the other said casually. "Item: Why did Mrs. Copperman take a pruning-knife for the altar flowers when she carries a perfectly good penknife round her neck which would have been quite sufficient to cut lupin stems? Item: Why did Giles Allen use the expression that the murder was 'too much'? What had been enough but not *too* much? A curious phrase. Item: Why did John Briarley not finish his brass-rubbing? (He's outside, Honeywether.) Item: Who was the girlfriend Magnuson went walking with last night? Was she with him today? Item: Why did Betsey Rowan quarrel with both Briarley and Magnuson yesterday? Item: Why does the Rector suspect the Verger and Mrs. Copperman suspect her husband?"

"Those aren't clues!" Honeywether exploded after a bewildered pause. "Those are just damn silly questions. And I've asked most of them myself," he added bullishly, "without getting any forwarder."

"Ask enough questions and you may get an answer," axiomised Cam. "If you answered all those the case would be over. I'd suggest also, however, that you don't delay Miss Rowan's talking-to. That quarrel with Magnuson before the service is very odd. I've seen him trying to talk to her often enough since he arrived last Monday, but she was always politely off-hand. Yet you have to know a person pretty well to quarrel with them."

"Yes, I was going to get after her," the other said gloomily. "And now he's dead. Did you hear?" Cam nodded. "He fell over the cliff. It took up most of my morning. I'm afraid it's not just a straightforward accident, Cam. The grass is torn away in his struggle a full four feet from the edge. There are only two reasons why he should have fallen with all that space to hold on to. Either he was pushed or he was drunk."

"You'll find some evidence on that outside," Cam interpolated. "Apparently Magnuson visited the hotel bar before his walk and was full of helpful hints about how to solve the murder. Probably just the usual amateur enthusiasm, but I thought it would be worth bringing his audience at the pub along. Poor fellow! You have to be dead to have your views appreciated by the police. Yes, he was drunk, I think, but not drunk enough to fall off the cliff of his own accord."

Honeywether nodded seriously. "Might be something in it," he said. "I've got something here, Cam." He emptied out of a brown official envelope a collection of personal impedimenta which Cam gathered must be the relics of Percy Magnuson. Honeywether picked out one object and held it up triumphantly. It was a plain red pencil, rather chewed about the end and with a rough stubby point. Cam raised his eyebrows and the local Inspector nodded.

"Not a doubt about it. The point has fragments of the stone paving still on it. Magnuson was our amateur artist at the church."

"Not surprised," Cam said. "He had that sort of humour, I should guess. But why? And when? Was it during evensong—after he parted with Betsey? He was probably in a bad temper. But what did he mean—if anything?"

"It can't have been since eight-thirty last night," Honeywether stated. "I've had a watch on the church ever since then. Only the Rector and the Verger have been allowed near."

"The American children saw him on the cliffs with a girl friend at six-thirty. It would be a quarter-hour walk from the church for that kind of man—especially with one arm round the girl. So far as we know he didn't go back to the church but he was seen there just before service quarrelling with Betsey Rowan. Perhaps it was some time round then."

Honeywether grunted. "In that case he did it before anything happened and it had nothing whatever to do with our murder. So let's not bother our heads about it. Though why any fool should draw stuff and nonsense like that I can't think." Cam raised his eyebrows. "Why should we think that Evensong was the beginning of the case—as if for some mystic reason it let loose the powers of the devil? You'll have to look further back, Honeywether, further back even than Magnuson's poor little drawings, if my guess is right."

"There you go again!" complained Honeywether. "Keep off it, can't you? This is bad enough without raking up the past."

"It will keep popping up," Cam excused himself. "But if you can explain to your own satisfaction why a not-too-clever little man should come down from London to draw rude pictures in the church and get pushed over a cliff, why, more power to you. But what you'll have to find out first is why he came to Trevelley at all. Not his cup of tea, I should have said! Margate on a Bank Holiday much more likely."

"What about that girl he was walking out with?" Honeywether asked. "Maybe they knew each other before he came down. Maybe that's why he came down. Who is she, anyway? Someone except the children must have seen them together."

"Yes," Cam agreed. "She's the person to find. Perhaps she could explain the drawing. He wasn't the sort of person to keep a good joke to himself."

The Inspector threw a pencil impatiently at his blotter.

"A good joke is right," he barked. "How do we know that he wasn't showing an infantile sense of humour—nothing to do with the murder? If we saw it in a public lavatory we wouldn't give it a second thought. It's a fine thing when we can't tell murder from a practical joke," he added bitterly. His eye lit on one item amongst Magnuson's relics and he picked it up to shake in Cam's face. "He was holding this in his hand. It's no hanky, is it? That's no joke, anyway. That's a clue, that is!"

Cam took the torn scrap of black cloth in his hands.

"What is it? Sail-cloth? Torn in a fight, you think?"

"Maybe, Anyway, he had it in his hand and it doesn't fit anything round the scene."

There was a pause while Honeywether gloomily put punctuation marks in the report before him.

"Still no idea who Number One is?" Cam enquired at last.

"Not a hint," the other said. "The only new thing I know is that he was very well-fed an hour before his death. Dress him up in a blue serge suit and he'd look like any prosperous shopkeeper under the blessed sun—soft-handed and shrewd-faced."

"Good Lord!" Cam blurted explosively. "A shopkeeper? That's it! Holy snakes!" he added no more explicitly and groaned with mortified amusement. "Oh, Honeywether, what will you say!" he exclaimed at the other's astonished expression. "I think I know him. Or his local friend, anyway. And he's *not* a Piccadilly flower-girl, damn it."

\* \* \*

Half an hour later a shaken Mr. Potts was emerging from the tiny back room which served as mortuary of Trevelley police station. Honeywether hastened him back into the inner office for a reviving glass of brandy. The big man gulped it down and looked dazedly at his still trembling hands.

"Can't believe it," he muttered hoarsely. "Saw it with my own eyes, I did, but I can't believe it. My God!"

"You say his name was Wilowski, Leo Wilowski, 10 Tull Street, London, E.C.3," Honeywether matter-of-factly read out of his notebook.

"'S right," murmured the other.

"He was a jeweller and antique dealer, specialising in mediæval works of art." Honeywether stumbled over the 'mediæval' and went on more rapidly. "Polish by birth; came to this country soon after the first World War; moved to the States in 1925, where he established a shop on Madison Avenue, New York. Did well and became a naturalised American. Returned here last November to set up a branch of the New York shop. So far as you know he was well to do. Has a wife in New York, but no children. Right?"

He stopped abruptly and looked grimly from his notes to Mr. Potts. The other nodded vaguely.

"Right. That's what he told me. Antique dealer. He bought here mostly and sold in the States. We had dealings ..."

"What sort of dealings?" Honeywether barked. "Now let's get down to it. How did you come to know him and what did he come down here for?"

"I've got a jewellery shop just off Covent Garden," Mr. Potts began slowly. "It's a small place and pretty crowded. I say it's a jewellery shop and do the usual watch repairs and silver work, but actually there's every oddity under the sun crowded into six feet by eight because I can't resist a bargain. Second-hand junk is what I specialise in, you might say, but it earns me a living. Well, I first met Wilowski when he came in to see me one morning about five months ago. There's a tray of odds and ends of rings, brooches, necklaces, in my window. It attracts the girls, y'know—'specially when they've got a boy friend in tow. They sell for anything from sixpence to half a crown. Well, Wilowski noticed a pin in the tray which he thought was tenth-century cloisonné. Looked like early twentieth-century Woolworth to me, not knowing that period, but he was right and I made a pretty penny out of it, I can tell you. I'm still living on it, to tell the truth. I gave him a cut-in, of course, but that shows what sort of a chap he was. He might have bought the pin for half a crown, for all I'd have known the difference, and made all the profit himself. After that we became quite pally. He was one of the ugliest men I've ever known—well, you've seen—but he was nice to me and we got on pretty well.

"He did a lot of travelling, buying stuff for New York, but whenever he got back from a trip he would drop in to see me and we'd talk shop all evening. There are a lot of yarns to tell in our business, gentlemen. I kept an eye open for his kind of bargain too, and once or twice was able to put a good thing his way. About a month ago I noticed Wilowski was looking pretty peaked—hands shaking, complexion bad, losing weight. He had been working hard and on the road all the winter. So I started suggesting he should take a holiday, and as I was pretty worn out myself, after that terrible winter we'd had, I said we might as well go together. I never really expected him to agree, because, although we were friendly, he was a reserved bloke in some ways.

"Well, he hummed and hawed and said he would think about it, and then two weeks ago a friend of his told him that he'd heard of vacancies in this hotel. That evening he came round to see me and we fixed it up then and there. We were going to meet here as he was off on another trip. He was to arrive on Sunday morning. I can't think why I didn't guess when he didn't.... And everyone talking about the murder.... I must have been mad...."

Potts covered his face in his hands in a sudden access of misery. "Who was the friend who told him about this place?" asked Cam.

Potts shook his head. "Haven't the faintest. Never knew any of his other friends. Didn't think he had any. He said this fellow recommended Trevelley as a nice quiet place for a rest—nothing ever happened!..."

Honeywether picked up the phone and summoned the landlord of the 'Three Fishers' to speak to him.

"Hello, Lathrop? Honeywether here. Can you tell me when a Mr. Wilowski wrote to you for reservations? Right, I'll hold on.... Hello? Two weeks ago. Right. And he booked for Mr. Potts too? Had you heard of him before—anyone recommended him? No one. Who else has arrived since then? Mr. Cam and Mr. Briarley. H'm. Uh-huh. Uh-huh. Well, all right. Thanks, Lathrop. By the by, you might as well cancel that reservation. No, he won't be coming. Well, it's a long story. Some time, perhaps!"

He turned to Potts. "Have you any idea, Mr. Potts, how your friend could have reached here if, as we believe, he didn't come by train? Did he have a car?"

"No," the other said. "He was always complaining that he couldn't get one here and wishing he'd brought his Buick over from the States. I haven't a clue. He hated walking—wasn't built for it. Perhaps he got a lift."

"Where was he coming from?" asked Cam. "Do you know where he had been visiting?"

Potts waved a helpless hand.

"No idea. He never talked about his trips. And in our business where you've got to depend on hush-hush tips about private collections and local 'finds' a fellow doesn't ask, you know."

"You know remarkably little about this man you were to spend a holiday with!" Honeywether exclaimed tartly.

The fat man looked miserable. "I suppose it does sound stupid. We hadn't known each other long, you see. Not having much of a family—no one close—I'm always picking up odd friends...And then I'd always wanted to come to Cornwall."

"Did Wilowski speak with an accent?" Cam asked abruptly. "Why—yes. Yes, he did. A sort of Polish-American accent which was quite difficult to follow. *He* was a bit lonely too, I think, with his family in New York, y'know."

Honeywether took careful note of Mr. Potts's business, residence and associates before he dismissed him with a curt: "Well, perhaps you'd like to cable Wilowski's wife, Mr. Potts, as you seem to be the closest friend of the deceased."

Mr. Potts was horrified. "Good Lord, no! That would be impossible! She doesn't know me at all. I couldn't do that! Isn't it your job? Surely the police will do it..." He seemed so perturbed that Honeywether gloomily accepted the responsibility.

After the unhappy man had left, the local Inspector looked sharply at Cam. "Pretty fishy, eh?" he barked.

Cam shrugged. "I just don't know," he confessed. "Maybe it's fishy or maybe that's how Covent Garden jewellers live. If I don't know what's normal," he said aggrievedly, "how can I tell what's abnormal?"

"It's mighty odd that he should plan to go away with a man about whom he knows almost nothing. That sticks out like a sore thumb. I'm not sure he's as bewildered as he seems."

"A second-hand jewellery dealer," murmured Cam. "I'd thought he was a fruit and vegetable man—Covent Garden, you know. Interesting."

"Did it strike you," pursued Honeywether, "that he and Wilowski might have had a closer association than he said? Both in the same line of business and all."

"Yes, it seems a curiously casual relationship, as he tells it. Far too casual for canny bargain hunters in that kind of business. But if there is a closer association it must be slightly crooked. Otherwise no need to be secretive. Q.E.D."

"Crookedness in that profession usually means fencing," Honeywether dogmatised. "Perhaps they specialised in selling stolen goods to the States. Potts could handle the English and Wilowski the American end."

"In that case," Cam said, "why should Wilowski set up shop here himself? And how did they get the stuff out?" There was a pause. "An expert in mediæval art," he murmured. "It strikes me that the traffic in mediæval bric-à-brac has been very lively in the last couple of months—very lively indeed. I wonder whether a travelling antique dealer mightn't fit into that picture rather neatly."

Honeywether was mystified for a moment, but then his expression cleared. "Oho!" he cried gleefully. "The Cathedral Robberies! That's quite a thought, Cam. Quite a thought! Let's see what's the score now? The Robarts' tapestry from Minchester—that was the main thing of course. But there's also been in the last four months the Jacobean silver ewer from Limpeter's Parish Church... the ewer from Monks Gabbington ..."

"And the Cons loving-cup which the family gave All Souls' Church in Upper Cons and the Welkin Book of Hours from St. Christopher's in Little Kittle," Cam concluded. "And in addition to these recent coups there was that little flutter of thefts eighteen months ago starting with the one at Wittington. Everything very tastefully selected and quite beyond monetary evaluation—at least the sort of value that the likes of you or me think of. And gathered at random about the South country, Honeywether. Not in the north, mark you, but peppered up and down from Land's End to the Wash. A man would have to do a sizeable amount of travelling."

"Like Mr. Wilowski?" nodded Honeywether.

"Like Mr. Wilowski," agreed Cam. "The indefatigable American tourist in person." He paused and looked at his friend in mock surprise. "But you're not suggesting that Mr. Wilowski stole those things, are you?"

"You suggested it," Honeywether protested. "And I'm not saying," he added tortuously, "that it mightn't be a quite reasonable suggestion. At least it might make some sense out of this pother. A motive, at last a motive for my murder! Of course, personally, I wouldn't leap to conclusions like you, but it bears examination, it bears examination. Where there's money, there's a motive."

Cam shook his head reprovingly.

"Always headstrong, Honeywether. Always over-enthusiastic. I just mentioned the Cathedral Robberies and you want to tie it in with your own local headache. But Point 1: I seem to recall that the Talisbury theft took place last October. According to Potts, Wilowski arrived here only last November."

"That means nothing," Honeywether exclaimed. "He might have been here much longer for all Potts knew. They only met five months ago. Or Potts may be lying. Or Potts may have handled the first job himself. He's by no means in the clear."

"Point 2: As one professional to another, Honeywether, I think we can be pretty confident that a peculiarly large and ugly man with a strong Polish-American accent could not have been in the vicinity of all these robberies without Scotland Yard having detected the fact. In any case we know that practically every art and antique dealer in the country has been under surveillance in connection with these robberies. An exporter like Wilowski wouldn't stand much chance of pinching tapestries and manuscripts scot-free."

"He might be good at disguises. Anyway, we'll check that," Honeywether growled defiantly. "Mistakes do happen. He may have assistants to do the actual work. It might be Potts himself for that matter. There are a thousand explanations. Anyway, *you* suggested a connection. Or did I? It doesn't matter. My God, Cam!" he exclaimed with sudden enthusiasm, "I'd like to be the man who solves those robberies."

"Unless," said Cam cruelly, "it turns out that Trevelley has been the centre of operations for all these months and you all unconscious of it."

"I'm not worried," Honeywether said stoutly. "I'd bet my boots that neither Wilowski nor Potts have been here before. It's my guess they just came down because this was a quiet place in which to talk things over—a place where they were unlikely to meet any London friends."

"That's likely enough," said Cam. "But they must have some contact down here—either a visitor or a native."

"I don't see that." Honeywether was obviously anxious to keep this crime on a London basis. "It only takes two to make a murder."

"But who murdered Wilowski? No, no, Honeywether. You've got to face facts. Potts has an alibi. He was sitting by the ferry with Briarley. And what's more, my imagination boggles at the idea of a man like Potts laying the body out with all that stage-play. Someone else is mixed up in this."

"Magnuson?" Honeywether suggested doubtfully. "Well, never mind that now. If we know what part Wilowski played in the Cathedral Robberies—and if we know who his associates were in that we can clear this up quick enough."

"How did Wilowski get here?" asked Cam thoughtfully. "No. Don't tell me. Let me guess. But if you can guess that yourself you may find who his accomplices were."

"That's it," Honeywether agreed. "That's more like it. Someone must have brought him here by car, killed him and driven away. We've got to start at the London end if we want to find who that someone was. The London end and the Cathedral Robberies end."

"You certainly make it sound very simple," Cam said admiringly. "But my money is on Trevelley. You can't tell me that a place like this would sit back and be taught about crime by London. Where's your local pride, man?"

Honeywether nodded absently. His mind was absorbed with the responsibilities of a crime of national—nay, international—dimensions. "The first thing," he said, "is to let London know of my discoveries here. The Yard may be able to help me pin down Wilowski's associates. But I had better read up the facts of the robberies myself. Something may have escaped their attention...."

"There's still the murder to solve," Cam suggested gently.

"Of course, of course!" Honeywether exclaimed impatiently. "I haven't forgotten. Cam, would you be a good fellow and do something for me? I must get in touch with the Chief Constable about these developments. And I've got those two blasted fishermen you brought me—and Lucy—to interview. And Briarley. Rundle can handle the first three. Good training. I'll see Briarley in half an hour. But there are still Red Cowdray and Betsey Rowan to talk to about Magnuson's death and I've no constable to spare. How would you like to be a good chap and see them for me? You might ask Miss Rowan a little more about her activities last night too. Incidentally," he added kindly, with a sudden recollection that this was, after all, Cam's holiday, "Red Cowdray lives on the fishing quay and you ought to see that. It's very historic, they tell me. And Miss Rowan's camp is a pretty walk along the cliffs. So it would be a nice way to spend the afternoon," he concluded generously.

"I have seen the quay," Cam pronounced as he rose, "and I have already today sweated along that cliff to the camp and my idea of a holiday is inaction, Honeywether—the contemplative life—not acting as unpaid constable for you. As between friend and friend, and in remembrance of the two more pints it will bring me, I shall do as you wish. (There's another pint due for Potts, don't forget.) But don't think you can gull me," he warned as he left the room, "into thinking that a murder investigation can be turned into a sight-seeing tour."

# CHAPTER VII

IN the waiting-room only the two old fishermen still waited a chance to speak their minds.

"Where are Lucy and Mr. Briarley?" Cam asked the constable in charge.

"She's taken the newspaper fellows down to the 'Fishers'," the man looked up from a thriller to reply. "He got impatient too and walked out. I couldn't keep 'em without no warrent."

"Of course not," Cam sympathised. "Everything happens at once in this case. But be sure you bring them in eventually. They're worth two pints to me."

He plunged out into the blistering sunshine of the High Street.

'Blistering' is not usually a suitable adjective for English sunshine, but Trevelley was now in the second week of a heatwave. The whitewashed cottages, the tawny-sailed fishing-smacks which could be glimpsed on patches of blue harbour water down, far down between the buildings, the brilliant green of the cliffs across the river—all these had a gay Adriatic bravado. Old fishermen sitting out on their front steps inspected with objective interest the remarkable brevity of tourist sun-suits. A plump farmer on a plump brown cob trotted by, hoofs beating a gay tattoo on the cobbles. Stout-bosomed fisher-wives with good red faces chatted and chuckled at their garden gates. There was languor in the air and all the girls seemed prettier and brighter, all the men larger and more lusty than normal. They moved with dreamy waltzing steps through the unaccustomed heat. In a moment, thought Cam, they will join hands and burst into a mazurka.

"Here's Mr. Cam," said a friendly voice at his elbow. "Glad to see you, sir. Not spendng all your holiday at work, I hope."

Two young men in gleaming white shirts and grey slacks were chatting in the shadow of the police station door. With their pleasant even-featured faces they might easily be the juvenile leads in the musical comedy. Giles Allen, carrying a fishing rod, represented healthy outdoor interests. John Briarley carried a book and the inevitable cricket bag—he could be the more serious lover. All the pair needed was a couple of charming *ingénues*. Cam sighed. He liked to have nice tidy human relationships, in the same way that he preferred well-arranged pew-racks. It was Giles Allen who had spoken to him so he related his sigh to the question.

"Well, it's a bit of a busman's holiday," he admitted. "But at least I'm seeing a new side of the village."

"And the villagers," Allen remarked, "are seeing you. You're the main topic of conversation, y'know. The general idea is that you're the Big Man from Scotland Yard."

He seemed to have completely forgotten the awkward scene at the Rectory. There was lurking youthful awe in his tone which Cam was too human not to enjoy. Really, he thought suddenly, what a lot of charming people are mixed up in this affair—honest young Briarley, pretty Betsey Rowan, the ingenuous Potts, the high-minded Mrs. Copperman, Allen—well, not the Rector or the Verger perhaps. But otherwise a very pleasing lot of characters.

"How are the Rector and Mrs. Copperman?" he enquired, with a conscientious return to business. "I'm afraid I rather upset them on my visit."

Allen flushed. "They're all right. It's been a bit of a shock all round, you know. I wish I could *do* something," he added impulsively. "Mrs. Copperman has been awfully good to me and this affair is getting on her nerves. You may not have thought so, because I know she always gives the impression of imperturbable calm, but I can see myself how worried and unhappy she is. After you left today I started asking questions about the murder—quite naturally, y'know, as I've only seen the press reports. She shut me up with more annoyance than I've ever known her show before. Of course she's always worried about Copperman being involved in anything troublesome, but she doesn't usually show it."

Mrs. Copperman, Cam pondered, seemed to have all the ability to inspire devotion which her husband lacked. He wondered at what point she had shown annoyance with Allen.

"She is worried about the pruning-knife?" he hazarded.

Allen gave him a quick, searching glance which indicated it was a lucky stab. "It's perfectly absurd," he muttered. "Copperman can get along without it for a few days—and any fool can see it was just an accident leaving it. She wasn't responsible for the use to which it was put."

Briarley was listening in the background with some impatience. He seized the opportunity of the ensuing pause to say hastily: "Well, Allen, it's been interesting meeting you again. Perhaps we'll see each other in London some time. I still hold to my case about the brass."

"You, there!" Cam stopped him imperiously. "You ought to be with the police giving evidence."

The young man shrugged impatiently. "They took so long. Why should I waste all my holiday trying to give unnecessary evidence about a case in which I'm not interested? If they want it they can come for it."

Cam looked at him reprovingly.

"That's not the right attitude for a Citizen and Voter. However I'm on holiday too, so I can't blame you." He looked from one man to the other. "Do you two know each other, then?"

Allen explained. "We've mutual interests, sir. Brass-rubbing, if you know what that is. Yardley has told me there was an enthusiast at the hotel and I thought I recognised Briarley when I saw him coming out of the station. We both belong to the same society in London. I had the pleasure of hearing him give a talk there last month. There's nothing," he added with a laugh, "like monumental brasses to bring strangers together, you know, except, perhaps, a mutual interest in stamps or speliology."

"Or microlepidoptery," suggested Cam. "Are you going to let him rub that blessed brass?" he asked the curate.

Allen shook his head regretfully. "No. Even if Honeywether would let him enter the church I'm afraid there's a strict prohibition against brass-rubbers. A moderate amount of rubbing does no harm to a brass, but when you have the responsibility of something as lovely as the Pollpen I'm afraid you have to be rather dog-in-the-mangerish. Otherwise it would be rubbed right away. The Rector is very emphatic on that point as he told Briarley last Friday."

"It isn't just the rubbing he objected to!" Briarley laughed. "I want to dig the thing up! I thought Allen might be my friend at court but he doesn't like the idea either."

The curate looked rather irritated.

"I'm sure you're wrong," he said abruptly. "It was tried in 1774, you know, by an antiquarian predecessor of mine and nothing whatever found. Why on earth should it *now* turn out to be a palimpsest? You must be reasonable."

"A what?" said Cam. "Sounds like a legendary monster! Why on earth should a brass turn out to be a palimpsest?"

"A palimpsest," explained Briarley in conscientiously simple terms, "is a brass which has been used once on one side and then turned over in a later generation and re-engraved. Actually the same term is used for parchment manuscripts which have been cleaned and then used again. They used to do it for the sake of economy. Brass and parchment were both extremely valuable commodities in times past. Some of our best early monumental brasses have been found on the back of quite inferior ones of a later century."

"Austerity methods, eh?" Cam sighed. "That's something, anyway, that we haven't descended to nowadays. Fancy turning over our grandparents' gravestones so that someone else could use them."

"*I* think," said Briarley stubbornly, "that there's another brass engraved on the back of the Pollpen. There are unusual irregularities on the surface of the plate which might be the traces of some impression made on the other side. And one of the deeper engraved lines seems to go right through the plate at one point. It's difficult to judge while the brass is fastened down, but I think there is at least a tiny incision. The most likely explanation is that the stroke on the side we see met another stroke on the other side of the plate. It's a reasonable hypothesis, anyway."

"But the 1774 investigation?" protested Allen.

Briarley brushed it aside. "There are no reliable reports about that. Only the curate and a couple of local workers witnessed it. And not a very reliable curate either! He was hanged, you remember!" he laughed. "No reflection on your profession, Allen! No records have been found about the incident except a brief note in the curate's diary that the brass had been relaid after examination."

"What more do you want?" exclaimed Allen. "If he had found a palimpsest he would have said so."

Briarley shook his head. "The records are too casual by half. I don't agree it's final proof. But you're the man in charge. If you won't, you won't." He patted Cam in friendly farewell upon the back and wandered off downhill towards the 'Fishers'. Looking after him Cam caught a glimpse of Mrs. Copperman, a market basket over her arm, also walking swiftly in the same direction. In the musical comedy atmosphere of sunshine and colour she moved like a grey shadow.

"Good heavens!" Allen was saying in wry humour. "Who would have any responsibility for a church containing historical treasures? Poor Copperman! You have no idea, Inspector, what a ravening pack of wolves antiquarians are. They would tear the rings from their dead mother's fingers if they had any historical or artistic value. Not for profit, you know. Just for the glory of possession or discovery. Not even glory, in fact. There are plenty who are so fanatical that the pleasure of simple personal possession, regardless of whether anyone else appreciates their luck, is all that counts."

"There's not a policeman in the country who doesn't know that now!" Cam commented and the other chuckled.

"The Cathedral Robberies? I bet that's got you in a stew! It looks as though cathedrals and churches with any precious muniments will have to be a jolly sight more careful at this rate. It's pretty scandalous how easy the robberies seem to have been, isn't it?"

"It's a tough case," Cam admitted noncommittally. "Fortunately it hasn't touched my area. Pretty valuable stuff, I understand."

"Priceless!" the curate said fervently. "I know most of these churches personally. Only an antiquarian could appreciate the treasures which have been stolen. The Archbishop is holding a conference on it next week, I hear. It's taking on the proportions of a 'disestablishment'!"

As a churchman the curate may have been concerned, but his voice betrayed youthful glee in the excitement of the case. Cam could not help smiling. "Mrs. Copperman," he said, "mentioned that you had your own views on the robberies."

The young man flushed. "Oh well," he apologised, "I suppose everyone has and you don't want to hear amateur theories. But," he took heart at Cam's encouraging attention, "as a matter of fact, have you noticed that all the robberies have been in the southern counties—and most of them in counties with a coastline on the Atlantic or the Irish sea? Well, it did occur to me that perhaps the goods were being smuggled to Ireland from here. After all, even during the War, little ships used to go back and forth pretty frequently, slipping through the naval patrols. It was common knowledge. Now there is no control—or not a tight one, anyway—what's to stop them?"

Cam forbore to mention, since Allen seemed so pleased with his contribution, that a route to Ireland had been accepted for some time by the police as an uncontestable fact in the case. The problem was—what route? He smiled encouragingly on the curate.

"That's an interesting theory, Mr. Allen. You know these coasts now. Would you say that smuggling on such a scale might be practicable? Would the gang—if it is a gang—be able to find men and boats able and willing to help?"

Allen laughed with open amusement.

"Well, that's a leading question, Inspector. Do you want me to point out any local parishioners who might help? I think I could, as a matter of fact, if it really came down to it! But no, even though they were capable of it I think all the fishermen and boats down here are pretty well accounted for in their daily comings and goings. But that's not vouching for all the villages along the coast. There's plenty of the old spunk and spirit left in Cornwall. You never know what we might do!"

Cam smiled. "I notice that smuggling has a soft spot in everyone's heart here. Even Honeywether was telling me it didn't count as a criminal offence!"

"It's an honourable profession," the curate agreed half-seriously. "But you haven't heard all my amateur theorising. I don't think these robberies are a normal smuggler's line of country. They help, but behind it all must be an antiquarian. The loot has been chosen with real artistic as well as monetary taste. There's a brilliant mind and judgment at work in the thefts I've read about—not just the usual criminal greed for cash."

"An antiquarian, eh?" said Cam. "Like a brass-rubber?" Allen laughed uneasily. "Let's not get specific. As a matter of fact I've noticed the robbed churches do, by coincidence, all have good brasses, but that doesn't mean a thing. They all have good bells too, but I'm not suggesting it's a campanologist's crime."

"Well," Cam said, "I've got to be going. Work to do. But if you've any more ideas let me know."

He turned away with a gesture of farewell to go down to the wharf on Honeywether's commissions. Giles Allen seemed reluctant to take this abrupt dismissal and walked along beside him.

"I say," he remarked with forced casualness after a few silent steps, "I suppose it's not good form to ask, but are you really suspicious about the Rectory? I mean, if there's anything I could do to help clear them I... I certainly would and perhaps I could save trouble by answering some questions."

Cam glanced at him sideways. "Suppose, young fellow," he said kindly, "that you just tell me what's worrying you up there and save me asking unnecessary questions. If you've got any information I don't mind hearing it if it'll make you any easier, but otherwise I'd just as soon talk about the weather or fishing or rose gardens."

Allen looked at him gratefully. "Thank you for guessing, Inspector. I *have* got something to tell you. I'm in a bit of a fix, as a matter of fact, and yet I don't want to talk to Honeywether, even though I suppose you'll relay the news to him." He took a deep breath. "You see, I've been an accessory to a crime—if that's the right phrase." He paused to see Cam's reaction but there was none except a polite inclination of the head. He plunged on. "The church suffered a robbery three weeks ago, Mr. Cam, and we never reported it. The seventeenth-century plate used for special church festivals—a ewer, a paten and a chalice—was taken after Vespers. It was in the vestry safe at the end of the service when Copperman put the collection plate there. He forgot to lock it. Half an hour later when he remembered and went back to do so the plate had gone. We— the Rector and I—didn't dare call in the police. You see—well, it's a pretty serious thing to happen and it placed Copperman in a particularly nasty position for after all it was he who had left the safe open. The Verger was ill, just as he was yesterday, drat him, and couldn't be responsible. I was at Powey that night on my regular visit." He stopped anxiously. Cam still made no comment and the curate stumbled awkwardly on. "I know it sounds appalling for ordained ministers to hide a thing like this. But you see, as it was Mr. Copperman's mistake he would be held responsible. He might even have to pay compensation—and the plate was awfully valuable—insured at £1,000. But it's even worse than that because he had neglected to renew the insurance on the things. In fact the whole situation is too awful to contemplate and there might be the most serious results for the poor chap if it came out. He's not too popular here, you see—nor with the Church hierarchy, for that matter. Somehow he has never settled down since leaving Minchester. People get tired of a misfit."

"Does Mrs. Copperman know about this?" Cam asked.

"No, I don't think so. Though I sometimes wonder if there's anything she doesn't know. Yardley doesn't know, either. Copperman told me first and, frankly, it was I who advised him not to report the affair. Robert isn't on too good relations with the powers-that-be; you've seen enough of him to know that he's a bit of a grumbler and that doesn't help in the Church. They might even take such an occasion to unfrock him."

Cam was shocked. "He's shown atrocious judgment, I agree," he remarked. "But I can't see why it's that serious. An unfortunate accident, but not a crime. Surely they would just move him to another parish."

Allen shook his head miserably, "I'm afraid it gets worse as I go along. You see, Robert *had* the money for the Insurance. He had put off paying it until the last possible moment when he happened to be going up to London. He decided to save postage—twopence halfpenny—by taking it in personally. His first errand, however, was to a bookshop. There he found a volume of an early history of Cornwall, one that he needed to complete a set. This purchase took most of his available funds so he promised himself to attend to the insurance when he returned to Trevelley. He forgot. Then, a week later, this awful thing happened." Cam whistled vulgarly. "That insurance money was church money, I suppose. It bears a remarkable resemblance to embezzlement, my friend."

"That's not fair. It's not as if it were a large sum. The truth is that until he came here the Rector never had to worry for a minute about money. He never had much, heaven knows, but he has simple tastes and can get along on very little. The living here, though, is only about £250 a year—and look at the Rectory he has to keep up! It's outrageous, really."

"It's hard," Cam agreed. "But it still looks bad."

"Now, perhaps, you'll understand why I advised him not to report the theft at once but to wait a bit in hopes that we might trace the thief on our own."

"And how did you propose to do that?"

Allen gave an airy gesture. "Oh, the usual sifting out of those who would be likely to take it and those who had the opportunity to do so. I've read all the books! Unfortunately those who would rob, couldn't; and those who could rob, wouldn't. All the rough types in the village one would naturally suspect were out of the question. The boy Colly Yardley was sitting on his father's garden wall that Sunday after service, during the half-hour the church and the safe were open— and he saw no one going up or down the road to the village. I questioned him as closely as I could without arousing his suspicion. Fortunately, he's too simple to be very suspicious. Yardley himself, of course, was ill—as usual in time of need— and would be no help. The unluckiest man in the world! If this had happened to him rather than Robert I shouldn't have been surprised."

"Unlucky?" Cam asked. "He seems comfortably enough set. Or do you mean his illness?"

"Nothing as serious as that," Allen laughed. "Yardley's trials are not on a dramatic scale. I sometimes think that he wishes they were. It would be more interesting. No; Yardley suffers from the pixies, they say. Milk upset; tools lost; hens don't lay;

clock always wrong; dogs dig up his seeds; cats have kittens on his porch—nothing at all important but sufficient to make life miserable for him—and, if truth be told, sufficient for him to make life miserable for everyone else."

"Some people," Cam said sententiously, "love their bad luck. Well, to get back to the theft, the only available thieves are the cottagers over the hill, who appear to be an inoffensive lot, and the people in the Rectory itself or the Verger's cottage?"

Allen frowned angrily. "It may look like that, Inspector, and I've no right to resent the suggestion, but as far as the Rectory is concerned it's impossible when you think a moment. The Rector and Mrs. Copperman obviously have everything to lose, nothing to gain from theft of the church plate. As for the Verger's cottage—Yardley is more likely to steal the Crown jewels than anything belonging to the church. Colly hasn't the sense or the inclination or the courage to offend his father."

"So everyone is obviously innocent and the plate still missing," Cam commented. "Your absence at Powey and the Verger's bilious attacks seem to be unfortunately synchronised."

"It's a miserable coincidence," Allen agreed. "You might think the thief planned it that way. But of course that's impossible. It must be. The alternative—that someone watches all our movements—is too awful. My absence is known ahead of time, of course, but the thief couldn't count on Yardley's stomach. My own view is that the plate must have been stolen on the spur of the moment. But that doesn't get us any further in *finding* it." He paused and then added miserably: "I suppose there's not a ghost of a chance of keeping the theft a secret, Mr. Cam?"

Cam shook his head. "You wouldn't have stood much chance of that even if there had been no murder, Mr. Allen." They strolled along for a few paces, Allen with an expression of deepening depression. "Have you known Mr. and Mrs. Copperman long?" the Inspector asked.

"Since I came here when I was demobbed in 1945. He has been a good person to work with because he lets me have a free hand. He's not very active himself nowadays, though he used to have a terrific reputation as a preacher." Cam looked surprised.

Yes, his type of sermon isn't very popular in a place like this. But he's quite a scholar and in a cathedral or university town that's appreciated. With a good audience he's still brilliant. He was the son of the Bishop of Minchester, you know, and he was raised to think of himself as a potential bishop, likely to fill his father's shoes! He had the intellect, certainly, but he didn't quite have the personality, I suppose, and one disappointment after another has rather soured him. People criticise him for not taking an interest in the parish. Well, the answer is that he isn't by nature a parish priest and that's no crime. In the Middle Ages there was more opportunity for the scholar-cleric. Robert would have been in his element in the Jarrow of Bede's day. Anyway, he does take an interest in the parish in his own way—is fascinated by its history and gave a series of talks on the subject last winter. The audience consisted of three old women nodding to sleep, one or two fidgety children, the atheist greengrocer come to get ammunition, Mrs. Copperman and myself. That sort of thing is heartbreaking for a man who *knows* he could do great things with the right opportunity. And it's heartbreaking for her too," he added. "She was made for a larger rôle."

"Well, I hope you have better luck yourself," Cam said with a friendly smile.

Allen shrugged. "I'm not ambitious. A nice little parish like this would suit me down to the ground. Where I can pursue both my antiquarian and sporting interests."

"Tennis?" asked Cam, glancing at the tennis racket.

"Yes, at this time of the year. But hunting and cross-country running are my passions."

Hunting, thought Cam, was an expensive pastime for a curate. But this was not one of the hunting shires and doubtless the farmers would have inexpensive local chases.

He returned to one random question about the murder.

"What about the Verger—Yardley? What makes you so sure he's trustworthy?"

"I would trust him in anything which concerns the church. I remember—I used to live here as a boy, you know—I remember when he was the worst reprobate in Trevelley—and that's saying something because the old smugglers left a strain of rank blood in these parts. But Banting worked a miracle with Yardley and the old man's a flame of the Lord now. He rather frightens me, to tell the truth, and he's made his son, poor kid, a raving lunatic."

"Not my kind of religion!" declared Cam, and the other laughed.

"Speaking as a clergyman, almost any sort of Christianity is better nowadays than none. But his conversion has certainly taken in a very violent way. And he's been getting worse lately. Will hardly let anyone in the church unless he will declare his faith upon the church porch. I've seen him chivying tourists about until they fled for their lives. That brass is a case in point. As a matter of fact, speaking as a brass-rubber I don't care who rubs it. If seven maids with seven brooms brushed it for seven years they probably wouldn't make very much impression on that alloy, but Yardley regards the whole operation as sacrilege—desecration of the dead—and I don't want to get into any argument with him on the subject."

"Oh, is that why?" Cam said. "I thought you were a bit severe. The Rector was the stumbling-block, didn't you tell Briarley?"

"He is too, as regards Briarley's wild idea for raising the whole thing," said Allen. "But for other reasons. It would cost something to move the brass and although the church would bear the expense the Rector feels, quite rightly I think, that the money could be used in better ways."

While they talked they had been strolling slowly down the High Street, stopping occasionally, moving on again, speaking quietly so as not to be overheard, but otherwise only half-conscious of the passers-by.

They reached a cottage now where Allen stopped.

"Mrs. Copperman asked me to call here," he said regretfully, "so I shall have to leave you. You will think about what I told you, won't you?"

"You can count on that," Cam said obligingly and Allen turned up a side alley to the cottage's front door.

"Hoy!" He was stopped abruptly by Cam having a second thought and turned back impatiently.

"Something else?"

"Yes. Two things. Do you swim?"

"Yes, of course!"

"And what was the subject of Briarley's lecture in London?"

"Cornish church towers."

"That's splendid," said Cam, and went off down the street, not much wiser himself, but leaving a duly-impressed curate behind him.

# CHAPTER VIII

CAM'S walk to the town quay was not to be uneventful. A few yards farther on were two other people in whom he had a lively interest and who seemed to be in unexpectedly close consultation. Betsey Rowan and Jessica Luigi were standing at a corner in impassioned discussion. They were speaking low, but the stubborn anger on Betsey's face and the tantalising amusement on Jessica's were unmistakable. Was it merely the operatic heat of the afternoon which gave to this chat between two girls such a sinister appearance? Cam approached as unostentatiously as police training can ensure and was within two paces before Betsey noticed him and broke off in the middle of an angry exclamation.

"You have no right to them! They're as much ours as yours....You have everything else...."

She looked up at the bland face of the Inspector with startled hostility. Jessica, following her glance, laughed.

"Isn't it the great inspector from London?" she said boldly.

"Aye, but it's honoured in Trevelley we are!" There was a faint affected Irish inflexion in her voice which Cam found rather attractive.

"I'm on holiday," he smiled. "And as a matter of fact, I'm the great inspector from Little Biggling, not from London— but there's not so much difference."

"Of course not," Betsey added bitterly. "You're all professional eavesdroppers."

"Those are hard words," Cam said wryly. As she was obviously anxious to give offence he replied in kind. "Fancy you two girls knowing each other so well. I'd no idea ..."

"Why should you!..." interrupted Betsey sharply, but Jessica again laughed it away. The village girl seemed at this moment to have far more poise than her more sophisticated companion.

"What are you suspecting, Mr. Cam? One of us? Sure, you're a cunning man to be after two young girls like us when the village is full of great wicked men and of murders to be solved."

"Just one so far, surely?" Cam said with a sidelong glance at her. "Or do you know of more? It's a hard thing when I can't speak to two pretty girls without their thinking I suspect them of crime. I'm just on my way to visit your father, Mrs. Luigi. Is this the right way?"

Jessica smiled charmingly. "Down the hill and ask on the wharf, Mr. Cam. I wish I could take you, but I be off to my Grans.' You should meet my husband too, Mr. Cam. Him and Dad be the most wicked men in Trevelley, so indeed you ought to be seein' them." For Cam's benefit she gave another amused look at Betsey and went on her way. The older girl turned after her a look of hatred that amazed Cam. Among his favourite illusions was one that nicely nurtured girls do not resort to violence, but if ever he saw latent mayhem it was on Betsey Rowan's face that moment. He was shocked out of silent observation.

"Why, Betsey—Miss Rowan! What's the matter, eh? She's just a silly village girl, you know. You mustn't take her seriously."

Betsey, with an effort, turned away from looking after the girl and managed to smile rather wryly.

"I'm afraid I can't help but take her seriously, Mr. Cam. But don't let it worry you. Are you investigating her family about the murder?" she added eagerly.

"Well," Cam said doubtfully, "I'm 'investigating' a lot of people but that doesn't mean they're responsible."

"It might be," the American girl murmured thoughtfully. "What about poor Mr. Magnuson's accident? Is that part of the case too, now?"

"What made you think that?" Cam asked sharply.

"I met John Briarley and he told me you thought it was murder," she replied blandly. "Is it a secret?"

"Well, it wasn't for publication," said Cam stiffly. "And it's still not definite. If you knew, anyway, why did you ask me?"

Betsey's eyes widened with alarm.

"Mr. Cam! You're so mean ... You aren't thinking ... Perhaps that's why John told me. I *thought* he looked worried."

Cam interrupted abruptly. "Well, you haven't been entirely straightforward with us, Miss Rowan. There was your story about meeting Briarley for a drink after Vespers, for instance. Now you know and I know it wasn't true—Briarley denies it himself—yet you didn't get back to Camp until ten. Discrepancies like that are very disturbing in a murder investigation."

Betsey laughed uneasily. "I told the children I was having a drink with John Briarley. I didn't tell you. Honeywether got it out of them, I suppose."

"The question is, why should you lie, not how we know you lied," Cam said patiently.

"I had to tell them something. And it was a half truth. Jack had asked me to have a drink and I had told the children I would be back late. When they asked if I had been with him it was easier to say yes. Actually he had been very rude at the church so I went for a walk by myself to get the bad taste out of my mouth." There was defiance in her tone and Cam could guess at the hurt pride which she suffered from Briarley's snub—if snub it had been. He doubted if Honeywether would regard pride as a valid excuse but Cam preened himself that he knew enough about women to realise that it was in these absurd little questions of personal prestige that they found most difficulty in being strictly honest.

"Briarley never mentioned that he had invited you to have a drink," he said gently.

"Well, perhaps I asked him," Betsey said ingenuously. "He said he'd like to—or at least I thought he did. Englishmen are so difficult to understand. Half the time you don't know whether they like you or not. He was really very polite at the church," she added bitterly. "But he made it clear he preferred a memorial brass to my company."

"Did you wait at all?" Cam asked.

"Certainly not! You won't find *me* hanging round church doors waiting for *men*!"

"So you don't know how long he stayed?"

"No ... Oh, I see!" But although she showed recognition of the implication of the question Betsey made no further comment.

"Where did you go for your walk?" asked the Inspector.

She laughed wryly. "Well, I had just finished resisting Mr. Magnuson's invitations before service to wander out on the Poltherow cliffs so I made tracks to avoid him and the children by taking the ferry over the river and walking about a mile towards Powey."

"See anyone?"

"Quite a few. It was a lovely evening and lots of visitors were trudging up from the coves along that path on their way home to supper. I didn't know any. I don't suppose any of them would vouch for me."

"Perhaps it won't be necessary," Cam suggested. "So Magnuson invited you for a walk, eh? I've never seen you around with him. You weren't with him this afternoon, I suppose?" There was a harsh ring to the Inspector's voice and Betsey Rowan looked at him anxiously.

"I was at the camp, Mr. Cam. Or about a hundred yards away, picking cowslips for the table. Seems silly picking cowslips for a vase when they're growing all over the dining-room floor, doesn't it? But that's the feminine touch for you. I heard Magnuson scream..." Her voice faltered. "I thought it was a gull at first. It had just that note of savage hysteria. But I had never heard a gull that sounded so terrified, so I went to look. He was down at the foot of the cliffs. ... I saw his blue pullover."

"Isn't it odd," Cam asked, "that you didn't see him coming along the top of the cliffs towards the camp?"

"You forget that there's a hillock just before you reach the camp. He would have been on the other side. I couldn't see Red Cowdray either until I got on top of that." She looked sharply at Cam.

"Where was he?"

"About five hundred yards farther down the cliff, strolling towards us. He was bringing gulls' eggs for the kids, he said. The boat was tied up in the cove."

"Didn't he hear the scream too—or see Magnuson fall?"

"He said," she reported non-committally, "that he had just climbed the cliff from the shore—had just reached the top when I saw him. If he were climbing, the rocks would have hidden Magnuson from him. And the wind was blowing to the southeast, so he wouldn't hear him either. He certainly had eggs from a gull's nest," she added unwillingly.

"Did he get the police or did you?" asked Cam.

"He did."

"Were you alone?"

"Y—yes. I was."

"Miss Rowan," Cam said with sudden severity contrasting sharply with his previous gentleness, "you're keeping something from me. I tell you now that murder is too serious for you to mix with your own personal problems, whatever they be. And I'm not having it." They had reached the 'Three Fishers' and he stopped at the door. "Would you like to come in while I ask Briarley about your invitation yesterday evening?" he added unpleasantly.

"I'd hate to," she said fiercely. "I'm beginning to have a curious dislike for Englishmen, and if you want my opinion I think that policemen should have better things to do than playing about with silly little murders of people who don't matter anyway while there is *real* suffering of *real* people going on in this world." Head high she marched on down the hill, leaving Cam pondering on the unpredictable scale of values of women in general and of Miss Rowan from Rhode Island in particular.

He went into the lounge in a thoughtful mood and after ringing the bell stretched himself out on the sofa. From there he could see through the french windows out to the harbour. The lounge appeared empty and no one answered the bell. In a moment or two he would have been asleep when a sharp voice from within one of the great arm-chairs of the room said bitterly, "What were you worrying Betsey for? Is *she* under suspicion in your monstrous mind?"

It was Briarley, hidden from all casual visitors to the room by the chair-back, but commanding a fine view of the village street which passed just before it. Cam got up and took a chair from which he could see the young man.

"I thought you were going to Powey again," he commented.

"I've finished at Powey. And if you thought that why did you ask Betsey to come in and see me?"

"Peeping Tom!" remarked Cam. "Because I wanted to torment her, naturally. So you heard our conversation. What do you think of her, then?"

"I think she's very nice," Briarley said stiffly, "and if she has a private life of her own, why so have all of us and it's none of your damned business."

Cam was nettled. "Don't be a fool. Of course it's my damned business. My business is to prevent people letting their private lives trespass excessively on other people's lives, especially when it reaches the point of murder. That's what you pay me for, isn't it?"

"Yes," said Briarley, "but the emphasis is on 'other people'. Nobody pays the police to interfere with their own life. Anyway, I beg your pardon. I'm afraid I learnt no manners in the Army."

"Betsey Rowan was complaining of it."

"Quite rightly," Briarley said. "I had promised her and I should have gone through with it."

This struck Cam as a strenuous way of referring to a friendly drink with a young lady, but he went on: "What I can't understand is why you didn't catch up with her on the way to Powey. There's only one road, isn't there?"

"There is an inland road, but no one goes by it except in a car. The shortest route by foot or cycle is the cliff-path. Yes, I followed her along that, but when I caught up there didn't seem much point in breaking up the conversation."

"What conversation?"

"With Allen. He wouldn't have appreciated it, even if she had been in a mood to forgive and forget!"

"So she knows Allen too." Cam scratched his head with growing perplexity. "That young lady certainly gets around."

"American girls are awfully friendly," Briarley agreed with warm approval. "I like them."

"She knew Magnuson too."

"Casually. He wouldn't be much help to anyone." There was a note of grim disapproval in Briarley's voice.

"Why," asked Cam, with honest interest, "would she be looking for help?"

But Briarley shrugged. Cam sighed. "So you like American girls," he said. "What do you think of the local variety?"

The young man looked at him with marked suspicion. "I don't know much about them. A lot of them had their heads turned during the War; that's all I know."

"That Jessica Luigi is a pretty piece," Cam sighed.

"You think so?" 'The old man is getting to his dotage' was implicit in Briarley's tone.

Cam laughed. "Yes, of course I think so. And you do too, so don't be sanctimonious, young man."

Briarley laughed too, but with a shade of bitterness. "All right. She is. But don't let that fool you, Cam. She's not very nice." He spoke too soberly to be melodramatic. Before Cam could explore the grounds of this statement he went on quickly: "When do you think the church is likely to be open again? I'd like to have another look at the brass to see if I can pick up any more clues."

"Clues?" asked the Inspector blankly. Was Briarley turning his hand to detection? "Oh, about the palimpsest. I don't know, but probably tomorrow. You'd better not let the Verger see you at it! After this affair he'll be more on his guard than ever."

"In defence of his church, you mean?" Briarley asked sharply.

"Of course. He's fanatic on the subject."

"That's what I've been led to believe." The young man was silent a few moments surveying Cam. "Look here," he said suddenly. "I'm not one to tell tales, but some things get under my skin. Here's one. Last night after I got back from Powey—about ten o'clock—I was passing the Verger's cottage when I heard an awful racket. Furniture being man-handled, a boy howling and some of the powerfullest swearing I've had the fortune to hear.

I stopped, hesitated about going in. Then I noticed there were sheets of printed paper lying scattered about the lane and under the hedges. They were very large sheets—about ten of them—being pushed along by the breeze and looking in the moonlight like icefloes on a river. I picked one up, and what do you think it was?" Briarley asked his question with too much horrified suspense for it to be a guessing game.

Cam shook his head.

"A page from the Bible! Torn out roughly yet not crumpled at all. Book of Elijah, I think. It must have been an old family Bible from the size of it. I picked up some of the other sheets. They were all torn in the same way. I don't mind telling you I felt rather sick. You don't expect to find that sort of thing lying in a country lane. It was getting dark. The swearing had suddenly stopped. I felt very much alone with the Devil."

Briarley looked grimly out across the blue harbour.

"Did you see anyone?" Cam asked.

"Yes, I was standing there with a page of the Bible in my hand when a gaunt figure appeared at the garden gate. It was the Verger. He was grey as a stone and I swear he was frothing at the mouth—a thin line of white froth round his grey lips. He didn't say a word. Neither did I. He snatched the page out of my hand, then stalked round picking up the others, holding them tight to his chest. When he had finished he just stood and looked at me. I went! Perhaps it was cowardly, perhaps I should have asked questions. But at the time there seemed none to ask."

Cam nodded understanding. "What do you make of it?" "Madness," the other said simply. "Stark, staring insanity. Either the Verger or his son. Poor wretched souls," he added in compassion.

"You heard no other voice? No third person in the quarrel?" "No. I heard footsteps running after the quarrel had stopped—running down the path on the other side of the hedge and out of the gate round the corner where I couldn't see. They were light and quick like a child though. It must have been the boy."

"It's a strange tale," Cam commented. There was a pause, then he added abruptly, "Did you know that villagers here used to practise Black Magic? Did you run across it when you were stationed near here?"

"Rubbish!" said the young man baldly. "Don't you believe those old wives' tales. A self-respecting witch wouldn't have wasted a spell on those adolescent brawls they used to call 'Black Magic' here. I attended one. It wasn't much more exciting than a church bazaar would be if held at night. One or two people got drunk and acted accordingly. Several more tried out a few halfbaked ideas about the Black Mass, but one could safely have taken one's grandmother there for the evening."

Cam thought with amusement of Honeywether's awe at what Briarley regarded with such contempt. He wanted to ask more of this eye-witness of wickedness, but at this moment Lucy came in.

"Did someone ring?" she asked sanctimoniously. The men looked at her blankly.

"Not us," Cam said, and it was not until she was shutting the door that he remembered that he had rung a long time ago for a cup of tea. He called her back and gave the order.

"Kitchen's busy," she said. "You'll 'ave to wait. And serve you right, it will, for gettin' me into trouble."

"What trouble?"

"Manager were mad right through, 'e were, 'bout me gallivantin' off leavin' th' bar wide open. 'E said 'e'd sack me if ever it 'appened again. All yer fault it wer too. Though I didn't tell 'im that, 'cause I'm no tattle-tale."

Cam gave her a half-crown in reward.

"Didn't the other girl keep watch for you then?"

"What, 'er? Nah! She never kept watch fer nothin' except a boyfriend—an' never found 'im neither." Lucy was so pleased by this reflection that she went on more philosophically. "Well, it might 'a bin worse. I guess I knows the fellers who'd take drink wi'out tellin' and most of em' be honest enow. Not but what some of 'em would surprise yer. That Yardley boy wot almost lives in the church—I met 'im coming up t'hill with 'is pot o' ale—wot 'e 'adn't paid for. Oh, I got 'is shilling quick enough!" "That would be for his father?" Cam asked.

"Of course. Boys like Colly don't drink strong ale like that. Even when they've got th' siller."

"He gets it regularly?" asked Briarley, catching the drift of the question.

"Every night like clockwork, an' never spills a drop, they say. Aye, there's much to be said for those simple-minded lads. They're into less trouble than the brainy ones."

Cam winced at this cavalier treatment of the saddest of human tragedies. But then the lounge was suddenly filled with the brassy clamour of a Chinese temple. As the call to worship began, Lucy turned and ran.

"Tea!" exclaimed Briarley, leaping to his feet. For a moment Cam struggled with professional conscience. He knew there were several things he should ask. But then the holiday passion for another meal seized him.

"I wonder what sort of jam today?" he said, getting to his feet.

"Strawberry, I think. The chambermaid told me."

"I hope they've got to the end of that chocolate cake. It tasted like soap."

"Yes, but lovely with jam on it."

"Then you don't have enough jam for the bread-and-butter. I'd rather have a good piece of pound cake myself."

"Or what about saffron cake? That's the local speciality."

"Or Devonshire cream on scones."

"I once had a tea in St. Austell ..."

And so, talking like sensible people about important things, they passed out of the lounge.

★ ★ ★

Hallelujah! Hallelujah! Halleluu-jah! Miss Cornthwaite was singing to herself. No sound issued from her thin close lips but within the chords crashed and crescendoed in passionate thanksgiving, and the sopranos soared triumphant, weaving golden threads of sound.

No one could have guessed, to look at Miss Cornthwaite, that within her the whole Hallelujah Chorus was throbbing with full orchestral accompaniment. In all the vivid colour of a Cornish evening she was a tiny sombre figure. Yet if the world exists in and for the mind of humanity it was in Miss Cornthwaite's mind that all this creation had its being. The golden path across the sea to the sun lay open for her. The white-whipped froth circling the oceanic bowl, the soaring flight of the gulls, interlocking in elaborate pattern, the cowslips beside her, the tawny fields undulating into a cloud-streaked horizon—all these were for Miss Cornthwaite. She looked upon them as sternly as she would upon a class of delinquent girls. Her back was straight and her hands folded upon her lap.

But her seat was upon a rock jutting precariously over the sea from the very cliff-top and her legs swung carelessly in mid-air. This was Miss Cornthwaite's holiday. Four more weeks, she was saying to herself. One whole month before returning to reality. Then one more year and again—six precious weeks. Then ten more years containing sixty weeks and then—the rest of a lifetime. It would all work out in the end. One day would come *the* day when she could sit here and know that she never need leave.

Miss Cornthwaite's soul was singing free. Now the clouds were marshalling for their triumphal procession into the sunset, piling up in reds and golds towards the west while long white streamers pointed expectantly across the sea-sky. In thanksgiving Miss Cornthwaite was praying: 'Lord,' she cried, 'oh Lord, I, Jane Cornthwaite, give thanks for the world. This world which belongs to me, this piece of earth and no more, for my possession six weeks of the year. This lovely, lovely world of mine!'

Miss Cornthwaite's eyes widened just a trifle as one golden banner of cloud caught fire and flamed to red. Behind her a lark burst into an evening song as desperately intense as though this were its last attempt to charm the world to admiration. And the world was charmed.

Miss Cornthwaite's eyes widened yet again but not from ecstasy. Miss Cornthwaite was slipping—slipping and sliding into greenblue eternity from the solid security of her rock. Urgently, desperately, she was snatching with frantic fingers at tufts of grass, cowslips, brown tendrils of heather. They all came to her kindly and gave way to her strength. It was not possible—not possible. She who had been so safe was now to die! It was not possible. She clawed in the earth, but the earth had no substance, and the pebbles rolled over the edge of the rock past her legs and rattled down a hundred feet to the rocks below. There was nothing to save Miss Cornthwaite—nothing except her two hands—only her hands against a rope, twisted relentlessly, tightening inflexibly around her two grey-stockinged ankles.

Miss Cornthwaite did not scream. There was no one to whom to scream, but she prayed in agony: 'God, don't let me die here—here, in the world you gave me. Save me! Drive away trespassers. Save me! Drive away trespassers. ....'

As she prayed Miss Cornthwaite struggled. She was half over the rock, lying face flat upon the cliff, when her hands found anchorage. A crack in the rock where her finger-tips just held. Once there nothing mortal could tear her loose. She felt renewed strength and desperate confidence. Her old body, hardened like seasoned oak through years of exercise and work, defied the rope. She drew her legs, inch by inch, onto the jutting rock. The rope came with them. Now her knees, now her calves, now her ankles, still desperately clutched. With savage effort she rubbed her ankles back and forth across the edge of the shelf. Now there was a voice as well as a rope—a voice groaning and swearing. She pressed harder and more viciously, rubbing the rope until it frayed, wishing it were hands, scratching them to the bone. There was an undistinguishable howl and she was free.

Miss Cornthwaite did not look round. She ran, by the inland path to Trevelley and she never looked back.

# CHAPTER IX

AFTER an ample and placid tea, chatting with Briarley about churches, cricket and Russia, Cam rose, stretched himself and decided to pass the time before supper by strolling down to the harbour. While there he would pay his visit to the Cowdrays. The local villain should certainly not be missed.

Perhaps that cake had been too rich for a ration-conditioned stomach. He felt pricked by uneasiness as he strolled down the twists and turns of Trevelley High Street, which seemed always to be seeking a route up the cliffs only to be dragged sharply back towards the sea. There came to Cam suddenly, with ironic amusement, the memory of how he had plagued Mrs. Cam to come to Trevelley. She had wanted to go to Bournemouth. They always went to Bournemouth. They knew Bournemouth. There was plenty to do in Bournemouth when it rained. But he would have none of it. Middle-aged nostalgia for the Cornish coast obsessed him. Trevelley it would be or nothing. They were getting into a rut. The children ought to see more of the English coast than Bournemouth. So it went on for weeks, ending in vistory for the Inspector— victory as unexpected as it was pleasant and largely due to Mrs. Cam's sudden realisation that there would be fewer people in Trevelley than Bournemouth, more privacy and even a beach to oneself. Her sober expectation was being gratified. The children and she were having a delightful holiday. So had Cam until today. Today it occurred to him that despite fifteen boyhood summers in the village all sense of familiarity had disappeared. He would feel more at home in Bournemouth.

He wondered, and the absurdity of the thought piqued him, whether he had ever actually been down to Trevelly harbour before. Of course he must have been there hundreds of times, yet it looked strangely unfamiliar. This must be the obverse of the familiar sensation that one has 'been here before'. Cam had trod these same cobbles, passed the same lace-curtained windows and blue shutters, nodded to the same casually-glancing fishermen and housewives, on countless occasions. This afternoon, however, going down to see Red Cowdray, he seemed to be passing from the good high-tea and shrimping-nets world of an English holiday resort into an atmosphere uncomfortably foreign. The several tourists he passed seemed out of place. A red-faced perspiring lot, he thought critically, intruders like himself poking hot fingers into the cool secrets of the fishing village. And what secrets! It was not so long ago, Cam remembered, since Trevelley was inaccessible by rail or road from the main body of the island, not so long since the only fresh blood in its population came from the progeny of shipwrecked foreign sailors, not so long since men, women and children in the village, snatching up sacks, buckets and other receptacles, would race at a familiar signal down to the rocky shore to salvage with conscienceless greed the remains of some ship which had foundered upon the coast as a result of their devilish misdirections. Cam did not find it difficult today to picture those plump, smiling fishwives and even their tow-headed children standing breathless upon the cliffs above a storm-lashed sea, watching the struggles of a desperate crew to bring their ship to port where the false beacon guided—only to crack sickeningly upon the sharp rocks. He could hear the chorus of savage shrieks from the remorseless gallery above the cries of the crew. Any sailor who survived the wreck could expect nothing better than to be thrown back to the waves by the devils on shore unless he himself took the fancy of a local maiden and was ready to join them in their barbaric occupation. Cam found himself glowering savagely at a small girl, dark-haired, slim and Spanish-eyed, who had placed herself in his path with obvious hopes of a penny from the tourist—so savagely that with a frightened glance she turned and fled. Conniving little beggar, thought Cam ruthlessly. He had lost his good humour.

He reached the wharf just as a group of fishing-smacks was tying up. While the men folded up the sails, lashed down the mainmast to the tiny decks and landed the haul they exchanged gay remarks with wives and friends upon the harbour wall. Cam joined the group for a moment and listened gloomily to the bursts of laughter which exploded spasmodically into the warm evening. He was conscious of curious glances cast in his direction and of nudges exchanged to draw attention to his presence. He was, he remembered, the Great Inspector from London. He wondered what impression, if any, the murder had made upon this section of the village or if their lives were so divorced from the church that even such a startling event within it would arouse only curiosity. Did they think of it as a village disaster or merely an event upon the hill? Looking up he could see the church towering head and shoulders over the terraced house-tops up the cliff. There was solid, earth-rooted power in the squared stone. I'll put my money on that, thought Cam vulgarly.

"You be Mr. Cam?" enquired a shrill old voice behind him, and he swung round sharply. A little nut of a man was looking up at him, head cocked on one side with aged pertness. Insignificant in size he was yet a startling figure by virtue of straggly, unkempt hair of a most unlikely orange. The backs of his horny hands, too, were matted with orange hair and his blue eyes peered sharply from under orange eyebrows which drooped to his cheeks like a pair of sideburns. His seamed face was clean shaven, but about the mouth and chin was the shadow of that pervading orange again. In the evening light the old man looked as if he had caught something of the reflection of the sunset and was storing it within himself for the next morning.

"That's right," Cam replied suspiciously. He was in a mood to distrust even the most feeble stranger.

"Darter tells me you bin lookin' for me, eh?" The old man cocked his head even further to one side at imminent risk of dislocation.

With a shock of surprise Cam realised that this must be Red Cowdray. He had drawn a mental picture which was so very different—a great broad bull of a man, red-bearded and complexioned, powerful with something of a swagger, a buccaneer of the old school. It was difficult to reconcile this little old man with the reputation for evil living about which Cam had heard so much. It was difficult, too, to picture him as the father of that graceful, dark-haired creature, Jessica Luigi. Illogically Cam felt cheated.

"Are you Red Cowdray?" he asked suspiciously.

"Course I be," the old man said with reedy petulance. "Ain't I red enough for ye? What dost want wi' me, Mister?" Cam glanced at the openly curious crowd.

"Well, we can't talk here. Is your home near?"

"Come along," said the old man abruptly and turning led the way towards a narrow alley. He walked with a catlike speed and surety. Stumbling after him on the uneven cobbles Cam could well believe that he was capable of climbing the local cliffs despite his age.

They arrived at a thinly whitewashed cottage tucked obscurely down an alley. Red Cowdray kicked open a wooden door which indicated by its battered condition that it had rarely been opened any other way. Inside stifling heat originated in the oil cookingstove and was intensified by a complete absence of ventilation. The concentrated odour of fish, oil and unwashed bodies overwhelmed rather than offended the senses. After two minutes of misery Cam's sense of smell succumbed to the unequal struggle and did not regain consciousness until Mrs. Cam complained bitterly of his personal habits later that evening. In a quick glance Cam could observe almost nothing which was not in need of some repair—the furniture was broken and scarred, the radio lacked any case and exhibited its inner workings with ugly exposure, the dirty china on the table, no two pieces matching, lacked handles or spouts. In curious contrast to the general squalor was one neat if unfinished object—a magnificent model of a sailing-ship, a threemasted schooner—upon the table. The care and precision winch were going into its construction were in remarkable contrast to the shoddiness of the rest of the room. Cam admired it openly and Red Cowdray, who had flung himself into a chair, nodded complacently.

"Aye, 'tes a fine thing," he agreed. "Six months I've spent on that an' et's twenty pun I could get fur et from one o' your visitors."

"Is it for sale then?" asked Cam. It would look nice up on the mantlepiece at home, though twenty pounds was out of the question.

"Nay, not thes un. I'm givin' et to the young Yanks—nice little lads an' lasses they be—an' t'ship may remind 'em o' many 'appy days in Trevelley."

The old man's expression and tone were too sanctimonious for Cam to refrain from puncturing his righteousness.

"And no doubt they'll be giving you fine presents in return," he commented dryly. Red Cowdray laughed shrilly and looked with more appreciation at the Inspector.

"No doot," he agreed cheerfully. "Sich as some new clothes an' good food from Amurricy w'en as they get back. Aye, I luvs such little kiddies," and he chortled happily.

"I hear you took them a present only this morning," Cam remarked.

"Did the young leddy tell you then? Aye, the gulls' eggs I was gettin' for 'em same time as yon poor feller were a-killin' 'imself. Me climbin' up cliffs while he were failin' down. Me so old an' him so young." The old man shook his head with wonder at the unaccountability of life.

"A funny thing you didn't hear or see him," Cam commented.

Cowdray shook his head emphatically. "I can show you easy how 'twas. The gull's nest is in Lully Cove an' 'twas up there I were climbin'. He wor round the bend of the cliff in

Pennypocket Cove. There wor a sharp sea-breeze, an' his yells would get carried away from me. So I'd neither hear nor see the pore feller."

"Where was Miss Rowan when you first saw her?"

"'Twas just arter I got to top o' cliffs when I saw 'er flyin' along, hair all which-a-way. When she saw me she hollered fer help. She wor in a great takin'."

"Who wouldn't be?" Cam asked sharply. "She'd just seen a man—or heard him, anyway—dashed to pieces on the rocks."

Cowdray shrugged. "It happens reglar 'bout this time o' year. Silly fools playin' on the cliffs, y'know. Not but what 'tis sad, o' course," he added hastily.

"You're pretty old," Cam commented frankly, "to clamber up and down cliffs. Do you often do it?"

"When I've a mind ter. I'm not feeble, Inspector, not in no way. I can still run up a sail wi' nobuddy's help an' climb a mast wi'out help."

"You have your own boat still?" asked Cam.

"Not fer fishin'," the other explained. "I takes the trippers out on fine days fer three bob an hour. An' wot wi' listenin' ter their silly gigglin' an' cleanin' up their sickness I lose by the trade. ..." He spat contemptuously at the cat which lay before the oil-stove.

"It must be a busy trade, though," Cam said. "At this time of year especially. How is it that you weren't taking people out this afternoon?"

"I must rest me old bones sometimes," the old man whined piteously. "Yesserday I were traipsin' 'tween here an' Powey wi' trippers from tea till ten. T'fools think 'tis romantical by evening so I charges six bob arter tea fer the Powey trip."

That's a nice alibi, thought Cam suspiciously. "And do you know your passengers? Could you find them again if the police wanted to talk with them?"

"Oo, aye," Cowdray said casually. "They be hereabouts, no doubt. But nobuddy ud want to talk wi' them. Pore simps they were."

"Did you know the young man Magnuson? Had you ever taken him out?"

"Never seen 'im afore."

"What about Miss Rowan?"

"Her neither. Though I've heard t'kids talkin', o' course, and ... No, I've never got to seein' her afore meself."

"But your daughter knows her well?" Cam hazarded.

The old man looked shocked. "What would the likes o' my darter know 'bout sich a young leddy?" A thoughtful look passed over his face. "Unless they might 'a met in Americcy. But Jessy never said nothin'. Not that I'd 'a asked her. Nay, but I don't hold wi' all this pokin' an' pryin' into folks' business, Inspector, thet I don't. In my young days folk did what they pleased an' asked nobuddy by your leave, but now you can 'ardly turn over in bed wi'out bein' had up 'fore the justices for disturbing o' the peace. In my young days ...'"

"This place was a sink of iniquity," Cam concluded rudely. The old orange head nodded delightedly and with some pride. "Aye, that's right. We were real bad, there's no denyin' et. Th' young men nowadays are nothin' t'what we were! Some of 'em are full o' bluster but they doesn't have th'ideas an' nat'ral wickedness we had."

"And they don't have your advantages," suggested Cam. "All these policemen about the place nowadays complicate things."

"'Tes true," said the old man seriously. "Things be much harder nowadays. I'm glad I wor active in a better day."

"Are there many of your old pals about?" Cam asked with interest. "I'd enjoy hearing you reminisce together."

"Most of 'em gone," sighed Cowdray. "Most of 'em in a Better Land. Died or drowned or hung arter th' railway come to Trevelley." The arrival of the railway was obviously synonymous with the coming of law and order. "An' then some o' th'ould hypocrites won't talk about th'ould days. Take Yardley. He's Verger now, Gawd 'elp us, though I remembers a time when he'd sooner rob the church than pray in et. Gone all religious he has now, an' won't hardly talk to hes ould friends except to curse 'em. He always wor a slipp'ry 'un, though. Never catch old Yardley, us use ter say. He'd a nose fer changes in t'weather like nobbut else I ever knowed!" The old man bobbed his head with mixed admiration and contempt. "It's nay his weaselin' I care abaht," he added. "It's hes tale-tellin' on t'other chaps when he done et. Aye, he a'most had us all in gaol an' pore Elijah Tomlin he did get took by reason o' him."

"You've not done so badly," suggested Cam. "Are you still practising or have the police and age proved too much for you?"

"Age!" sighed Red Cowdray. "That's et. I'm old an' decrepit now, mester. Just a pore weak feller. Gawd knows what I'd do wi'out me pension, nobbut et's small enow an' hardly enough to keep a cat." He shrivelled in self-pity momentarily but brightened as soon. "Et's not a few policemen would be worryin' me; no offence, Inspector. Why, they ain't even found who killed thet feller in church yit, though et's plain as the nose on your face. Pore old Honeywether!" the old man added contemptuously. "What would ye be 'spectin' of a furriner like him?"

"It might be worth your while to help him along," suggested Cam. "There'd be a reward—or is it a friend of yours?"

Cowdray laughed. "'Tes no friend o' mine, but I'll not be tellin'. 'Twould be takin' the glory from ye, Inspector. That's your job."

"It wouldn't be you?" suggested Cam hopefully and the old man roared at his wit.

"Nay, nay; look a little further, Mr. Inspector. I were never a good hand at proper killin'. Some do, some don't. That's how 'tes." The Inspector could not but agree with this observation.

Cowdray was watching him closely. "But dunna' forget," he said suddenly, "that et's a mad thing been dun there an' 'tis a mad man you want, eh? All thet pilin'o' t'body on t'altar, thet warn't sensible, eh? Nay, you won't have to look far, that's sartin."

Cam chose to ignore this. He asked some more questions about Magnuson's death, but Cowdray's connection with that mystery seemed to be as entirely casual as he claimed. Nor could the Inspector extract any more information about the relationship between Betsey Rowan and Jessica Luigi. Cowdray shook his head sadly when the subject was raised again.

"Aye, Inspector, you knows fer yerself what these young gels be like. All skirt an' flirt. Et be more than an old man like me can do to keep an eye on her. She be married now, thank Gawd, an' another man's worry. But don't be askin' me 'bout her doin's 'cause danged ef I know ought o' them an' don't want to know nothin'."

Cam looked without sympathy on the old man whose drooping shoulders and shaking hands seemed now to epitomise the helplessness of all men before their wayward daughters. A slight twitch of his eyebrows, however, revealed eyes peering upwards to see the effect of this lament. He seemed slightly abashed by Cam's cool stare—but at this moment the door was kicked open and another man entered to share the burden of the inquisitive Inspector.

The new arrival was so unmistakably and even ostentatiously American that Cam wondered that he had not noticed him before amongst the small village population. A tall, slim-hipped young man, with hands thrust deep in his pockets, he looked around him with a permanent expression of contemptuous composure. Dark hair and eyes, an olive complexion, even, perhaps, the brightness of his yellow shirt and green trousers, suggested Italian ancestry, but there was only New York in his voice when he spoke to Red Cowdray after one casual glance at the Inspector.

"Hey, Dad, have you seen Jess? We were supposed to meet at the movies. What the hell d'you suppose has happened to her?"

"She's gone to her Gram," the old man said calmly. "Gram's ill an' Jess took her a pasty. She'll be back soon."

"She might have let me know," the young man grumbled. "I could have gone in earlier instead of missing most of it." He went over to the sink, stacked a few dirty dishes out of the way and started to wash his hands.

As there was no sign of an introduction forthcoming Cam spoke up himself.

"Is this your son-in-law?" he asked Red Cowdray.

The old man sighed noisily. "He be," he said. "Vic, this be Inspector Cam." There was a hardly detectable emphasis on the 'Inspector'. That the young American half turned indicated some interest—but it was not detectable in his expression and he kept his hands deep in the water.

"Hiya," he said. "Are you the cop from London who's working on the church murder?"

"I'm interested in the case," Cam replied indirectly. "Your father-in-law has been giving me his views on it. I gather he could solve it himself for us if he wanted to."

Luigi's smile was not very pleasant as he looked towards Red Cowdray again.

"Set a thief to catch a thief. I guess Dad could clear this up quick enough if he wanted to! Me, I'm baffled. It's not the kinda thing you'd expect in a one-horse town like this, is it?"

"I'm not so sure," Cam demurred. "It's not Shanghai, I'll grant you, but there's plenty goes on under the surface in Trevelley."

"Are you kidding?" scoffed the young man. "I spent eight months here during the War and even then the only things that happened here were what us guys made happen. And now! ... It's death warmed over!"

"Well," said Cam, "I think your father-in-law could tell you more about that side of the place than I can. Cut your hand?" he asked abruptly. The water that the young man was throwing down the sink was red with blood. Luigi scowled and shrugged.

"That damn wharf. It's slippery with fish-guts and I barked my knuckles falling down the steps."

Cowdray laughed unexpectedly. "Clumsy!" he commented. "Marries a fisherman's daughter an' can't keep 'is feet on dry land!" Although he smiled there was an unpleasant vindictiveness in his voice and Luigi flushed defensively.

"I'd like to see you crossing Sixth Avenue," he muttered, but Cam noticed that he said it furtively. Red Cowdray was still master in his own house.

"Are you planning to settle here?" the Inspector asked Luigi. "Not likely! What a dump! I'll give Jess another month or so and then back to the good old U.S.A."

"I suppose your wife misses her own home and family," Cam said sentimentally, surveying the disreputable room and its most un-fatherly owner. "After all," he added conscientiously, "be it never so humble there's no place like home."

"You suppose so, do you?" said Luigi contemptuously. "Well, I can tell you one thing, this is Jess's last visit here. From now on the U.S.A. is her home and she'd better remember it. After all—I've got my kids there," he added, rather as an afterthought.

"Yes, twins, I hear," Cam remarked with friendly admiration, but the young man looked at him with quick suspicion.

"Who was telling *you* about them?" He scowled blackly. "Lot of old hens here can't do nothing but gossip, I guess. No wonder I won't be living here. Guess I'll take Jess away where people mind their own business. You let me catch anyone talking about my kids and there'll be trouble, I'm telling you. ... And when I say trouble I know what I'm talking about!" Under a veneer of sophistication the young man appeared very sensitive about his wife's reputation.

"What *do* you know about trouble?" Cam asked curiously.

Red Cowdray replied. "Ask Mr. Honeywether. Our Leo can be a rough boy sometimes. Now, Leo, s'pose you go along an' meet Jess. Forget your fingers, can't you? Anyone'd think you'd broken 'em."

Luigi stuck a considerable amount of sticking-plaster on his hands and with a curt nod to Cam left the room. Cowdray shook his head sadly after him.

"Not bright!" he remarked sadly. "Poor Jess. But 'tes 'er own fault. ... She'd offers enough. ... An' ef he's not sharp, p'raps it's all fer t'best."

There could be no doubt that the old man was under no delusions concerning his daughter. Nor did he appear to care much.

It had not, thought Cam, as he left the cottage, been a fruitful visit. He had no faith in the old man's veracity, but— well, it might be worth checking whom he had been ferrying round the harbour yesterday afternoon and evening.

He stopped at the wharf again by a booth which advertised harbour trips for visitors and in the course of booking a fishing trip for his children made discreet enquiries about Red Cowdray's tourist trips. It appeared that old man had a legitimate business, but he was warned seriously against entrusting himself or his family to such a reckless sailor. It appeared that most of the retired fishermen who devoted their declining years to the profitable pleasures of tourists gave their clients a brief run round the harbour and back again. Old Red, true to character, would, at a price, take you on more adventurous trips out to sea and around the coast to neighbouring villages if you wished to risk your life in his ancient smack.

"The old pirate!" a fisherman standing near Cam exclaimed bitterly at this. He came, apparently from Poltherow and explained that there was great resentment in that village because Red Cowdray would pick up tourists there as well as in his native harbour. This modern form of piracy was against all the ethics of the local tourist traffic and Cam guessed that the consequent friction gave a certain zest to the otherwise tedious legality of the old man's latter-day occupation. He declared that an apocryphal friend of his had commented unfavourably on a sea-trip he had taken yesterday evening. Could it have been, Red Cowdray's boat—was he out last night? Yes, he had been, the booth attendant reported. Busy all the afternoon. Two of the American lads had wanted to go out with him, but from four o'clock when he left for Powey with a party of hikers he had never touched the Trevelley wharf until ten. He'd been about the harbour all right though from about six, with tourists aboard. Sometimes he used the ferry slip as a pick-up point. Always a lone wolf, but the old devil never lacked custom, Cam's informant complained, despite the derelict in which he sailed.

Following the other's glance Cam saw a fishing-smack, suitably named the *Red Ruin,* tied up near the wharf. It was an apt if unpromising name. A man in yellow shirt and green trousers was tinkering with the auxiliary engine. Luigi had apparently given up his idea of meeting Jess at the cinema.

"Cowdray's lucky to have an able-bodied son-in-law to help him," he commented before he left the booth.

The proprietor shrugged. "They say he's sick as a dog every time he goes out but he's pretty handy with engines. Red useter run on sails only but the Yank fitted him in a fine auxiliary motor last summer. Stole it from the U.S. army, I reckon."

"'When the coster's finished jumping on his mother, on his mother,'" thought Cam as he trudged uphill, "'He loves to hear the merry village chimes, village chimes! When Luigi's finished robbing the U.S. army, U.S. army, He loves to give his wife's dad little gifts, little gifts. Take one consideration with another, with another,'" he sighed, "'A policeman's lot is not a happy one, happy one!'"

# CHAPTER X

C AM'S melancholy was only deepened when, reaching the police station to report upon his activities, he observed Honeywether's occupation.

"Ah," he said hastily after one glance, "you won't be wanting me to interrupt. I'll see you later, old man ..."

Honeywether halted him with a pudgy but imperious hand. "Hold on!" he said. "Why so fast? I could use your help." He corrected himself. "There are one or two little details, Cam, which I haven't had time yet to look into myself about which you may have an idea worth hearing."

"When you put it that way ..." Cam sighed, dropping into a chair. "But if there are three things in this world I abominate they are charts and analyses and time-tables."

"I wish the Chief Constable had the same views," Honeywether said gloomily. "He dotes on them. Never mind, my boy. I'll look after all the complications and you just tell me what you know." He took his pencil delicately between thumb and forefinger and held it poised over the foolscap sheet before him. His bottom lip was pouted gravely and with his free hand he gravely stroked his chin.

"Now," he said. "What have we here?"

Cam peered reluctantly across the desk and examined the elaborate pattern of writing upside-down.

"Well, if you don't know," he remarked sardonically, "no one else ever will. Very pretty, however. Very few erasures."

"There are few erasures," Honeywether remarked frankly though with no relaxation of his dignity, "because there are a great many blanks." He swivelled the page round so that Cam could see it.* In the left-hand column were names now familiar

---

* The chart was as formidable as Cam feared, and as it only contained information which has already been given to the reader we can spare him a reproduction.

to Cam. The other columns were headed: 'Opportunity to murder Wilowski'; 'Motive to murder Wilowski'; 'Opportunity to murder Magnuson'; 'Motive to murder Magnuson'; 'S.C.'.

"What does 'S.C.' mean?" Cam asked.

"Suspicious circumstances, of course."

Cam read the list of names with interest and then, picking up another pencil, scribbled in a few comments on the sheet under the Inspector's anxious eye. He added one more name, wrote some questions and then, returning the document to Honeywether, leaned back and closed his eyes.

"That's that," he said. "You can go on from there."

Honeywether wrinkled his brow in awesome thought over the finished product.

"Mrs. Copperman!" he said eventually with shocked surprise.

Cam shrugged. "Yes, Mrs. Copperman. Unlikely perhaps, but you know as well as I, Honeywether, that often the unlikeliest people commit the most effective murders. She had opportunity enough to murder both Wilowski and Magnuson. And I think Allen has shown me that she had a motive also."

Honeywether looked up with startled interest and Cam shook his head sadly. "I'm afraid you won't like it, old man," he said. "There has been dirty work in your precinct." He proceeded to tell the Inspector in the gentlest possible terms the tale of the stolen church plate which Allen had revealed.

"Ha!" said Honeywether with curious mildness when he had finished. He wiped his face with a handkerchief and looked at Cam with an expression into which many emotions were crowded—amusement, distrust, puzzlement and downright anger. His friend for a moment thought that the complications of the case were proving too much for him.

"Have you made all this up yourself?" the Inspector finally burst out. "I don't think much of your sense of humour if so, Cam. Never heard such a rigmarole in all my born days!"

It was Cam's turn for surprised annoyance. "What the dickens do you mean?" he exclaimed. "Just because you don't like the idea of your local church being robbed without you even knowing about it, there's no reason to accuse me of making the whole thing up. That's Allen's story. It's up to you to do what you like about it. Damn it, it's not *my* headache," he added in sudden exasperation.

Honeywether threw his pencil down and leaned back with a gesture of despair. "But why should he tell such a tale?" he exclaimed. "What possible conceivable shadow of a motive can he have?"

"Remorse," Cam suggested. "Fear of discovery. Desire to clear himself as far as possible. Alarm at the sequence of murder to simple robbery. I don't see any difficulty in *that*."

"But it's all a lie," Honeywether explained desperately. "It's none of it true. There wasn't any robbery. The plate is still there. I saw it myself this morning when I visited the church to question the Rector. He was examining it. Part of the chalice is broken and has to go for repairs. I saw it with my own eyes."

"Good God!" said Cam. There was no other relevant comment.

The pair looked at each other in mutual bewilderment.

"What possible motive ..." Cam repeated at last. "Honeywether, the only solution that I can see is the very improbable one that he was telling the truth. Perhaps the stuff *was* stolen, perhaps Copperman had found it and returned it to the church, perhaps he had had no chance yet to let Allen know. After all, Allen was away until lunch and I was there when he returned. When I left Mrs. Copperman was with them and Allen says she was ignorant of the affair. I met Allen again, after an hour and a half during which he had been talking with Briarley some of the time. So it's quite likely that in all that hour and a half he hadn't had a minute with the Rector alone."

"On that basis," asked Honeywether, "where are we to suppose that Mr. Copperman found the church plate?"

"That's a nasty thought," Cam said, and the Inspector nodded gravely. Then he gazed back quickly at Cam.

"But you said that the robbery provided Mrs. Copperman with a motive. I don't see it. How do you get that?"

"Well, this has rather taken the wind out of my sails. But let's just suppose the robbery had taken place as Allen says. Then all three—Allen, the Rector, the Rector's wife—had excellent reasons for murder. Allen—well, perhaps he's short of money. He has one expensive taste at least—hunting—and who knows what other secret vices. If he steals the silver he can not only get ready cash from their sale but he can persuade the Rector not to report the loss. He may even get a little blackmail money on account."

"But he was in Powey when the robbery took place," Honeywether pointed out.

"That's what he says. There's no evidence that the silver was actually stolen that night. Do you know how many keys there are to the safe?"

"One," said Honeywether definitely. "The Rector keeps it on his personal key-ring. I know that because I checked up after a couple of village thefts we had here last year." He shook his head doubtfully. "I still don't see where the murder comes in.

"We know now that Wilowski may have been a fence. Perhaps Allen had stolen the silver. Perhaps he used Wilowski to get rid of it and was now being blackmailed. There's a motive."

"But Allen was in Powey at the time of the murder—and there's no doubt when that was committed."

"Perhaps he had accomplices. Anyway," Cam protested, "I'm only citing motives now, not making a case."

"How about Copperman?"

"There again a shortage of money might be the root of the trouble. Perhaps he had pawned the plate, to cover some purchase. Then Allen discovered the loss so he had to cover up by pretending there was a robbery. No wonder he would accept Allen's suggestion not to tell the police! In his case Wilowski may have been a blackmailing pawnbroker who had to be disposed of in self-defence."

"Copperman or Allen," Honeywether argued. "I fail to see why either should have laid on that body-on-the-altar hocus-pocus. It seems even worse if ordained ministers are responsible."

"Worse than I like to think," Cam said gravely, "because the only reason for the stage-setting would have been to throw suspicion on another man—Yardley, the possible religious maniac."

Honeywether shivered. "Well, do you accuse Mrs. Copperman of such calculations? What motive do you give her?"

"Protection of her husband," Cam replied. "Perhaps she knew he had stolen the chinch plate or that Wilowski was blackmailing him. Anyway, I think it is quite in character for her to go to extreme lengths in his defence. Perhaps she had tried to regain the silver from Wilowski. As for 'body-on-the-altar hocuspocus'—I can only think that if Mrs. Copperman did commit murder she would regard it more as a sacrifice than a sin."

"I deny that," the other said stoutly. "Perfectly normal, though she does have a rough time of it, I grant you. Anyway, Cam, the trouble with you is over-enthusiasm. By finding motives for all you've weakened the effectiveness of your case against any single one."

"I repeat," the other said wearily, "that I'm not trying to make a case—only to show who might have had reason for murder, only to let my imagination play round a little."

"Imagination!" Honeywether said contemptuously. "Rubbish. What we want are *facts,* man. The people I look for in a case like this are the criminal types. Magnuson now; there was a man I didn't trust at all. Shifty-eyed, comes from a poor part of London. No good."

Cam was smiling slightly to himself, but he nodded agreeably. "But he's dead, unfortunately. What about Potts? He has the additional S.C. of being friendly with a foreigner and a corpse. A disarming chap, but what would he be doing at Vespers? I wouldn't have thought it at all his type of interest. And he told me that the Rectory garden was delightful. Now, he'd have to go in to see that—it's not visible from the road. Why should he be snooping around? He has a good alibi for the time of the murder—chatting by the ferry, but on the other hand he is the only person who really knew the victim."

Honeywether nodded gloomily. "But why the pruning-knife? The sacrifice? The general hocus-pocus? And where does Magnuson come in?"

"Yes," agreed Cam. "The sacrifice would be very odd if Potts were responsible. That wouldn't fit in at all. I'm not suggesting that he'd be top man in this. That's unlikely. He's obviously in a supporting rôle. The whole affair is too big for his boots if he's the sort of man I think he is." He paused a moment and then he added: "What was Magnuson's line of business? Have you looked into that yet?"

Honeywether sniffed contemptuously. "London's supposed to be doing that for me. Just had a phone call that they'd 'located' his lodgings (I *gave* them the address!) but that his landlady didn't know anything more than that he was a shop-assistant somewhere near Kingsway. Now they've got to find the shop."

"Wilowski; Potts; Magnuson," murmured Cam. "All working somewhere near Kingsway. You might suggest that they concentrate on Covent Garden, Honeywether."

The Inspector's eyes brightened and he scribbled a note on his chart. "Not a bad idea," he muttered.

"It's a far cry," Cam mused, "from a Covent Garden shop to the church of Trevelley. That's what I can't make out. There seems no sense in a case with Wilowski, Potts and Magnuson on one side and on the other the Rector, Mrs. Copperman and Allen—and Briarley. He frequents the church too. ...What did Briarley have to say?" he asked after a pause. "Did you get hold of him eventually?"

Honeywether snorted triumphantly. "That I did, but not because of his helpfulness. Rundle caught him just as he was slipping away to Poltherow. I had him here just half an hour ago. He sticks to his story that he was in the church only twenty minutes and all alone. He saw no one except the Verger. Certainly he had plenty of time to do the job, but how do you get round the fact that when Yardley went in after Briarley there was no sign of a corpse?"

"I can't," confessed Cam. "Nor see any motive, either. Betsey Rowan has a new tale," he added, and told, with a wry expression, the story of her meeting with Briarley and subsequent walk to Powey. "Potts confirms that she crossed over," he added.

Honeywether sighed. "Briarley seems a gruff sort of chap. She's a pretty girl, too. I can't make out who's chasing who of that pair—who's the fox and who's the hare. Maybe they're both foxes, eh?"

Cam nodded thoughtfully. "Surely they would take more care to concoct their stories if they were really working together. Did you know that Betsey Rowan knew Jessica Luigi, incidentally? Well enough to be quarrelling with her in the High Street. That brings her almost into the local crime circle."

Honeywether rubbed his chin hard. "Y'know there must be a heap of American girls who would have good cause to quarrel with our Jess. She raised Cain with the G.I.s here. But I can't imagine a girl coming all this way to speak her mind."

"There's an American angle on this case, don't forget. Wilowski was from America. Perhaps he didn't come over alone."

"It would be a dirty thing," Honeywether protested, "to use a bunch of children as red-herrings for a job like this. Not," he added gloomily, "that the whole case isn't dirty enough. Well, I'll ask the Yard to check on Miss Rowan's antecedents too."

"And that's the lot," Cam said. "Except Luigi. What about him? Ever had any trouble here at all?"

"During the war, once or twice. Took a big part in a couple of pub brawls we had here and I suspected him of being one of those to use a knife, though that couldn't be proved. He took part in those Black Masses too. I think our Jess used him to lure in some of the more gullible Yanks. That was before they were married, but not before they were walking out together."

"Did you ever attend one of those services yourself?" Cam asked curiously.

"In disguise," Honeywether said complacently and the other wondered with considerable interest how one disguised a figure like his. "Rundle and I went and Allen, who was visiting the Rectory at the time to talk about his new curacy, came along too. I wanted to have a churchman there and of course the Rector wouldn't come. We got there rather late so we missed the sacrifice—they used a cock, I believe—and just arrived for the dance. It was hot! I've seen some pretty nasty things in my life, but this beat all. Quite nice girls from the village dancing round in nothing but their slippers. There had obviously been a rich supply of liquor to get the thing going—if not worse. We stayed about fifteen minutes while I tried to pin down the ringleaders—but they must have had warning and escaped. When my men came on signal there was no one to arrest except a few shamefaced village girls and a score of bewildered servicemen. It wasn't one of my best efforts." the Inspector confessed, "except that we didn't have any more trouble with witchcraft after that!"

"Who was your informant?" Cam enquired.

Honeywether looked towards the door before he replied. "I don't talk about that. As the ring-leaders are still free it might cause trouble, but Will Yardley was the man. God knows how he found out the time of the ceremony, but he worked closely with us. To him, I suppose, it was something of a crusade. He was mad with rage that we didn't get the ringleaders—and a bit uneasy too, if truth were told."

"Did he go with you?"

"No. He would have been too conspicuous."

"I should have thought," mused Cam, "that Yardley would have been the very last person to hear about such a ceremony, in view of his God-fearing reputation."

Honeywether shrugged. "News gets around through odd channels in a village like this."

"What a rich variety of crime you have here," Cam commented admiringly. "Nothing too good for you—Black Mass, murder, church plate robbery. ..."

"Church plate robbery!" Honeywether sniffed. "But you're right, Cam. You're right. I don't know what's coming over this place. I swear I don't. A few years ago we had as quiet a little village as you could hope to see. And now what? Black Mass, murder in church, clergymen robbing the parish, young men being pushed over cliffs, cathedral robberies! It beats me, it beats me!"

"It's pretty hard," Cam sympathised, "but at least you've had it all, Honeywether. After this, anything else that happens here will seem like a picnic. You can relax—you have reached Nirvana."

But Cam was wrong and he was proved wrong on the moment. There was a sound from without of argument and protest. Then the door was flung open and, with Constable Rundle still protesting, Miss Cornthwaite battered her way in. She was slightly flushed and very dishevelled. Her stockings were badly ripped and her legs cut.

"I have a complaint," said Miss Cornthwaite, fixing a stern and desperate look on Honeywether. He began to protest that he was busy—Rundle would deal with it—but she stopped him with a warning hand. "I don't know," she said, "what Trevelley is coming to, upon my soul I don't. But I do know that unless I get some positive assurance, Inspector, that it will not take place again I shall have to cancel my reservation for next summer."

Only Cam, perhaps, appreciated the dramatic implications and serious nature of this statement. He had talked with Miss Cornthwaite about her plans for retirement here.

"What," he asked gently, "has happened?"

Miss Cornthwaite swallowed nervously.

"Someone," she said, "someone has just tried to murder me. And I won't have it. Indeed I won't have it! It's quite intolerable!" Whereupon she sat down very suddenly in the nearest chair and began to cry.

# CHAPTER XI

THE sigh of a soul tried beyond endurance came from Honeywether's direction. Distressed as he was by Miss Cornthwaite's tears, Cam could hardly suppress a grin at his colleague's accumulating trials. The silence into which fell explosively Miss Cornthwaite's unpractised sobs became increasingly oppressive. Cam got up and put a gentle hand upon her shoulder.

"That's all right, now," he said kindly. "You're safe now, whatever has happened. But cry a little more and you'll feel better."

The head-mistress blew her nose firmly, adjusted a hatpin which had held her felt hat in position throughout and looked at Cam with cold rebuke. "I've no intention whatsoever of crying," she said. "Cry indeed! What rubbish!" With a deep breath she recovered her poise and she turned again to Honeywether with grim self-possession. "Well?" she enquired. "What *do* you intend to do about it, Inspector? Is everyone in tire village to be murdered without the police raising a finger? Is assault and battery to become the official Trevelley pastime?"

"Madam," replied Honeywether aggressively, "if you would have the goodness to tell me what has happened I may be able to help. You come in here and say that someone's been trying to murder you! Well, I can't just take your word for it, you know. You'll have to give me some evidence." The Inspector's tone was that of someone who is sick and tired of people rushing to him every other minute with murder to report.

"Is it likely," Miss Cornthwaite asked with acerbity, "that I should tell such a silly story unless it were true? You aren't suggesting that I am a notoriety seeker, I hope—an exhibitionist?" She paused for a moment to glare at Honeywether, who merely repeated:

"Well, ma'am? Your story; your story."

"Half an hour ago," Miss Cornthwaite recited in a businesslike way, "I was walking along the cliffs towards Poltherow. I was alone. There was no one in sight. I had met no one since leaving the village except Mrs. Copperman, who was returning to the village from the American children's camp. Just before you reach the camp there is a rock in the cliff-top which juts seaward some three feet. Although it looks precarious it is very comfortable and perfectly safe. Quite often I watch the sunset from there and indeed at all times of day you will find someone or other—usually visitors, of course—sitting upon it admiring the view. You call it Peter's Perch locally, I believe. When I reached this spot I sat down. It was very quiet. I saw no one either upon the cliffs or down below me on the sand at the foot of the cliffs, although, in admiring the view, I looked all round me." Miss Cornthwaite took a deep breath and went on rather rapidly. "I had been sitting there about ten minutes. My legs were hanging over the side of the rock. Suddenly I felt a rope tighten round my ankles. At first I could not believe my senses and I was almost over the edge before I began to put up a struggle. I managed to dig my fingers in somehow—I couldn't tell you how. After what seemed like hours I felt the rope give and bit by bit I dragged myself back. When I was firmly anchored I rubbed the rope back and forth on the rock. Somebody swore. Then the rope broke. I ran back as fast as I could to the village. I was terrified," she ended simply.

Honeywether had taken a new pad of paper out of his drawer and had been making notes. "You felt this rope, you say. What sort of rope was it? Thick or thin? What happened to the bit round your ankle?"

"Thick," said Miss Cornthwaite. "Very hard. The bit round my ankle must have fallen off while I ran."

Honeywether looked at her severely on this confession of carelessness with important evidence. "You heard someone, did you? Man or woman?"

"Man. But he only swore rather incoherently. His hands were probably cut."

"Who knew you were going for this walk?"

"Anyone who was sufficiently interested to watch my movements, I suppose. I took the same walk every evening after tea."

"Yes, yes," Honeywether said impatiently. "But is there any particular person who you suspect might be especially interested in your walk and who could have known about it?"

"I repeat, anyone could have known about it. I suspect no one. What you really want to know," Miss Cornthwaite said patiently, "is whether I know of anyone who might have wished to murder me. Yes, of course I do. Plenty of them. Not all my girls are properly appreciative of the opportunities for reform in our school. But I certainly don't know of any such girls round here and on the whole my enemies are women—not men."

"But there might be some local boy-friend of one of your old girls who bore you a grudge?"

Miss Cornthwaite shrugged. "It's possible. I certainly don't know all my student's friends. Heaven forbid! But it all seems rather far-fetched, Inspector. How could the creature have known I would actually sit down there? I don't always, by any means. I can think of no one who hates me sufficiently to wait like a snake under that rock all the afternoon—all day—on the off chance that I might sit down. I repeat I did not see anyone during my walk and it would have been impossible for anyone to get there without my seeing them—so he must have been waiting a long time."

"Apart from any personal enemies, can you think of anything you may have seen or done during this holiday," asked Cam, "which might have made you the victim of such an attack?"

"Not a thing," said Miss Cornthwaite. "And if you think I have the solution to the church murder in my pocket you're unlucky, Mr. Cam. I'm as much in the dark as anyone—even the police," she added, with a nasty look at Honeywether. "It's my opinion," she went on, "that you shouldn't waste your time looking for a rational explanation of this affair. Obviously the creature is a lunatic—a homicidal maniac. I don't believe that he ever saw my face—ever needed to see me. I think he was curled up under Peter's Perch waiting for anyone who chanced to come along and when I was so careless as to dangle my legs I became the victim. It would have made no difference whether it were me or the butcher's boy or an American child or Mrs. Copperman. I can only thank God it was me and that He gave me sufficient strength to overcome the devil."

"Hear, hear," exclaimed Cam feelingly. "But if your idea is right I'm surprised that you got away at all. These madmen have fantastic strength—and the pain to his hands would not discourage a lunatic."

"He must have been very uncomfortable and insecure," reasoned Miss Cornthwaite. "I didn't stop to look, naturally, but any foothold beneath Peter's Perch must be quite precarious. When I was able to put all my weight on the rope no doubt he was thrown off balance."

"There's a cave there," Honeywether contributed unexpectedly. "A well-known ex-smuggler's den, fairly high up the cliff. A tall man standing on the entrance might be able to throw a lasso up to Peter's Perch if he were handy with such things. But you're right that he wouldn't be very secure—a false step and he would be over the edge."

"And could someone in the cave see Miss Cornthwaite approaching?" asked Cam.

"Impossible. And it's a difficult climb which takes about ten minutes so it isn't likely that anyone could have raced ahead of her to get into position, even if they'd guessed she was going to sit there."

"Can you tell us more about your conversation with Mrs. Copperman?" Cam asked after a pause, turning back to Miss Cornthwaite.

She looked at him narrowly but answered without hesitation. "We only exchanged a few words. She said what a lovely evening—that she had given herself a treat by going out to see the American camp. I remarked that she deserved an airing after yesterday's tragedy. She merely remarked that she thought the police would probably clear all that up very soon. Poor woman! Then she added very simply and nicely that she had been praying for the murderer. I was quite touched. I said that I should do the same and she seemed pleased. Then we parted."

"Did you mention Peter's Perch?" Cam asked.

"No, of course not. I never thought of it until I was actually there."

"Come, come," said Honeywether impatiently, getting to his feet. "This isn't getting us anywhere. If there's anything in your idea, Miss Cornthwaite, and I'm not saying there is, we ought to be getting out to the scene as soon as possible. The fellow may still be there. In any case I want to explore the ground. We must find that rope. Cam, you'll have to come too as I may need help and Rundle will have to stay on duty here. James is up at the church. Two constables on a case like this!" he added bitterly, herding Miss Cornthwaite and Cam through the door before him. "I'd like to have the Chief Constable take a week of duty here. It would teach him to appreciate how much work I put into the job."

"Just suggest that he takes a week's holiday here," Cam advised, but the other was not listening in the bustle of telling Constable Rundle his change in plans.

The three of them climbed into the tiny police car and then Honeywether paused. A shadow of apprehension crossed his face and Cam read his thoughts.

"Yes," he agreed. "If it's a homicidal maniac two middle-aged men and one lady are going to be hard-pressed to deal with him."

"I shall certainly take no part in it myself," Miss Cornthwaite announced. "I never was a feminist and I have always claimed every privilege of womanhood."

"And I'm on holiday," Cam declared, "so my family wouldn't get any pension if I were hurt. Mrs. Cam would be very cross if I got killed off duty."

Honeywether looked at them sourly. "It's every citizen's duty ..." he began, but stopped abruptly as he saw someone crossing the street in front of the car. "Allen!" he shouted. "Hoy!" He drew his head in to say confidingly to Cam: "If it's a religious maniac it may be useful to have a representative of the Church along. He's an active young man too."

The curate turned back with cheerful unconcern. Honeywether opened the door and beckoned him in imperiously.

"Someone has just tried to murder Miss Cornthwaite at Peter's Perch," he exclaimed hastily. "I am going to arrest the fellow if he's still there. You'd better come along."

Allen stood one dazed moment surveying the posse. But at Honeywether's repeated urgent injunction he climbed in obediently. From then until they reached the scene he made no comment except to murmur to Miss Cornthwaite that he was frightfully sorry. She nodded impatiently and he subsided into further bewildered silence.

Honeywether drove them at a rapid pace down the High Street and then with more caution out along the hill-path. In the small confines of the car there was little room to bounce, but every hillock over which they passed jarred the occupants to the roots of their teeth. The Inspector slowed down to four miles an hour—more out of care for his car than his guests—but the discomfort was still extreme and after a particularly vicious jab from the driver's elbow Cam demanded his freedom. The car still moving he opened his door and jumped out. Walking very quickly he kept in front of the others and breathing the good sea air reminded himself that cliffs were made for holiday hikes and artists' brushes, not for the skirmishes of cops and robbers. He walked close to the cliff edge and looked all around him. Far inland he could see some village boys playing cricket in a field. They were the only human figures on the horizon as long as he kept his eyes averted from the incongruous police car bumping along behind. He looked down to the cove. There was no one on the sands, but standing off shore was a small fisherman's smack turning out to sea. The sailor was hidden by the single sail now being hoisted, but the colour of the hull was unmistakable. It was the *Red Ruin*—Cowdray's boat. Straining his eyes to see who was handling her, Cam gazed after the boat. It was remarkable how swiftly the little vessel slipped across the cove water and around the peninsula towards Trevelley. Ramshackle it might be, but obviously built for speed. Cam shouted once, trying to arrest the attention of the pilot, but there was no reply or sign of recognition and in a few moments the boat had disappeared.

Cam reached the jutting rock, Peter's Perch, as Honeywether drove up, and he was already on his stomach peering over the edge as the others got out of the car. Miss Cornthwaite did not approach the edge. She pointed with one thin hand.

"You can see where I snatched at the rocks," she said. "The flowers are all torn away. And here," she said with satisfaction, "is the rope." It was, in fact, not much more than strong string, but Honeywether snatched it with a gleam of pleasure. He liked tangible clues.

"There's some blood on the rock," he remarked.

"From my knees," Miss Cornthwaite said. "They are badly scratched." With a gesture of sudden shyness and distaste at the whole melodramatic affair, she twitched her skirt further down. Her grey stockings were ripped and stained with blood. Allen was looking at them in bewildered interest.

"Was someone pushing you?" he asked. "Who was it? How did you get away?"

"Some man tried to pull me from below," she explained. "I didn't see his face."

"You know who it was?"

"Not yet!" she exclaimed tartly. "And if we wait until the Inspector gathers courage to go down and inspect I never shall."

Honeywether, however, did not hear her as he was lying beside Cam.

"See that ridge?" Honeywether pointed to a spot six feet down. "Doesn't look like anything from here—or from below—but it's the mouth of a cave."

"I remember it," Cam recalled. "Small, but very dry and a nice cool place on hot days. Now what?" he asked. "For all you know a homicidal maniac is lurking down there. Do we lower you by a rope to investigate? You'll go first, I suppose. Obviously we can't all go together."

Honeywether looked at his friend sourly. "Hoy!" he shouted tentatively down to the cave. There was no response.

Cam laughed. "Put a little more gusto into it," he suggested.

"This may be your great opportunity to get a medal. I can see the fulsome obituaries already."

"All right, all right!" the other grumbled. "I'm going over. Don't you fret." He got up with grim resolution.

Cam relented. "Don't worry too much," he said kindly. "I doubt if you'll find anyone."

"Why not? How d'ye know that?"

"Look," Cam pointed. "That's the end of a rope dangling against the rock." Honeywether looked down along the line of his friend's finger and saw now against the grey rock a grey rope, practically indistinguishable in the evening light. "I saw Red Cowdray's boat slipping out of the harbour just as we arrived," Cam added. "An odd place to bring trippers."

"Get the rope out of the car," Honeywether called to Allen, now in an agony of eagerness to get down to the cave. He ran to do it himself. Allen, who had been standing shyly in the background, helped him pull open the boot and extract the coil of heavy rope which lay there.

"Let me go down!" he exclaimed. "With all respect, Honeywether, I think I could handle a maniac better than you."

Honeywether refused the offer with a new zeal.

"It's my job," he said. "Cam, if anything happens to me I leave you in charge."

They tied the rope round Cam's waist. Allen took a coil of the slack and the end was thrown over the edge of the cliff.

"Here goes!" Honeywether proclaimed and twisting a length round his arm he went over the edge with middle-aged bravado. Cam gasped at the sudden pressure round his middle, but thanks to Allen's efforts he found the strain not too difficult to bear. He could see nothing of the descent, but he heard all Honeywether's puffs and exclamations as he lowered himself to the cave mouth, hitting his elbows on obtrusive rocks, and then the grunt of satisfaction as the Inspector reached his goal. Miss Cornthwaite was standing a little farther along, peering cautiously over the edge now and reporting on progress. "He's there," she announced. "He's standing on the ledge looking in. Do you see anything?" she called down. There was a muffled cry from below. "He's going in," she reported. "He can't see anything yet."

There was a sudden release of pressure round Cam's middle. He joined Miss Cornthwaite at the edge. They strained their ears, but heard nothing except the waves lapping on the sands below. Cam had a sudden reminiscent vision of himself as a boy reading *Westward Ho!* in that long-forgotten cave, lifting his head occasionally to hear the same rustle of water over pebbles and the shriek of a seagull.

The seagulls reminded him of Magnuson's death and Betsey Rowan's confusion of his screams with those of the gulls. It was near here that the Londoner fell. He thought with sudden nostalgia of the days when murder had all been in his imagination and when the dead had been straightforward villains, not scruffy little clerks from London shops.

They had not long to wait. Honeywether's red face, bright with mingled perspiration, triumph and relief, appeared below and he shouted imperiously that they should pull him up.

"Have you got anything?" Allen cried. "Can I help?"

"Pull me up," Honeywether repeated. "I've done all I need down here."

Two minutes later he was on the cliff edge with the rope (heavier than the one used to trap Miss Cornthwaite) over his arm but still uncommunicative. "Come on," he said brusquely. "Back into the car. I've got work in the village."

"This is all very impressive," Miss Cornthwaite said scornfully as they followed obediently, "but I do not see why it was necessary for all of us to traipse out here in order to watch the Inspector being clever."

"Come on, Honeywether. Tell us what you found," Cam pressed.

The Inspector was easily persuaded and told them curtly as they drove back along the bumpy route.

"There was no one in the cave," he said unnecessarily, "but the debris on the floor was quite freshly kicked around. Apart from the rest of the rope, which is a kind that every fisherman in Trevelley uses, I found two objects tucked away in corners of the cave—one near the entrance and another near the back. Number one I found just by the cave mouth ..." He produced from his waistcoat pocket a ring—its thin silver band roughly broken at the point where it was welded to the stone setting. The single stone was a large and vivid but very improbable emerald.

"I've seen that before," Allen announced excitedly. "Luigi wears it. I've often thought it was rather gaudy."

Miss Cornthwaite shuddered suddenly. "Who is Luigi?" she asked. "I don't know him. I'm sure I don't. He couldn't be ..."

"Number two ..." Honeywether announced, and he produced from another pocket a tiny silver object. Cam took it from him.

"*Very* nice!" he murmured. It was the head of a bear, beautifully wrought, even to the details of the bared fangs and shaggy eyebrows, yet not more than an inch in height and half an inch in breadth. The base was jagged as though torn from the rest of the body. "Now why," Cam asked of the world at large, "should anyone tear the head off a silver bear? That's a very curious thing."

Allen snatched the head from him with a cry of surprise.

"Good Lord!" he exclaimed in bewilderment. He looked at Honeywether's back. "Do you recognise this?" he asked.

"I do," said the other grimly, holding a hand over his shoulder for the toy. "You and me will be having a little talk about that, Mr. Allen. And the Rector, too, when I have the time."

"Well, what is it?" asked Cam tartly. He disliked other people's mysterious exchanges.

"It's the crest from the cover of the church ewer," Miss Cornthwaite explained unexpectedly. "What on earth is it doing here?" she asked suspiciously, but none of the men answered her.

So it *was* stolen, Cam was thinking. I wonder if Allen knows yet that the rest of the plate has been found again. The curate's next question answered him.

"Was this all?" he asked eagerly. "Did you really search the place? Perhaps there was—something buried."

"The cave has a solid rock floor," Honeywether said stiffly. "I know my job, Mr. Allen, which is more, I may say, than you seem to do."

The curate subsided into unhappy silence again, but Miss Cornthwaite, who had been looking from one to another during this exchange, took up the enquiry.

"This makes no sense at all to me," she exclaimed angrily, "and before we go any further, Mr. Honeywether, I should like to know where you are taking me now. It's perfectly absurd being rushed all over the countryside, hither-thither, without any idea of what it's all about. I for one won't stand for it and unless you tell me in a civil way what we are doing I shall get out."

"All right," said Honeywether. They had reached the beginning of the village street and stopping abruptly he got out to let Miss Cornthwaite pass. "Thank you very much for your help," he said politely. "I hope that in an hour or two we may have your assailant under lock and key."

Miss Cornthwaite got out with stiff disapproval.

"Judging by what I have seen of your methods so far," she exclaimed, "nothing could be more unlikely," and marched off towards the 'Three Fishers'. Her tiff with Honeywether had at least had the advantage of restoring her composure. Allen made no move to follow her, but the Inspector peered in again through the door and said with an air of finality: "And thank you for your help too, Mr. Allen. I'd be grateful if you and Mr. Copperman would call at the police station in, let's say, half an hour to discuss this church plate matter."

Unwillingly, the curate climbed out. "I'd like to explain about that ..." he began.

"Not now, if you please." Honeywether stopped him. "One thing at a time. I'll see you later, if you'll oblige." He returned to the car and without more ado drove on.

"That was telling them!" said Cam appreciatively. "Are you sure you wouldn't like me to leave too?"

"You can stay," the Inspector said generously. "But I don't like these witnesses who think that they have a right to criticise the running of my case simply because they contribute a few odd clues." This seemed to Cam an understatement of Miss Cornthwaite's rôle, but there was an air of complacent purposefulness about the way Honeywether re-started the car that indicated he would brook no argument. He turned confidently towards the harbour.

"So Luigi's the man," Cam said thoughtfully. "That makes it all quite simple, doesn't it? Funny we should have had such trouble. Now you thrink of it he's an obvious type."

Honeywether ground his gears angrily.

"I haven't had so much trouble," he exclaimed. "Matter of fact, I've had my eye on Luigi all the time. But there was no point in startling the covey before I was ready to fire."

Cam sighed. "I wish I had such foresight. Why, even when Luigi came into Cowdray's cottage while I was there with his knuckles dripping blood I never guessed he'd been trying to murder Miss Cornthwaite! He just seemed to me like any young man in a bad temper at missing his girl at the cinema and then hurting himself in a fall. He looked savage, certainly, but then so would I."

Honeywether expanded. "The most difficult thing," he said, "in our profession is to put one and one together and make two. Years of experience," he continued, waving a cavalier hand. "Look out, blast you! ... Did I hit him? Never mind. Can't stop now. ... Important business. ..." They swept on, leaving a grey-faced Mr. Potts backed against a house wall, looking after them with alarm. Cam turned and gave him a cheerful wave of encouragement.

"Wonder where he's off to now," he remarked idly.

"Perhaps we should have stopped to gossip," Honeywether said with heavy irony. "You're a regular old woman, Cam—poking your nose into everyone's business."

"Isn't that what we're paid to do?" Cam asked mildly. But there was no time for an answer because they had arrived at Red Cowdray's alley. Honeywether leaped out of the car and strode up the narrow passage, his expression becoming more consciously rugged with every step. These Yankee gangsters, he was thinking to himself, can't treat them with kid gloves—they're used to third degree and suchlike—must show him I'm as tough as he is—but not so tough that they ask awkward questions at the trial. The last thought was so disturbing that he was looking positively ferocious by the time he knocked with all the pomp and circumstance of the Law upon Cowdray's door. The door, obedient to such heavy-handed treatment, swung inwards and the Inspector was face to face with Cowdray himself, who looked up with aged timidity from the model ship to which he was now attaching the sails.

"Hey, Hey!" he quavered. "Here's a fine thing! Bustin' into my house like 'twar the pub! Beatin' down my door. ... Breakin' the lock. ... Actin' like a blamed Nazzy! I'll have th' law on ye, Inspector! I've got my rights, I have, though I be so pore an' old. ..."

"Stow it!" said Honeywether who was peering round the room anxiously. "Have you seen your son-in-law?"

"Course I 'ave! D'ya think I'd let me darter marry a man I hadna seen? Now yore insultin' me, Inspector. ..."

"Brutal and licentious. ..." contributed Cam from the door. "Breakin' an' enterin'," the old man added with relish.

"Shut up!" Honeywether exploded. "I'm looking for Luigi, Cowdray. And you needn't pretend that you don't know why. Either you tell me where he is or I'll cart you off to gaol on suspicion and let you improve your memory there."

"Suspicion o' what?" asked the old man mildly.

"Attempted murder—that's what."

Cowdray's malicious amusement stiffened into sudden attention.

"Whose?" he asked earnestly.

"A lady at the hotel. Miss Cornthwaite. And as Luigi was in the vicinity I intend to have a talk with him, Cowdray, whether you like it or not."

Cowdray was looking more puzzled than shocked.

"Miss Cornthwaite?" he repeated. "Now why? ... Where was it?" he asked. "How d'ya know Vic was there?"

"Peter's Perch. Someone tried to pull her over the edge ... someone standing in the mouth of the cave there. And Luigi left his ring there so as to cause us no trouble."

With a startling passionate rage, as if the red thatch of his hair had suddenly set his nature afire, Red Cowdray tore at the thread which he had been meticulously threading through slender masts of his model ship and in a moment's fury wrenched down the whole superstructure. Cam gasped with horror at the wanton damage. Even Honeywether was taken aback. Cowdray hurled the fragile sticks to the floor and trampled on them with aged hysteria while a stream of almost meaningless blasphemy spattered through his trembling lips.

For a minute or two Honeywether was silent, hoping that out of this delirium would come some words of enlightenment. Impatient at last, however, he thumped angrily with his fist upon the table. Outside the neighbours were already gathering and he did not wish the whole village to be alive with the news before he had laid his hands on Luigi.

"That's enough; that's enough," he exclaimed. "Save that for later. What I want now is to find Luigi. Then we can talk about him. But a man isn't guilty," he added painstakingly, "until he's proved guilty by law."

Cowdray stopped as suddenly as he had begun. For a moment he looked at the Inspector thoughtfully and then dropped to his chair with decrepit exhaustion.

"A disgrace to the family!" he sighed. "What a turrible, turrible thing to happen to be sure. A murderin' villain—that's what he be—a murderin' villain."

"What did you think he was?" asked Cam suddenly.

The old man shook his head sadly. "A thief," he said. "Just a thief. I niver thought as how he'd do no one no harm. Et's a turrible shock, et be, mister. At my age 'tes pretty hard to bear."

"Who persuaded him to return the church plate?" Cam asked. "Or who stole it back from him?" Honeywether looked at him with puzzled annoyance, but Cowdray was unmoved.

"So you know about that? 'Twarn't nothin' to do wi' me, mister, that I'll swear. I didn't know ought about et till the Rector's leddy come down an' threatened to report him unless he give it back. She wor real upset, she wor. But he give in, o' course—he would—and give et back here afore me very eyes.

So why he should want to be murderin' folk is more than I can tell. Seems plain foolish-like, don't it?"

Cam agreed that it did, but Honeywether broke in again.

"That's all very well," he said angrily. "And I'll attend to it later. I'm sick of all this playing around behind my back, by God! But in the meantime—where is Luigi for the last time of asking? Have you seen him in the last hour, Cowdray? And if not, where might he be?"

"I haven't seen him," said the old man simply. "And as for where he moight be, I should think he moight be well on his way back to Americcy if he's any sense."

He spoke now as if there were no need for further palaver and as if he wished them to be gone with no more delay. Turning suddenly, Cam looked at the chattering group of villagers in the alley. Yes, Jessica was there too, just arrived apparently. When she saw him looking at her she came forward with a shrug. Honeywether turned too and saw her with sudden suspicion. "Hi, you!" he said brusquely. "Where's your husband?"

"Why d'ya want him?" she began, but this time the Inspector broke her off abruptly.

"None of that!" he exclaimed. "I've wasted enough time as it is. Either you tell me where he is or have done."

She looked past him at her father and a faint mischievous smile coloured her expression. But she said demurely enough:

"Down at t'wharf, I think. He war there five minutes ago." Honeywether charged bull-like out of the cottage and up the alley towards the wharf. Cam was on his heels and most of the village behind him. Red Cowdray, forgetting his decrepitude, took a short cut through his back door and was there with Jessica before any of them arrived. It looked as if the Inspectors were too late. Standing out from the wharf, headed for the open sea, was Cowdray's little boat, its engines purring gently under the soothing hand of the tall young American. As the Inspectors reached the water's edge he looked up from his work and gave them an ironic salute. Honeywether spat out an order to a nearby fisherman and the pair sprang down into the nearest dinghy. Cam followed in boyish delight—there was nothing he liked more than a chase—and felt someone stepping on his heels. There was Briarley grinning with excitement and clambering down too.

"Let me help!" he exclaimed. "This is grand fun! Who are we chasing?"

The chances of the row-boat catching up with the motor-boat seemed slim indeed. They might, however, get aboard an anchored launch and carry on the chase in that. Cam felt, however, that they were chasing more on principle than in hope.

A stroke of luck suddenly made the odds more even. The purring of Luigi's engine turned to a hoarse growl and thence to a cough, with which it stopped completely. The pilot threw off the cover of the engine and desperately threw himself to some adjustment, while the row-boat, propelled by Honeywether and the fisherman, ploughed through the water to the cheers of an ever-increasing audience. Cam, who was facing backwards, could see Cowdray and his daughter dancing with anxiety, but whether in fear or hope of the suspect's capture he could not tell.

They were within ten yards of the motor-boat when its engine again began to splutter. Honeywether, perspiring heavily, called to his fellow-oarsman to put more into it. Cam turned in his seat to be ready to grasp the other's gunwale if ever he had the chance. Briarley too was feverish with impatience and unexpectedly he discarded his shoes and plunged over the side of the boat to swim the rest of the distance. After a moment's unsteadiness at the sudden change of weight the oarsmen gathered speed again, but Briarley was already ahead and with a few powerful strokes he had reached the side of the motor-boat as the engine again burst into full-throated power. He clung on valiantly, trying to climb aboard as the motor-boat gathered speed towards the sea, leaving the row-boat struggling vainly behind. But Luigi, abandoning the purring engine, now seized an oar and battered at the young man's fingers until he was forced to let go and sink back into the wash of the boat. Three minutes later the row-boat picked him up and he fell over the side half muttering with agony at the pain of the salt water on his cuts, half laughing at the excitement of the affair.

Once he was aboard the fisherman lay back on his oars and looked after Luigi's wake with admiration in his eyes.

"When you come down to it," he said dreamily, "there's nothin' so useful as a motor-boat—nothin' to beat 'em."

"Aye," said Honeywether grimly. "Nothing except another and a better one. Let him go now. But back to shore, man—and as fast as we came. I think the Coast Guard will have engines as good as that."

Cam took the other Inspector's place at the oars on the return trip and as he pulled with creaking muscles Briarley, still breathless, gave him a friendly wink.

"I don't know what it's all about," he said blithely. "But at least I'm on the side of the law."

"It's always best," said Cam. "I'm coining to that conclusion myself."

# CHAPTER XII

C AM woke up on Tuesday morning with a disturbed feeling that life was not as free of care as it should be on a fine June holiday. He had retired to bed early the previous evening, physically exhausted by all the activity of the day, and in a dreamless sleep the details of his discomfort had become obscured. But now they crept back into his consciousness again one by one. A fellow hotel guest had been murdered—another had almost been—a body had been found in the church—a suspect had escaped—the church silver had been passed from hand to hand in an unbecoming manner. ... He drew the sheets closer round him and resolved not to get up until lunch. Last night he had refused Honeywether's invitation either to join in interrogation of the Rectory folk or to join the Coast Guard in their chase of Luigi. Today he would hold to his resolution of not allowing murder to encroach upon his personal peace of mind. ...

His protective covering was snatched ruthlessly from his hands and three small faces, pink with expectation, peered down at him.

"Are you awake?" they asked anxiously, climbing onto him to investigate. "We haven't woken you, have we?" jabbing sharp knees into his ribs. "It's jolly late, you know, so you can't really be asleep, and you wouldn't want to miss what's happened. There's a naval sloop down in the harbour—and all sorts of big cars have been arriving at the police station—Miss Cornthwaite has said that none of us should go out on the cliffs alone. Is that because we might get killed too? So *do* get up, Daddy, and show us where she almost was murdered. And couldn't you get Mr. Honeywether to take us on the sloop? It's been hunting all night, they say, and it will be going out again soon and we'd like to go too. And we'd like ..."

"Silence!" shouted Cam, rising suddenly from his shelter and casting children in all directions. "Can't you see I'm resting? And I have no intention of showing you gruesome sights when you ought to be down by the seashore building sand-castles. This is no way to spend a holiday. Bothering your heads about death and murder when you ought to be out in the fresh air and sunshine."

"We can do both at the same time," reasoned one, but Cam made a threatening gesture.

"I don't want any lawyers in my family," he exclaimed. "So be off with you and don't give your poor father as much trouble as a Royal Commission."

There was a disconsolate shuffle and then peace again for a quarter of an hour. Cam shielded his eyes from a stray sunbeam and was falling again into the trance between waking and sleeping when another hand pulled back the sheet and a familiar voice said critically: "You must be the laziest man in all creation. For goodness' sake get up and come for a walk. Or are you going to spend the rest of your holiday in bed?"

"Yes, I am," he said grumpily. "Every time I move someone is murdered so it's best for everyone that I just stay here. You might ask Lucy to send up breakfast before you leave."

"Rubbish!" Mrs. Cam said, ignoring the suggestion. "People will get killed, if they must, whether you're up or down. And if you exercise a little will-power there's no reason why that Honeywether should drag you into his troubles."

"When I see suffering humanity crying out for help …" began Cam, lifting his head slightly with momentary enthusiasm.

"Rubbish!" repeated his wife. "You know it's just your horrid curiosity. A walk is what you need to clear your mind."

"And where would you like to walk?" asked Cam with sudden suspicion.

"Oh, anywhere. It doesn't really matter. Out to Poltherow, perhaps. That's pretty."

"Ha!" exclaimed Cam with malevolent triumph. "So I'm the one with horrid curiosity, am I? I don't suppose *you* want to see where Magnuson fell over the cliff. I don't suppose *you* want to see where Miss Cornthwaite almost died. How much did the children bribe you then?"

"Don't be silly!" Mrs. Cam said, but she flushed slightly. "I certainly don't want to go there. It's a beastly way to spend a holiday. And though I don't suppose it will hurt the children I certainly don't want to encourage them in following your professional interest."

Cam ignored the jibe and concentrated on the main issue.

"In that case we don't want to walk out towards the camp, which would remind us of all those horrid things, and as I can't think of anywhere else I want to walk suppose you leave me in peace to recover from yesterday's exhaustion."

His wife sighed. "How difficult you are. Well then, to tell you the truth, Betsey Rowan asked me to bring you out to her camp. She wants to tell you something. She seems a nice girl—and very worried—so I thought I'd try to help."

Cam stirred uneasily. "If she wants advice," he complained, "the police are the people for her. It's just misleading her to pretend that I can help. She'd do much better to talk to Honeywether."

"That big goose!" said his wife scornfully. "Well, it's up to you. I've delivered my message, anyway. And now I'll try to dig sand-castles."

Again Cam was allowed to sink into slumber, but not for very long. This time it was Lucy with a cup of tea, some toast and a conspiratorial air who pulled back the sheets to see if he were really asleep. He opened his eyes at the tempting scent of tea, but shut them again quickly after a glance at her hopeful expression.

"Just put it down, my dear," he said faintly. "And close the door after you. I'm not feeling too well. Any noise disturbs me."

"Mr. Allen was here to see you," she said firmly. "'E would be grateful if you wud call at the Rectory. And Mr. 'Oneywether wants you to phone 'im as soon as you're awake. It's eleven o'clock already. Don't you think you'd better get up now? You're missing all the excitement."

"That was my intention," Cam muttered gloomily. "If anyone else calls you can tell them I'm not well."

"Mr. Potts has run away," Lucy told him with relish. "And Mr. 'Oneywether's as mad as a wet 'en about it. I saw 'im sneakin' out this mornin' about seven w'en I was dustin' the lounge. But 'ow was I to know he was Wanted? Nobody never said nothin' to me about it. They can't expect me to know ev'rything 'bout ev'rything. 'I'm not a pliceman,' I says to Mr. 'Oneywether. 'You can blime me all you wishes,' I says, 'but that won't bring your Mr. Potts back again. An' what's more,' I told im, 'I don't care if you *never* finds 'im,' I says, 'because it ain't none of *my* business,' I says. 'Finders keepers, losers weepers—an' you oughtn't ter be so careless with yer witnesses; you that's paid by the Public,' I says."

She looked in vain for a sign of appreciation from the Inspector, but he seemed to have fallen asleep again.

"Your tea will get cold," she said and he woke up.

"Well," he said sourly as he reached for the cup. "Thanks for all the news. When you bring lunch you might like to get me a newspaper. Not that it can ever have more to say than you."

Lucy took this as flattery and bridled.

"Get along with yer! But there *is* another thing, now you mention it. The Rector's gone an' 'anded in 'is resignation. 'E told Mister Trefusis, the butcher—'im as is churchwarden—this very mornin' and Mister Trefusis told me not an hour since w'en I were collectin' the meat. Mister Copperman told 'im 'isself, just arter 'e'd posted the letter to the Bishop, Mister Trefusis says, an' 'e wor proper 'umble, 'e wor. 'E told Mister Trefusis that 'e feared 'e'd never bin a good pastor to Trevelley an' that 'e thought 'twas best for all that 'e should leave. 'E said 'e 'oped everyone would try to forget an' forgive 'is mistakes an' that 'e'd allus pray for the village isself an' for whoever took his place. Mister Trefusis said 'e didn't know which way to look, 'e wor so taken aback like, but 'e spoke up bestways 'e could an' said 'e couldn't but say that relations 'adn't bin as good as mighta bin 'oped, but, notwithstandin', 'e 'oped as no one in t'village wouldn't remember Mister Copperman with all respect an' for '*is* part 'e 'oped that 'e were 'uman enough to say that all th' 'arm 'adn't bin on *one* side, not by a long shot it 'adn't, an' mebbe th' village 'ad 'ad its comeuppance by these 'ere un'appy events, for which the Rector certainly warn't t'blame an' 'e 'oped 'e'd 'ave the kindness therefore ter stay on until a successor 'ad bin found an' these un'appy events bin ended an' over."

Until the end of this breathless expression of unaspirated hope even the resolutely uninterested Cam could only wait with fascinated attention. When Mr. Trefusis had had his say, however, he merely took a long sip of tea and murmured: "That's certainly the best solution."

Lucy searched for other news with which to entertain him.

"Mr. Briarley was out before breakfast. But Miss Cornthwaite's still in bed too," she volunteered. "Not feelin' well neither. Though she's got more excuse than you 'ave, pore lady."

"I shouldn't have expected her to take it," Cam commented. "I'm glad she has so much sense. And I only hope she's getting more rest out of it than I am!"

"Hoity toity!" Lucy tossed her head. "Well, I think I knows when I'm not wanted, thank you. An' don't blame me when everything 'appens an' yer don't know about it. You can sleep throught the Day of Judgment, if that's 'ow yer feel about it, for all that I'll tell you different!"

"Nothing," Cam murmured sinking back luxuriously into his pillows, "could please me more on that occasion."

The hot tea induced torpor through his relaxed limbs. He lay sprawled in the vast double bed listening to that most comforting of summer sounds—a lawn mower being toiled up and down beneath his window. It is good, he thought, to be one of the leisured classes. Work is the grave of the intellect. Here I am, he thought, with a chance to think great thoughts when I might be sweating after criminals for nobody's glory but Honeywether's. But before another great thought came he was asleep.

Not for long. This time the intruding hand was hard and hairy. "Still asleep?" asked an incredulous voice. "Or just shamming? Good Lord, man, I've been up for hours. You *can't* be still asleep."

"You're right, I can't," Cam exclaimed peevishly in the bad temper of sudden awaking. "Not if no one will let me. Otherwise I could quite comfortably. And when you have a holiday, Honeywether," he added in sudden vemon, "I swear I'll find you out wherever you are and wake you at five every morning to say there's a corpse in the next room."

"It's half-past twelve," said the Inspector. "Afternoon. I've never been in bed so late in my life, holiday or no."

"That explains why you aren't a great thinker," Cam muttered, and he tried in vain to remember the great thought that had been in his mind just before he fell asleep. Honeywether swallowed an angry retort and said in bluff conciliatory tones:

"Well, well. There's no corpse in the next room, anyway, Cam. Nor anywhere else in Trevelly this morning for a change. So you can get up and have your lunch and then you'll feel much better."

"I couldn't possibly feel better than I was feeling before you came into this room. I shall feel just as well again when you're gone—after I've rested a bit."

Honeywether looked at him incredulously.

"Where's your enterprise, man? Aren't you even interested in this case? Surely you must have some professional pride. Here you lie sleeping the day away while all the world rolls past your doorstep and you won't even raise your head to look at it."

"There's no need!" the other exclaimed, flinging away his coverings in sudden desperation. "All the world stops rolling when it gets to my door and comes in and tells me its story and then goes out and rolls on again. What I say is: let it Roll! But it won't so I might as well get up and face it like a man. Well?" he asked, shoving his feet into bedroom slippers and staggering blindly across the room to the washstand. "Well? What do you want? I'd thought you'd solved the crime. Is Luigi found and under lock and key? If not you can't expect me to find him. I'm a great detective mind, not a bloodhound."

"I did not come here," Honeywether said with tremendous dignity, "to ask your help. Or to be insulted. I came, as one friend might to another, to tell you the latest facts in a very interesting case. If you do not want to hear it—then I know where I stand. I'm sorry to have disturbed you, Cam. You can return to bed and sleep till hell freezes over for all I care."

The last words were uttered more in anger than in dignity and the Inspector strode to the door. Cam, however, withdrawing his face from the basin, intercepted him and with one wet hand on his shirt-front, the other on his sleeve, forced him back into the room's one chair. Having vented his wrath and washed his face he was already looking more peaceably on the world. He delighted in Honeywether when the latter was in turkey-cock mood and not for the world would he have let him go off now.

"I'm very sorry," he said. "I apologise. I wasn't nice. Of course you don't want help and I should be delighted to hear all that you have to tell me. Only what you can tell me," he added with a flicker of dying resentment, "that I haven't already been told, I cannot possibly imagine."

"Who's been telling you anything?" Honeywether asked suspiciously. "I haven't issued a statement."

"Do you really think," asked Cam, "that the village waits till you've issued a statement to talk about the case? I've heard, for instance, that the Rector has resigned."

"So he's done it!" said Honeywether. "I didn't know that myself. He said he would last night but she protested and I didn't think he'd go through with it."

"She protested!" Cam said with surprise. "Now that's odd. How did your interview go?"

"Oh, all right. It's never much fun interrogating the clergy somehow. He—the Rector—spoke up rather well, as a matter of fact. Yes, he confessed that the silver had been stolen and that he hadn't said anything about it for fear of scandal. He also said that as soon as it was back in the safe he wrote right off to the insurance people, sending a cheque to cover it. So that's all right. He also wrote to the Bishop to tell him the story and offer his resignation. He recognises that he's lucky to get out of it all so easily."

"How *did* she get the stuff back?" asked Cam. "How did she know Luigi had it? How did she make him give it up?"

"I thought everyone had told you everything," Honeywether said smugly. "Well, apparently up to Saturday night she didn't even know that the silver had been stolen. But as Sunday was coming along, when she was more than likely to look into the church safe and might notice the empty box, Mr. Copperman had a change of heart and he told her what had happened— told her before they got up in the morning. Naturally she was dumbfounded—didn't know what to do. So she did what every sensible person in a quandary does—got up and went about her work. It happened that she was going that afternoon to visit the Cowdrays—Jessica in particular—on some parish duty. Not being one to coddle herself she went off about her duty, though she couldn't have had much of a heart for it. She knocked at the door, just as I did last night, and it flew open. (They really ought to have that latch mended if they're going into high crime!) There at the table sat our Jess busy packing up the church silver. It was quite a stage-setting! What they had to say to each other I leave to your imagination, but the long and short of it is that Mrs. Copperman told Jessica and Jessica told Luigi that she wanted that silver back then and there—and if it were returned there would be no more trouble."

"So Luigi gave in." Cam murmured. "Did she take it with her?"

"Of course. There was no reason not to. She had a shopping basket with her, packed the things in there, put a tea-towel over them and took them home."

"Was her husband delighted?"

"Speechless, anyway. She says he all but fainted away from relief, Allen, of course, had already left on his tour of duty to Powey so didn't hear the good news. That's why he made that blunder about telling you the whole story. When you think of it, I should never have known anything about it if he hadn't done that."

"Why didn't they tell him after I left them all on Monday morning, I wonder. They were alone together, the three of them, for long enough."

"That's obvious. When the Rector told his wife about the theft he didn't tell her that Allen knew about it. Apparently he thought he should not drag the young man into something which was mostly his own mistake. After you left them yesterday the two men were never alone together, so Copperman never had a chance to tell Allen the latest developments."

Cam nodded. "Well, that, I suppose, is that. There's one crime the less for your books, Honeywether. Unless, of course, you propose to prosecute, anyway. It would be rather a difficult court case to handle, but interesting, very interesting."

"I've got quite enough interesting cases to last me a lifetime. Maybe it's all wrong. Maybe I ought to prosecute and see that justice is done. But somehow I can't pull myself to do it.

Just stirring muddy waters it seems like. Won't do anyone any good. Maybe I'm wrong. ..." For once in his life Honeywether was in doubt. Cam sprang willingly to his rescue.

"Of course you're right," he said firmly. "It's all very well to be ruthless when you work in a town and half the crimes go unpunished, anyway, but life is different in a village. You can't go tearing it to pieces and mending it with legal sticking-plaster all the time. Let sleeping dogs lie—that's the motto."

"That's what I say," Honeywether agreed with some relief. "Trouble with me is that I've been with London police all the morning and the way they want to probe and peer into things would get on anybody's nerves. I said to them—right in front of the Chief Constable and all—I said to them, it's no good you coming here and thinking that in two days you can find out all there is to be found out about this village. I've been here ten years, I said, and still I don't know all the ins and outs of it, though there's no one living who knows more. I'm not pretending, I told them, that there isn't something funny going on here ..."

"A concession!" Cam murmured.

"... but it's outsiders, Londoners, who have done it—that I'll swear to in any court of the land. If you can clear up your end, I said, if you can clear up your end we'll be getting somewhere. But don't come barging round here, I said. Trevelley people need careful handling and it's best to leave them to them as knows them."

"Straight from the shoulder!" said Cam appreciatively as he drew his razor carefully over the loose fold of his chin. "Did they take it lying down?"

"Oh, you know what they're like," Honeywether sighed in disgust. "Always picking holes. 'This file doesn't seem quite complete, Inspector'; 'You didn't cover that point in your report, Inspector'; 'There doesn't seem sufficient warrant here for that assumption, Inspector'—little points, little nattering points!"

Cam gathered that his friend had not had a happy morning. "Did they tell you anything useful?" he asked kindly. "Or were they just throwing their weight around?"

"Oh, we cleared a few loose ends up—got the general picture a bit clearer. When I had explained the facts of life to them they didn't do too badly. We went over the five church robberies one by one—Minchester, Limpeter, Upper Cons, Monks Gabbington and Little Kittle—looking for the Highest Common Factor—the facts common to all of them. One thing stands out a mile," the Inspector said with satisfaction. "The newspapers have played them up as if some master mind were at work, but there's nothing remarkable about the robberies really, except their success."

"There was nothing remarkable about Arsenal's football record last year," Cam commented, "except that they won the Cup."

"What I mean," said Honeywether, "is that there's nothing magical about the case. They are quite ordinary thefts by some quite ordinary thief—or gang of thieves. Anyone with a lot of nerve and luck could have pulled them off by walking in and taking the stuff. It's not the crime of the century. At two of the villages, Upper Cons and Little Kittle," Honeywether went on, "the records say that a dark Italian-looking fellow was seen about the place with a car at the time of the robbery. The description would fit Luigi. We are sending his photograph to the police there and in other places, but for my part I'm sure they'll recognise him. There's no doubt about it—he played a part in this."

"But not the master-mind, eh?" said Cam.

"What I say is that there *is* no master mind," said Honeywether grumpily. "But the Londoners aren't so sure. Of course *my* views aren't of any importance. It seems to me that when you get an American who lives in New York and has a criminal record there for assault and robbery (for so he has) and who comes over here for no reason at all except to see his old blackguard of a father-in-law, and who's half Italian to boot, so is probably arty and interested in church relics—well, when you've got someone like that I say, you ought to grab him. He's master-mind enough for me."

"Any success in the hunt?" asked Cam, ignoring the higher flights of fancy in this exposition.

"Neither hair nor hide of him. It's my guess that he's still somewhere about these coasts. There are plenty of small caves where he could lie for days without being found. But he's not in *my* district, that I'll swear."

"I shouldn't think that he's very much at home in this part of the world," Cam suggested. He was dressed now and opening the window still wider; he leaned out to survey the prospect of village, cliff tops and sea which his room commanded. A sunny, serene prospect.

Suddenly the church bell tolled. Two limpid treble peals in quick succession, like murmurs of warning, fell from the church to the village, rolled in alarm through the streets and faded into the soliloquy of the sea. Two strokes only and in a minute even the echo had gone.

"What's that, eh? ... No more? ... That's funny." Cam waited as if for an explanation.

Honeywether, solid Honeywether, laughed at Cam's startled expression.

"An accident," he said. "Often happens. Someone pulled on the rope by mistake. Now where was I?"

"You were wondering where Luigi was," Cam said, but he was still looking up at the church with a puzzled frown.

"Oh yes! Well, it's only a matter of time and routine before we get him. What I really wanted to tell you was about the method of disposing of the stolen church property. The Londoners don't think that Luigi actually carried out the robberies. He was seen in local pubs, as I've said, about the time they were carried out, but there's never been any mention of him in or near any of the churches themselves.

So what they drink now is drat he was the driver, the carrier, and that someone else, who actually took the stuff, passed it to him in some local pub or shop. It was Luigi's job to bring it back to the coast. All the churches which were robbed are within a day's drive of here. This village is half a day's sailing from Ireland. Scotland Yard has evidence that a dealer in Eire is in touch with an American about the stuff. The Irish police have watched that dealer. We know the Cons loving-cup went that way and is now in America. But what about the rest? We're pretty certain he hasn't received the Robarts Tapestry or the Welkin Book of Hours. The idea is that Trevelley is the half-way house for the smugglers and that the stuff is here. It wouldn't be the first time she's played that part."

"An old stager," agreed Cam. "What about the unfortunate Wilowski, and Magnuson, and Potts? Have you fitted them in at the London end?"

"Roughly, Wilowski is, as I was just about to say, the American dealer in the case. There's no doubt whatever. Presumably he came over here to ginger up the local boys or to make sure that he was getting a fair deal. He started his shop in Covent Garden as a front. Magnuson was his clerk there and probably knew well enough that the shop wasn't Wilowski's source of income. He must have got suspicious of the latter's business methods. It's not likely he was in on the game. His bank balance and wardrobe prove he wasn't. But he may have been finding things out. Whether he meant to force Wilowski to give him a cut-in, to try a little blackmail or whether he was going to report him to the police and sell the story to the papers we don't know and probably never shall. Anyway he landed himself in a pretty pickle, poor young fool."

"And Potts? ... Is he as guileless as he appears?"

Honeywether shook his head. "This escape from the village doesn't look guileless, by a long shot. Did you hear about *that*?"

"Stale news. Stale news."

"Well, he must know something. Or perhaps he is just frightened. I can't see why Wilowski should saddle himself with a mere holiday companion on a trip which was obviously going to be pretty difficult to handle, anyway. But the Londoners say that there's no evidence in Potts' past that he would get mixed up in a crooked deal like this."

"Perhaps Wilowski thought he would be a useful screen. Perhaps he had some plans for using him which never materialised owing to his own death."

There was a silence in the bedroom. Cam turned from his window and saw with sudden displeasure the unmade bed, the tossed blankets.

"For heaven's sake," he said accusingly, "let's get out of here and into the sunshine. You don't want to spend all day cooped up, do you?" He charged out of the room and downstairs, while Honeywether followed at a slower pace. Down the stairs they went, through the polished hall and into the paved courtyard about which a pair of seagulls strutted arrogantly on the stone wall. Cam looked approvingly upon the scene and rolled up his shirt-sleeves as a sign not of readiness for work but of abandonment to the luxury of heat.

"What I wanted to see you about ..." said an aggrieved voice behind him.

"I know! I know!" Cam exclaimed, turning angrily. "You wanted to see me so as to tell me the story and get me to say how well you're doing. Well, you're doing wonderfully. Neither Poirot nor Holmes could do so well. But in the name of all friendship, Honeywether, leave me out of it. I'm on holiday, man. I don't want to work at murder and no one shall make me. Get off about your business, won't you, and let me enjoy my leave. I don't see what is troubling you. Everything seems to be working out satisfactorily. Find Luigi and the case is solved."

"That shows how much attention you've been paying," his friend retorted. "Don't you realise there's all that loot from the church robberies probably lying round Trevelley waiting for a chance to get to Ireland? We've got to do something. ..."

"Find Luigi and I bet you ten bob that he'll spill the beans. Do you expect me to tell you where it is?"

There was a crestfallen expression on Honeywether's face which indicated that indeed he had hoped for assistance of that kind, though not in so many words. Cam suddenly felt something of a false friend. He himself knew that anxiety to discuss a case with a colleague—to put the facts before a fresh mind to whom the solution would appear with crystal clarity while to himself it was still a dim mass of irrelevant facts. He had not, he acknowledged, been paying attention. Mrs. Copperman's visit to Jessica; pages from a Bible; the bear's head; Miss Cornthwaite;—all these pieces must be fitted in. There was no short cut if justice were to be done. The guilty feeling overcame him that if he would only turn his mind to it the solution of the mystery was already within his grasp. He knew the answer, but he wouldn't give himself the trouble to produce it.

While he was still chastising himself, however, there was an interruption which removed the immediate cause of his discomfort. Inside the hotel a telephone had rung and been answered. There was the sound of a short distant conversation and then Lucy appeared on the doorstep, all conscious importance.

"A message for Mister 'Oneywether," she announced. "Six constables from Plymouth have arrived at the police station. Will 'e please return there to give orders."

The breath of confidence inspired Honeywether visibly. Like a general receiving the news of a new army arrived in the nick of time to strengthen the lines, he swelled with hope and vigour.

"Very good," he said to Lucy. "Now we shall see about this crime wave. Give me the men," he added with sudden inspiration, "and I shall finish the job."

"If I *can* help ..." Cam began, still suffering from a sense of guilt.

His friend looked at him coldly. "I need constables, not Inspectors, to help me," he said. "Of course, if you *had* had any views I should have been willing to hear them, but since you aren't even interested I shan't bother you. Good afternoon."

Lucy looked at Cam triumphantly as the Inspector turned out of the yard.

"There!" she said. "Now you're out of it an' won't know no more than what the likes o' me does. That's what comes o' bein' lazy."

Cam stretched himself luxuriously. "That's that," he agreed. "I have been given my freedom from duty and conscience. Six constables have taken over my work. A flattering proportion. Now back to my holiday." He rubbed his hands with sudden glee. He felt just in the mood for a long walk. "Where are my wife and the children?" he asked impatiently. "I thought they wanted to walk somewhere."

"Hours ago," Lucy pointed out. "And they've gone. Towards Poltherow, if you wanted to follow."

Cam scowled. That would mean the American camp and trouble again.

"If they couldn't bother to wait," he said with dignity, "I shan't trouble them with my company. I'll go to Powey myself. And don't expect me for lunch."

With exhilaration pricking in his heels he marched out of the hotel, up the cobbled hill through the market, past the police station where six police constables were marshalled in force before the Inspector, along a lonely stretch and then round the corner where the verger's cottage and the Rectory on one side, the church on the other, presented a united clerical front, down the narrow path behind the church to the ferry-stop. From here on, he said firmly, let the holiday spirit be unconfined.

# CHAPTER XIII

THE ferry, a large rowing-boat with benches for passengers round the sides, was drawn up to its wharf. Cam stepped smartly aboard with a nod and good-day. The ferryman, a craggy dour man, nodded back silently. Beside him sat a good-natured chunk of a girl who smiled a greeting. Cam sat down. The ferryman and his sweetheart resumed their love-making. Since this consisted merely of sitting elbow to elbow and gazing solemnly into the middle distance silence settled again over the scene. Occasionally the girl introduced a little variety into what might otherwise have been a tedious occupation by nudging her lover and giggling shyly. He, however, was not one for playfulness and made no reply to these overtures except to say brusquely: "A' right! A' right! Dunna be giddy."

Cam had great sympathy with young love but he did not see why this kind of flirtation could not continue equally well while the ferry was in motion.

After a minute or two he shuffled his feet. A little later he coughed noisily. Then he whistled a little tune. The ferryman and his sweetheart remained unmoved.

Cam picked up courage to break the peace.

"Waiting for someone?" he asked shyly.

The ferry looked at him carefully before answering.

"Waiting for t'proper time," he said at last.

"Oh, you run to a time-table," Cam said with disappointment.

He was so full of zest now that he hated the thought of sitting actionless. "I rather thought you just carried people across when they arrived. The fellow before you did," he added with sudden resentment.

"Old-fashioned," commented the ferryman scornfully. "No Plan. Now with me folks know when I'm going t'cross and act according. If they want ter arrive early they kin wait."

Cam sighed. "Well, what's the time-table?" he asked.

"On the hour from Powey; half-past from here."

Cam looked at his watch. It was one o'clock.

"You ought to be leaving Powey now," he pointed out triumphantly. "What's happened to the Plan, eh?"

The ferryman raised his eyes briefly to heaven.

"Nobbody there," he explained condescendingly. "What would be t'sense o' me crossin' ter pick up nobbody, eh? Plans," he added, "has ter be elastic ter meet circumstances, ain't they? We've got ter keep adaptable, ain't we?" His sweetheart looked at him admiringly and empassioned by his own oratory the ferryman went so far as to squeeze her hand. Then he recalled himself and threw it roughly away.

Things have come to a pretty pass, thought Cam, when Cornish villagers talk like leader writers. He looked without pleasure on his Charon. "If you adapt your plan to passengers *not* coming," he pointed out brutally, interrupting the romance, "why can't you adapt it to passengers arriving early? Then it would be as elastic as you please."

"Then suppose someone arrives here at one-thirty sharp and finds me not here. They'll think I don't know me own business. They'll start expectin' me ter be at their beck an' call just as they please. Then where's my Plan?"

"But suppose someone arrived at Powey side right now—at one—and saw you sitting here. Wouldn't *that* be the same thing?"

"They should've planned to get there earlier, so I'd know there was a passenger," the ferryman growled. "They can't expect me to be t'only one wi' a Plan."

There was a baffled silence while Cam turned this question confusedly over in his mind. The girl was now so heady in her admiration for her lover's eloquence that she went so far as to place a hand upon his knee. He removed it coldly and turned again to Cam.

"Be you t'Inspector from London?" he asked.

Cam, hoping that this might lead to special privileges, said boldly that he was. The other just nodded, however, and turned again to contemplation. The Inspector thought that he might drive the point home. "You've been questioned already?" he asked portentously.

"I have," the other returned. "An' I've told Mr. Honeywether all about me passengers on Sunday. So there's no more to be said."

"There was one young lady in the evening," Cam said. "An American. You remember her?"

"I do."

"What time did you bring her back?"

"Ten-fifteen o'clock."

"According to your time-table," Cam pointed out, "it must have been ten sharp." He looked at the other with inspectorial suspicion.

"I'm human," said Charon. "It wor gettin' late so when he called across I changed the Plan."

"'He'?" asked Cam. "I'm talking about the American lady."

"Do yer think she'd be alone at that time o'night?" said the other with a leer. "'Twouldn't be safe. Mr. Allen called across, an' seein' as I knowed he an' 'twas a lady I made an exception. It's just as I was sayin'. A Plan's got to be elastic."

Cam was interested. "Did Mr. Allen cross with her?"

"No. He wor spendin' t'night at Powey, he told me."

"There can't have been many people about at that time of night."

"Nobbody except an old fat chap sittin' beside t'wharf here. A Lunnoner. He followed th' American lady up the lane an' arter that I closed an' went t'bed."

"Did you now? So no one could cross from then onwards." "Not unless they wanted to swim."

Cam measured the distance with his eye. "It looks a longish pull."

The ferryman shrugged. "They learn swimmin' young round here," he said moodily, "so as to save my twopences."

"Twopence?" asked Cam. "The fellow before you used to charge a penny."

"Sweated labour," retorted the other. "An' prices have gone up."

"They certainly have!" Cam said with sudden decision. "And I, for one, can't afford it. So I think I'll walk to Poltherow, thank you."

The ferryman shrugged and turned to spit overboard. Cam got out of the boat with all the dignity which is possible for that operation. In the enthusiasm of energy again released he was half-way up the lane before an unexpected shout from behind stopped him. He turned, half hoping for contrition, but it was not the ferryman. A rowing-boat manned by John Briarley had paddled round the corner of the cliff.

"Want a lift?" he shouted. "Going my way?"

"Any way you want," shouted Cam, and marched back triumphant to the ferry-slip.

"Blackleg!" muttered the ferryman without venom. "Don't you pay him nothing. It's agin the Law if money changes 'ands." Briarley manoeuvred unskilfully up to the shore and Cam clambered aboard, rocking the boat violently. The two men laughed at their own clumsiness. "I'm all right in the open water," Briarley boasted. "It's going round corners that's difficult. Where can I take you?"

"To the other side, if that's not out of your way," Cam replied. "What are you doing? Fishing?"

"Just paddling round," Briarley said non-committally. But he looked at Cam sideways. "Mind if we take a look at the church from the water before crossing? It's quite striking, they say."

"Good idea," said Cam, but it seemed rather odd all the same as Briarley had just appeared from the direction in which lay the part of the harbour from which one saw the church.

They were actually directly beneath the church at this point, but hidden from it by the overhanging cliff. To see it Briarley paddled round the corner of the rocks and out towards the deeper water. Fifty yards from shore he rested his oars.

"There," he said. "What do you think of that?"

It was a fine view. The small and unaspiring tower looked lofty and remote—literally towering above the water. The stone of the cliff and the stone of the tower melted into one impregnable wall, rising up and up into sky-high distance. The sun at this moment was glittering on the windows which shone like gold plates.

"It's like a castle on the Rhine," admired Cam. "What a fortress it would make!"

He became aware suddenly that Briarley was looking not at the church but at him—looking at him with a curious intentness that was disturbing. It occurred to Cam that they were fifty yards from shore, that he was never a strong swimmer and that Briarley was a powerfully-built young man. He stared even more strenuously at the cliff and tried hard to think of something distracting to say.

"Pretty little flowers," was all that would come, with a cheeriness which sounded false even to his own ears. "See the pretty flowers?" Briarley hissed faintly and Cam knew without looking at him that he was not admiring the yellow cowslips which had planted themselves on the cliff-side below the church. "No chance of picking them," he babbled on feverishly. "They know where they are well off … Wonderful the way those little things can cling to a sheer wall."

"Would you like to get closer?" Briarley asked in what seemed to Cam a venomous tone. The young man picked up an oar and swung the boat a few yards nearer the shore. A step in the right direction, thought Cam. He mustn't let this murder prey on his mind. He looked conscientiously at the cowslips and discovered suddenly that one clump was hanging by its roots. The wind, he thought; but there was none and had been none for days. A rockfall? Yes, he could see a gash now in the soil where a rock had been recently displaced. And another.

"I wonder," he said thoughtfully, "whether it is as sheer as it looks. Possibly one could get up it with a little luck—or knowledge."

"Do you think so?" asked Briarley with surprise, and steered the boat a few yards further in. "I wonder if you're right." Cam had an uncomfortable sensation that he was being led by the hand down a pre-arranged train of thought. "In that case," he mused obediently, "the tower door would not be as useless as it appears. There would be some sense in keeping the lock oiled."

"So there would," Briarley agreed. "But who would use it? Who would have the key?" He steered the boat even nearer the shore, but this time it was Cam who was looking at him and ignoring the yellow cowslips.

"And what do you know about the door being oiled, eh?" he fired. "Who told you about it? You seem to know a good deal too much for a summer visitor, it seems to me!"

The young man, recovering from his first surprise, laughed uneasily.

"Was that a trap?"

"A heffalump trap," said Cam. "You built it for yourself. What do you mean," he exclaimed with rising anger, "by trying to teach me my business? I don't need young whipper-snappers like you to show me that the murderer might have got into the church this way."

"Had you thought of it?" asked Briarley defiantly.

"I would have," declared Cam. "And much more interesting to me is how *you* thought of it. Eh?"

"Common sense," said Briarley who now, seizing his oars, had started pulling hard for the opposite shore. "And the fact that I talk with the people who really know this village— every inch of it. Do you know who they are? No, of course you don't. But as you'll think of it anyway I won't bother to tell you."

"The villagers ..." began Cam.

"The villagers!" Briarley exclaimed. "What do they know about the place? And what they know they take for granted and don't talk about. I have a better source than that."

"You ought not to know too much," said Cam mildly. "It's unwise sometimes in a case like this."

"To tell you the truth," said Briarley violently, "I don't want to know anything—not a thing. I only know what any fool couldn't help seeing and I tried to get rid of that rapidly by passing it on to those who don't see anything."

"Oh, I see a reasonable amount," Cam said tolerantly, "I see that you're very anxious that Betsey Rowan shouldn't get involved—though I don't see why you think she would. I see that you're not at all anxious for Luigi to be captured and that you did him a good turn last night by rocking the boat just when we might have caught up with him. I see that your knuckles have recovered very nicely from the rapping he gave them. I see that you know as much about church towers as about monumental brasses—and about this church tower in particular. I see enough to think you're a very peculiar fellow and to wonder why."

Briarley laughed uneasily. "You're right about my knuckles, anyway. I didn't hold on long enough for him to hurt them much. I'm no fanatic."

"Or you choose your friends well," said Cam.

"That's slander!" the young man exclaimed. "Luigi is no friend of mine. Far from it."

"Then why help him get away?"

Briarley did not deny or affirm the suggestion. He merely said grimly as they drew up to the ferry-slip on the Powey side: "It's sometimes better to let a tiger go free than to catch hold of it by the tail."

Cam sat for a moment in the boat turning this over in his mind, fitting it in with the other pieces of the puzzle. His eye wandered absently over the heavily wooded banks on this side of the river. He had lost his slight nervousness of Briarley.

Whatever the young man's purpose he was obviously relying more on words and persuasion than on force. Nevertheless he started violently when the young man suddenly laid a heavy hand on his shoulder. On this side there was not even the ferryman to call to his aid. Briarley, however, was also staring at the banks.

"There's someone watching us," he whispered hoarsely.

"Well, there's no need to watch back," Cam exclaimed in irritation. "Do you want to frighten him away? Whereabouts?"

"Under the chestnut tree half-way up the path."

Cam cast a sidelong glance in that direction. A rather inexpert rustling of bushes confirmed Briarley's suspicion.

"Pull the boat on shore," he ordered, "and come along with me. Only try not to look as if you are a bloodhound."

They beached the boat and Cam in the lead sauntered casually up the path, talking with careful articulation about the weather. The rustling of bushes ceased altogether. If it were a rabbit, thought Cam, he would feel very foolish. He reached the chestnut and paused idly to wait for Briarley, who was loitering almost too naturally, to catch up with him.

"Hist!" said a conspiratorial voice from the bushes. "Hist!"

"'Hist,' yourself!" Cam exclaimed in normal and irritated tones. "Who the devil are you? Come out of those bushes, damn you!"

Briarley, arriving at this juncture, plunged violently into the undergrowth. "I'll get him!" he exclaimed excitedly. "Leave it to me! I'll get him!"

"Don't you lay a finger on me!" a shrill voice protested.

"Not a finger. I'll have the law on you."

But Briarley had him now and marched out of the bushes propelling a dishevelled and perspiring Potts. Both men looked at each other with annoyed surprise and Cam surveyed both with scorn.

"It's heartbreaking," he exclaimed, "for a professional policeman to see such amateur goings-on. If you want to hide, hide! If you want to hunt, hunt! Which of you is clumsier I really couldn't say. You're a good match for each other, anyway."

The two men shuffled shamefaced. "What were you doing in the bushes, anyway?" demanded Briarley.

"That's my business," Potts declared. "What right have you to say who shall or shall not walk where he wants to? This is a free country, isn't it, eh? Answer that if you can!"

"I thought you were Luigi."

Potts started and looked round him nervously. "Why? Is he over here?"

"We don't know where he is. The police can't find him."

"Well, it's about time they did," Potts exclaimed indignantly.

"It's scandalous having a brute like that at large. We might all be murdered in our beds."

"Is that why you've left the 'Fishers'?" Cam asked. "It doesn't seem to me you're much safer over here. Honeywether is very worried about you," he added pointedly.

"I've got a right to spend my holiday where I want," the Londoner said with justice. "I left the money for my bill, didn't I? And I don't know how *you* feel about it, but two murders and one attempted is more than my ration for a seaside holiday. I've had enough of Trevelley and it will take more than the police to get me back there. My best friend," he added, rather as an afterthought, "was murdered in Trevelley. Doesn't that make you understand how I feel about it?"

"You ought to choose your friends better," Briarley said brutally. "Mine don't get murdered."

"No?" asked Potts. "Only your enemies?"

The two men looked at each other with naked antagonism for a few seconds. Then Briarley shrugged, turned on his heel and started back to his boat. "You can get the ferry back," he said abruptly over his shoulder to Cam. "I don't think you'll need any protection against this fellow."

So that's what he was doing, Cam thought with amusement. Protecting me? Protecting me from harm or protecting me from seeing what I oughtn't?

"What *is* that young fellow about?" Potts echoed his thoughts.

"He's a rum sort of holiday-maker."

"You're pretty rum yourself," Cam pointed out. "Saying 'hist' out of bushes when you might be sunning yourself on the beach."

"Sunning on the beach!" Potts sneered. "Not on your life! I'd hardly close my eyes but someone would sneak up and cut my throat."

"Not without reason," Cam suggested. "Not unless you're worth murdering for some reason."

"Miss Cornthwaite? Magnuson? Why were they worth murdering? I'm no better—or worse—than they."

Cam looked at him sharply. "What am I supposed to gather from that? That your good friend Wilowski *was* worth murdering?"

Potts shrugged. "I guess he might have been. For someone. Your Inspector friend thought it was queer that I didn't know more about him. Well, it was queer. I'm no fool. I know you think that if I don't talk about him it was because I won't, not because I can't. That's not so. He never told me anything about himself. I thought it was odd myself and now he's dead like this—well, I guess it proves he had something to hide."

"So you've no idea why he wanted to come to Trevelley? I have never doubted, myself," Cam said frankly, "that you were as ignorant as you say about Wilowski. But I haven't been able to figure out why you let him persuade you to come here. You don't really like Cornish fishing villages, do you?"

Potts looked round the shadow-patched lane and then across the blue harbour waters to the packed houses of Trevelley. "No," he said at last, "I guess I don't. I thought I would. I used to be a great one for the bloods and I thought Trevelley might turn out like that. Smugglers, treasure trove, piracy! I got quite sentimental to think about it—before I came. That was partly why I said I'd come."

"What was the other part?"

Potts fidgetted under Cam's eye. "I never knew Wilowski very well," he repeated uneasily.

"But he asked you to do something for him—to meet someone—to arrange a deal?" Cam pressed.

Potts sighed. "I knew it would come to no good. Of course, I wasn't going to do it for love. I'm no sucker and I don't pretend to be a saint."

"So you offered to collect something for him."

"Silver Jacobean plate. He didn't want to get it himself, because they knew him and knew how much he could pay. If I went along, he said, they would ask half what they'd ask him. It was true too; only fifty pounds and well worth five hundred. And I'd get half the profit. What a loss! What a loss!"

"Who were 'they'? Red Cowdray and family?"

"So you knew, did you?" Potts said with satisfaction. I thought you would. Someone else was after the stuff of course. So they said, anyway. They wanted to get rid of it quickly. That was all right by me."

"Who was the other person?" Cam interrupted.

"I never knew. And as it turned out it doesn't matter. We both got a fly in the ear. I arranged to collect and pay for the complete set—three pieces—there at the cottage on Sunday. They were to bring the silver and I was to bring the cash. At one o'clock sharp, when everyone ought to be at Sunday dinner, I strolled along. I passed a lady with a shopping basket and didn't give her a second glance. If I'd known what she was carrying I *might* have been mixed up in a murder case! There was bedlam let loose at the cottage. The old man cursing his son-in-law, Luigi swearing like a blue streak and the girl crying. When I got some sense out of them it turned out that the lady was the Rector's wife, that she had come in unexpectedly while they were getting the silver ready for me, had thrown her weight around and had the ruddy cheek to take the stuff away with her under threat of a police summons. Sheer daylight robbery!" The jeweller paused in indignation.

"What the ...?" asked Cam. "Did you call it a day—or the police? A Rector's wife is a formidable opponent."

"A day!" Potts said emphatically. "I wasn't out for trouble. And I didn't know enough about Wilowski to want to call the police in. They might ask too many questions I couldn't answer—or Wilowski wouldn't want to."

"But you called on the Rector," said Cam.

"What makes you say that?"

"You admired his flower border."

Potts laughed. "You don't miss a trick, do you? Well, since you're so clever I'll confess. I thought I'd go to church that evening to take a look at the old lady. Just as I got there I saw her and her old man leaving their house. The garden gate was open so I slipped in there, just to have a look round." The fat man paused a moment, wiped his forehead and looked shyly at the Inspector. "I guess this was pretty irregular. We're all human, y'know."

"I'm not easily shocked," Cam consoled him. "It's great fun being burglars once in a while."

The other frowned. "I wasn't burgling. Nothing like that. Anyway, if I had seen the stuff lying around and taken it, why not? It was as much mine as hers. She had no right to it. ... Well, there I was in the garden with no one about, but the french windows wide open. So I looked in and if the silver *had* been there I might have taken it. But it wasn't and I didn't look far. All I took was a piece of their cake. Then I went off to church myself, just to see what it looked like. It was on my way over that I saw Magnuson and the American girl yapping at each other—much too hard to notice me coming out of the garden gate. I sat through that service and though I'm not a churchy fellow it made me sick in the stomach to see that old woman sitting there as if butter wouldn't melt in her mouth. Such wickedness!" The Londoner's whole face wrinkled with shocked distaste.

"Dreadful," Cam agreed absently. "And after the service you went and sat by the ferry slip, eh? Alone with Briarley."

Potts shot him a sharp look. "Part of the time. He wasn't there when I arrived. And he didn't stay with me all the time. He went for a stroll. No, I haven't a foolproof alibi because the ferryman wasn't there all the time, either." He looked downcast.

"You and Briarley," Cam said wearily, "told me a fine story about being together there until the ferry went. What about that?"

Potts sighed. "Do you remember he and I had a talk when I asked him to join us in a drink? He was saying it would be a good idea for us both to have alibis so as not to get mixed up in this business. It struck me as sound sense. After all, it was only an accident that we didn't sit there all the time together, so the alibi he suggested was just to tidy things up and not confuse everyone."

"Confuse!" exclaimed Cam grimly. "Well, I hope you're right."

"I wanted an alibi," Potts said manfully. "We're all human, aren't we? And I didn't have any reason then to think young Briarley was up to anything."

"Have you now?"

Potts did not reply directly. He was watching Briarley's boat slowly disappearing up stream. "Do you know what he has been doing all morning?" he asked. "Paddling round the harbour below the church. He beached once against the cliff and tried to climb up. Didn't get far. Now, why should he do that? Was he just after a thrill? I watched him for two hours. What's he after?"

"And then he picked me up so you watched us both," Cam commented without replying, "which brings me back to the main question. What are you doing over here, anyway? If you want to leave Trevelley, why not leave? Is it just for morbid curiosity that you sit over here watching the place? If you want to get away from it all, why don't you go home, eh?"

Potts pouted. "My friend has been killed. That's one reason. I want to know why. He may have been a bad 'un. I'm beginning to think he must have been. But I want to know."

"That's the reason you're staying near, then. But what's the reason you don't stay in Trevelley?"

"Luigi," said Potts simply. "The old red devil's son-in-law. He threatened me. Yesterday afternoon I went along to see Cowdray—after I knew it was poor Wilowski who had been killed. I wanted to find out what he actually knew about this silver deal. I wanted to know whether there was any reason why the police shouldn't know about it. Wilowski had told me it was a family heirloom that he wanted me to buy for him. Well, I'd seen the family now and they weren't the kind with heirlooms!"

"Pretty rash to go and ask them."

Potts shrugged. "I didn't think of that. Not till I got there and started asking questions. The old man didn't care. He just sat there building his ship. The young one, though, he came at me with a knife and swore that if I opened my mouth he'd tear my tongue out. He said a lot of other things too. I left quicker than I came. When I got back to the hotel I heard about this thing happening to Miss Cornthwaite. She told me herself it was Luigi. I knew I'd be next. So I went while the going was good."

"You gave the local police the wrong impression," Cam pointed out.

"Fine! Maybe they'll set a watch on me and that will protect me from Luigi. I'd like that!"

"I'll tell them," Cam promised. "Perhaps they'll oblige."

The ferry was coming in and he sauntered down to it, Potts plodding at his side and gazing longingly at the forbidden land on the other side.

"I'm staying at the Blue Moon in Powey," he volunteered. "You can always find me there. Keep me in touch, won't you? And keep your eye on Luigi. He's the man you want, don't make any mistake."

"I'm on holiday," Cam shrugged. "Too tired to put two and two together." He was getting hungry. It was not too late for the tail end of cheese at the 'Three Fishers'. He planned his time rapidly. A quick lunch—a visit to Honeywether to tell him this intriguing tale—and then find the children wherever they might be and enjoy in peace and quiet somewhere a real holiday picnic. Pleased with the prospect he smiled kindly upon Potts. "I can't promise," he said, "how the police will take your story. It's a bit outside the routine, y'know. Anyway, I shall tell them exactly what you told me. But next time you take a holiday keep away from fishing villages, eh?"

"Wattlebury Holiday Camp for ever," Potts said fervently, and as Cam got aboard the ferry he stood there wistfully, an urban blot against the greenery.

Cam looked at his watch as he climbed aboard.

"Two o'clock," he said cheerfully. "Target time! Good work!"

The ferryman, mopping his brow, had just seated himself for a rest after the toil of pulling ten husky athletes across stream. He gave Cam an unpleasant look, but braced himself resolutely to his work.

"Plans," he said as he pulled wearily back, "is all very well if you dunna let 'em master ye. Ye gotta know where to draw the line."

"It's your Plan," Cam pointed out, leaning back luxuriously. "I liked the old, planless days myself. But you're possibly right. One must move with the times."

The ferryman set his chin. "I don't want to be at nobody's beck an' call," he said stubbornly. "I'll set me own times, thank you."

They finished the trip in silence and Cam, having paid his twopence, climbed out and started up the narrow lane. He was halfway up the hill for the second time that day when an unexpected yell from the ferryman stopped him. He turned, half fearing that Potts would be asking for his return. But this time the opposite bank was empty and the ferryman, though he beckoned violently with one hand, was leaning far over the side of his boat, peering into the water. For a wild moment Cam thought he was being seasick. He ran back.

"Look here!" the other exclaimed urgently. "Summut funny here. Never noticed it afore, neither. Summut nasty!"

Cam knelt by his side and together they looked through the green shadows of the river into the tangle of weeds and boulders of its bed. One shadow there was darker than the rest and one shadow lighter. A grip of horror clutched his heart. Two empty sleeves were reaching languidly up to the surface of the water from the seaweed bed on which they rested.

# CHAPTER XIV

LOOKING back over this eventful holiday Cam wondered at the curious way that murder had poisoned each of the special joys of Trevelley. The cool sanctity of the church stained with blood. The sea winds of the cliff-top rendered ominous by the death there of a city clerk and the narrow escape of a headmistress. And now the water itself, the ever-present water stroking the shore, always to be associated with a bundle of old clothes soaked in blood. There seemed no escape from death in this bewitched village. Sitting an hour later in the spiritless gloom of the police-station waiting-room he thought moodily that this was the proper environment for his holiday. Here beneath an ancient brown photograph of the Parthenon, upon a hard bench looking out through a dusty window to a grey brick wall two feet away—this was the true reflection of his holiday spirit. He sighed with self-pity.

His companions in the waiting-room seemed in low spirits too. Jessica was after news of her husband, she said. Gaudy in her red slacks and high heels, she sat tearing at a handkerchief with nervous hands and looking more frightened than distressed. Every once in a while she darted defiant glances at the others in the room as though they had come to reprove her personally. Mrs. Copperman, sitting by her side, patted her gently on the shoulder once, but otherwise seemed lost in private thoughts.

Mr. Copperman had retired to the window, from which he stared out at the wall opposite. As he passed Cam, the Inspector caught a glimpse of his face, scared by an expression of bewildered helplessness.

"Are you all right?" he asked suddenly and the old man turned with surprise.

"'All right'?" he repeated. "Is anyone 'all right' here? What an extraordinary question. Will any of us be in our right minds again until the devil has been driven out of Trevelley? Of course I'm not 'all right'! I hear," he added, with an incongruous laugh, "that one of the hotel guests was almost murdered yesterday at Peter's Perch."

Cam nodded. "You see!" exclaimed the other with an almost hysterical triumph. "Then I was right! The Devil is back indeed. Did you know the story of that place—of Peter's Perch? Of course not! And a police station is no place for stories. But it is part of the case. You should be told. And possibly I'm the only person who can tell it, for I'm the only one who cares. It's such an old story. No one else would care. It goes like this: Years ago, before Trevelley was Christian, before even our Lord came to Glastonbury, this part of the earth was ruled by a devil—the Devil. His seat of power was in Trevelley itself, but all the world for a hundred miles around was his demoniac realm. You've heard the famous couplet about the pre-historic earthwork further north:

> "One day the Devil, having nothing to do,
> Built a hedge from Lerryn to Looe.

"The brutalities of his rule are written in all local legend. Caves in the cliffs are where he hurled rebellious villagers; rocks out to sea were thrown by him at drowning sailors; the rocks shaped like women—there are always some!—are the remains of local girls he took to himself. It is a grim story to cherish!

"But God loved Trevelley also, because it was beautiful and its people oppressed. He sent an angel one spring day to save us and in a titanic fight on the cliff-tops the Angel and the Devil wrestled for mastery. The Angel won and he stood out there on Peter's Perch in all his glory watching Satan fly southwards across the sea in a cloud of scalding spray. But that isn't the end of the legend. Before the Devil disappeared he turned once and cursed the Angel and cursed Trevelley. 'I shall be back,' he said. 'As long as two stones of my palace remain on the other I shall return. Trevelley has not seen the last of me.' And indeed we hadn't," the Rector concluded grimly. "Trevelley is still possessed."

Cam smiled uneasily. There was something ridiculously earnest about Mr. Copperman's recital, even as though he half-believed the tale himself. "How do you account for the story?" he asked.

"Account for it?" the old man asked blankly. "Oh, you mean explain it historically. Quite easily. There are the remains of an old Stone Age settlement in the hill just behind the American Camp. Cornwall is littered with such places. This one may have been ruled once by a chief evil enough to be remembered with awe long after his name was forgotten. And there's a quoit near here—or the remains of one—which is quite famous. It is one of the largest in Cornwall and was certainly the burial place of some great ancient king. Some of the stones were used in the building of the church, whereby the legend arose that the Devil still has his home here—and in the church itself! Oh, you can explain it easily enough. ..." Mrs. Copperman had come over to them and interrupted him with a soothing hand laid upon his arm.

"Robert," she suggested. "I think that poor girl would appreciate your comfort now. She is very much distressed about her husband."

The Rector nodded jerkily and went over to sit by Jessica. Cam wondered as he looked at the pair which was most in need of comfort.

But Mrs. Copperman was demanding his attention.

"Have you seen Giles today?" she asked.

"No," Cam replied. "I have done nothing but soothe Honeywether and supplement the visiting constables. It hasn't been a very sociable day."

"He wants to see you very much. He is afraid that you may think that he intentionally misled you with that story about the stolen silver."

Cam was surprised. "You know about his part in it? Did he or your husband tell you?"

"He did. This morning."

Cam nodded. "Well, I wasn't suspecting him. I'm not suspecting anyone. It was bad luck for your husband that he told me the story though. No one need have known if he hadn't."

She shrugged slightly. "Better have the sin out in the open. Confession is good for the soul—even unwilling confession. We were more fortunate than we deserved."

"If you had known earlier about the theft, would you have made the others confess?" Cam asked. "Do you blame them for what they did? I have been wondering what I should have done. It was a painful predicament."

"Of course, I should have confessed," Mrs. Copperman said bluntly. "I blame Giles," she added abruptly. He should have known better. Robert would never have dared a trick so foolhardy without Giles's encouragement. There's too much of the daredevil in him."

"But he was right in a sense. You found the silver, though admittedly by the barest chance."

"Yes, *I* found it. Not Giles, despite all his clever detection. And my husband's good name was not saved. I heard too late for that."

"Mrs. Copperman," Cam asked abruptly. "Why did you say that you took the pruning-knife to church? Why did you tell that untruth?"

Every vestige of colour escaped from her face at the shock of this assault. After a moment of aghast silence she whispered: "How do you know? What do you know?"

"I know you lied," Cam said bluntly. "I want to know why."

She shook her head. "I can't say. I can't say. I lied because I wanted to explain it, because I wanted to be safe—not because I understood what was happening. I know nothing, Mr. Cam. My husband knows nothing. Giles, I am sure, knows nothing.

But we are frightened and frightened people do foolish things."

"Obviously. Why did you go to visit Jessica Luigi on Sunday, Mrs. Copperman? Are you sure you had no knowledge of the whereabouts of the silver then? Was the timing of your visit pure coincidence?"

She shot a startled glance at the sulky girl across the room before replying firmly: "I went on parish duty only, Mr. Cam. I had been asked most earnestly to visit her. I had to go. I had no idea that the silver would be there."

"*Who* asked you to go?"

"It was parish work," she repeated. "It can make no difference. No," she added. "I shall tell you so that you don't get a false impression. Yardley asked me to see her. He thought she was corrupting his son."

The idea was so ludicrous—that seductive creature wasting her time over a simple boy of fourteen—Cam almost laughed.

"You didn't believe it?" he asked incredulously.

"Of course not. Yardley has what they call a persecution mania. He thinks all his bad luck is the result of personal vindictiveness. But I saw Jessica in order to warn her not to give him any grounds for suspicion."

"What did she say?"

"Why not ask her?" Mrs. Copperman asked in sudden anger. "Why must you ask us to convict each other? If you must know, her husband was there and was very angry. He's a jealous man, I think. Poor fellow." There was no interpreting her sympathetic coda.

"And are you here in connection with his disappearance?"

She shook her head. "My husband wished to talk about reopening the church."

"So you came along?"

"Why not? My husband and I like to face problems together."

Cam felt convicted of intolerable impertinence. Mrs. Copperman got up then abruptly as Honeywether swept into the room, imperially escorted by two constables. The gloomy stillness of the room escaped through the open door and was replaced by brisk efficiency. One by one the visitors were interrogated in the inner room. Jessica first. She came out red-eyed and grim-chinned after Honeywether's voice had been heard at a threatening pitch through the thin door. He had got small change out of her, Cam thought. When Mr. and Mrs. Copperman went in voices were courteous and subdued. There was no argument there. Honeywether himself ushered them to the door after a few minutes, then turned briskly from this polite interlude to summon his constables and with the aid of a wall map of the region give them brisk deployment orders. It appeared to Cam, who had retired into a corner out of range of the new brooms of organisation, that soon no one would be able either to leave or enter Trevelley without a signed warrant from the police. What with policemen and murderers a man would be very lucky to get out of the village alive. A wild desire to escape seized him, but as he was edging surreptitiously towards the door Honeywether, now high on the tide of administrative zeal, saw him.

"Cam?" he exclaimed. "Just the man I want. I've got an appointment with the Chief Constable, but Yardley wants to have an interview. He claims he has important evidence. Perhaps he has. Anyway, will you see him here for me and take a statement, if necessary? Then I can deal with the important points later if it seems necessary. I can let you have a constable," he added as a generous afterthought.

Cam sighed, but this was no time to be unhelpful. Honeywether had his hands full. "I'll see him," he agreed mildly. "I don't want a constable. Is he here?"

"In the hall. You can use my office. You'll find the bundle on the table in the corner, but don't mind that."

Cam, who was still wearing his wet trousers, grimaced. He did mind. There was to him something as repulsive about that bundle of old wet clothes, of the clinging river weeds and the weight of the water in them, as about a drowned body itself.

"Why don't you put them with the body?" he complained. "Haven't you finished with them?"

"We've found out they'll fit Wilowski," Honeywether said. "I'd still like proof by someone who saw him in them. In other words—Potts. He'll be brought in any time now. I've found him. And where do you think he was? In Powey! He had run just two miles away and was established cosily there. I'm looking forward to hearing his explanation."

"I can give you his explanation," Cam said smugly. "He has just been telling me about it."

Honeywether's jaw dropped. "You've been talking to him yourself? Well," he brightened, "I'll probably get a report from my detectives soon that Potts has been seen consorting with a criminal type. What did he have to say?"

"How much time have you?" Cam asked cautiously.

"Six and a half minutes."

So in four and a half minutes Cam gave a precis of Potts's story—a feat made possible by many years of telling Chief Constables improbable and complex tales between two holes of golf.

Honeywether was remarkably attentive towards the end of the recital and where Cam had expected an explosion of incredulity came only a mild, "Well, that's a queer tale!" as he finished.

"Potts," Cam explained, "is a romantic soul. That's his excuse, perhaps."

"Certainly," Honeywether said absently. He looked at Cam slyly. "One alibi goes up in smoke if Potts is telling the truth."

"Briarley's?"

"Right. Did he suggest their little story just so as to escape inconvenience? Pretty rash, as he hardly knows Potts."

"When did he go?" Cam asked. "Had he forgotten anything? Was he going to meet someone?"

"Can't we guess?" asked Honeywether. "I never trusted him. Do you remember? Right from the beginning I've said he was a queer one. What was he going over to Powey for, anyway? To catch up with that girl and apologise? Then why didn't he? Why did he carry his brass-rubbing stuff with him? Those cricket bags are a nuisance to carry. Couldn't he have left it in Trevelley? It was too dark to rub brasses in Powey if it was too dark to rub them in Trevelley. Yet he carries all the equipment with him. It's my guess he had something else in that bag. Wilowski's clothes! *That* would explain why we found them there—right by the riverside where he sat."

"Where everyone and his brother sat," Cam said firmly. "And probably the bundle had drifted from its original anchorage. Have you figured out what the iron weight with it was?"

"Not yet," Honeywether confessed unwillingly. "It looks familiar, somehow, but I can't place it. A clock weight, perhaps."

"Something like." Cam nodded. "I've another idea. No," he shook his head, "I'll see first if I'm right. Tell me, did you have that analysis made of the specimens of dust round the sanctuary?"

"The first analysis. They'll be sending a full one tomorrow. It is fairly straightforward churchyard dust, mixed with a good bit of sand—just as you'd expect round here—nothing very remarkable except one peculiar element."

"What, then?"

"Silver-dust."

"Silver-dust!" Cam burst out laughing. "No golden guineas; no Spanish doubloons? Not even a little gold-dust? Now, Honeywether, your local blackguards aren't living up to their promise! Silver-dust, by God. Cheap skates!"

"Only a flake or two," Honeywether said defensively. "Not enough to make all that song and dance about. Never would have found it if I wasn't very thorough in the way I collect my evidence. Anyway, what does it prove? Only that the fellow who stole the church silver—Luigi—was mixed up in the murder. I guessed that, anyway. At some time or other a piece of the silver must have been scratched and some flakes left in his clothes. Later on they dropped off in the church. It's just another piece of evidence against Luigi. There are several deep new scratches on the chalice and the crest broken off. He hadn't treated it any too carefully. No, we won't have any difficulty there."

"It's easily checked, anyway. The silver of the chalice can be analysed."

"Of course. It's on its way now." Honeywether looked impatiently at his watch and started for the door.

Cam stopped him. "One other thing. What about Briarley? Have you checked his record?"

"Yes. Apparently he's an old Trevelley visitor. For the last year before 'D' Day he was a liaison officer with the Americans and he spent two months of that in the embarkation station at Powey!"

"He told me," Cam said doubtfully, "that he was near here during the War."

"Of course he did. He must have known we would find out. But that doesn't make it less odd that he should come here of all places for his demob. leave—this fellow who pretends to be shattered by his war experiences and wants to get away from it all."

"It doesn't seem quite reasonable. What happened after 'D' Day?"

"Ah!" said Honeywether triumphantly. "Now there you have the best part of it. He was wounded in the landings the very first day and after a couple of months in hospital he was appointed Army Education Inspection Officer with Southern Command! His own car to potter round in, his own master to all intents and purposes, able to visit any cathedrals or churches he wanted any time he wanted. A good job!"

"And all the Cathedral Robberies took place in Southern Command. I see your reasoning. But it's far from proof in any court of law, y'know. You'll have to do better than that."

"I'm doing better," Honeywether growled resentfully. "He is being watched of course. I'll give him a little more rope."

He looked anxiously at his watch. "I must go. I'm opening the church this evening. Just agreed that with the Rector. You may like to come. Rector's holding a service at half-past six."

"I'll come," said Cam. "Did you know that Briarley has a theory, which Allen denies, that the monumental brass in this church is a—well, that if you turned it over you would find another engraved on the back. I think it would be interesting and instructive for all concerned if you had a look."

Honeywether shook his head doubtfully. "It sounds like sacrilege to me. Wouldn't I need an Order from the Home Secretary—like a disinterment?"

"It might be interesting," Cam insisted. "You could have all the Rectory people there. I'm sure there's no question of an Order—there's no body to be touched. But of course," he added, "I can see your point. The Rector and Allen, not to mention Yardley, are dead set against it, so you won't want to rub their backs the wrong way."

Honeywether, a noted and complacent wrong-way rubber of backs, bristled. "That's got nothing to do with it. If it's my duty I'll do it, whoever objects. I shall ask the Chief Constable. If he doesn't object, I don't."

Cam gave the flattery asked for. "That's the right enterprise! Now what about the Verger?" he asked. "Let me get at him and get it over."

"Right," said Honeywether. "And I shall be back in about an hour so you can tell me then whether I should see him myself "

"Long before then," Cam declared, "I shall have gone to my tea. But I shall come in afterwards." It was past three o'clock and after his meagre breakfast he was beginning to feel peckish.

"I can send a constable to get sandwiches for you," Honeywether said grandly, but Cam refused. He remembered now that it was today that he had promised to lunch at the

American camp—on hamburgers and coca-cola. The police station and an empty stomach were a poor exchange. Perhaps he would go later—there might be some left over.

Yardley was sitting in the narrow hall, starkly erect and contemptuous of his surroundings. A gangling, tow-haired, simplefaced boy—obviously Colly—stood by his side. The Verger, still wore his official gown. It would have been improved by a wash and a few stitches. There was a curious and rather pleasing scent about him, however. Cam decided with some surprise that it was lavender—a trace in the air of Mrs. Copperman's perfume.

Cam directed the pair into the Inspector's office. The damp clothes of Wilowski were folded neatly upon a table. Cam and Honeywether had already examined them with care. Found a little sooner they would have helped to prove Wilowski's American background. Even his sodden passport was there to confirm identity. Apart from identity the clothes showed nothing. When dry perhaps some tell-tale threads or traces of dust might indicate where the fellow had been before he came to Trevelley. But prolonged soaking would have destroyed most of these. No, the only lingering mystery to titillate the mind about these damp garments was why they had been found at all, when it was so easy hereabouts to commit a weighted object to the deep sea.

"So you've found his clothes, eh?" Yardley said behind him. "Will you bury him decent, then?"

"We'll bury him decently," Cam said in disgust, "with or without clothes." He seated himself abruptly behind the desk. A sense of authority possessed him. Until now his ambition had been to play a spectator's part in the case. He had brought his mind to bear upon its problems only intermittently and with distaste. The governmental desk was to him, however, what the clerical gown was to Yardley, a symbol of authority—and of his place in society. An old familiar urge to come to grips with the case seized him.

212

He always associated this with the eternally frustrated civil servant's aspiration to get a heap of papers out of his in-tray into his out-tray. Yet here where there were, as far as he was concerned, no papers, no reports, no files, no memoranda, the very action of placing himself behind the bulk of a Ministry of Works desk brought back the thoughts as well as the appearance of authority. He turned with some gusto to Yardley.

There was no need for searching questions, however. Yardley needed only to know that he had Cam's attention to burst full blown into his declaration of wrath.

"You be no good to me," he started unpromisingly. "Nobody can help me here but t'Inspector and he wullna. Et's bringin' in of strangers like you which have brought misery to Trevelley, et is. Foreigners everywhere! Foreigners in the inn; foreigners in th' police station; foreigners in the Rectory. Et's gettin' so there's no place where a good Trevelley man can lay his head in peace. How ye creep like serpents into our bosoms! How ye writhe your way into the bowels of our life! Be there no peace from ye? ..."

Colly was listening with awestruck attention to this blossoming jeremiad. Cam was less impressed.

"Rubbish!" he said firmly, rapping on the desk. "I'm no serpent and you'd better remember it if this interview is going to last any longer. I'm a deputy of Mr. Honeywether and you can speak to me as you would to him. So tell me what you want to say and have done. If it's only to make a sermon, then do it outside."

Yardley shifted resentfully in his chair but after a brief pause under Cam's steady eye, he took the suggestion and went on in lower key.

"Et's about the church. Almost two days now et's been shut, wi' dust and untidiness creepin' over et and the bloodstains still lyin' in the sanctuary and me wi' never a chance to do my bit o' cleaning. 'Tis a cryin' scandal, that's what et es. Will God look mercifully upon His people when they let His House fall to rack an' ruin? Will ...?"

Cam stopped this too. "I'm sure He will. I very much doubt if a little dust looks as important to Him as to you. Anyway, why don't you leave it to the Rector to look after that with Mr. Honeywether? It's none of your responsibility, you know."

"I've waited," the other said bitterly. "An' what's happened? Nothing! *He* won't do nothing, that I know. *He's* in no hurry. *He* wouldn't mind if the church never be opened."

"What are you suggesting?" Cam asked sharply. "Why shouldn't he care? You had better be more careful about your references to Mr. Copperman perhaps."

"If all the world knowed what I knowed," Yardley muttered, "there wuldn't be a Mr. Copperman here much longer." He paused and moved forward onto the edge of his chair. "If I tell you summat private-like will you promise not to let on who told ye?"

Here, thought Cam, is the village informer in person. This was the purpose of his visit. "I make no promises," he said. "But if you have something of importance to say, you had better say it and have done. You won't gain anything by prevarication."

Yardley leaned even further forwards. There was an eager glitter in his eye. "Rector has stolen the church plate," he whispered in hoarse triumph. "He dunna know I knows et, but I does know et! Three weeks ago et wor stolen an' he took et. I knows he took et."

"How do you know?" Cam asked cautiously. "That's a serious thing to say without proof."

"I got a key to t'cupboard," Yardley said in triumph. "Mr. Banting give et me when first I joined th' church. He give et me as a sign of his faith, he says, an' many's the time I've remembered those words. Rector don't know I've got et. I never told him. What for should I? None o' his bus'ness. Three weeks ago when I'd bin ill on the Sabbath I looked in the cupboard on the Monday an' the siller warn't there. So I thinks to tell the Rector, but somehow without comin' right out fer fear he'd ask me how I found out an' take away my key, which be rightly mine, et be. So I goes to him an' I says thet I wants to clean the plate, so will he come an' give et to me like always. You never seen a man turn so yeller in all yer born days. I thought he'd pass off, I did. Then he tells me that he hasn't time—that he'll do et later—that I mustn't bother him. Ever since then, mister, I bin askin' for th' plate an' ever since then he bin puttin' me off—till he runs at t'very sight o' me." The Hound of God, thought Cam. Yardley would take grim pleasure in the rôle. "Have you asked Mr. Allen too?" he asked.

"No. He be a Trevelley lad. 'Tes no bus'ness o' his. 'E wouldna do sich a thing. I hav'na plagued him."

"But if he knew nothing about it, then he would certainly open the cupboard for you and then the theft would be discovered and the police would start looking for the culprit."

"An' find the wrong 'un," Yardley said scornfully. "Nay, I prefers to do et me own way."

"What you mean is that you enjoyed tormenting a probably innocent man until he couldn't bear the sight of you. I know one thing. Mr. Banting wouldn't have approved of what you're doing. He was always a straight man and all this peeping and spying wouldn't have pleased him one bit."

Yardley looked stubborn. "He told me to guard t' church an' thet I'm doin'—from th' enemy within an' without. Et be th' duty of ev'ry Christian man to chastise the unrighteous."

"Didn't you confide in anybody? Mrs. Copperman, for instance? Surely you don't regard her as one of the enemy?"

"She be wife to the man hisself. I trusts nobody. This village nowadays be full o' thievin' rogues an' hypocrites comin' pest'ring round my church, pryin' at the great brass. There be thet young man down at the 'Fishers'—what wor he a-doin' of, I'd like to know, last Sabbath evenin'? I 'most caught 'im at et, I did."

"'At it'? At what? You met him coming out of the church after Evensong? That's no crime."

"Ay, but he looked all flustered like, he did, an' that's not all. Tell him what yer saw, lad."

Yardley turned to his son more in threat than invitation and the boy, who had been staring for some time with lack-lustre eyes out of the window, sprang to attention.

"I dunna know nothin'," he began promisingly, but a gesture of Yardley's fist reminded him. "'Cept that summun had moved the rug afore the Table. I saw thet. Lyin' there all heaved into a corner, et wor, an' th' brass wi'out no cover on et."

This confirmed Briarley's story of starting to rub the brass. He must have been in a considerable hurry to leave without covering it up again. Cam looked unimpressed.

"You seem a keen-sighted lad," he said kindly. "What about after evening service? Didn't you see anyone wandering round the church then—anyone at all—someone you knew or someone you didn't?"

The lad shook his head with a glance at his father.

"No, I wor home wi' Dad," he muttered.

Cam nodded as if this were all he had hoped for.

"And what about the Sunday that the silver disappeared? You've heard about that, haven't you, though you're too good a fellow to blab? Did you see anything queer then? Or anybody? Can you remember what you did after church, for a starter?"

To his horror Colly burst, for no apparent reason, into a flood of tears, bordering almost on convulsions. His father, showing neither anger nor pity, looked upon the boy with a proud complacency.

"For God's sake!" exclaimed Cam. "What on earth is this about? Is the lad ill?"

"A bit touched," said Yardley, not without pride. "He sees further nor you an' me, Mr. Inspector; further into the wickedness o' things than ye, wi' all yer police spies. An' sometimes he gets took away by it all. I dunna worry. 'Tes the Lord's work an' we mun abide by it."

"Or the Devil's!" said Cam. "If you ask me, what the boy needs is a few years tying knots in the Boy Scouts." Colly was now almost choked with his sobs and the Inspector, with an angry look at the complacent father, rapped on the desk.

"Come off that!" he said firmly. "You're a big boy now. There's no call to be crying!" This had no effect so Cam tried his usual final argument with his own eight-year-old. "Here's a shilling. Buy yourself some sweets." The lad, his simple mind seizing gratefully upon this unexpected kind of sympathy, stopped sobbing as suddenly as he had begun and looked at the Inspector agape. "Go on!" said Cam. "Take it and be off with you." Colly snatched the shilling and ran, oblivious for once of the black looks of his father. The latter turned his frown, therefore, upon Cam.

"You've no call to be givin' him shillin's," he growled. "I can look arter me own. 'Twill make him think on fleshly things, 'twill, an' blind him to the glory o' the Lord."

Cam swallowed his anger. There was no point in launching a child-training argument.

"Well, what was he crying about?" he asked. "Is he often like that?"

"I beat him rare hard that Sunday," Yardley said complacently. "Black an' blue, he were, an' he won't forget et fer many a day."

"What had he done?"

Yardley's voice sank to a lower key. "He talked wi' the whore o' Babylon—afore me very house I saw him. Was fer his own good I done et so as to set sinful thoughts a-flyin'."

"Talking with who?"

"The Devil's daughter. Jessica, she calls herself. A turrible torment she be to godly men."

Cam was surprised. "Jessica Cowdray—Luigi? Now, why do you think she would want to talk with Colly? Perhaps for old times sake," he added mischievously. "You and old Red were great friends once, I hear."

"Before I saw the light," Yardley growled. "When I still walked in darkness an' me companions were toads an' vermin."

"Do you see much of him now?"

"Everywhere!" the Verger bunt out furiously. "Everywhere I see him grinnin' an' leerin' et me. The Devil 'imself, he is, as I've often telled me lad. Never a word do we speak to each other, but he's always about leerin' at me—tormentin' th' life out o' me. Black wi' sin though he be he doesna fear to look in th' face o' virtue. Ay, he would sneer in the face of the Lord hissen if t' chance offered. He be long overdue fer burnin' in hell," the old man ended with sinister meaning.

"Are you afraid of him?" Cam asked abruptly. "Are you afraid he may try to pay you back for spoiling his game of witchery out near Peter's Perch?"

A veil of unknowing dropped over Yardley's face. "Dunno what you be talkin' about. I know nothin' of et."

"Is that why you don't like Colly and Jessica talking together?"

"She'll corrupt him—young as he be," the Verger said grimly. "He's a simple lad, is my Colly. He wouldna know what she's up to."

"So you beat him so that he shall know. Splendid!" Cam felt a wave of dislike for this grim old man, with no mercy in him. "You seem to take more care of your boy," he said maliciously, "than of your Bible. What games were you playing with that the other night, eh?"

Yardley got to his feet in startled passion. For a moment Cam thought he would explode in speech, but second thoughts intervened and after a glare of fury his eyes dropped.

"'Twere an accident," he muttered. "Nobbut an accident."

"I see," Cam remarked. "You were reading the Bible in your garden and a sudden breeze shot some loose leaves into the road. Very likely!"

"'Twere an accident," Yardley repeated, stepping towards the door. "I didna come here to talk about thet."

Cam looked at his watch. The afternoon was getting on—time to be on his way to the camp. "What *did* you come about?" he asked ingenuously. "Yes, I remember. Opening the church. Well, Mr. Copperman and Mr. Honeywether fixed that up just before you came. The Rector's holding a service. It's to be opened tonight. He's probably waiting to tell you all about it even now."

Yardley looked at him unbelievingly, one hand on the doorknob.

"Tonight?" he said. "The Rector hisself to preach tonight? Oh no, mister; 'tes unheard of!" Then suddenly he wrapped his gown round him and without another word turned from the room and ran with long strides out through the waiting-room, through the door and up the hill. Cam, watching him through his window, saw only a raven, flapping back to its graveyard nest.

Then he saw Colly, profoundly intent upon a large lollipop, come up the street and trudge after his father, kicking a pebble carefully in front of him. Concentrated upon this sucking and kicking process, he jumped with surprise as Jessica Luigi came up behind him and put a hand on his shoulder. A quick glance after his father and he slipped with her down the nearest alley. Cam watched with astonishment. There was something customary about the way they went off without a word. Yet what could such an ill-assorted pair have in common? For the first time he felt a twinge of sympathy for the Verger. Something hateful was going on behind the old man's back—something Cam did not like to think about. Resolving, therefore, not to think about it he turned savagely out of the police station and started off to his long-deferred meal with the Americans.

# CHAPTER XV

O N his way to the American camp Cam walked very slowly, pausing from time to time to gaze moodily at the sea, so magnificently, so profoundly self-concerned. There were clouds this afternoon. It might rain before evening. Quills streaked across the vivid blue, splattered there out of the deep bowls of cumulus which were piling up in the north. There was no break yet in the sunshine but it had taken on a softer texture; the burning heat had turned to a glow on sea and landscape. How green it all is, Cam thought, and then impatiently abused the English language for confining in the word green all the varieties of colour which were extravagantly displayed there. The sea was green and every field and tree was green, yet there was not one which was like another. There was the translucent layered green of the sea, like very ancient glass which has been buried a thousand years. There was the mossy yellow green of one field, the sharp electric of another, the pale pastel of another. And even the colour of each field varied according to the angle at which it reflected the light, and the sea, when he looked again, had changed its appearance completely and was now a menacing green-blue as the shadow of a cloud skimmed across it. How green it is, he repeated contemptuously. Yet how to express the infinite variety of the generality? It was impossible. Anyway, send a postcard home saying that everything is very green and people will know what you mean. No one expects you to be exact. People will think you're rather a bore if you try to be. People understand, without having every 't' crossed and every 'i' dotted. That's all very well, Cam argued crossly with himself, as long as you don't take yourself in. As long as you don't think you've said everything when you've said this looks green—or when you say a man is a man or a church is a church or a dog is a dog—as long as you don't let the meaninglessness of words make the things themselves unmeaning to you. Who was that woman, he thought, who said that a rose is a rose, yes (Gertrude Stein)? Well she had a point there. Makes you stop and think. Well, what is a rose, anyway? When you think about it a rose *is* a rose and that's something special. But you have to think. The word means nothing.

Cam's expression became increasingly grim as he pondered over the greenness of things, for while the front of his mind was arguing linguistically, in the back of his thoughts lay another application. He had been conscious for some time of a tendency on his part to treat the case as though it were a stage plot with all the traditional cast types. There was the old Rector, just as narrow and self-centred as every stage Rector must be (unless he is soft, silly and absent-minded). There was the self-sacrificing Rector's wife; the handsome, aimless curate; the maladjusted ex-serviceman; the pretty *ingénue* American; the wicked old smuggler; the Covent Garden shopkeeper (a humourous part that); the fanatical Verger (who might get a humourous part in the last Act); the local badgirl and all the rest of the tried, true and rather tired character parts. Maybe they were really like this, Cam bullied himself, but had he bothered to find out? Hadn't he just taken it for granted that the Rector was a rector and a curate a curate and a smuggler a smuggler, and allowed all his preconceptions and prejudices to form his idea of what the individuals concerned were actually like?

Scandalous, he said to himself. Just because you're on holiday you've no right to treat human beings as though they were creatures in a seaside vaudeville. You've got to pay attention, eh? Maybe they're all cast wrong. Maybe the Rector should be a smuggler and vice versa. Well, he modified his criticism, probably not vice versa, but still you never know.

He walked on more vigorously, digging his heels in at a brisk pace going down the hill and leaving deep footprints in the sand as he strode across the beach of Pennypocket Cove. He had swung one leg over the stone stile which began the steep path up the hill again when "Boo!" said three young voices from beneath him and the heads of John, James and Gillian Cam shot up over the wall that he had been about to cross. Cam manifested horror and shock to the required degree, threatened to box all their ears and asked where their mother was.

"If you'd only look about you," she said from some distance behind him, "you wouldn't miss so much. Come over here and have some tea, dear."

So he turned round and there on the other side of the cove, cosily sheltered behind a jutting heap of rocks, were gathered Mrs. Cam, Betsey, the eight young Americans and, when they were not busy frightening the life out of their old father, the three young Cams. There was a driftwood fire burning strenuously under a kettle of water; there were sandwiches, cakes and pots of jam spread generously about on the old rug which served as tea-table; there were cups and mugs of every shape, size and state of wholeness and, although Cam had obviously come near the end of the party, there was still plenty for him to eat with many exclamations about his famished condition.

"What nonsense," Mrs. Cam ridiculed, pouring him another cup. "I don't suppose you got up until half an hour ago and probably Lucy brought you a hearty lunch in bed. The way that girl pampers you is disgraceful."

Cam was about to defend himself hotly by giving an account of his strenuous activities of the afternoon, when it occurred to him that he did not want to spoil this scene by remembering the sodden clothes of Wilowski. Instead he said mildly that he had actually been up some time and busy talking with Honeywether.

The children, who had been discussing amongst themselves the technicalities of fishing, here stopped talking abruptly and turned upon Cam grave expressions of profound respect which he found difficult to bear while munching a bun.

"Any developments?" asked John in a deep confidential tone. Cam guessed that his elder son had been taking advantage of their relationship to boast a more intimate knowledge of the crime than was actually his. Loathe to betray him, he said gravely: "Nothing new to you I think. Except they're opening the church again."

There was a stir of excitement and when Cam added that a service was to be held that night there was instant unanimous demand that they be allowed to attend. Mrs. Cam looked displeased, but before she could speak, Betsey, who until now had been lying silently on her back, looking into the sky, leaped to her feet angrily.

"What little ghouls you are!" she exclaimed. "Don't you even know what a church is for? You certainly shall not go if all it means to you is gawping at the scene of a terrible crime. Churches are for prayer and if ever a church needed praying for it's this one. There'll be enough sensation seekers there, anyway, without adding you to the crowd. If it really meant anything to you, if you had an ounce of feeling about it, I'd want you to go just to make the balance more even. But as it is you can bet your lives you won't."

The children were impressed and even had the grace to look ashamed. There was an embarrassed hush.

"You're right, Betsey," Bert said at last. "We had it coming to us. Sure we won't go. Let's forget it."

Betsey, always unpredictable, looked at him approvingly.

"If you feel like that," she said briskly, "I think you ought to go. There'll have to be some people there who take it seriously. So go along and get dressed. Only don't forget who's side you're on, and what you're going for."

The children, half excited, half awed, trooped up the cliff to their camp. John, James and Gillian immediately clamoured to join them but were brusquely told by their mother that they were too young and to start packing the tea things. Betsey looked at her anxiously.

"Do you think I shouldn't let mine go?" she asked. "Only I think they'll really be serious now—and I hate to dunk of that service without anyone there to really pray."

"And eight makes quite a good score," Mrs. Cam said ironically. "But no, Betsey. I think you're right. They're old enough to go and as you say, someone with a conscience must back up the church's side. I'm going myself," she added firmly.

She went off to patch up a quarrel which had started amongst the children and to help them up the hill with the tea things. Betsey sat down again beside Cam.

"I've been wanting to see you," she said rather hurriedly. "There are some things I have to explain."

"How about this evening?" suggested Cam. "Come around after the service and have a drink with me."

"No, now!" she exclaimed fiercely. "Bright away! It's nothing criminal and you might be able to help." Cam lay back resignedly and shut his eyes. This seemed to be his day for hearing stories. Betsey told hers, plunging in with the maximum resolution and the minimum art.

"What I've got to tell you isn't really about me. It's about my brother—Jim. My people aren't very well off—Dad's a high-school teacher and teacher's pay isn't too good. But we had a nice shabby house, a big back yard and the things we liked doing didn't cost money, anyway, so I guess we were as happy a pair of kids as any. You know the sort of family you see in our magazine advertisements—Mum and Dad and Junior and Sis, all looking happy and bright and hygienic, with nice clean teeth, no complexes and well-brushed hair—that was us! We live in a small town where everyone knows everyone else. There aren't many stuffed shirts because you can't stuff a shirt when everyone knows what's really inside. We all grow up together there, in the same grade school, the same high school and the same college, so friendliness just comes about naturally. I'm telling you this so that you know why our family liked being together and didn't like it one bit when the war broke us all to smithereens. Jim and I were at college; me a junior, he a freshman. He was president of his class and going great guns as the most promising physicist they ever had in college. We were all pretty proud of him. But though he could have been deferred—most of his class were—Jim just couldn't stay out of a fight and he joined up one day without telling Mum or Dad. That was bad. I suppose we knew right then and there that the family was broken. Nothing could mend it. And as a matter of fact we never had the chance, anyway. Six months after Jim joined up he was shipped overseas. He was killed in the Normandy landings."

Cam murmured a few orthodox words of sympathy. He was, in fact, sorry to hear yet again the story of what war meant to individual families, but it could only confirm his impression that war was the devil. He could not be shocked any more. But Betsey was not waiting for condolences.

"Now I guess you're wondering," she went on, "what all this has to do with Trevelley. Maybe it'll give you a clue if I explain that Jim was stationed here for six months before he crossed over to Normandy. You know this was one of the springboards, I guess. Jim's outfit was one of the first to arrive. Six months they were here, boys from every state in the Union; big towns, small towns, mountain hilly-billys, Brooklyn lawyers, garage mechanics from Wyoming, drugstore clerks from Reno to Kalamazoo, all cooped up in a village the size of a pocket-handkerchief, all being trained and re-trained until they were pretty near crazy, I guess. You know what happened—not only in Trevelley but a hundred other places. There were fights and brawls and kids got drunk and all of them got to figuring they must be in love with someone or other and if it turned out it wasn't love with a capital L, well, they were all going to be dead next week or next month, so who cares. I suppose it all looks pretty unimportant now against the fact that we won the war, but it added up, then, to a lot of pretty miserable human beings." Betsey's chin jutted out defiantly as if to challenge any sneers from Cam. He did not feel like sneering. He was wondering if it were her own history or Jim's she was talking about now.

"Jim was more level-headed than most. He'd been raised right. But at that he wasn't too steady. When he joined up without telling Mum or Dad it was a shock to them, but it was pretty bad for Jim too. It was the first time we'd had a real breach in the family front, you see, and, with him going across so soon after there wasn't really time to patch it up properly. Jim must have felt cut off from his moorings for the first time in his life. He was a domesticated sort of kid and he wouldn't be happy that way. So I, for one, wasn't surprised when he wrote to us that he'd fallen in love with a local girl here and wanted to marry her. Well, that was all right as far as we were concerned. We trusted Jim. But he was very cagey about her. Never told us her name or what she was and we didn't hear from her family or anything. That was kinda worrying—but not for long because he wrote a month later and said he'd broken the engagement off and would we please not bother him with questions. So that was that! I just about forgot all about it and so did Mum and Dad, I suppose, until the day after we had the telegram that Jim had been killed on the beachhead. That day there was a letter from him. We knew that it had been written and mailed before he left England, before he even knew that he was being shipped out, but it seemed to us like a voice from the grave. It said that this girl friend of his was going to have a baby and that he was responsible. He said that he was not going to marry her—she was already engaged to someone else—but that he wanted to have the child, because he didn't think she could give it the right sort of home. He asked Mum and Dad if they would forgive him please and rally round like they always did when he was in trouble so he could bring the child home when the war was over. The girl had agreed, in fact would be glad to get rid of it. He couldn't bear to think of her having the child—she wasn't fit to.

"Well, of course even if Jim had been alive there wouldn't have been much question about what the answer would have been. Mum and Dad were shocked and unhappy, but if it was a question of a child's life, their own grandchild's life, there wasn't any real doubt in their mind. And coming as it did, right after Jim's death, they didn't even worry too much about the disgrace of it. In fact Mother told me that in her heart of hearts she could only thank God that she had something now in return for her Jim. So the only question was how to collect him or her. You see, Jim had never mentioned the name of the girl, even in this last letter. He must have thought we knew—or that he'd tell us when we agreed. We knew she must live in or near Trevelley—Jim had never been anywhere else—but for all we knew then Trevelley was the size of Chicago.

"I should have liked to come straight over to fix things up. But I was in the W.A.C.s then and, as luck would have it, got posted to Hawaii. We wrote to the Rector here. He didn't reply. I think it must have arrived during the interregnum. All we got was an anonymous letter cursing us for wishing to foster ungodliness and nourish the unclean. That was nasty coming at the time it did."

"The Verger," Cam said positively, looking up from the sandpile he was carefully constructing.

"That's my guess too," Betsey shrugged. "It was a rotten thing to do. We were in trouble enough. But it doesn't matter now. Well, in the year after the War Dad was very ill with pneumonia and the bills we had then ate up all the money which was to have paid for my trip. He got better slowly, but it didn't look as if I ever would be able to afford to get here. I knew by then, through reading all the guide books I could get hold of, that Trevelley was in a pretty nice part of this country and well-considered by tourists. So, I thought, why not give some American kids a chance to see it and at the same time pay a visit there myself. So I advertised and this trip was the result. Of course I had to throw in a few other places for the money but, as far as I was concerned, this was a tour to Trevelley with one purpose in mind—to find Jim's ex-girl friend and to get the child."

Betsey stopped suddenly and stared very hard over the sea, biting her lip. Cam concentrated on his sand-pile until she seemed under control again and then asked: "What luck?"

"Well," she said grimly, "I found the girl friend. That was due to John Briarley's help. I couldn't go round the village myself very well, asking which girls had been engaged to Americans and had illegitimate babies during the war. I didn't like to go to the Rectory, because I thought then that they'd been pretty mean not replying to my letter. But the very first night I was here I met John in the hotel and we got talking. As he had been posted near here during the War I asked him if he knew Jim. He didn't, but one thing led to another and gradually I told him the whole story. He's very easy to talk to," she explained rather shyly.

"I asked him if he would make tactful enquiries about the local girls. He had luck the very next night. He brought me a list of three possible girls and by comparing dates I managed to narrow it down to one—Jessica Cowdray. Then I saw her— saw her in the hotel bar—and I realised she must be the girl. She had the looks to attract Jim and from what I heard about her, once I started asking questions, I could tell why he was so violently against her raising his child. Gosh, I was happy that day. I thought I'd been so clever! I'd found the girl and what's more I'd found out that the children—for she'd had twins— were already in the States, for she'd married an American. All I had to do was tell her that I was Jim's sister and wanted to take over the children as arranged. It was going to be too simple.

"That afternoon I went to see her, hated her from the start and told her my story. Perhaps I showed I didn't like her. Perhaps she just felt contrary. Perhaps I was too confident. In any case she listened to all my story and then said calmly that she had changed her mind about the whole thing. That she wanted to keep the twins; that in any case she didn't know what I was talking about because Luigi, her husband, was the children's father and she would sue me for slander if I dared say otherwise and that she would be glad if I'd get out of her house at once. If ever I was near to murdering someone it was then! How I hated her! I tried to argue, but couldn't make sense, even for myself. And I saw she was enjoying it all. I had to leave the house before I hit her or burst into tears."

Betsey almost burst into tears again at the memory, but she brushed them angrily away and went on grimly.

"Well, from then on there's nothing to tell except that I've pestered her everywhere she's gone, begged her to see reason and that she's had the time of her life. Sometimes she admits the twins are Jim's children. Sometimes she swears at me for a liar and threatens to complain to the police. The last time I went round, Luigi—to think of him raising Jim's children!—turned me out of the house. In fact it's my guess that he's the real stumbling-block, for he insists on believing the children are his and she isn't likely to contradict him to his face. I asked Mr. Allen to help me, but he's had no success either, though he has been to see them. To him her story is that I'm a mad old maid trying to steal her children and I guess he's starting to believe her," she laughed, without amusement. "When did you ask Allen?" Cam asked.

"On Sunday evening, when I went over to Powey-side after service. I met him on a cross-country practice run. That's his hobby, you know. One of the local sights is to get up at five and see him racing solemnly through Trevelley in shorts and a singlet. Anyway, I'd hardly spoken to him before, but I was so steamed up that I stopped him then and there and insisted on telling my story. He was 'the Church', you see. Though he didn't help much, as it turned out, he was very nice about it."

"What about Briarley? Is he still helping?"

Betsey flushed and turned her direct gaze over the sea. "No," she admitted. "He's changed. Ever since he discovered who the woman was. Probably he's fallen for her too! He told me he thought the root of the trouble was Luigi and that he was the person 'we' ought to concentrate on. But since then he hasn't done a thing. So there's no one I can rely on now, while my poor folks sit at home waiting for their enterprising little daughter to bring home the grandchild. It's too mean!"

Cam shook his head. "It's a grim situation," he agreed. "And what's more, I don't see what you can do about it if she won't give the children up. Even if you proved they're your brother's—and that would be tough enough—she has a right to them as long as she can provide decent care. If Luigi backs her up I don't honestly see that you have a hope. When did you last see her, by the way?"

"I saw her this morning, shopping. She wouldn't even answer me this time. Just glared and walked on. Luigi I saw late last night, about ten, here in Pennypocket Cove, in that boat of his father-in-law's. He waved. I was on the cliff."

Cam raised his eyebrows. "Did you know the police of the whole county are looking for him?" he asked. "Was he alone?"

"Yes, I know. But that wasn't my business. There *was* someone with him, but I couldn't say who. It was too far away."

"Man or woman?"

"It was in trousers, but that proves nothing nowadays."

"Was Magnuson also drawn into your enterprise? You two knew each other, didn't you?"

Betsey looked at him with a trace of suspicion.

"Just. Yes, somehow or other he got to know what I was after. Perhaps John Briarley told him. He chased after me on Sunday and offered to help. Said his 'influence' might be useful! I didn't think much of him. We have that type at home too. But leave no stone unturned was my motto! It was in the morning he offered to help me. Then in the evening, just as I was talking to John going into church, he came along and butted in. John left us together with mistaken tact.

Mr. Magnuson started right in telling me I was wasting my time and would do much better to forget about the babies and settle down to a nice holiday—with him. Boy, did I let fly! I guess I was pretty rude, but I wasn't in the mood for that kind of line. We parted on bad terms!"

"I can imagine," Cam said dryly. "And those were the last words you had with him?"

"The very last," she replied firmly. "Except that he said a few words to me on Monday—to which I did not reply."

"When was that?"

"At breakfast yesterday, after you had gone. He came up to my table and muttered something about wanting to come along and explain things. I wasn't having any, and didn't even reply. I feel bad about that now, but he couldn't help me."

"You're a determined young woman." Cam remarked. "Do you only talk to people who can help you?"

Betsey turned on him with a flare of hurt anger, but before she could speak her mind a hail from the cliff-top drew their attention to the children.

"Come along!" they shouted. "Hurry up! We're all ready."

"You'd better get dressed," Cam said kindly. "I'll wait for you. Tell them to go ahead."

Betsey nodded, picked up her towel and trudged up the cliff-path. She looked weary.

Cam gave her a few minutes to get the children off and herself dressed. Hugging his knees he gazed round Pennypocket Cove.

It was so still that even the quietest water lapping seemed to intrude noisily upon the peace. Yet round the corner to the west was Peter's Perch, where Miss Cornthwaite had been attacked and a few steps further Magnuson had died. That sort of thing, Cam thought sternly, did not happen when he was a child. The neighbourhood was going down.

The children on the cliff had received their marching orders from Betsey. They shouted, "So long! We'll be seeing you!"

and went off in crocodile round the edge of the cliff. Mrs. Cam and her three, with a special wave for Cam, followed too. He watched them with a sudden tightening at the heart. Very small against the sky they looked, parading along the cliff-top—very small and very near to danger. Some mad, strange things were happening in Trevelley. Something lunatic, indeed. A body on an altar; a harmless young man pushed over a cliff; a Bible torn to pieces; an elderly woman almost murdered by someone who could not see her. What could all this mean but lunacy? No subtle plot for wholesale robbery, no unlikely Satanism and black magic, no personal feud—just plain, everyday lunacy and homicidal mania.

He got to his feet impatiently. As he did so a mellow sound dropped soothingly down from the cliffs, putting his thoughts to shame by its gentle civility. Church bells, the bells of St. Poltruan's, were sounding the call to service and the gently insistent peals came as clearly to this secluded cove as they would to Trevelley itself. It must be something to do with the shape of the hills, Cam thought—providing a trough through which the sound would roll unimpeded. He listened a minute, allowing the anxieties of his mind to settle. A curious hesitance in the peal caught his ear. Four strokes there should be. But dang dong doom, they went; dang dong doom. No 'ding', he realised; no treble. He struck his fists together triumphantly. So that, of course, was where the weight for Wilowski's clothes had been found—the bell-clapper. Dang dong doom, went the other three bells imperturbably; dang dong doom. This morning, Cam reflected, this morning it had been 'ding'. He could swear that as he stood at the bedroom window this morning overlooking the town and heard two bellnotes sounding from the church, that those notes had been treble, thin and boyish. His ear would not be mistaken in such a thing. But did that mean that the clapper had not been removed from the church and attached to the clothes until this morning? Where were they in the meantime? And why, after so elaborate a weighting of the clothes, were they put so obviously by the ferrystop? For all theories about tide movements, on which Honeywether had been making such elaborate calculations, became nonsense if the clothes had been put in this morning. They must indeed have been put where they were found. And that was lunacy, for a ferry stop was no place to hide evidence. Lunacy again. Dang dong doom, went the bells, dang dong doom.

A voice from above hailed him. Betsey was ready, bright in her red jumper and white skirt. He started up the cliff-path, his steps heavy with thought. When he got to the top he stopped stark still, gazing inland at the clouds piling in the west.

"Come along!" Betsey exclaimed. "We don't want to be late."

"Can you always hear the bells here so well?" he asked abruptly.

"Yes, I suppose so. They are quite loud, aren't they? Someone in the village told me they were made that way so as to warn the Devil if he's near Trevelley that he'd better not show himself during service."

"This place is riddled with devil stories," Cam said harshly. "Who uses this cove except you?"

"No one much. A few hikers stop off for a bathe. A few yachts anchor for an hour or two, but usually we have it to ourselves."

"What sort of yachts? Big ones?"

"Oh, no. Not much more than dinghies or fishermen's smacks, really. It's not a rich man's sport round here, is it?"

"When did you last see a yacht here?"

"Sunday. There was one in the afternoon."

"Yesterday?"

"No, there wasn't one yesterday that I saw, but I don't stand here all day with my eyes pinned on the sea. This morning one passed in and out, but it didn't stay."

"Was one here when you saw Luigi?"

"No. I guess not. I didn't notice one. You ought to ask the kids. They watch these things."

"Excellent idea," said Cam. "Come on. Let's get off to church." He turned on his heel and set off at a round pace.

"Hi!" said Betsey, half running after him. "Don't forget me."

Cam flung back a mirthless grin over his shoulder.

"I won't," he promised. "I won't. Just keep up with me. For by God I'm going to clear this mess up today if it takes me till midnight."

# CHAPTER XVI

IT had been many years since St. Poltruan's had held a large congregation. Perhaps never had it received such an awestruck one as entered hesitatingly, fearfully and yet with dreadful fascination, through the south porch that evening. Every pair of eyes swung automatically to the sanctuary on entry and then sought for a pew which would offer a safe distance but a good view of the scene of the murder. The Trevelley villagers were there in strength—the young, for once, as well as the old. They looked round their parish church with eyes as furtively curious as the London journalists who occupied in force a central pew. They inspected the bench-ends and the spandrel carvings and the stained glass windows and the choir-stalls with the interest of something entirely strange in their experience. They did not whisper, because they had been taught not to talk in church, but they gave each other little nudges and pointed out oddities as busily as tourists in a great cathedral. Between curiosity and respect there was a constant nervous rustling in the pews. From time to time members of the congregation tried to look as if they had come here to pray, but they made a lamentable job of it.

Yardley was there, hating them all and darting furious glances at those who dared to put their heads together for an exchange of soft words. The reporters were most remiss in this and he hovered ominously round them, longing for an excuse to tell one of them to leave. Poor Colly had been delegated the responsibility of showing people to their seats. Tom three ways between the congregation's desire to see everything, Yardley's intention that they should see nothing and the sudden demands of local dignitaries from the nearby 'big houses' that they should occupy the pews for which they had so long paid without using, he was having a very unhappy time. Cam, as he entered with Betsey, spotted a pair of empty seats near the back and managed to take them without Colly's assistance or Yardley's obstruction. He was struck by the uneasiness of the atmosphere. There was something in it of the many police court cases he had attended—the tense waiting for the *dramatis personæ* to step on to the stage, the spotting of prominent characters as they appeared and the nudging and peering which followed, the morbid staring at the evidence on display. Yet, because this was a church and because it was a rector, not a judge, who was awaited, and because these people had all been raised with respect for the Christian tradition, this curiosity had to be furtive. There were perfunctory little prayers on entry and hasty shuffling of prayer-books, as though this were primary motive of their attendance at church. Only the children were candid enough to look round with unabashed curiosity. Only a few regular churchgoers were sufficiently unselfconscious to pray without reference to the unaccustomed crowd.

Cam spotted the persons in whom he had some interest, or with whom he was acquainted. There was Briarley, hunched in the corner of a pew—which indicated that he had arrived early—reading with obstinate concentration an obscure portion of the prayer-book. Miss Cornthwaite had somehow found herself in the middle of a tourist family party—Mum and Dad and three small children—who poked each other across her kneeling body in order to draw attention to possible bloodstains. She appeared unconscious of these goings-on, however, so raptly was she lost in prayer. Lucy, on the other hand, very gay in a hat of blue and mauve roses, was missing nothing. Her bright cockney eyes travelled restlessly round and round the church and congregation. She forgot herself sufficiently to wave in comradely fashion at the Inspector and even Yardley's savage glare only quelled her lively interest for a minute. Jessica and Red Cowdray were there too—he looking very salty and rakish and managing to swagger even while sitting in a pew. Jessica, in contrast, was remarkably subdued. Her hands were folded in her lap and she kept her eyes firmly fixed upon them. Cam wondered why she had come. Apparently not out of curiosity, probably not out of desire for spiritual comfort. Another glance at Cowdray's 'master-in-his-own-house' air suggested to Cam that she was there under compulsion. Cam's expression stiffened.

He looked for Potts, but that character was absent. So, he observed with more astonishment, was Mrs. Copperman. The American children were there, sitting very demurely, trying not to look too curious but taking everything in. Mrs. Cam was with them, praying quietly with closed eyes. That reminded Cam, so he shut his own eyes. ...

The organ music started—rather shakily at first—and the brief processional walked up the aisle. Six boys, Allen and the Rector. The congregation sprang to its feet as though released. The play had begun. But there was apparently to be a prologue before the first act. As the choir shuffled into its places and Allen took his seat by the lectern, the Rector turned and faced the congregation from the chancel steps. Cam, who had seen many people in trouble, started with dismay. Mr. Copperman's face was ploughed with sorrow. It was hard to believe that one day could create such a contrast to the anxious, self-centred peevishness which Cam had seen in him only yesterday. There was, however, a dignity and staunchness in his bearing now which was also new. He surveyed his audience gravely and carefully before he spoke.

"This is," he said at last, "no ordinary church service. You are no ordinary congregation. I am no priest. This church has been unhallowed by the monstrous deed which was done here, a desecration against God and man. The Bishop, therefore, will this coming Sunday hold a special service of reconsecration and atonement at which we shall pray for the restoration of godliness. Until that service I cannot regard this building as a holy place. except in so far as all places are holy where men truly pray to God. Neither can I regard you as a congregation in the true and deeper sense of the word. Let us not deceive ourselves. You are no body of people gathered together for the united purpose of prayer and thanksgiving. Instead, you are inspired by an infinite variety of motives—curiosity, superstition, vanity, perhaps a little pity, perhaps a little awe. But there is no common ground amongst you. You are spectators, not participants. You have come to take all you can and to give nothing." The Rector paused to survey his audience as if awaiting some challenge. Eyes swung away as his came to meet them. The point was well taken.

He went on in a sterner voice. "But if your claims to be a congregation in the sight of God are small, what are mine to be your pastor? I have sinned as no layman should, let alone an ordained minister. No, I shall not burden you with the story, I am not one of those who believe in passing on the responsibility of conscience to others. But I want you to know that in denying your claim to be in the House of God I am not trying to exalt my own. For we are all sinful people gathered together in a place of desecration. All sinful, though some of us are worse than others. I count myself very low and yet there may be others here, one other in particular, whose sins weigh even heavier, God help him!"

The Rector paused here and a sign of uneasiness ran through his audience. "No, I name no names," he went on quickly. "Let us, in fact, dismiss names from our minds tonight—all names but the name of Jesus. Let us, I beg you, my good people, together tonight in this desecrated place, purge our souls so far as we are able by honest, heartfelt prayer, a hymn or two, a few passages from the Bible and a little silent contemplation. This is no church service. We are not fit even for that. But let it be a private service of our hearts and minds, sincerely felt and honestly expressed. Let us now beg forgiveness for all the sins which have been committed here in Trevelley so recently; for our own individual sins and for those of all of us and each of us."

As he finished the Rector turned to his seat and, kneeling at the desk, covered his face with his hands. There was a profound hush in the congregation, half surprise and half awe. Allen came forward now and, perhaps a shade too robustly to be in tune with this present mood, announced a hymn.

'Lead us, Heavenly Father, lead us,' they sang in the straightforward, unmelodic fashion of village churches. The music rose like smoke to the upper crannies of the roof and came back all the stronger. Trebles and cracked old voices, doubtful soprano and gruff bass—all contributed to the artless volume of sound.

After the hymn Allen read some verses from the Book of Job. "...Yes, the light of the wicked shall be put out, and the spark of his fire shall not shine. ...The steps of his strength shall be straightened and his own counsel shall cast him down. ... For he is cast into a net by his own feet and he walketh upon a snare. ...The snare is laid for him in the ground and a trap for him in the way. Terrors shall make him afraid on every side and shall drive him to his feet. ..."

Cam glanced round for the Verger. He was crouched in a corner seat shaken violently by soundless sobs. Everyone else, the Inspector noticed, was concentrated on Allen at the lectern. The curtain to the vestry was at his left. In a silent movement he got up and slipped through.

Alone behind the curtain he could hear Allen's voice intoning on and on. He glanced round him. The safe was open. Probably it was always open during service since no one could enter the vestry without passing through the congregation—unless he came through the door to the turret staircase. That was open too, though the door beyond onto the cliff-side was well bolted. He preferred to take the ladder to the belfry, which was flat against the wall, instead of the shadowy stairs and he went up in handover-fist nautical style. There was a gap at the top of the vestry curtain through which he caught a glimpse of packed heads, and he thought he detected a halt in Allen's recital as though he had, himself, been seen.

The trap-door was only a square of wood which could be lifted bodily out. Bearing it before him Cam entered the first floor or the tower. In the absence of Yardley's care a layer of dust already covered the floor. It did not need much skill to detect footprints in it. Cam snorted with triumph and plunged up the second ladder. The next floor was the tower clock. Apart from the slow-ticking clockwork there was nothing here except, again, a few footprints in the dust and a solid door to the tower staircase in the corner.

Up the ladder he went again and now he was in the belfry itself. The black mouths of the bells gaped down on him.

He could not hear Allen's voice up here. It was very quiet. The only sound was his own breathing. Getting old, he thought critically. Puffing like a grampus after three short ladders. He held his breath for a moment. But the breathing went on. He was not alone.

There was a pause while he looked round casually, trying to see behind what beam a figure lurked. No darker shadow appeared. He held his breath again. The breathing went on—apparently from behind the turret door now. Cam had an uneasy impression of an eye watching him through the keyhole. He examined the bells absent-mindedly. The treble bell gaped toothless without its clapper. There was one more ladder, one more trap-door to the roof of the tower. Cam sighed, for he wished he knew whether the being behind the door was larger or stronger than he. But there was no half-doing-things for him. Up again he went. The trap-door here was a stronger one, to keep out the weather, but its two large bolts were already drawn.

He pushed open cautiously and poked his head out. It was met by a rush of fresh air and a positive roar of sound after the dusty stillness of the tower. Emboldened, he climbed through and his eyes swung sharply to the door of the turret. It was ajar.

"All right," said Cam casually. "Come out now, like a man." There was a shuffling and a sniffing in the turret. "I were just watchin' ye," said Colly, sidling through the door. "I meant no harm."

Cam relaxed his tense muscles. "Why are you spying, then?" he asked indignantly. "Did your father send you, eh?"

"When the service gets too long for me," Colly said humbly, "'tes here I allus come. See," he waved his hand. "Et's pretty."

It was indeed. The river, the hills beyond, the village and the sea beneath looked like an animated miniature. Cam leaned against the parapet and looked down into the river. Seen from above the cliff did not look so impregnable as from below. He could trace, in fact, a worn, narrow little path up the side.

"Have you ever climbed that?" he asked Colly.

The boy flushed as though he had been very naughty.

"Nay, never!" he exclaimed. "I wuddna do thet. 'Twouldn't be right. Only bad chaps 'ud do thet."

"Does your father say that, then?" Cam commented. "Does he also say only bad chaps would use the turret door to the cliff-side?"

Colly looked with respect at the man who knew all. "He beat me when I found et open," he confessed. "He said I opened et. P'raps I did," he added as an afterthought. "I've forgot."

"So that was why you cried when I asked you about the Sunday before last," Cam said in matter-of-fact tones. "But would you have the key?" The boy shook his head doubtfully. "There's a key," he muttered. "I'm sure there's a key. But I ain't got et."

"Do you love your father?" Cam asked abruptly. "Would you want to do him harm?"

Colly looked at him in amazement. "'Course I love him!" he gaped. "Don't et say I must in the Book? 'Love yer father', it says, don't et? I'm a good boy, I am. I wouldn't do him no harm."

"So it wasn't you who tore up his Bible? You wouldn't do a naughty thing like that?"

The boy's expression became secretive and shifty.

"'Tweren't nothin' to do wi' me. I didna touch et. 'Twar lyin' on the table when I left an' I didn't touch et."

"Where did you go to then? To meet Jessica? Was she waiting for you?"

But the boy would answer no more questions. He pouted childishly and kicked his shoes. Cam shrugged and took another look at the view before turning to go down the turret stairs. Little people were passing up and down the village street; little boats were anchored in the harbour; little cows and horses browsed in the green fields and little men with hoes worked in their brown gardens. Coming down the river he could see a little red boat. Colly was watching it too with furtive attention. Cam laughed.

"So much," he said aloud, "for Honeywether."

Followed by the boy he went through the door of the turret and clattered this time round its turns back to the vestry. As he came into it the sound of the congregation's last hymn burst upon him in full force after the stillness of the tower. There could have been no sermon.

Yardley was waiting at the foot of the steps.

"Whar have ye bin?" he whispered harshly. "What ye bin doing?"

Colly ducked under his outstretched arm with experienced skill and was out through the curtains before another word could be said.

The Verger looked after him with gloomy suspicion.

"Dunna believe a word he says," he warned Cam still in a whisper. "The boy be full o' t' devil's pisin. Bewitched, he is. I wouldn't like everybody to know he be so queer."

"Beating won't help him," Cam retorted. "Even to mend torn Bibles. He says he didn't."

Yardley shrugged. "All, he's a turrible liar. 'Tain't his only trick neither," he added, now that this secret was out. "Up to 'em all, he be. Spillin' me milk; lettin' the chicks out; tramplin' on the cabbidges; p'isinin' me beer—"

"Poisoning your beer?"

"Ah. 'Tes that gives me t' belly-ache," the Verger said resignedly. "Puts pisin in me beer, he does, a-bringin' et from the 'Three Fishers'."

This struck Cam as the most far-fetched tale he had yet heard. He snorted unbelievingly. "What tommy-rot! A boy of sixteen! Where would he get poison? And if you think that, why don't you get the beer yourself?"

"Me go to the 'Three Fishers'!" Yardley was shocked. "Nay, I'm no reveller. I'll teach the lad in time. Till then I mun bear me cross."

"But ..." Then Cam gave up. This was too deep for argument. He raised his hand in defeat. "He's your boy. It's your stomach. Have it your own way. And what," he added as an afterthought, "has happened to one of your bells?"

"The clapper's lost," Yardley said sullenly.

"Queer thing to lose. Have you been dusting that too?"

"'Twarn't nothin' to do wi' me. *I* never touched et. 'Twar thet murderin' beast last Sunday."

"It can't have been last Sunday. I heard that bell this morning. Who rang it?"

"I never touched et," Yardley repeated. "'Twarn't nothin' to do wi' me."

The Rector's voice, clear and confident, was raised in the Benediction. The *sotto voce* conversation ended.

Yardley muttered something about 'keeping an eye on them' and disappeared through the curtains, brushing past the procession of choir, curate and rector. Cam could hear outside a pause, a murmur, a shuffle and then the welling sound of the congregation moving towards the door. He tried to appear oblivious of the curiosity of the choir in examination of the campanological records on the tower wall. Allen chivvied the boys along in the process of removing surplices and hanging them on hooks and, as soon as they were ready, pushed them out through the curtains. At last there were only the Inspector, the Curate and the Rector left.

Allen turned to Cam with relief.

"Well there we are!" he exclaimed. "How good of you to come. I've been wanting to see you—to explain why I told you that story about the silver. ..."

Cam was annoyed by the young man's assumption that this visit was entirely for his benefit. "I've already spoken to Mrs. Copperman about that," he interrupted curtly. "It's quite all right. By the way," he asked, turning to the Rector, "I hope she's well. She wasn't at the service."

Mr. Copperman looked at him with a trace of the old anxious suspicion. "She's not very well," he said shortly. "She couldn't come."

Allen laughed abruptly. "For heaven's sake," he said angrily, "who are you trying to fool, as our American friends would say? You forget Mr. Cam is one of the police—deep in Honeywether's bosom. He'll know within the hour so why not speak up now?"

The Rector looked at him with sudden anger which as suddenly melted away into an expression of compassionate understanding.

"Giles, Giles!" he exclaimed. "There's no cause for us to quarrel, is there? Things are difficult enough, God knows, without that."

Allen had the grace to look ashamed. "I know," he said. "I'm sorry. It doesn't help. But I feel so confoundedly helpless that I must fly off at something."

"I suppose we both do," Copperman explained to Cam. "But we show it in different ways."

"Of course," Cam agreed. "But you forget that I haven't the slightest idea what you are talking about. What makes you both feel helpless?"

The Rector looked at him squarely. "My wife refused to come to the service. She told me before the service that she believes I am guilty of this crime."

"Are you?" asked Cam.

"No."

"Why does she think you are?"

"She won't explain. She says that she knows. I don't know what she knows. I don't understand it. ..." The Rector turned his face away very suddenly. Fool! exclaimed Cam mentally. He was not thinking of the Rector. He turned to Allen. "What do you know about this?" he demanded. "Any idea what she is driving at?"

"Not a clue. It's just the last day or so she's been rather odd. At first I think she suspected me. She was very abrupt and I found out that she phoned my friends in Powey to see if I had really been there Sunday night. Why she changed over to Robert I cannot imagine."

"Neither can I," said Cam, "because you weren't at Powey all evening, were you? You could have come over here."

Allen looked at him defiantly. "Have you been talking to Miss Rowan? You're right. I could have. I could have swum the river after she left me. I could even have clung on behind the ferry in the dark and had a tow. But as a matter of fact, I didn't. Why should I? Where's my motive?"

Cam ignored this. "If you don't mind my asking," he asked, not caring in the least whether he minded, "why are you two at loggerheads?"

Allen laughed curtly. "Do you think it's a case of thieves falling out?"

"Don't be a fool!" the Rector said unexpectedly. "No, Cam. The difference of opinion is whether to leave my wife to make her own way back to understanding or whether to try to argue it out with her."

"And your view?"

"She must make up her own mind. There is something more profound here than misunderstanding of facts. She misunderstands me. I had not expected that. But I think she will see things more clearly in a little while." There was a quiet authority in his voice which surprised Cam.

Allen, however, seemed irritated. "That may be very manly and dignified," he exclaimed. "But what worries me is the thought of her tearing her heart out when a few words of explanation would solve the whole thing."

Mr. Copperman went white. "I don't think that I need any lesson from you, Giles, on how to treat my wife!" He paused and then added with more control. "In any case the point is that until she explains her suspicions I cannot clear myself."

"It's that blessed pruning-knife, I suppose," Cam said thoughtfully. The other two looked at him in surprise but the point was not pursued for at that moment a great clatter of boots heralded the entry into the church of Honeywether and his myrmidons.

The three in the vestry went out to meet them.

"There you are!" Honeywether greeted Cam heartily in a normal bellow. Then remembering where he was, "There you are!" he repeated in a sepulchral mutter. "I wondered if you'd turn up. Never miss the dramatic points, would you? You were right about an Order in Council not being necessary. We can go right ahead."

Cam puzzled this out in a minute or two. The monumental brass was then to be turned over at his request. He looked round anxiously. "But Briarley isn't here. Or Yardley. You aren't going to do that without them here, are you?"

Honeywether raised his eyebrows. "And why not? I don't mind Yardley being about if he doesn't interfere—and that I wouldn't lay a bet on—but what's Briarley got to do with it? We don't want every bystander in the village gawking."

"He originally suggested it. That's one reason. The other I leave to your own intelligence." Cam looked at Honeywether with such meaningfulness that the Inspector dared not fail to show his understanding. He nodded knowingly.

"Very well. Rundle, go and collect Mr. Briarley at the inn and bring him back as soon as you can. We won't start till you get back."

The constable marched briskly off and the others strolled out into the evening light. They stood in front of the south porch, looking over the roof-tops to the harbour and to the sea beyond. There was a great deal of the gentle noise that sounds like silence—the sea sliding up and down the shore, some crickets chirping, the melancholy, distant bellow of a cow for its calf.

Cam could not help sighing. Allen looked at him sharply.

"Yes," he said. "'Where every prospect pleases and only man is vile.'"

The Inspector shrugged. "No, I wasn't drinking that particularly. In fact I've always had a special dislike for that aphorism. If the prospect pleases it's usually fifty per cent due to the work man has put into it—certainly in this case."

"And who dares say that man is 'vile'?" added the Rector. "Silly, perhaps. Rather sad, certainly. But the smugness of whoever wrote those lines is the only vile thing about man that I know."

Cam looked at him with interest. He would have expected the Rector to collapse completely when deprived of the starch and stuffing of his wife's support. Instead, the man had apparently recaptured his own independence of character. Allen now was the one who was anxious and on edge.

"Pst!" a surreptitious whisper came from behind. The whole group turned sharply toward the south-west corner of the church. Round it peered the cautious head of Mr. Potts. He ducked back instinctively when faced with such a battery of stares, then, rather shamefacedly, produced his whole body. "Well, well, well!" he exclaimed with forced geniality, coming down the path. "Here we are again, eh? I never thought to see such a crowd. And Mr. Honeywether too, eh? Well, well!"

"Yes," said Honeywether. "Mr. Honeywether too! And so you've decided to come back, have you? Very good of you indeed! And where have you been gallivanting to, may I ask?

Don't you know there's an investigation on and we don't like our witnesses roaming loose round the country?"

"I have been very foolish," Potts said meekly. "But I guess Mr. Cam will have told you my story." Cam nodded in reply to his enquiring glance. "I heard a little while ago in Powey that Luigi was on the run so I thought it would be safe to look in. I got back during the service and didn't like to barge in so I sat round the corner on a gravestone overlooking the river."

"Where's my detective?" asked Honeywether suspiciously.

"I lost him some time ago," Potts said innocently. "Not having anything else to do after leaving Mr. Cam I thought I'd try that. It wasn't very hard really."

Cam checked Honeywether's swelling indignation with a kind thought for the unfortunate detective. "Perhaps he has gone after Luigi," he suggested. "I saw the *Red Ruin* coming up-river half an hour ago. I guessed one of your chaps would be on his tail."

Honeywether wavered between pride in the ability of his forces and fear lest they fail him. "Maybe I'd better go ..." he started, but was diverted by Rundle, returning with Briarley. The latter brightened on hearing the purpose of the gathering.

"How splendid! And how decent of you to let me watch! This is going to be worth seeing. How do you feel about it now?" he asked Allen. "Is this your doing?"

The other shook his head. "No, but I admit I'm looking forward to it. I've never been quite sure how brasses are laid, for one thing. Now we'll see."

"Come along, come along," Honeywether said impatiently.

"The light won't hold for ever and I've got other things to do."

They trooped into the church, not without a certain embarrassment at the oddity of the task on which they were engaged. Honeywether, ill at ease, cast anxious glances at the Rector. Work of this kind was not rightly in his province. The Rector, however, stayed resolutely in the background, watching what was going on with distant tolerance. Only occasional glances towards the door suggested that his mind was still at the Rectory.

Rundle rolled up the carpet from the great brass and he and Honeywether got to their knees to examine how the plate could be lifted.

"Well?" the latter said impatiently to Briarley, having looked in vain for a screw to attack. "This was your idea. How would you set about it?"

Before the young man could reply there was a choked cry from the other end of the aisle and Yardley, eyes blazing, came striding towards them.

"What be going on here?" he exclaimed passionately. "What sort o' heathenism is this, eh? I thought I'd seen the worse, I did, but this beats all. Be ye tearin' th' church to pieces now, eh? I wullna have it, I wullna!"

He had overlooked the Rector in his onslaught, but now the other came forward.

"You forget yourself, Yardley," he said sharply. "I'll look after the interests of the church here. Stand back and let the Inspector go on. There is nothing evil happening, I assure you. We are merely examining the brass."

Yardley looked at him with obstinate hatred.

"Wherefore be the police here, eh? Ef et be just th' brass you want to look at, what for be they here? 'Tes no concern o' theirs, be et?"

"You heard what the Rector said," Honeywether interfered brusquely. "Out of our way now and let us get on with it."

Cam, however, saw fit to be more communicative. "We think," he said kindly, "that we may find something of interest beneath the brass. You wouldn't, by any chance, know how to set about moving it, would you?"

Yardley looked at him suspiciously. "You do yer own work," he said rudely. "I dunna want to have no hand in et. If Rector wullna protect God's own, 'tes none o' my business." He withdrew to the background and contented himself with evil glances and unuttered anathema.

Briarley meanwhile had joined the two policemen on the floor and together with them was pushing and prying at the brass.

"There should be some grooves down which the molten lead was run to fix the pins which held the brass in place. They were bedded on pitch too, but after all these years that may have crumbled. Look! Here's the beginning of one of the grooves. The stone edges of the indent are chipped, but the brass is still firm. ... It must be held somewhere. ..."

Honeywether put a heavy hand on one corner of the brass and it wobbled slightly. "Now here's something!" he exclaimed. "Looks to me like a hinge underneath. Were the things hinged down?"

"Never. That's quite impossible," Allen explained, and he too went down to the floor. "Good lord, so it is! I've never seen anything like that before. Look, Briarley!"

"Something new has been added," Briarley declared firmly.

"That has nothing to do with the original brass. Someone at some time has been fiddling around here."

The group round the brass pressed nearer. There was a sense in the air that they were on the verge of discovery. It came quicker than expected with a sudden 'Ping' as Briarley, who had crawled round to the opposite end from the hinges, inserted his penknife blade beneath it. Something gave and the end of the brass, suddenly released, sprang up a quarter-inch from its bed.

"That's impossible!" Allen and Briarley, the experts, repeated simultaneously.

"Now, now!" Honeywether warned. "Not too fast here. Leave it to me." He pushed Briarley out of the way so that he could get to the open end. The great sheet lifted back as if a lid, lifted back to reveal not merely its matrix but a large hole beneath it, where one of the paving-stones had been removed.

"Look there!" Briarley exclaimed with triumph and excitement.

Was it the secret hole which aroused him? Cam followed the direction of his finger to the back of the uplifted brass. There was engraving, hardly decipherable with mould and dust, but still detectable. This was indeed a palimpsest. But only Briarley seemed to take any interest in this discovery. The attention of everyone else was riveted upon the dark hole, some two feet by three across, which had been concealed by the brass plate.

No one had a torch. Honeywether prostrated himself and thrust his arm down into the blackness. It was a long stretch. The hole must be five feet deep at least. More than a paving-stone had been removed to make it. Rundle held his superior's legs while he reached further. Then the Inspector, after much muttering and groping, wriggled back. From the glint in his eye it was apparent that he had found something. He sat cross-legged and surveyed his discovery. It was a key. Somehow, Cam felt disappointed. Some golden guineas, ancient jewels, a faded manuscript or map would alone have satisfied him. And this key was not even one of those rusty, foot-long ancient instruments which seem to promise open doors to a thousand good stories. It was, in fact, a simple Yale key. Honeywether held it up so that all could see.

"Seen this before?" he asked at large. One Yale key looks very much like another. No one answered.

Cam, however, had a thought. He swung round suddenly to face Yardley. The old man was cracking his knuckles with desperate anxiety. He said nothing, but his eyes were fixed upon that key with dumb yearning.

"Is this where you kept it then?" Cam asked kindly.

The Verger looked at him with startled suspicion. Then he averted his eyes sulkily and said nothing. Honeywether glanced from one to the other. "Is this his?" he demanded.

Cam nodded. "I think you'll find it is the key of the safe. Mr. Banting gave it to him years ago."

"That's impossible!" the Rector interjected. "There is only one key and I have it. Let me see that!" He held out a hand but Honeywether shook his head cautiously.

"No, you let me see yours," he said. "That's more the way of it." So the Rector fished out his key-ring, selected the safe key and passed it to Honeywether. The other examined them side by side and returned the Rector's with a nod. "That's right," he said tersely. "You'll have some explaining to do, Yardley."

The Verger still said nothing. Allen was showing anger as well as amazement.

"Well, this is the limit!" he exclaimed. "It may explain a few little things we didn't know before, eh? How about ..."

"Hush!" said Cam sharply. "Save that till later." He turned again to the Inspector who was wrapping the key in his own handkerchief. "Is there anything else in there? Is that all?"

"Give me time! Give me time!" Honeywether said ponderously. "Rundle, let's have a light." He took a match and lit it in the hole. Cam peered over his shoulder, Allen from the other side.

"It must have been a smuggler's cache," the latter suggested. "A good dozen cases of claret or rolls of French silk would fit well in here. I'm afraid I see the hand of my smuggling predecessor in all this."

"Maybe," Briarley commented from behind. "But that hinge isn't eighteenth-century work. It's been mended quite recently, too—see how it shines."

"What's that?" exclaimed Cam sharply. The match flickered on a hint of gold thread caught in the hinge. It was a gold thread.

"Shavings of silver and threads of gold!" Cam said disgustedly. "All these hints of treasure and never anything to show for it."

"Well, it shows that something's been hidden here," said Honeywether. "The Manchester tapestry ..."

"No et ain't," the Verger interrupted with desperate anxiety. "Et ain't never bin there. I ben usin' thet hole fer years an' nothin' ben hid there, never. 'Tes all a plot, et be, to trap me. There ain't ben nothin' sinful in thet hole."

"I'll come to you later," said Honeywether ominously.

He lowered himself again to the hole, this time with a penknife to scrape the floor of the cavity. At first he brought up nothing but dust. The next attempt, however, produced a dark reddish flake upon the blade. He sniffed it, dampened a piece, sniffed it again and looked round with great satisfaction at the wondering group.

"Blood!" he said proudly.

"There's some more!" Cam, who was also upon his knees now, pointed out. This was on the stone which still formed the bed of the brass. Dust and dirt had already blended with it to make it almost undistinguishable, but a few strokes of the penknife soon revealed that it lay there in thick clots.

Cam looked at Briarley. The young man showed a perfunctory interest in the discoveries, but now that Honeywether had finished his explorations he came forward tentatively and ran his own finger over the palimpsest brass. "Look, Allen!" he said proudly, "fourteenth century, knight in armour. The head gone and the legs, but you can see where the gambeson begins under the cyclas. Very fine, don't you think?"

But the other made an impatient gesture.

"This is hardly the time," he exclaimed, "for antiquarian gossip!"

Briarley looked suitably admonished and withdrew his finger quickly.

"Nevertheless," he muttered aside to Cam, "it's very interesting and it shows that curate deserved to hang!"

Cam was uncertain whether this denunciation referred to the curate's villainy in using the church for illegal purposes or hiding the existence of the palimpsest.

He took Honeywether aside.

"Well," he said cheerfully, "it's all becoming a little clearer, eh?"

"I suppose so," the Inspector said doubtfully. "Yes, I suppose so. Yardley's definitely mixed up in it. That's clear. And did you notice how Briarley found that spring without too much trouble, eh?"

"I did," Cam replied. "And, I cast a glance over all their faces when the brass opened. Delighted horror—that's what I saw on most of them, though which showed more delight and which more horror I wouldn't like to say. Have you ever thought how like horror is an expression of delight? But Briarley—he was watching the others just as I was. And he was so enjoying their surprise he hardly bothered to look himself. No, I'm sure he had opened that spring before. But what does that prove?" he asked hastily, as his friend turned impatiently towards Briarley. "After all, he's an expert on these things—these brasses. We know he had examined it. He'd be quick to spot something queer about the way it was laid. The fact that he knew the hole was here proves nothing as far as the murder is concerned."

"Oh, doesn't it!" exclaimed Honeywether truculently.

"Don't we know now that the hole must have been open when the murder took place? Otherwise, how do you explain the blood in it? I'll bet my last penny that's Wilowski's blood! And how many people know of that hole that we know about?—just Yardley and Briarley."

"There may be dozens more," Cam warned. "Let's not be too hasty. Give them a bit more rope."

Honeywether might have argued. He was on the point of doing so. But at that moment there came the sound of running boots upon the path and, even more arousing, the shrill whistle of a fire alarm from the village below. A policeman appeared in the door.

"There's a fire, sir. A big 'un. Along at Pennypocket Cove. The American camp there—all the tents be alight an' there's a reg'lar panic afoot, there be. You'd better come quick, sir, you better 'ad. Summun's needed."

# CHAPTER XVII

ONCE again Cam was crowded into Honeywether's inadequate car and once again he was being bounced miserably along the cliff-road to the American camp. This time, however, he was too anxious about the immediate crisis to trouble about his own discomfort. It was darkening rapidly. Peering between the heads of Honeywether and Briarley in the front seat he could see a glow upon the horizon, red and livid. He felt a particularly sharp jab of an elbow in his side. Allen, muttering that he was sorry, bent down to look ahead also.

"It's so terribly dry," he said. "What else can one expect after a drought like this. One dropped match and the whole cliff will flare up."

It appeared indeed, as they approached at a reckless speed, that the fire was much more widely spread than the camp alone. All over the hillsides were little clumps of fires with occasionally the dark figure of a man trying to beat out the flames. It looked, Cam thought, like the aftermath of an incendiary-bomb raid. They were not the first on the scene. They passed single figures fighting small fires and then, as they neared the centre of the conflagration, groups of men and women hard at work with sacks, rakes, spades and shovels thrashing at the flames. Little rivulets of fire trickled downhill from the blaze at the camp. Honeywether parked the car as the fire seemed to threaten the road and the group of men clambered out. Briarley was half-way up the hill before Cam had extricated himself and Allen was on his heels after him a moment later.

By the time the older men reached the wall from which the camp could be seen, Allen and Briarley had already found sacks and had joined the dozen or so fire-fighters already at work. At first in the glare Cam could see nothing but shadows moving fitfully. Then with a sigh of relief he saw Betsey. He ran over and she seized his arm.

"Mr. Cam, I'm so glad you've come. Isn't this terrible? We're all safe, thank heavens, but the baggage is all gone—or most of it. It was on us in a minute. ... We didn't have time for anything. ... Oh, look! Now the other tent is going. ..." The main tent of the group was now being threatened by a low wall of fire and the fighters turned their attention to it. Cam seized a rug lying on the ground and joined them. "No water?" he asked breathlessly. His neighbour shook his head grimly. "Nary a drop! This danged drought be the trouble. Even th' wells be dry hereabouts."

The fire gained steadily. It advanced on so many fronts that it was impossible to forestall it. "Let's try and save the stuff," Cam cried at last, and a couple of men joined him as he dived into the tent to bring out what was portable.

"Aye, 'tes a game!" a cheerful voice said behind him, and as he glanced round he saw Red Cowdray, teeth gleaming in a black face above which his red hair glowed with startling effect. He looked as if the fire had spread to his own person—or had it started there? There was something impish—devilish— in his delight in the excitement. Cam snapped back: "It's no game for poor Miss Rowan," but he could not resist a sudden lift of the heart at the sense of drama which Cowdray brought to the scene. The old man was undisturbed by his short reply.

"'Tes t'queerest fire in the world that ever I sees," he rambled on, filling his arms with clothes and camp chairs the while. "Just sprung up, et seems, in a dozen places all at once. I never seen nowt like that afore."

Cam stopped his own work for a moment to look at him.

"That's very true. It's very odd—or is it? He looked at Cowdray shrewdly. "You wouldn't know anything about it, I suppose?"

"Me?" said the old man in shocked surprise, but with a grin which belied his tone. "What should *I* know about it, except that we're goin' ter be burned alive next minute if we don't look snappy." He darted out and Cam, grabbing a last handful, took his advice.

"Are you missing your boat?" he asked, as they piled the rescued things near Betsey.

Cowdray shrugged. "It'll return in a little while. What I'll say to thet Luigi when he turns up! 'Twas a nice little service up'n yonder, eh?" he added with a sly look at Cam. "First I ben to in many a year."

"Quite a change," Cam agreed. "I'm surprised your old friend Yardley let you in."

The fisherman grinned evilly. "I've as much claim ter be holy as he, ain't I? An' I wouldna be waitin' on his orders whether or no to go nowheere. Nay, Yardley would never try ter keep me out. He darsn't do't!" They were now back with their sacks and rugs beating again at the burning heather. Cowdray paused a moment to look round ostentatiously. "I dunna see Mister Yardley hereabouts! What be he up to, eh? Aye, I wudna tak me eyes offen that old man if I were thee!"

He disappeared in the smoke. Cam stopped his labours a moment to look round. Yardley was indeed not to be seen, but Cam recalled that when they left the church the Verger had appeared to follow them down the street. He caught sight of the Rector organising a team of men to rescue the camp's portable possessions out of one of the remaining tents. Allen and Briarley were there too and Betsey, of course, trying to prevent her excited children plunging into the flames. These, plus some eight or nine fishermen and farm workers, were still managing to hold the flames at their main point of advance, though at risk of encirclement themselves. Normally, Cam would have recommended a retreat all along the line to a point several yards away, where they could dig a trench which might effectively stop the flames advance. But to do that would mean sacrificing the tents to the fire.

Honeywether was acting as the chief of another crew. Cam took up a station near him so that he could ask, *sotto voce*, "Any chance of getting more help?"

Honeywether, perspiration streaming down his face, shook his head grimly. "Did you notice I sent all my constables, except these two, off? There's another fire at the cottage over the hill. Even worse! I've got to go and have a look. I knew we would have heath fires after such a dry spell—but so many at a time! It's queer."

"It's more than queer," Cam said energetically. "It's malevolent. Somebody has been having fun and games here, if you ask me. They'd find it easy enough with the heath dry like tinder, but someone has been dropping not just one match but dozens. You'll have to look into this, Honeywether."

The other grunted ferociously. He need say no more. Of all crimes in a country district that of arson is most hated and most feared. The work of a whole season can go up in flames, wooden-beamed cottages which have lasted for centuries be destroyed in an hour, and, because the distances involved make fire protection difficult, defence is just as difficult as the danger is terrible.

Bert Bellenger was working near the two men and overheard their exchange. "Dirty work?" he asked with interest. "Gee, you sure have a lot of nice lines in crime round here, Mr. Inspector." He made a few more strokes with his sack and then added: "Luigi has been round here. As we were coming back from church I saw him cutting inshore towards the village. He dodged behind a hedge but I saw him. D'ya think mebbe he had something to do with it?"

"What are your Coast Guard up to, eh?" Cam asked Honeywether. The Inspector shook his head gloomily.

"They can't be everywhere. There are as many places to hide here as there are holes in a rabbit burrow."

"He may have been using the cave where the silver was found."

Honeywether grunted. "Tonight I'll have a watch on it."

"What cave?" Bert asked excitedly. "One near here we didn't know about? There isn't one in Pennypocket Cove, is there?"

"Just around the corner," said Cam. "I'm surprised that your friend Cowdray didn't tell you about it."

Bert looked round for Cowdray to accuse, but the old man was disappearing in and out of the smoke too rapidly to be pinned down.

"Well, so am I!" he exclaimed sadly. "I specially asked him about caves and he took me to one or two near Poltherow, but be said definitely there wasn't one near this cove. Isn't that the limit!"

"Has he given you that model ship yet?" Cam asked curiously.

The boy beamed. "He sure has. Boy, what a beaut! Won't I just show it off when I get home! I've never seen anything like it. He gave it to me this morning. Say!" he whistled. "I wonder where it's got to in all this. I'd better find Mr. Cowdray and ask him." He disappeared in the smoke.

Coming up the hill Cam had noticed a slight freshening of the wind and had wondered absently if this portended a break in the weather. Since his arrival on the scene of action the breeze had been freshening rapidly to the advantage of the fire winch sparkled merrily under its stimulus. But now there came another and more welcome change. Cam felt a few drops of rain on the back of his hand. Shouts from a few of the other men indicated that they too had felt it. They paused a few seconds to look hopefully up. Briarley, his face beaming, came up to Cam flourishing his sackcloth triumphantly.

"We'll save one of the tents!" he exclaimed. "What a day! But I'd like someone to explain how the fire started in a dozen places at once. Looks to me as though the local police had yet another job on their hands. No one," he added mischievously, "could say Honeywether has a soft job here."

"You leave Honeywether's name out of it," advised Honeywether from the background. "You'd be better advised, Mr. Briarley, to think about your own problems. You've got a powerful lot of explanation to do. And I'll expect it to be a good one when I've time to listen."

Briarley looked abashed. "I've no idea what you're talking about," he said. Then, as he caught Cam's unbelieving stare, he laughed. "Oh, well, yes. I suppose I wasn't very subtle. I'll confess it all. I did know about that hole. I found it on Sunday, when I was pottering around after Evensong. I told you about that. But I couldn't very well rush round saying: 'Look what I've found! Come and see my palimpsest!' when I'd been expressly warned off by every representative of the clergy in Trevelley. So I thought my best line was to get *them* to find it for themselves."

"And was there any blood there when you found the hole?" asked Cam.

"I didn't notice any. Of course that wasn't what I was looking for! The palimpsest was what mattered to me, though naturally I was intrigued by finding such an ingenious little cubby-hole ..."

"The fire's still burning," Allen interrupted pointedly. The drops of rain were rapidly turning to a promising little shower, but still not sufficient to quell the fire. Briarley and the two policemen went dutifully back to their flailing. Cam was next to the Rector this time. He looked at him out of the corner of his eye and saw, with some surprise, that the man was enjoying himself. Copperman caught the glance and laughed with some embarrassment.

"Say what one will," he said, "about the danger and destruction, there's something stimulating about a fire. Even in the War I used to get a thrill out of them."

"Were you in the blitz?"

The Rector shook his head regretfully.

"I was offered a city parish in London in 1940. But my— we thought it would be too much for me. I have always led," he added rather bitterly, "a very sheltered life. Perhaps that's why I enjoy these moments of excitement."

The rain was coming down with increasing intensity, until, with a sudden crack of thunder, it turned into a downpour. Seeing that the rain was now doing their work for them, the fire-fighters retired triumphantly to a little bank overlooking the scene of devestation. It was a sad sight, becoming rapidly sadder as the rain added dreariness to the destruction by fire. Three sleeping tents had been completely destroyed, one damaged and the main tent scorched and torn. A pile of salvaged clothes and other belongings, having been rescued from fire, was now in danger of being soaked. Briarley ran to put a tarpaulin over it and Betsey smiled at him gratefully.

"We've really had it!" she said gloomily, running harrassed fingers through her hair. "What a mess! Where are we going to sleep, for one thing?"

"That's all right," Mr. Copperman interposed. "You can stay at the Rectory as long as you like. It's far too big for three people. And though it will just be camping out, that's what you came to do, isn't it?" He brushed away her thanks. "What grieves me is the ruin of all this splendid equipment. There's been some wickedness in all this, I'm afraid. Those fires were no act of nature."

There was a general murmur of agreement and all attention was turned to Honeywether. "All right, all right!" he exclaimed desperately. "Give me time to think, can't you? It's just one thing after another, that's what it is. I don't know what's got into Trevelley."

"Where's Cowdray?" Cam asked abruptly. The old man was not in their group.

"He's gone to put my ship in a safe spot," Bert replied. "He told me so. I saw him with it."

"Where was he taking it?"

Bert looked blank. "I don't know. Somewhere round here, I guess."

But at that moment they were distracted from the old fisherman's disappearance by a sound winch for the second time was to set Cam's nerves tingling with alarm. Two tolls of a church bell—one of St. Poltruan's bells—came quickly on each other's heels, beating in their ears. The fire-fighters looked at each other with surprise.

"What's that?" Honeywether exclaimed sharply, and held up his hand for silence in case more came.

"It's the tenor bell this time," Cam muttered in consequentially. "Do you remember it was the treble before?" No more tolls came but he started off down the hill at a rapid pace. "Come on," he shouted. "We've no time to waste."

Honeywether caught the alarm and Allen, Briarley and the Rector were all on his heels. At the car, however, there was a brief altercation between the Rector and his curate.

"You must stay here and look after the Americans," the Rector ordered. "We can't possibly leave them alone here in the rain without any cover. Look after them and bring them down to the Rectory as soon as possible like a good fellow."

"What, stay here while you look after the church by yourself? I should think not! There are plenty of people here. I'll come back later."

The Rector's expression darkened, but fortunately an explosion was prevented by Briarley who volunteered quickly to take on the responsibility of Miss Rowan and her charges.

"I'll enjoy it," he said cheerfully. "But for God's sake see that nothing has happened to that palimpsest."

"Why else," asked Cam as he climbed into the car, "do you think we are in such a desperate hurry?"

The drive back to Trevelley was probably as uncomfortable as any that Cam had yet taken, but he was cushioned against its full impact by a preoccupied mind. A jumble of odd facts were churning within him, possibly stimulated by the churning movements of the car. The scent of lavender, the key in the cache beneath the brass, the bell-clapper which held Wilowski's clothes beneath the water, Cowdray's model boat ... each piece seemed to be falling into place with a satisfactory mental click. He laughed aloud in delight and then, as Honeywether shot him a startled look, said shamefacedly: "No, I shouldn't laugh. It's very wicked really."

"What the devil are you talking about?" Honeywether exclaimed petulantly, snatching his car from disaster under the wheels of a passing truck. "If you want to exercise that mind of yours, why don't you figure out who started those fires and why? That's the next case facing me, I suppose. What a life!"

"But it's the same case, of course," Cam assured him. "Just another ramification. I don't think you'll find that very difficult."

"No more difficult than the rest, eh?" the Inspector said bitterly and then, remembering the rest of the company, added hastily: "Though I'm on the trail. It won't take long now."

"Not another hour," Cam agreed and his friend looked at him anxiously. He did not want anyone to get in first.

They were wriggling up the deserted village street now. Darkness had come with almost tropical suddenness. The roar of the engine drowned all silence but Cam could feel it pressing in upon them. Thus must it have been for excise men on the heels of a smuggling gang—not a door open, not a word spoken, not a glance of friendship. Had it been like this for the Rector? He half turned in his seat and gave him a look. The old man was deep in his corner, staring blankly out of the window into darkness. His thoughts were unreadable. Allen was in the same grim posture. The only obvious thing was the space between them, the resolute gap across which they did not touch and the way they looked sternly in opposite directions. Something had happened here too to destroy friendship and trust. Cam turned again, muttering angrily under his breath. The stain of these murders seemed to spread endlessly.

A shadow running in front of the car lights stopped and dissolved into a figure of waving arms and screamed words.

Honeywether put on his brakes and stopped with a squeal of tyres just two inches short of the would-be suicide. It was Colly, all wild words and terrified mouthing, unable to give any reasonable statement, but pointing with desperate gesture towards the church. Honeywether pushed him to one side of the road, leaped back to his seat and drove on. The two church bells seemed not to have awoken the village. It was only on the open cliff that those two notes would impress themselves upon a listener in all their solemnity. In the village they would be lost amidst the activities of the villagers in their homes. There was a strange connection, Cam thought, between the church and the cliff-side which bridged the intervening village. He remembered with a chill of distaste the Rector's story about Peter's Perch and the construction of the church out of remains of the Devil's palace. If the two were linked it was certainly by the powers of evil.

None of the alarm which the occupants of Honeywether's car felt seemed communicated to the village as they sped through its silent streets. Now the church itself seemed to stand deserted as they approached it past the lightless Verger's cottage. In the Rectory was one light in an upstairs window. Otherwise all was still.

Honeywether was first up the church path, not running now, but stepping very silently. The others imitated his precautions. Their feet made only a shuffle on the gravel. Yet they heard nothing. It was not until they had reached the dark porch and Allen had kicked over a spade which leant there that movements within were heard. Then Honeywether leaped into action. Pushing open the door he burst in, flashing his torch and calling for lights. As he advanced a flying figure hit him amidships. When the lights were switched on by the Rector, Honeywether was seen, a prostrate form, gasping in pained indignity, while an equally furious Verger lay near him, holding his head in his hands. But the attention of the others was not for these. They looked instead towards the sanctuary.

Upon the floor there, silent and desperate, locked in close embrace as though each would immolate himself in the other's death, rolled the figures of Luigi and Mr. Potts.

Cam advanced up the aisle, taking his time, to where the men fought. Then he took up his stand above them, still without making any attempt to stop the fight. It was left to the Rector to do this. He rushed towards the combatants, seized each by the collar and attempted to wrench them apart.

"Not here!" he exclaimed in horrified tones. "In the name of God, not here! Not again!"

Apart from the sound of tearing cloth, his efforts had no immediate effect on the men, who remained locked in an agony of hatred. But some consciousness that they were no longer alone did ensue. Luigi, who was now underneath, shifted his eyes from glowering into Potts's face into Cam's, bent over the pair in interested benevolence. He snarled in response and slightly relaxed his grip. The older man followed suit and took the occasion to glance up. When he saw Cam's face his own became, if possible, a trifle redder. Gradually, as by mutual consent the two men released each other and fell apart, exhausted and silent. Beneath them as they parted lay the brass which had been their wrestling mat. The happy couple whom it commemorated still gazed into eternity.

Honeywether, extremely breathless, staggered up the aisle at this point. "You're all under arrest!" he gasped violently. "Yardley for assault; Potts and Luigi, you for fighting in church and I don't know what else. Where's Jones? Where's my policeman? If anything's happened to him ..."

"I know whar he be," Yardley said glumly. "He be up in the tower, whar they put me to be safe when me senses were gone. He's still senseless, though. His head bain't so tough as mine, I guess."

"Who hit you?" Honeywether asked, not without approval.

"He did." Yardley pointed at Luigi vindictively. "I saw lights here when ev'rybody war gallivantin' up to the cliff, I did, an' when I got here 'twar him what knocked me down. I know 'cause I seed him do et, I did."

Luigi, scowling as he still lay on the floor, said nothing. Potts, however, padding at various cuts with a handkerchief, nodded carefully. "That's right enough," he said. "I saw lights back here too, when I was following you on foot. So I turned back because I thought someone might still be around to whom I could talk. Imagine my feelings when I found it was Luigi! He attacked me, of course, and knocked me out. Then while he was away, carrying Yardley up to the tower, I suppose, I came to again. I crouched behind a pew and saw him open up the brass. He was looking for something. I knocked over a prayer-book and he saw me. He came after me. We had a chase round the church and then he got me. That's when you came—thank God!"

"So that's how it was," said Honeywether curtly. "Then where were those lights you all saw? It was pitch black when we came along."

"*I* turned 'em out," said Yardley. "As I were cummin' in I thowt there be nobbudy knows church better than I so 'twill be a 'vantage ter me ef they bain't a-blazin'. I turned 'em off in porch but he were in t'door an' I hadn't no chance."

"In front of you?" asked Cam.

"Bang in front."

"Then why are you holding the back of your head? He couldn't have hurt you there."

Yardley removed his hand and looked blankly at the blood upon it.

"Ask Potts," Cam suggested to Honeywether, "how he got in." The shopkeeper looked at him defiantly. "Through the front door, or whatever you call it. Same as Luigi here."

"Luigi came another way, I think," Cam remarked.

The young man, still lying with casual ease upon the floor, nodded.

"I came up the cliff and in through the tower," he said casually. "Same as usual."

"Don't forget," Honeywether said rapidly, "that anything you say may be taken down and used in evidence against you."

"What is happening?" asked a quiet voice at the door. Mrs. Copperman came slowly towards them, like a grey nun. "I heard voices—the lights. What are you doing?"

"Clearing things up, I hope, ma'am," said Honeywether.

"Is this the first you've heard?" asked Cam. "Didn't you hear Mr. Potts shouting a little while ago?"

"No."

"Did you hear two bell tolls about twenty minutes ago?"

"Yes, I heard that. I supposed it was Yardley. He sometimes does it by mistake when he is cleaning."

"I didna," said Yardley indignantly. "Never have I done et." She looked at him coolly. "You once told me you did, Yardley. I asked why the bell had rung and that was how you explained it."

He flushed and looked away. "I'd forgotten," he muttered. "But I didna do et this time. 'Twas the wind maybe."

"Do you know?" Cam asked Luigi. The young man laughed. "Yes, I know. But I'm not telling."

"You'll tell," Honeywether promised.

"It'll be too late then," Luigi said cheerfully.

"Not too late to hang you!" the Inspector exclaimed unprofessionally. Avoiding Cam's shocked gaze, he turned directly to the Verger.

"And now we've got this far I think it's about time you explained yourself, Yardley. Everywhere I turn you seem to be mixed up in it. You say you didn't ring the bell. Who's to prove it? You're the only one—except Briarley—who knew about the cache under the brass. You had the key to the safe and could have stolen the silver—or let someone else steal it. You are the one who always manages to be ill and alone at home when anything's happening. You are the person with access to the church here any time you want—or access to any church, for that matter, in that black gown of yours. And who but you would use the church as a hiding-place, anyway, eh? Was it fighting with Magnuson you lost a piece of your gown?" The Inspector's accusing hand pointed to a gaping tear in the Verger's robe of office. The garment was so ragged that it had not been conspicuous before. But now it seemed like a vast accusing mouth, giving evidence against its wearer. Yardley pinched the edges together with trembling fingers. He looked round with despair. His defence was pathetic.

"Et warn't me," he whispered. "Et warn't me. Et's allus me in trouble but et warn't me done it."

"No more was it Colly," Cam said abruptly. "Yes, I know what you've been thinking, Yardley. Don't deny it. Do you really believe he poisoned your beer? What sort of a boy do you think he is, eh?"

"'Tain't him," the Verger said passionately. "I never thowt et! 'Tes the devil in him for all to see. I dunna blame the lad hisself, poor critter."

"Then why beat him?" Cam asked, but prevented an answer.

"Yes, I know. They used to beat the devil out of witches, didn't they? Better ways have been found since then, Yardley!"

"What's all this about?" Honeywether interrupted. "Why did he suspect the boy? This is no child's crime, God knows."

"He blames the boy for his sickness—thinks he poisoned his beer," Cam explained, watching the Verger all the time. "He believes the boy tore his Bible to pieces. For all I know he believes the boy stole the church silver and the boy murdered Wilowski! We all know the boy is simple. His father thinks he's *mad*." Honeywether shook his head firmly. "Rubbish! True enough that the boy could probably get in and out of places where an adult couldn't and so might have been able to commit the murder. But he wouldn't have had the brains or the strength to fix the body up like it was. Anyway, Colly is a good lad—he wouldn't do that sort of thing."

"No," agreed Cam, "even though he's been brought up to believe that the devil was in him and to act accordingly. No; Colly's trouble is that he has the wrong friends."

"My wife, do you mean?" asked Luigi and laughed malevolently.

"That's right," Cam nodded vigorously. "It was she who used to 'poison' Yardley's beer, wasn't it? No, you needn't even agree. I'm sure it was. I saw her with him one day. They were old friends. I don't suppose she did him any harm beyond giving him sixpences to buy sweets while she held the beer. What did she use? Just ipecacuanha? Nothing lethal, of course, for the reason was just to give you the run of the church once in a while."

Yardley was looking from one to the other in bewilderment. "It's bin a-goin' on fer years," he said miserably. "'Twarn't just latterly. I bin sick fer years."

"That's right," Mrs. Copperman interpolated. "Poor Yardley has been a chronic invalid ever since we have been here. I think this poisoned beer story is rather absurd, Inspector. Perhaps beer just doesn't agree with him. And in any case what can it have to do with the murder? Can't we get that cleared up?"

"Agreed!" Honeywether exclaimed. "We're getting off the track. Now let's get back to it. Yardley still hasn't explained anything that I know of. ..."

"Can't we explain it all and have done?" Mrs. Copperman asked in a weary tone. She was looking at her husband, asking him.

He replied gently. "Yes, of course. But you tell them, dear. You know I am quite in the dark."

"I wouldn't mind," she said passionately, "I wouldn't care, if others were not being implicated! But how can you let others suffer for you?"

"You tell them, dear," he said encouragingly.

"Very well." She turned from him. "If I must. You should know, Inspector," she said in level tones, "that I did not bring the pruning-knife to church. My husband did. Mr. Cam has found this out already."

"I knew that you didn't," Cam corrected her. "I did not know your husband did."

"What do you say to that?" Honeywether asked the Rector.

"She is right. She did not bring it—I did. But I took it back to the garden after Vespers. I lost it there. That is the truth, I swear."

Cam was angry. "Disbudding at this time of year! It serves you right!" he exclaimed disgustedly and took a turn down the aisle and back, conscious that Honeywether was delighting in his confusion. The Inspector, however, carried on with his duty.

"That's a helpful admission, Mrs. Copperman. Though I must say that it doesn't speak well for you that you lied about this—or your husband, that he allowed you to do so."

"A just remark," the Rector said. "My only excuse is that she told her story before I could tell mine and once the he was told I could only support her."

Only Cam, who had returned to the group, heard this without open disbelief. Allen, in fact, barked with disgust.

"So it was her fault after all!"

"I didn't mean that," the Rector said patiently. "I knew she was trying to protect me, though for the life of me I didn't see why."

"Neither did I know what it was all about then!" exclaimed his wife. "I only did instinctively what I thought would prevent you getting involved in these hideous things."

"I am more capable of taking care of myself," Mr. Copperman said, "than you have ever known."

"Well, what then?" Honeywether asked angrily. "What more do you know, ma'am? Anything to the point?"

"My husband stole the church silver," she said. "I only knew that this week. He told me last Sunday that it had been taken on the previous Sunday evening—that it had been stolen after evening service when the safe was left unlocked. But I knew it had not been unlocked. I had seen him lock it himself with

270

his own key. I watched to make sure, because he is sometimes forgetful. So the safe *was* locked, and he had the only key."

"Except Yardley," reminded Honeywether with a searching glare at the Verger.

"Yes, but wait. I remembered all this in bed that morning when he told me his story—while he waited for me to advise him."

"Why on earth didn't you say so!" her husband interrupted. "You know my memory. I hadn't the faintest recollection. When I found the safe open I presumed I had left it open. ..." She went on determinedly. "Then I remembered other things—that my husband had been in Minchester on the day the tapestry was stolen, that he had been away from home on other days when these church robberies have taken place, that he has often said that churches deserve to be robbed when they don't lock up their valuables—and that one of the few men he likes in the village was Red Cowdray—a notorious old smuggler."

"My dear," said the Rector with mild irony, "you must re-read *Northanger Abbey!*"

"It wasn't just accident that I visited the Cowdray's that morning. I knew if there were trouble of this kind that they must be mixed up in it. I wasn't even surprised when I found the silver. Cowdray, himself, of course placed all blame on his son-in-law, but I didn't believe that for a moment. Anyway, whether it was Cowdray or Luigi or both, it was my husband who helped them—who opened the safe."

"Cowdray told you that?" Cam asked.

"Yes. He told me that it wasn't the first job he had done for him, too."

"And you believe him? Even now that you know there is another key in existence which might have been used?"

"I believe him," said Mrs. Copperman, "because I know he is right. There is one more thing. My husband knew about the hiding-place beneath the brass. I don't think he told you that. He has always admired the brass—he has told me frequently it was the thing he cherished most in this village. He told me—told me that he thought the couple reflected our own happiness. Sometimes he comes across to the church just to look at it. Last week, last Tuesday, I came into the church rather quietly and saw him examining it. He had a knife in his hand which was inserted under the brass. Just then he heard me. He got up very quickly, hid his knife and said something hasty about being spied upon. ..."

"Was that guilt?" asked her husband with a wry laugh. "As a matter of fact, I had just heard Briarley's suggestion that it might be a palimpsest and was looking to see if there were any support for the theory. My dear, when I said 'spying' I meant rather crudely just that. Your care for me, much though I appreciate it, is a little too watchful sometimes."

Mrs. Copperman looked at him without comprehension. "I have never nagged, Robert, have I? You can't say that. Only you say yourself that your memory isn't good so I have to look out for you."

The Rector sighed. "I am very well taken care of," he said sadly.

His wife was silent, looking at him with puzzled eyes.

"All right, all right!" said Honeywether brusquely. "Go on, please." The Inspector was forgetting that his witness was also his Rector's wife.

She turned back slowly and somewhat uncertainly.

"Oh, yes. Well, after Robert left the church I looked at the brass too. I also loved it. I wondered what Robert had been feeling for. Out of the vainest curiosity I took my own penknife," she fingered her chatelaine nervously, "and slipped it round the edge of the brass. More by luck than any skill, I suppose, I touched a spring. The brass sprang up. I found the hole beneath. And I thought that Robert had been using it ... He looked as if he were ... And he was so strangely cross."

"I thought you were certain," remarked Cam.

"I thought I was," she murmured. "I was sure I knew."

"And was she right?" asked Honeywether of the Rector.

"No," he said simply.

"Then I have been very stupid," his wife said.

"Yes," he agreed. "Exceedingly so. But then so have I." Their eyes met.

Allen burst in abruptly. "What about the tapestry? How is that explained away?"

"What tapestry?"

"So you know about that!"

Honeywether and Mrs. Copperman spoke simultaneously. Allen nodded.

"The Minchester tapestry. I saw Mrs. Copperman wrapping it up last week. I recognised it through the french window. I assumed she was covering up for the Rector. You see, I suspected him too."

"I found the tapestry in the cache," she said simply. "I have put it in the safe. I thought I would return it later by post to the Cathedral."

"Will you kindly open the safe," the Inspector requested Mr. Copperman. The group marched down the aisle into the vestry and Honeywether stood over the Rector while he unlocked the safe. Inside it was full of parish registers and a number of small cardboard boxes labelled 'Mothers' Union picnic'; 'Red Cross collection'; 'Dues', etc.

"It's in the large one marked 'Girls' Guild Banner'," Mrs. Copperman said sadly.

Honeywether drew the box from the back and unfolded its contents on the vestry table. It was St. Christopher bearing a golden Christ child on his shoulders, crossing green and vicious waters in which silver threads glittered temptingly like the silver halo round His head.

There was a shriek of laughter from behind them. Potts was glaring at the tapestry over the Rector's shoulder.

"So it was the old lady did it!" he sneered. "After all everyone's cleverness 'twas she that got it! Oh, what a lot of clever chaps!" He collapsed in a chair, half sobbing with hysteria.

Allen turned on him savagely. "You shut up! Whoever is guilty in all this, it's not Mrs. Copperman. Let's face it." He turned back to Honeywether. "We still haven't explained the Rector's part in the affair. He has merely denied it. Yet what about the knife? If Copperman didn't bring it here, who did? Isn't some proof of his denial necessary?"

Cam looked at him curiously.

"So you suspected him too? I thought you did."

"Why not? He almost got me into trouble myself over the church plate robbery. I drew the same conclusions as Mrs. Copperman over that—and had the added injury that he tried to implicate me."

"There are only four points," said Cam, "which make your theories unlikely. First; if Copperman was engaged in smuggling, where did all the money go to? It certainly doesn't seem to have stuck to him. Second; would he hide the loot under the brass where Yardley might find it? For if he knew the cache he knew that Yardley hid his key there. Third; would he have used his own pruning-knife on Wilowski—a knife particularly associated with him? For the knife, remember, was only an afterthought. Wilowski was adequately dead before it was used. And fourth, and final, if he had planned to steal the church plate he would certainly not have neglected to renew the insurance."

"So my bad memory served one good purpose!" said the Rector.

"Quite!" said Cam. "Look out for Luigi!"

There was a wild scramble on the chancel steps as Luigi, who had been listening with a supercilious smile to the conversation, made an unexpected lunge for freedom. Potts grabbed at him and seized instead Rundle's leg as the latter was about to intercept the fugitive.

"Get him! Get him!" the Londoner shouted undismayed, still clinging to Rundle. Yardley did, in fact, get him with an outstretched foot as the young man was racing down the aisle.

"Well, that's settled that," Honeywether said vigorously. "The sooner I get Luigi locked up the better. And you too," he added hastily to Potts. "Let's clear the rubbish up, that's what I say.

"Not me," Potts declared. "You can't lock me up. You haven't got a case. No more than what you've got against half a dozen people, anyway. It's all guess work."

"You were fighting in church," Honeywether said doubtfully. Cam interrupted softly.

"Ask him whether in his business he doesn't have a great deal of experience with broken locks."

Potts heard, as he was meant to, and looked savagely at his interrogator. "That's neither here nor there. You know my story. Why say things like that? Are you trying to frame me?"

"Ask him," murmured Cam, "whether he doesn't remember picking up a knife in the Rectory garden after Vespers last Sunday."

"Before," said Potts firmly. "That's when I was there. And not picking up knives either."

"Ask him," murmured Cam to Honeywether, "why he went to so much trouble to lose your detective when he was still frightened of being attacked by Luigi. He told me that the detective was a welcome protection."

"Oh, I got over my first fright," Potts said bluffly. "And losing the detective was just a bit of fun and games. I'll lose *you,* if you like," he offered, but no one else laughed.

"Ask him," Cam said ruthlessly, "what he has got in his hand."

Potts clenched his fist spasmodically and put it behind him. Then, repenting of this instinctive gesture, he brought it forward again and held it open.

"Must have picked it up somehow in the fight," he said with surprise. Honeywether removed the wire and placed it in his pocket.

"That may be as may be," he said. "Might be used for unlocking a catch."

"Ask him," persisted Cam, "to turn his collar round."

"Who's handling this case!" Potts protested, turning desperately to Honeywether. "Are you going to let him ask me silly questions like that? This is your district, isn't it, not his?"

Honeywether scowled at Cam who smiled pleasantly back.

"Ask him," he suggested, "whether he has done any fine silver repairs in his shop recently, so he might have silver-dust hanging about his shoes."

Potts stared at him, breathing heavily. "Ask him also," continued Cam urbanely, "whether he is really such a fool of an antique dealer that he can't tell mediæval cloisonné from Woolworth's bric-à-brac."

With a mutter of fury Potts threw himself at this tormenter. They went rolling down the steps in a confused mass of arms and legs.

"Look out!" Allen shouted in horror. "He has a knife!" and he too joined the pair on the floor, seizing hold of Potts's uplifted hand. Honeywether circled the group like an anxious referee for a second or two and then saw his chance. He grabbed Potts's other arm and with an expert twist turned him somersaulting over to land moaning on his back in the nave.

"I must warn you," said Honeywether over his shoulder as he turned to help Cam up, "that anything you say may be taken down and used in evidence against you."

"That's all right," Potts growled bitterly. "I'm not saying a thing until my lawyer gets here. You'll pay for this, though."

Luigi, from the corner where he had been lying calmly surveying the scene, laughed unpleasantly. "A damned lot of good that will do you when I start talking," he said.

Potts looked as though again he would hurl himself upon Luigi, but Honeywether rapidly clamped a pair of handcuffs upon him and at the same time there came the welcome sound of police boots on the gravel outside.

"Come in here!" the Inspector shouted, and then remembering for the first time in many minutes their surroundings he added sternly in a softer voice, "Quietly now!"

In ten minutes the police had effected a notable spring-cleaning. Potts and Luigi had been led away; the constable, recovered from the church tower, was carried out. Before they left, however, Honeywether looked doubtfully at the remainder of the group—the Rector and his wife, Allen and Yardley—especially at Yardley.

"I don't think so," said Cam softly. "I think he's been put upon too much already."

Honeywether, remembering his own limited lock-up space and the problem of getting his prisoners to Plymouth, shrugged. "Well," he declared loudly, with a comprehensive look, "I'll know where to get them, anyhow."

As they left the church Briarley came bounding up the path and stopped short when he met them.

"Betsey and the children are deposited," he said cheerfully. "The door was open so I just went in. I hope that was all right."

Mrs. Copperman, holding rather tightly to her husband's arm, looked puzzled. The Rector hastened to explain.

"The American children," he said, "and Miss Rowan. They've been burnt out. Nowhere to live. I invited them to spend the rest of their time in Trevelley with us."

The Rector's wife, Cam now realised, though not a clever woman—indeed rather a suspicious, stupid woman—was a great woman.

Ten guests were set upon her without warning. Meals to be prepared, food procured, beds set up, hot water provided. ...

Mrs. Copperman pulled herself together.

"How splendid!" she said. "Then what am I thinking of! I ought to be there, helping them." She nodded rather stiffly to the Inspectors then, hand in hand like a couple of children, she and her husband hurried off to the Rectory.

Briarley looked anxiously at Honeywether before he followed them.

"I say," he said tentatively, "I hope the brass was all right. I mean, I hope it hasn't been damaged in any sort of rumpus ..." Allen laughed, but rather harshly from the background.

"I can assure you," he exclaimed, "that whatever was damaged in the rumpus did not include the brass. It is in perfect condition. And as far as my word counts for anything here, which isn't much, you shall be the first to rub it. Anyway I shan't exercise my claims."

Briarley looked at him with shining gratitude.

"That's damn decent of you. ..."

Allen waved it brusquely aside and laughed with histrionic bitterness. "Don't bother. I wouldn't want to now, in any case, as things are."

Briarley departed but Allen lingered gloomily with the group of police until Honeywether shot him a frankly enquiring glance.

"Well, what would *you* do?" he asked desperately. "Do you think I'll be welcome at the Rectory? Copperman will forgive me, I think, though it'll be a bit awkward. But she! The very fact that she had the same suspicions as I did will make her dislike me the more. It's intolerable. I can't possibly go back."

"You're right," Cam agreed. "I'm afraid she won't forgive you. But I think you might go back this evening. As long as Betsey and her brood are there she will have to keep up a front of good relations."

"Do you think she'd ever do otherwise?" asked Allen indignantly. "She's not the type to start slanging matches, I assure you. What will be intolerable will be her blasted good manners. She will freeze me out. And rightly, too. Lord, I have been a fool!"

"So was she," Cam suggested, risking an angry glare. "I think you would find life much more tolerable if you remember that she is not perfect. Her judgment is not necessarily the same as that of heaven. If I were you, I should go back to the Rectory and discuss your future plans with the Rector and the Rector alone. He's a good sort when he calls his soul his own and doesn't let so much weighty virtue oppress his spirits. Stay on until your plans mature. It may help him to re-establish his position and you can live with Betsey's side of the household for the next few days."

"Briarley wouldn't like that!" Allen said mischievously. "Never mind! Perhaps you're right about Copperman needing help—if he'll take it. Thanks, Cam."

He strode off into the darkness. Cam and Honeywether turned down the hill. At this late hour the village was almost asleep, but the thunderstorm was developing splendidly now. In flashes of wild lightning they could see the whole village in silhouette, just as it had been for three hundred years and more, self-contained, gallant and resolute.

"It's a good little place," Honeywether said complacently. "I'm glad we've cleared all these Londoners up. Do you remember that right from the beginning I said this was a foreign crime? That's what I said. 'Cam,' I said, 'mark my words, this is no Trevelley crime.' And I was right. Well, you can't find a substitute for local knowledge. There's no two ways about it."

Cam looked at his friend sideways. "So you think it's all over?"

The Inspector stopped in alarm. Rain streamed down his face and neck into his collar, but he was indifferent.

"Over? Of course it's over! Except for the trial, I mean. But although I haven't studied the fine points yet it's obvious enough we have the members of the team—Potts, Luigi and the late lamented Wilowski. English, American and Pole! Not a Trevelley man amongst them. And that's that. What other thing are you suggesting now?"

"Have you forgotten Yardley? I thought he was one of your favourites."

"Well, the way I look at it is that this murder was done either for fanatical or for business motives. We pretty well know now that Luigi and Potts were mixed up in it. They wouldn't know anything except business motives. And that rules Yardley out, because he'd only act through fanaticism. He's not the type to be one of a gang either. So if Potts and Luigi are in, he's out."

"And yet," Said Cam, "as you yourself once justly remarked, at every turn he's in."

"Coincidence!" said Honeywether grandly. "Plus his usual bad luck. Though," he added thoughtfully, "how *did* Magnuson come to have a piece of his gown in his hand? For that's what it must have been, mustn't it?"

"And there," said Cam, "you have the key to the case. Honeywether, you have a kindly, simple mind. You have solved the crime, or will when you've thought it out, but you haven't cured the evil. There are trimmings in this case which are Trevelley pure and simple. Yardley is innocent. That I know, but the fact that he is so deeply implicated is the most significant part of the affair. I'm not going to discuss it in the rain. I'm not going to discuss anything in the rain. I'm going to run home and have a hot strong drink. This is my holiday, you know. But in the meantime I suggest you look for one other person to complete your team. What has happened to Red Cowdray? Find him, then everything may fall into place."

But although Honeywether looked, he looked in vain. For the storm that evening developed to homeric proportions. Boats in the harbour itself were torn from their moorings and dashed against the harbour walls. All night the wind howled furiously through Trevelley, reaching new tempestuous climaxes every hour. It was the worst storm that coast had seen in fifty years. And in the morning peace came, the storm subsided and everything was washed clean and fresh in sunshine which came up assure of a welcome as if it had never basely deserted the world. Only the piles of driftwood, tom trees and broken boats along the shore recalled the anger of the night.

In Pennypocket Cove there was a larger pile than elsewhere—a rust-red tangle of planks and rigging and torn red canvas, of ships' supplies and sailing gear. Villagers came for miles to stand on the cliff-side and look down with awe upon the wreckage. For these were the remains of the *Red Ruin* and, broken amongst them, the body of Red Cowdray, last of the Trevelley pirates.

# EPILOGUE

CAM was on holiday. He reminded Mrs. Cam of this regularly once every ten minutes.

"Yes, dear," she would say amicably. "That's right. Relax. Enjoy yourself."

"What else?" he would reply and shut his eyes again.

They were all picnicking at the beach. The Cam family, the American children with Betsey and John Briarley, and the Honeywethers. It was one of those splendid all-day picnics—a mass movement of baskets, bottles, thermoses, rugs, books, extra sweaters, towels, balls, bats and essential paraphernalia—starting just after breakfast and due to end only with the end of the day or of the sunshine. At the moment it seemed as if neither would ever end. Life would go on for ever in a sunny haze of sand and sea, cricket and tea.

Cam and Honeywether in their bathing trunks lay side by side like two stranded porpoises, the unconscious objects of many amused and affectionate glances from the more active members of the group. Cam, it is true, opened one eye for a moment to catch Briarley examining him superciliously.

"Look on," he said placidly. "Take your fill. And please heaven that you may one day be like me. Fat, over forty and free from the need to prove I'm a man by excessive athletics." He glanced complacently at his indefatigable children and took another nap.

Honeywether was more restless. Try as he would to sleep yet the consciousness that this was for him an unofficial holiday plagued his mind.

"It's all very well," he said crossly at last, bouncing up to a sitting position. "But I agreed to this outing so that we could talk things over and all you will do is lie there, going red as a lobster. I can't waste my time. There's every manner of thing to settle about this case. And to tell the truth," he added in

282

painful confession, "I'm still not sure what's been happening here."

Cam sighed. "Now that Cowdray's dead," he said, "I doubt if we'll ever know the full truth."

"There you go again," complained Honeywether. "Why is Cowdray so important? Is *he* the ringleader? I'm not denying he knew about it and probably took part. How else could they have used his boat? But now that we know Luigi and Potts had this all figured out even before Luigi came to Trevelley...."

"But the trouble is," said Cam, sitting up too, now, "the trouble is that there were two quite different crimes here and they kept tripping over each other's heels. One crime was your crime—the robberies. You can have them. There won't be much difficulty there. If it hadn't been for the other crime— my crime—you would have cleared it up in a couple of days." Or would you? he suddenly thought. You might never have discovered it at all.

"Was the murder 'your' crime?" asked Honeywether suspiciously.

"Oh no! That was part of both of them." Cam caught sight of Honeywether's mounting fury and added hastily: "Well, let's get it straight now or we shall go as mad as Potts. Poor Potts! Will you start or shall I?"

"You can," Honeywether said generously.

"Right! Well the robberies are simple enough—now that we know all about them. Wilowski's records have explained the plot. Everything falls into place. Luigi, the employee in Wilowski's shop in New York, who, as he starts off to the wars, is offered a handsome dividend on any antiques he can pick up in the old world. He picked up a good deal—they were going cheap during the War. A couple of cartons of cigarettes on the continent could get you the crown jewels and a pretty box to keep them in. It was all quite legal—at first. Perhaps it was even a good thing. A great many precious things were saved from total destruction by removal to the quieter continent of

America. So far so good. But pickings were too easy. Luigi got spoilt. He served first on the continent and then when he returned to England, where sellers weren't so desperate, he found prices unconscionably high. It hardly paid him to ship them across the Atlantic. Wilowski began to grumble about the bad service. Luigi spent all his leave pottering round the antique shops, trying to pick up bargains, but the dealers usually knew more than he about prices. Then one day he wandered into Potts's shop. It looked the sort of down-at-heel junk shop where you could find Charles I's private toothbrush amongst the odds and ends. He didn't have much luck but he got to talking to Potts—who as we know is a sociable man— about his collecting exploits on the continent. Probably he laid it on pretty thick about the amount he earned in commissions and doubtless Potts goggled. We've no reason to believe Potts had been dishonest up to then. But there was certainly a streak of frustrated adventurer in him. And as bad luck would have it he had recently been reading about a church robbery in Wittington. Do you remember? Maybe it was that very day. Anyway it was fresh in his mind.

"'That's the way to get rich quick,' he may have said to Luigi. 'Treasures are lying round thousands of English churches, locked up in wooden cupboards or not locked up at all! Well, well!' he may have sighed. 'It's probably better to be honest and safe.'"

"And so it is," Honeywether said staunchly. "Though Luigi wouldn't believe it. I never did trust that fellow."

"Neither did Potts, I think. But as I said, there was always that streak of the Boys' Own Annual in Potts. Or maybe he was short of cash. Whichever it was, he and Luigi were soon hand in glove figuring out ways to rob the Establishment."

"So they had a trial spin at the end of the War just before Luigi left for home," Honeywether interrupted again, "and he smuggled some of the loot out with him when he was demobilised."

"The rewards of three robberies that was," Cam agreed. "That was why we then had a rest from church thefts for a few months. But Wilowski in New York got a good price for the stuff and thought this was too good a thing to stop so early. After all, he didn't risk anything. So he persuaded Luigi to come back here to try his luck again. Probably offered him a higher rake-off. Luigi wasn't too keen. He is really a domestic type of lad and wanted nothing more than to settle down at home with his wife and kids—or his wife and someone else's kids—he wasn't particular. But the bait was too tempting and perhaps Jessica was a bit homesick. So he came back. To keep an eye on him Wilowski came too a couple of months later. He opened a shop so as to make everything seem quite proper and Potts hired Magnuson to run it.

"Potts wasn't very happy about trying their luck further but by this time didn't dare refuse. Luigi and he tried three small churches successfully, but each time the public outcry was louder. So the two of them, getting nervous, calculated that by one really big job they might clear as much as through several small ones. Then Luigi could go home and Potts, having had his fill of adventure, could settle down comfortably on the proceeds. That's why they picked on the Minchester tapestry."

"Same old story!" commented Honeywether. "The bullfrog wanting to be a bull."

"But they were so near success," Cam pleaded. "If they'd kept it to themselves they might have done it. The robbery went off perfectly. Potts can impersonate a clergyman to perfection—a chubby country parson admiring the treasures of his diocesan cathedral, with his collar turned backwards and a skeleton key in his pocket. Mr. Copperman himself told me how easy it would be to rob Minchester. To make sure doubly sure, Potts would slip the loot to Luigi in some side-street and Luigi would get it away. They chose their times well—holidays when lots of tourists would be about and at lunch time so that

Potts could expect to have the church to himself for a few minutes as hunger conquered sight-seers' curiosity.

"But it was getting the stuff out of the country winch was the rub. The disposal of their first lot of acquisitions had been solved by Luigi smuggling the stuff back to the States with him. Customs authorities didn't inspect returning conquering heroes very thoroughly. And what Luigi didn't carry, Jessica, who travelled separately on a G.I. brides' ship, did. Luigi didn't want to risk that again though. He wanted to get safely back to the domesticated life. Unfortunately for him the solution was too obvious. His father-in-law had told him many stories of his one-time smuggling activities. What more natural than to ask the old boy to re-live his hey-day for a brief time and, for a small percentage, to assist his daughter and her husband in their praiseworthy efforts to earn a dishonest livelihood?

"Without asking Potts, Luigi explained the situation to Red Cowdray. After a few scruples about the size of his percentage the old man agreed to call on his Irish contacts again and to help in getting the tapestry and other loot to safety. Everything was set. Potts was furious about having another conspirator in the plot, but it was too late to do anything about that. And so they started off."

A cricket ball landed hard between Cam's legs, throwing up a spurt of sand. He lobbed it back to the game on the tide-water mark bearing phlegmatically the children's jeers when it fell short by several yards. A couple of seagulls swooped down to share the joke and shrieked their scorn.

"Magnificent," said Cam of them, "but lacking kindliness. They remind me of old Red."

Honeywether looked at the birds closely. "Don't see the resemblance," he announced. "Except that they're a nuisance and so was he."

"A nuisance! A nuisance! You call those specimens of uninhibited delight nuisances? Pull yourself together, old man! The truncheon is entering into your soul. Cowdray was like them. He had no morals, none of the virtues we policemen like, but by God he managed to enjoy himself. He made adventure out of his most pedestrian activities. Even his tourist traffic was turned into an excuse for boot-legging visitors from other seaside places. When I heard that I knew there could be no shadow of doubt that whatever trouble was afoot here Cowdray would be mixed up in it."

"*I* knew that," Honeywether said scornfully. "*That* was no secret. Wasn't he at the root of the Black Magic trouble we had here? I told you that myself. But as far as this is concerned you've already said that he only came into it towards the end. He was ready to help, I've no doubt, in getting the loot over to Ireland. But he wasn't the source of the trouble."

"He didn't plan the robbery," conceded Cam. "But from then on he was on his own. Why do you think Wilowski and Potts came to Trevelley, anyway? Why, because everything became so bedevilled from the time Red Cowdray joined their forces that they didn't know whether they were on their heads or their tails and had to come down here to check up. Luigi gave the tapestry to Cowdray. Why didn't he put it under his mattress or in his boat until he could get it to Ireland? Nothing so simple! He hides it in the old smugglers' hole in the church that he has known about since he was a wicked young man. Can you imagine Potts or Wilowski or Luigi doing that— even if they knew about the hole—which they wouldn't? Of course not. Such dramatics are pure Cowdray, pure Trevelley!"

"Pure rubbish," said Honeywether. "No, go ahead!" he added hastily. "It's an explanation but I don't see *why*. Why use the church at all? It's not exactly handy. Why complicate the simple problem of getting the tapestry to Ireland? Why be so elaborate? It doesn't make sense."

"Cowdray liked elaboration. He hated the ordinary everyday way of doing things. Look at his cottage. Everything which should be neat and clean and tidy left to go to rack and ruin. But a useless toy that he wasn't even going to sell,

287

a model ship that would never sail, being put together with endless patience and care for detail. Nothing was too much trouble for him if he were interested."

"And he was interested in the tapestry?"

"Not in the least. He was only brought in at the last minute. He would only care about a thing which he had created. No, his only interest was to use the robbery for his own ends. And that he did to everybody else's wild confusion."

"Then what were his ends?"

"Oh, wait a minute. That would spoil my story. First let's see what actually happened. Luigi gave the tapestry to Cowdray. That would be three weeks ago. Cowdray put it in the Pennypocket cave ..."

"I thought you said he put it in the church!"

"Not then. Later ... in the cave where he could pick it up any time with his boat. He left it there a couple of days, then had second thoughts and removed it on a Saturday night to the cache in the church, reaching it by way of the cliff and turret door. He knew the way well and had a key to the door, for he and Yardley when they were lads used to hide things under the brass in church."

"Ah, Yardley!"

"That's right. While Cowdray was in the church he took the opportunity to steal the church silver, using Yardley's key to open the safe. I think that was just a momentary inspiration when he found the key in the cache. He thought it might be fun. The tapestry was in the church for three days. Then Mrs. Copperman surprised her husband, or thought she did, at the brass and discovered the secret of the cache."

"That was pretty clever of her."

"Only a very stupid person," said Cam, "would have such an untrammelled imagination. Sensible people don't think about such things. Anyway, she removed the tapestry, convinced of course that her husband had stolen it and hid it in the Rectory until she decided what to do with it. Meanwhile Cowdray had told Luigi of his own cleverness. Luigi was beside himself with rage. The fact that Cowdray had stolen the silver too only made things worse, since it meant that suspicion would fall upon Trevelley, when the theft was reported.

"Luigi could do nothing with his father-in-law. For one thing, he was frightened of him and with good reason! So he sent an SOS. to London, asking Potts for advice. Potts told Wilowski and they agreed to risk a meeting in Trevelley to clear the whole thing up. I think they hoped to bribe old Cowdray to be good. That's why Potts had a good sum of cash with him.

"Since the tapestry was in the church it was there the crew had agreed to meet. That was certainly Cowdray's idea. The others were just simple, straightforward thieves who would cook their plots in furnished bed-sitters for choice. Only Cowdray had a sense of atmosphere. Perhaps Potts too. Yes, perhaps Potts.

"Cowdray, who had studied the question, promised a clear run of the church from seven-thirty onwards. If the south door was locked, as it should be, he could get in by the turret. He arranged that Yardley would be out of the way by having Jessica waylay Colly and drop a little something in the old man's beer...."

"That too!" exclaimed Honeywether. "Draw the line somewhere, old man; draw the line somewhere!"

"That is probably," said Cam complacently, "the most significant feature of the whole case. Anyway, that's how it was. They met at the appointed time and place. Cowdray brought Wilowski by sea from Powey and landed him at the ferry-slip while the ferry was taking Briarley across the river. Then he tied the boat up at the foot of the cliff and climbed up through the turret door. Perhaps Luigi came that way too. Potts came up from his seat by the ferry. He almost met Yardley as the Verger was leaving the church and slipped through the Rectory garden gate so as not to be seen. That was when he picked up the pruning knife that the Rector had dropped on the path. So they all met in church for the first time.

The obvious thing to do was to take a gander at the tapestry. Tableau! Cowdray touches the spring. The brass opens—cache revealed empty! Consternation! And I've no doubt that Cowdray laughed and that was why murder was precipitated. Who actually did it in the free-for-all no one can tell, unless Potts or Luigi do. But the man morally responsible was certainly Cowdray. If they had stopped to take a vote it would probably have been he who died—not Wilowski, who got in the way of the fatal blow."

"What then?" asked Honeywether after a pause.

"Why then they hid Wilowski in the cache, which would just hold him and, while Luigi and Cowdray retired down the cliff to the boat, Potts went back to the ferry-slip to think things over.

"Cowdray, climbing down the cliff, has second thoughts. His genius for making the obscure chaotic rises to the surface. He mutters something to Luigi about having left the knife which Potts had dropped in the skirmish and returns to the church. Out comes Wilowski again and when all his clothes are removed he is laid out on the altar and a candle lit at his head. The clothes are put back in the cache and Cowdray goes off again, satisfied with a good night's creative activity and just in time to miss Mrs. Copperman."

"So perhaps he *did* believe in that Black Magic hocus-pocus!" Honeywether exclaimed. "Perhaps it really meant something to him."

"Perhaps," said Cam. "But I doubt it. Except that he loved the atmosphere of evil."

"I should like," Honeywether said wistfully, "to have seen the faces of Luigi and Potts when they read the story!"

"I saw Potts," confessed Cam. "I thought he was cross about the lateness of his breakfast sausage. It shows how little police training teaches us."

Honeywether's expression indicated clearly that *he* would have detected guilty fury, but he only said: "Did he think Luigi had done it? Is that why they quarrelled then?"

"Possibly. Probably he thought Luigi and Cowdray really had the tapestry and were trying to cut him out. Anyway from then on the team broke up. It reached the stage where Potts was forced to choose between risking his own life by staying in Trevelley or risk suspicion of murder by leaving it."

"And that was why he fled to Powey and then took you in with that fantastic story about buying the silver for Wilowski. Trying to put me off the track. What a fandango of lies it was! Well, well," said Honeywether, "we all make mistakes. And what about the stolen church silver, anyway? Was it really as simple a story as Mrs. Copperman makes it?"

"I think so. Cowdray had put the silver in the Pennypocket cave along with other loot from various church robberies. But Luigi didn't trust him. He was sure the old man meant to take the stuff off to Ireland on his own. He went along to collect it and bring it back with all the other loot to the cottage where it would be under his own eye. But the box was too heavy to handle by himself. So on that trip he only took the Trevelley silver. He was in such a nervous hurry that he knocked the crest off the ewer. He had reason to be nervous. That was the time he killed Magnuson—but that's by the way. Mrs. Copperman walks in while they are wrapping it up for the trip to Ireland. They wouldn't make a fuss—the position was too dangerous. So she takes it home believing, poor fool, her husband was really responsible, as Cowdray told her."

It beats me," exclaimed Honeywether, "the way she wanders in an out confusing the issue."

"You ought to be grateful," Cam admonished. "A most useful repository for stolen goods; quite an asset to the village. But Luigi was particularly incensed. The domesticated life he longed for was retreating further and further. Now this wretched woman took one of his last hopes of a net profit.

He went off to the Pennypocket Cove to brood and to collect the remaining stuff. While he brooded he looked up and saw a pair of grey-stockinged legs hanging over the edge. He had no doubts—his obsession was too strong. It was Mrs. Copperman who always went in grey like a nun. Probably he had seen her set off on her cliff walk. It must be she. He had brought a rope with him to lower the case of loot to the boat. He made a lasso and tried his hand at trapping her. Thence poor Miss Cornthwaite's trial of strength."

"I've never compared their stockings," Honeywether said doubtfully. "I suppose you're right."

"Of course I am. The greyness of Mrs. Copperman's dress is conspicuous. Miss Cornthwaite's lower extremities are the only grey thing about her. But on this occasion that was enough."

"You haven't explained Magnuson."

"Only Potts can explain Magnuson. He was responsible for bringing the poor fellow in. Wilowski paid him for running his 'shop' but it was Potts who hired him. And it was Potts who felt a little timid about this trip and wanted a bodyguard. Magnuson was handy so he was offered a free holiday all expenses paid on the understanding that he kept close to Potts, but pretended not to know him, and didn't interfere unless told to. That was asking for trouble. Magnuson was intrigued and bored at the same time. After two days Jessica, whom he had seen often enough while following Potts round smiled at him. That was on Sunday just as Potts had gone into the church for Vespers, and Betsey had snubbed Magnuson. Perhaps Jessica had been told to find out who Potts's shadow was. They went for a walk during Vespers—do you remember the children saw them? Before they went Magnuson tried to show off that he knew some dirty business was afoot in connection with the church by drawing his little sketch.

"Jessica told the folks at home and Luigi, who was jumpy by now, thought it would be best to see how much Magnuson really did know. So our Jess was instructed to take him out to

Pennypocket Cove where he could be examined. Luigi was going by sea to collect the loot in the cave and Cowdray went with him to keep an eye on things.

"Jessica would have no trouble with Magnuson. Probably the fellow overplayed his hand, pretending to know more than he did, committed himself before he knew the risk involved. Luigi came up the cliff to join them. I don't suppose he wanted to murder Magnuson. All he wanted was a domestic life. Perhaps the Londoner got frightened, or blustered, or was rude to Jessica—anyway, there was a fight. We know that because of the torn grass. And that, incidentally, proves that Jessica herself couldn't have done it because, though Magnuson was no Olympic champion, he could have stood up for himself against a slip of a girl."

"So over he went," Honeywether concluded.

"And down into the bottom of the boat went Jess and Luigi to hide until the coast was clear. Fortunately Cowdray was there to assume ownership of the boat and explain away its presence in the cove. When he left they left, unseen by anyone."

"Cowdray, I suppose," said the Inspector, "was just sitting back enjoying the confusion all the while."

"I'm not sure about that. It wasn't *his* confusion so he wouldn't enjoy it so much. Anyway, the affair was getting away from his own interest ..."

"Which was ...?"

Cam ignored him. "Cowdray's own contribution came on Tuesday morning when he got into the church by his usual route, removed the clothes from the cache, tied them round the clapper of the treble bell, ringing it in the process, and deposited the bundle in the river at the ferry-slip while the ferry was on the other side. I think he had given up hope that we would ever find the cache under the brass."

Honeywether took this in after a few seconds. "'Hope'? But you're suggesting," he said, "that he *wanted* us to find the clothes. Why should he be such a fool as that?"

Cam ignored him. "Luigi hid in the Pennypocket cave when he got away from us on the Monday night. Cowdray relieved him of the boat during that night and kept it in an obscure backwater of the river about a quarter-mile upstream."

"*I* found that out," Honeywether interjected.

"Luigi, of course, wanted to get away as soon as possible and Cowdray was willing to transport him. But unfortunately Luigi had lost all trust in his father-in-law and could not screw up courage to get on the same boat with him. Moreover, he still wanted the tapestry and was not convinced by Cowdray's story that someone unknown had stolen it from the cache. They probably quarrelled about this point of difference. Cowdray was not a patient man. At length he agreed violently, probably on Tuesday afternoon, that he *had* got the tapestry and that he had put it back in the cache when he had removed Wilowski's clothes. The police would not look for it there under their own noses, he would say!"

"But we had ..." said Honeywether.

"Luigi didn't know that. He only knew what Cowdray told him. And Cowdray was feeling malicious. Luigi believed this story. He thought he had beaten the old man down. Cowdray was a born actor; I can just see him as he would have appeared then—dejected, frightened, cajoling. So Luigi laid down the law. He would himself go to the church that night and collect the tapestry. As soon as he got there he would ring the church bell twice as he came through the belfry. That would warn Cowdray to bring the boat from its hiding-place in the river and come under the church. The ringing of the bell would cause no surprise in Trevelley. Everyone knew it rang occasionally for no reason at all and no one paid any attention—even the Inspector of the Police. No, don't interrupt. ... In any case, in order to get the village out of the way and especially the police, Luigi planned to start heath fires on the cliff towards Poltherow. Better still, he would fire the American camp and some cottages. So the coast would be clear for them to escape to Ireland with the tapestry, and the rest of the loot that was in the boat from the time of Miss Cornthwaite's misfortune—and even the silver if they could crack the safe. You've got to give Luigi full marks for effort!"

"Would he leave Jessica?"

"He would have had to. That was why she was so miserable at church, of course. But she could come over afterwards to join him in the States—or in Ireland—or wherever he decided to settle. But it didn't work out that way, of course, because Cowdray didn't mean a word he said. The bell signal merely warned him that it was time to get aboard his boat and take the case of loot that still lay there over to Ireland. While Potts, who thought Luigi knew where the tapestry was hidden, prowled round the church, while the pair of them fought it out in the sanctuary, while you and I were wasting our time trying to make reason out of everyone's mutual suspicions, old Cowdray was sailing happily off to Ireland with all the profit of the transaction stowed in his hold."

"If it's true what you say—about him liking complications—he must have died happy. Everyone suspecting everyone else. Miss Rowan didn't help things, of course, with her goings-on." Honeywether looked critically across at the girl being taught to bowl googlies on the sand.

Cam sighed luxuriously.

"That's come out all right in the end, too. Jessica will be only too glad to give up the children. It was Luigi's desire for a domesticated life that caused the trouble there, too. It was he who wanted to keep them, not our Jess. But Briarley didn't help to clarify poor Betsey's story. He had decided that Luigi might be persuaded to give the children up—and that to persuade Luigi would be the best way to help Betsey. So he tried to win Luigi's trust by helping him to escape from us—not knowing then that we were after him for murder. As he never saw Luigi again it didn't get him far! And as for Betsey she was sure he was guilty in his refusal to go walking with her after evensong. So her tales and counter-tales to shield him merely confused the issue."

"But of course he knew nothing about the murder," Honeywether said. "All that mattered was his blessed brass." He looked doubtfully across the beach. "I hope they'll be happy but I don't see much chance for it unless he gives up brassrubbing."

Cam laughed and shut his eyes and sighed. He had been looking forward to the picnic as a chance to forget the murder. But Honeywether would not be stayed.

"I still don't see ..."

"Yardley, of course!" exclaimed Cam. "That's why Cowdray did it! Just because of Yardley!"

"Yardley at the bottom of it!"

"Yes, but not the way you mean. Didn't Cowdray hate Yardley? Of course he did. That's why he made spiteful fun of him. Wasn't it Yardley who spilt the beans on what was probably Cowdray's most profitable larceny—Black Magic? Hadn't the pair of them been friends and thieves together? What are all these curious doings about 'poison' in Yardley's beer, the church bell that rings and turns him white with terror though nobody else notices, the bad luck that spills his milk and lets cows into his garden, the torn Bible pages lying round the road, his fear that his son is being corrupted? Why, they're all part and parcel of the fact that for years Yardley has been tormented by the devil. All these things started long before the robbery. Cowdray had made it a full-time occupation for years—so long that everyone thought Yardley had persecution-mania and paid no attention. He, indeed, half thought it was the devil, wasn't sure if it was his son, feared it might be Cowdray. He likened himself to Job. There was a certain virtue in being so chastened. But at heart he was sick with terror because he had a sense of sin. So he went in suspicion of everyone and kept his most precious and symbolic possession, the key to the safe, in the church itself and in the cache. Perhaps he had forgotten Cowdray knew of it—or that Cowdray had a key to the turret. Or perhaps he thought the church would protect its own.

"Cowdray, knowing his fear, played it to the full. For years he teased and plagued and bedevilled the Verger. Then with the robberies came an even riper thought. Cowdray wasn't particularly interested in the tapestry, but it would be a rare joke to throw the guilt on Yardley. That's why he put the tapestry in the cache which he and Yardley had discovered and why he stole the church silver when he found the safe key under the brass. That's why he laid the body out on the altar, partly to mock at Yardley's beliefs, partly to suggest that a religious maniac was at work. That's why, when things didn't move fast enough, he took Wilowski's clothes and wrapped them round a bell-clapper. Wasn't a verger the most likely person to lay hands on a bell-clapper? That's why he told Luigi to ring the bell as a signal on Tuesday night. For didn't he know by now that Yardley was driven to desperation and would regard the bell as a signal to himself to come and meet his devil? Of course he did—he had studied his subject for years—and he was right. Yardley came when the bell rang and was almost killed. Then when we arrived on the scene Yardley was so obvious. Yardley—the man with the key, the man who knew the cache, the man who might conceivably regard murder as a sacrifice to his own ruthless God—or who had, alternatively, if his religion were a fraud, most opportunity to steal the church silver. How were we to know? There were any number of reasons why Yardley could have been the murderer or thief. But, fortunately, what Cowdray didn't realise—and probably could have done nothing about if he did—was that we have to prove a man actually did commit murder. It wasn't Yardley's job to prove that he didn't."

"No," said Honeywether doubtfully. "I wish he could have though."

"He can't," said Cam firmly. "And don't try to make him. He's had enough trouble. Let's hope that the next rector proves understanding and that an end to his 'bad luck' makes him a more contented man. Mr. Copperman would probably understand him better than anyone now, but he's off to Minchester again soon.

"Ah!" said Honeywether. "As for Mr. Copperman I'll admit I misjudged him, but he'll be happier in the close again, anyway."

"I suppose so," said Cam uncertainly. "I hope so. More comfortable but not happier. The reason he left the cathedral was to strike a blow for his spiritual independence. Now he goes back beaten."

"She's learned a lesson. They're more on equal terms now. He knows her weaknesses."

"For the moment. She'll forget and then he will. But it doesn't matter. They are deeply fond of each other. They'll find happiness in that, however things work out."

Honeywether let the sand dribble through his fingers. Mrs. Cam and Mrs. Honeywether were enjoying the women's share of a picnic—trying to build a fire in a sheltered corner of the cliff so that in the utmost discomfort and inconvenience they could set about preparing tea for the younger and male members of the party. They would get no credit for it. The flavour of the meal would be credited to the fresh air, the exercise, the ozone. "I could eat anything," the others would say, wolfing down the most exquisitely baked rock buns. "Why doesn't the cooking taste like this at home?" would be the cook's reward for effort. Nevertheless, Mrs. Cam and Mrs. Honeywether seemed content as they burned their fingers and spread their skirts in attempts to coax a flame in the driftwood.

Cam's eyes followed Honeywether's abstracted gaze. Being a kindly man he rose wearily to his feet. "Funny thing about women," he said. "Never can light a fire. I swear they'd freeze to death if it weren't for us."

"Quite helpless," agreed Honeywether, but he was thinking of something else. "Yardley," he said, "you're quite sure, are you? I mean he *could* have been mixed up in it. Perhaps he and Cowdray had patched things up. Perhaps ..."

"No!" said Cam quite violently. "Absolutely no! Because even if he can't prove his innocence, I can. It's perfectly simple. I've known it all along."

"Then prove it," challenged Honeywether.

The other looked at him humorously a moment and then laughed.

"Do you remember," he asked, "once telling me that crime had no smell?"

"I certainly do," said Honeywether confidently.

"And I said that Trevelley crime smelt different from any other?"

"Some such nonsense," the Inspector agreed.

"But the tapestry had a strong scent, did you notice?"

"Yes, like lavender. But you'd expect it of a tapestry."

"Would you? Not lavender, surely? That's Mrs. Copperman's perfume."

"Is it? Well, then! That's the explanation. When she got it out of the cache she probably kept it tucked away in one of her drawers with one of those bags of smelling things women have."

"Sachets. I think you're right. But I don't think she felt that was safe for long. After all, she suspected her husband of the crime. Could she be sure he wouldn't look in her drawers? The best regulated husbands don't, but obviously he wasn't perfect."

"Then she put it back in the church safe. We know that. That's where we found it."

"She hadn't got a key. Her husband had it."

"But she must have had access to it. She could take the key."

"It was on his watch-chain. How could she ask him for it when she thought he had stolen the silver? Would he suspect she knew? How could she explain?"

"They have their ways," Honeywether said with a glance at his wife.

"Her's was simpler. She took Yardley into her confidence. He was devoted to her. She thought she could keep him from betraying her husband. She was wrong, because he tried to tell me—but without implicating her."

"That's easy to prove," declared Honeywether. "We'll ask her. And if she admits it I'll agree that Yardley's part in the affair is explained."

"I've asked her," said Cam. "She denies it. She always will. The one thing she cannot admit to her husband is that she distrusted him enough to plot against him with the Verger. That would be too much."

Honeywether raised his eyes to heaven. "Then where are we? Do I just take your guess for fact?"

"That's no guess," Cam said. "I know. You see I have a sensitive nose. Yardley is not a very cleanly man. Not nearly as clean as his church. It struck me, therefore, as rather odd when he appeared in the police station on Tuesday afternoon smelling strongly of lavender. I could not explain it. But now it's abundantly clear."

Honeywether's brow was wrinkled with formidable thought. "Lavender?"

"Lavender. Like the tapestry and like Mrs. Copperman. You see, he had had the tapestry overnight. And to hide it from Colly's eyes he had wrapped it up in his Verger's gown and put it on the chair by his bed before going to sleep. The tapestry was impregnated with lavender. Therefore so was his gown the next day. I will even bet," said Cam, "that he went round all that day with the tapestry tied round his middle. So he had it in his possession. If he had wanted to steal it nothing would be easier. But he didn't. He slipped it back into the safe when the Rector was getting out the offertory plate for evening service. For don't forget he no longer had his own key."

"He might have told on her," said Honeywether.

"Not he. He had promised. He couldn't even tell on her husband if it implicated her—much as he longed to. For he

300

believed her story, of course, that it was the Rector who was the villain."

"He deserves a medal, poor fool!" said Honeywether with unofficial enthusiasm.

"Just some peace," suggested Cam.

"Tea!" called Mrs. Cam.

Her husband looked with surprise. "Why, they've lit the fire!" he exclaimed. "I was going to help them."

Honeywether got up stiffly.

"Lavender," he was muttering. "Lavender."

"I agree," said Cam. "The last smell in the world I'd associate with this affair. But lavender it is, so let's be thankful. And let's have tea and forget about murder. For after all," he complained for the last time, "this *is* my holiday."